Marcie's Murder

Also by Michael J. McCann

THE DONAGHUE AND STAINER CRIME NOVEL SERIES
Blood Passage

SUPERNATURAL FICTION
The Ghost Man

Marcie's Murder

A Donaghue and Stainer Crime Novel

Michael J. McCann

The Plaid Raccoon Press

2012

This is a work of fiction. All names, characters, institutions, places and events portrayed in this novel are either the product of the author's imagination or are used fictitiously. Any resemblance to actual persons, living or dead, events or locales is entirely coincidental.

This book is dedicated to the memory of Joan Clark Lord and Janet Clark Parker, two wonderful women who are sorely missed.

1

Hank Donaghue was asleep in a motel room in Harmony, Virginia at 2:21 a.m. when the door went flying off its hinges with a crash. He jerked awake, shocked. The dark room filled with sudden noise and movement. The lights came on. Strong hands gripped the front of his t-shirt and pulled him upright.

"Son of a bitch!" a man screamed into his face.

Hank chopped upwards with his forearms, trying to break the man's hold. They twisted sideways together and Hank fell off the side of the bed. The man fell on top of him, pinning him down. Hank worked an arm free and groped above him.

Someone swept Hank's clothes off the chair next to the bed and shouted, "Gun!"

Hank looked at the yellow stripe along the outer seam of the second man's trousers. Cop. He looked up at a young man with blue eyes, a blond brush cut and a trimmed blond mustache. The officer pointed his weapon straight at Hank's forehead in a business-like two-handed grip.

"Freeze, asshole."

Hank let himself go limp. "I'm a police officer. From Maryland."

The man on top of Hank pushed off and grabbed a handful of Hank's t-shirt. "You're a goddamned killer and your ass is busted. Get up or we'll shoot you right here and be done with it."

Hank got to his feet. Another cop stood on the far side of the bed, gun leveled. He was a few years older than the blond cop, with short dark hair and thick eyebrows. He stared at Hank with flat brown eyes.

They moved Hank down to the end of the bed where there was more room to work. They turned him around and cuffed his hands behind his back. They weren't gentle about it.

Hank was wearing only the t-shirt and boxer shorts, but the blond cop patted him down anyway.

"He's clean, Chief."

"He's dirty, the son of a bitch." The chief took a fresh grip on

Hank's t-shirt. He was about five inches shorter than Hank and was about fifty years old, judging from the crow's feet at the corners of his eyes and the amount of white that was beginning to shoot through his thinning red hair. The body beneath his white shirt and khaki trousers, however, was muscular and fit, and the look in the man's eyes betrayed a meanness and aggression that Hank immediately recognized. This was a cop who always traveled in a straight line, demolishing anything in his path that threatened to prevent him from reaching his objective.

This was his town, his law, and his moment.

Hank took the punches without making a sound. The first one struck him in the stomach, bending him over. The second clipped his jaw as he rolled his head, trying to minimize the impact, but the third caught him on the left temple and he dropped like a shot steer. After that it was a blur, a series of punches and kicks that ended with the chief's hands around Hank's neck as someone else tried frantically to pull him away.

"Billy, that's enough!"

"Chief Askew! Let go!"

The hands jerked away from Hank's neck. He dragged air down his throat like a fish gulping water.

Other hands gripped Hank at the armpits and pulled. "Get up! On your feet!"

Hank made it to his knees, still breathing heavily. He opened his eyes and looked at a uniform with a single gold bar on each black shoulder flash.

"I'm a cop," Hank mumbled, "from Glendale, Maryland. There's been some kind of mistake."

"Close your mouth right now," the man told him quietly. He was younger than Chief Billy Askew, in his middle-thirties, ruggedly handsome, with wavy black hair, green eyes, dark complexion, high cheek bones and a dimpled chin. "I'm going to put you in the cruiser, so just let it happen."

"Branham, get him the fuck out of here!" Chief Askew shook his bruised hand. "Get him out!"

Branham got Hank on his feet and hustled him outside.

The Harmony Motor Inn consisted of a central lodge and two long single-story wings, one extending north and one extending south. Hank's room was three doors from the end of the southern wing. His rented vehicle, a Grand Cherokee with Maryland plates, was parked in the spot directly in front of his room. Beyond it, blocking the driveway on the left where it wrapped around the end of the south wing, sat a darkened police cruiser. Another cruiser sat two doors up on the right, also on an angle. A third vehicle was parked close enough to Hank's car to make it impossible to open the driver's side door. This one was a black Ford Explorer with a Town of Harmony Police Department crest on the doors above the legend *Chief of Police.*

"Move," Branham urged Hank, guiding him around the Grand Cherokee to the cruiser on the right.

Hank's bare feet stumbled on a crack in the asphalt.

Branham caught him, hauled him up and promptly stuck a knee into the back of Hank's knee, taking him off balance again long enough to push him over the trunk of the cruiser. It was a fairly impressive maneuver, given that Hank was six feet three inches tall and weighed two hundred pounds.

"Don't move." Branham opened the back door of the cruiser and hauled Hank upright. "In you go."

Hank tumbled into the back seat. Branham pulled him up and swiftly released one of the bracelets, dragging Hank's arms around to handcuff him in front.

"Sit tight. Stay calm." He slammed the door on Hank and went back into the motel room.

Hank sat alone in the dark interior of the police cruiser. His left cheek felt wet from a cut that was bleeding. His left temple ached madly and his rib cage, his buttocks and his left thigh were sore from having been kicked. His right shoulder, which still wasn't one hundred percent thanks to a four-month-old gunshot wound, throbbed dully. He looked down and saw that his t-shirt and boxers were spattered with what he assumed was blood.

He wasn't exactly dressed for company.

He'd done nothing wrong and it was obviously a case of mistaken identity, so Branham's advice to sit tight and stay calm was solid, the kind of advice he himself would have given a suspect he felt was not the person he wanted. The chief had said something about a killer, so there must have been a murder in town. They'd jumped on Hank's handgun, a Glock 17, but since it hadn't been fired in a while Hank was confident it wouldn't take them anywhere they shouldn't be going. They would find his identification and badge in his room and know he was telling the truth about who he was.

Stay calm. It'll get sorted out.

Branham got into the cruiser and threw the transmission into reverse, looking over his shoulder.

"So if I'm under arrest, what's the charge?" Hank asked.

"Just keep your mouth shut and don't say anything," Branham warned, avoiding Hank's eyes as he swung the cruiser around and accelerated out into the street. "It's going to be a long night and you're in a shitload of trouble already."

9

2

Hank was on vacation. Although he was wealthy thanks to his maternal grandfather, whose will had made him a millionaire at the age of eight, he didn't own a car and never drove anywhere himself, preferring to scrounge rides or take taxis wherever he needed to go. Vacations were the exception. Every autumn he went on vacation for three weeks. He rented a car, threw a bunch of books into the back seat and drove somewhere. He stopped wherever he felt like stopping, soaked in his surroundings, read a book, and passed the time quietly.

As a twenty-three-year veteran of the police department in Glendale, Maryland, a city of just over a million people, Hank had devoted half of his life to his job, given that he'd just passed his forty-sixth birthday. His father was the late Robert Vernon Donaghue, a criminal defense attorney and university law professor. His mother was Anna Peach Haynes, former state's attorney, the daughter of a state governor and grand-daughter of a state Supreme Court justice. The youngest of four children and an academic prodigy, Hank accelerated through school and entered State University in Glendale as a fifteen-year-old freshman. He majored in criminology and criminal justice, earning a bachelor's degree, and then went back for a master of arts. The completion of a law degree was a logical progression, and at the age of twenty-two Hank passed his bar exams at the top of his class and accepted a job in the local state's attorney's office.

He worked for a year at the bottom of the ladder, married a fellow assistant state's attorney, and learned the ropes. Before long, however, he realized he was much more interested in investigation than prosecution and decided to change course, applying for admission to the police academy. It was a move that disappointed both his mother and his wife. He passed with flying colors, put in his eight weeks of field training, and received his assignment as a uniformed patrol officer. His wife filed for divorce soon afterward.

Hank quickly ascended the ladder, earning promotions to detective, sergeant, and lieutenant in the minimum time allowed, but politics eventually caught up with him and he had remained at his current rank for the past thirteen years. He was now working with

Detective Karen Stainer, who was without a partner after transferring into Homicide from Family-Related Crime after a suspension for insubordination. Although Hank outranked her she did not report to him, as the supervisory lieutenant position in Homicide was currently occupied by someone else.

While working with Stainer on a case in May involving the local Triad society, he'd been shot in the shoulder while protecting Peter Mah, a Triad official, from an assassination attempt. Vacation, when it finally arrived, was a welcome break.

He drove across West Virginia and south into Kentucky. He followed what was known as the Bourbon Trail, a circuit that included six distilleries. He toured each one and bought the three liters allowed per day under Kentucky state law. Some would be for him but most was for his mother, a bourbon enthusiast.

He started for home by passing through the Cumberland Gap down into Tennessee and then northeast up into Virginia, following a scenic route through Scott and Russell Counties into Tazewell County, enjoying the countryside and stopping to read for an hour here and there at rest stops which cropped up along the way.

Yesterday he'd followed Highway 460 to Tazewell, the county seat, where he ate lunch. He got back onto 460 and drove as far as Harmony, about a third of the way from Tazewell to Bluefield, before deciding he'd had enough for the day. At the edge of town he stopped at the Harmony Motor Inn, booked a room for the night, grabbed a shower, and took a short nap.

Lacking ambition, he ate his evening meal in a Pizza Hut and wandered along Bluefield Street, Harmony's main thoroughfare, window shopping as he strolled, hands in his pockets. It was a warm, pleasant evening in mid-September. He approached a store with a small seating area out front enclosed by a low wrought iron fence. Three men sat at a table watching the traffic in the street. As Hank approached he caught the unmistakable scent of cigar smoke. It was a tobacconist's shop. He went inside and spent an hour talking to the owner, trading stories and shopping for cigars. When he left it was 9:00 p.m. and the store was closing. Smoking one of his purchases, he walked slowly back to his car in the parking lot of the Pizza Hut and returned to the motel.

On television the Orioles were playing the Angels at home. He stretched out on the bed to watch the rest of the game. At 11:00 p.m. when the news came on he was bored but couldn't sleep, so he decided to drive over to a convenience store he'd seen on Bluefield Street for a six-pack of beer and a bag of potato chips. The store was closed. On the way back through town, still craving a beer, he pulled into the parking lot of a run-down bar called Gerry's. He parked in the spot closest to the sidewalk and got out.

As he walked through the parking lot to the bar entrance he passed two bikers standing next to their machines. They were discussing compression and tuning. One had a reddish-blond beard and tattoos on his forearms that Hank couldn't quite make out, and the other had a brush cut, a long mustache, similar tattoos, and wore sunglasses despite the darkness of the night. Both bikes had Pennsylvania license plates. Out of habit he memorized the numbers.

As Hank approached the door of the bar he saw a woman standing in the shadows on one side. She stepped forward to look at him and quickly stepped back again. She was in her forties, with wavy, shoulder-length black hair, prominent cheekbones, a high forehead, dark eyes, dark complexion, long slender legs, and a good figure. She wore a light-colored dress with large flowers on it and black shoes with a slight heel. She looked upset about something.

Hank stepped inside the bar and looked around. There were a few middle-aged men sitting at tables and one younger guy hunched over the bar. There were two waitresses, one about Hank's age and one in her early twenties. There was a man behind the bar. Faces turned in his direction and eyes looked him over.

Hank went to a table along the far wall and sat down facing the room. According to his watch it was 11:19 p.m.

The young waitress smiled as she went by with a tray of beer for three men on the other side of the room, but it was the older woman who eventually served him. He ordered a beer and drank it slowly, watching the room. He was now being completely ignored. The bikers came in and settled down at the bar, one of them fooling around with a cell phone. A few minutes later an athletic-looking middle-aged guy came in. He wore a black sport jacket and jeans. It was 11:25 p.m. He sat at a table and ordered a beer from the young waitress. When it arrived he drank it quickly. While he sat there he kept looking around, as though expecting to meet someone. He left in about ten minutes.

Hank ordered a second beer. When it was done he got up, went to the washroom, came back out, left his money on the table, and went out. The woman he'd seen outside the door was gone. He hadn't seen her come into the bar while he'd been there. The parking lot was empty. It was a couple of minutes before midnight. He got into his rented Grand Cherokee and drove back to the motel.

He watched television for about a half an hour, after which he turned out the light and fell asleep.

At 2:21 a.m. they kicked down the door, dragged him out of bed, beat the living crap out of him, and threw his sorry ass in jail.

3

The Town of Harmony Police Department was headquartered in a small, single-story building a block from Bluefield. Set back about twenty feet from the sidewalk, the station building was fronted by parking spaces. Branham swung the cruiser into an empty space in front of flagpoles set in a broad concrete base. Hank heard flags fluttering above him as Branham led him by the arm from the cruiser to the front door. Inside, they crossed a shallow lobby area and passed through a waist-high cattle door at the end of the front counter. There were four cluttered desks behind the counter. Branham stopped at a little fingerprint station attached to the wall with metal brackets.

"We don't have a Livescan," Branham said. "We just do it the old-fashioned way, with ten-print cards and ink. Got a problem if we take yours now?"

Hank shook his head and let Branham fingerprint him. When it was done he led Hank over to a heavy metal door. There was a small window set in the door with safety mesh embedded in it. Branham pressed buttons on the number lock and opened the door.

"Just rest quiet for a bit." Branham guided him by the arm into the corridor and down to a cell. "Think you can do that?"

There were only four cells in total in the lock-up. The other three were empty. Hank allowed Branham to push him into the cell. The deputy chief locked it and went back down the corridor and out through the metal door. Hank looked around. The cell was six feet wide and nine feet deep, with a metal cot bolted to the wall on the left. That was it. There was a mattress on the cot that looked reasonably clean and a folded brown blanket and a thin pillow stacked at the foot of the mattress. Hank spread the blanket out on the cot, propped the pillow against the wall, and sat down to wait.

After what felt like an hour, the metal door opened again and Branham walked down the corridor to the cell. With him was a small, balding man in a brown suit with narrow gold-framed glasses. He was carrying a large black bag. Hank didn't move from the cot as Branham opened the cell door.

"This is Dr. Justice," Branham said. "He'll look you over."

"Sit forward on the edge of the cot," Justice instructed. He knelt down and opened his black bag to remove a notebook and pen. He opened the notebook to a fresh page, wrote the date, checked his watch, and wrote the time.

"What time is it?" Hank asked.

"Three forty-seven," Justice replied. "Don't speak, please." He took Hank's pulse, made a note, then removed a blood pressure cuff and took Hank's blood pressure. That called for another note.

"I imagine it's up a bit," Hank said.

"Shh." Justice took out a stethoscope, shoved it under Hank's t-shirt and listened, moving it around. "Breathe deeply." He listened and moved the stethoscope. "Again." He moved it once more. "Again." He put the stethoscope away and made a few more notes. He lifted up the t-shirt again and examined Hank's rib cage. He palpated a spot on Hank's right side and looked at him expectantly.

"That hurt?" he prompted when Hank said nothing.

"No," Hank said. "Don't think they're broken, just bruised."

He ran his fingers gently over Hank's throat. "Swallow."

Hank swallowed.

"Hurt?"

"No."

He nodded and made a note. He flicked a light in and out of Hank's eyes, made a few more notes. He put down the notebook and examined Hank's hands, wrists, and forearms, both sides, finding nothing out of the ordinary. He made another notation, then removed some supplies from his bag and cleaned up the small cuts on Hank's forehead, left cheek, and lip.

"Head ache?"

"A little," Hank admitted.

"What day is it?"

"Saturday night. Sunday morning, actually, September 18."

"Okay," Justice said. "The lip's stopped bleeding. It'll be okay if you rest your mouth a bit. I'll put a plaster on your cheek."

He applied a small bandage to Hank's left cheek, packed up his black bag, and stood up, nodding at Branham. "He's fine."

"Thanks, doc," Branham said, stepping aside as Justice left the cell.

Hank watched him lock the cell door. The two men went down the corridor and out through the metal door.

Hank slowly slid back against the wall and closed his eyes to wait it out.

4

The sound of the metal door woke Hank from a light sleep. He was lying twisted on the cot, his head at the top and his bare feet sticking out over the side. He sat up and swung around as Branham walked down the corridor and unlocked the cell door.

He motioned Hank to his feet and held up a plastic bag. "Brought some clothes for you," he said. "You can use the washroom at the end of the hall."

Hank stood up and walked stiffly to the open cell door. His entire body ached. He took the bag and looked inside at a pair of jeans, a yellow polo shirt, a pair of gray tube socks, and gray boxer shorts. Each item still had the store tags attached.

"Crime scene team gave me your sizes from the stuff in your suitcase," Branham explained.

"I appreciate the thought."

"Petty cash," Branham said. "You can reimburse us later."

"I'll be sure to."

Branham pointed. "Down here." He led Hank down the corridor past two other cells to a washroom at the end. There was no door. Hank looked at a toilet and sink. There was a small metal shelf bolted to the wall. On the shelf were a white face cloth, folded white towel, and a bar of soap. "Sorry about the lack of privacy."

"I'll survive." Hank stepped into the washroom. "What time is it?"

"It's 6:40 a.m."

Hank used the toilet and then stepped in front of the sink. There was no mirror on the wall. He ran his hand through his frizzy hair and scratched his scalp. He washed his face, trying to keep the water away from the small bandage on his cheek. He kept his beard trimmed at about a quarter of an inch and so wasn't bothered by the lack of a razor, but he could have used a tooth brush and tooth paste. He settled for rinsing out his mouth several times.

"I checked you out and confirmed your ID back home," Branham said. "I'm sorry about this, Lieutenant, but you'll have to stay in the cell for a while longer. I hope you understand."

15

"If you're trying to tell me it's police business, then, yeah, I understand." Hank dried his face with the towel. "If you're talking about the situation itself then shit no, I don't understand at all. What the hell's going on?"

"Wish I could say more, I really do. Best if you just hang tight a while longer. I appreciate it."

Hank shook his head. He wiped his hands, folded the towel, and put it back on the shelf. Then he stripped off the blood-spattered t-shirt and briefs, put on the clothing Branham had brought him, and stuffed the t-shirt and briefs into the plastic bag. "Your name's Branham, is it?"

Branham pushed off the wall and motioned Hank to precede him back down the corridor to his cell. "That's right. Deputy Chief Neil Branham."

"Well, Deputy Chief Neil Branham," Hank said, handing him the bag, "you forgot to bring me shoes."

Branham grunted. "We'll set you up with some later. What size do you wear?"

"Thirteen."

"I'll find you something later."

"Thanks, Branham. Appreciate it." Hank sat down on the edge of the cot.

"No problem."

"Pretty quiet place," Hank observed. "Get much business?"

"Not really. The odd DUI or what have you. Not a lot of serious crime around here. That's one reason why things are a little tense right now. So just sit tight and wait it out."

Branham locked the cell door. With a brief look into Hank's eyes, he went down the corridor and out through the metal door.

5

Some time later Hank heard the metal door open again. He watched Chief Askew and Deputy Chief Branham walk down to his cell with a man between them. The man was small and thin, like a jockey. He was in his fifties, had short gray hair, a high, wrinkled forehead, and small hands and feet. He wore a blue plaid shirt with the sleeves turned up on his forearms, faded blue jeans, and beat-up white sneakers.

"Take a good look," the chief ordered brusquely.

Hank folded his arms across his chest and considered telling the chief how his lawyer would discredit the use of a show-up identification procedure when Hank was sitting alone in a cell displaying obvious signs of having been beaten and when a lineup or photo array procedure would not have been all that difficult to arrange, even in a backwater town like Harmony. Instead, he kept his mouth shut because the witness was already shaking his head.

"Could be, Chief, but I don't think so." The little guy spoke in a distinct Appalachian accent. "This fella's big but the other fella was bigger. This fella has a sorta beard, but the fella I seen had a real beard." He looked at Askew, who glared at him, then turned to Branham, who merely watched with interest. "Know what I mean? A big bushy beard like Moses, not like this fella's. And the clothes is wrong."

"He wasn't wearing those clothes," Chief Askew snapped, turning his glare on Branham.

"Even so," the little guy insisted.

"But this guy got into the car you described," Askew said. "License plate and all."

"Yeah, most like. But this hain't the fella walked by the window. That fella was bigger, and his face was longer and bonier than this fella's."

"Jesus fucking Christ." Askew pushed by them and went back down the corridor and out the metal door.

"Come on, Pete," Branham said. He glanced at Hank without expression before guiding their witness down the corridor after the departed chief of police.

About two hours later Branham came in with a paper bag and a

Styrofoam cup. He opened the cell door and handed them to Hank.

"Sorry we missed breakfast," the deputy said, "but I brought you some lunch compliments of the town of Harmony."

"Thanks." Hank took the paper bag and sat down on the edge of the cot. He took out a smoked meat sandwich on light rye bread. It tasted good. He washed it down with a mouthful of decent coffee as another man walked into the cell. This one was medium height and thin, with wavy steel gray hair. His cheeks and nose were red-veined. He had the look of a confirmed alcoholic. He wore a rumpled dark green suit and scuffed black shoes. His hands were shoved into his pockets and his eyes roamed around the cell instead of meeting Hank's.

"This is Ansell Hall, our detective," Branham said. "We only have the one. I imagine you have quite a few."

Hank swallowed a mouthful of sandwich. "A few."

Branham nodded.

"You guys care to tell me what I'm doing here?"

"First, why don't you take us through what you did last night? When did you get in town?"

Hank walked them through it, from checking into the motel to where he ate, the walk he took, the cigars he bought, what he watched on television back in his room, the final score of the ball game and what he thought of the Orioles, his trip back out for beer, and the stop at the run-down bar where he had two before coming back to his room and going to bed.

"What time were you at the bar?"

"Got there at about 11:20 p.m. and left about midnight." Hank put his empty coffee cup into the paper bag and handed it to Branham.

"What'd you do while you were there?"

"Sat at a table, looked around, drank a couple of beers, went to the can, and left."

"Just two beers?"

"Just the two. Nothing else. Then I left."

As he talked, Hank kept glancing at Detective Hall, but the man steadfastly refused to look at him. Hank wondered what the hell kind of a detective he was.

"You didn't go around to the back of the place at any time?" Branham asked.

"The back?"

"Outside. Did you go outside and around the side of the place to the back?"

"What the hell for? Of course not."

"You were seen by a witness passing the kitchen window," Hall said in a raspy smoker's voice.

"The hell I was," Hank retorted testily. "That witness already changed his tune. You need to keep up on current events, Detective."

Hall looked in confusion at Branham, who merely rolled his eyes.

"Come on," Hank said, "I'm trying to be real patient here, but there's a limit. What the hell's going on?"

"A woman was killed last night at the back of that bar where you stopped in for a couple of beers," Branham said. "Right around the time you were there. Someone strangled her and left her body down the ravine behind the place."

Hank digested this for a moment, then looked at Branham. "If she was strangled, you don't need my gun, right? You'll be returning it as soon as I get out of here, right?"

Branham sighed. "Tazewell took it. They'll release it in due course."

"Tazewell?"

"The County Sheriff's Office. We're too small for crime scene technicians and all the sort of stuff you take for granted, so we call the sheriff's office and they send their crime scene processing van. It's only the second time this year we've needed it. There's not a lot of violent crime around here."

"So you're telling me my weapon's in another part of the state somewhere and I'll get it back God knows when?"

"It's just down the road in Tazewell and it'll come back real soon if you stay patient and let this all work itself out."

"Well, now I feel a hell of a lot better. Are you going to keep me here or transport me somewhere else?"

"Lucky you," Branham replied. "You get to stay here as our guest. Normally we'd ship you to Tazewell but the chief wants you to stay handy."

"Lucky me," Hank echoed.

"Who was at the bar while you were there, Lieutenant Donaghue?" Branham asked, changing the subject.

Hank looked at Hall. "You want to take notes while I'm talking?"

Hall looked confused again, but Branham cleared his throat. "Detective Hall has a photographic memory."

"I'll bet he does." Hank shot his hand through his frizzy brown hair. "Two women were serving, an older one and a younger one, both white. Older one was in her middle forties, five-six, one fifty, wavy dark hair, looked exhausted. Younger one was in her early twenties, five-nine, one thirty, short straight brown hair. Cute and flirty. Guy behind

19

the bar was white, middle thirties, five-ten, two hundred, short straight blond hair. The girls got their own orders so I figure the guy was the manager."

"Customers?" Branham prompted.

"When I got there, there was a young guy at the bar. White, early twenties, maybe five-ten, two twenty, pudgy, short, light brown hair, kept to himself. At a table by himself was a white guy, middle forties, looked like a construction worker or something, five-nine, one sixty, short gray hair. At another table were three white guys, maybe in their thirties, all medium height, medium build."

"Any of them leave before you did?"

"None of them did. They were there when I walked in and they were still there when I walked out." Hank paused. "When I got there, there were two bikers outside in the parking lot shooting the shit. They came inside a few minutes after I did and sat at the bar. They were still there when I left. No gang colors, just leather jackets with Harley crests. Tattoos, but I wasn't close enough to make them out. Pennsylvania plates." He dictated the license plate numbers from memory. "Some other guy walked in while I was there. Guy about forty but still athletic-looking, as though he'd been a big deal back in the day. Wore a black sport jacket and jeans. Short black hair, thin face, pale blue eyes, big hands, five-ten or five-eleven, one ninety to two hundred. Drank a beer and left before I did."

Hall stirred. "Sounds like Morris."

"Morris?"

Branham looked uncomfortable. "David Morris. Former chief of police."

"A cop," Hank mused.

"Former." Branham looked at him. "Anything else?'

Hank thought for a moment. "No. Oh, wait. Yeah. A woman was standing out front as I walked in. She took a look at me like she was waiting for someone. Nice looking, early forties, five-nine, maybe one thirty, good figure, dark complexion, dark wavy hair, pretty dress with big flowers on it and black shoes with maybe a one-inch heel. Looked upset about something."

"Oh, hell," Hall said softly.

"What?" Hank asked. "Someone you know?"

"Yeah," Branham said. "The victim."

"Who was she?"

"Marcie Askew," Branham told him. "Chief Askew's wife."

6

It was the middle of the afternoon when the metal door down at the end of the corridor opened again. A heavy, middle-aged woman wedged it open with a chunk of wood and pushed a trolley cart down the corridor to the washroom at the end. She wore a pale blue dress that looked like the uniform for a cleaning company, white sneakers, latex gloves, and white terry cotton wristbands. Whistling softly off key, she went into the washroom to clean the toilet.

"Afternoon," Hank called out.

The woman ignored him, whistling and scrubbing as though completely alone in the universe.

"What time is it?"

The tune was "Jingle Bells." She was whistling "Jingle Bells," for chrissakes, in the middle of September. Enough was enough.

Hank stood at the door of his cell and looked down at the open metal door. "Hey!" he called out. "Hey, Officer!"

Oh what fun it is to ride....

"HEY! OUT THERE AT THE DESK! *HEY!* HEY, ARE YOU DEAD OUT THERE?"

A uniformed officer stuck his head through the doorway. "Shut your fucking mouth."

"Hey! Tell Branham it's time for my phone call! Right now!"

"Deputy Chief went home, now shut the fuck up."

"Is Hall out there? Tell Hall I want to talk to him right now!"

"You don't need to talk to nobody, mister. Don't make me come down there and bust your fuckin' head for you."

"Hall! *HALL!* Get the hell in here right now!"

The uniformed officer disappeared and Detective Hall shuffled down the corridor to Hank's cell.

"You don't have to yell, Lieutenant. They can hear you clear to Bluefield."

"I want to make a phone call, Detective. Right now."

Hall looked dubious. "Chief Askew's got to give his permission for that, and he's not around. It better wait."

"It's not going to wait, Detective, and that's that. I make a

21

phone call right now or my attorney's going to be filing lawsuits with your name on them. Now let me out of here and let me make my call."

Hall sighed and went back down the corridor. He returned in a moment with the uniformed officer, a big, beefy specimen who glared at Hank as though daring him to try something. The name tag pinned to his shirt said *Grimes*. Probably an offensive tackle on the local high school football team. Lots of upper-body strength, quick feet, and the mentality of a mean dog on a short chain. The officer unlocked the door and jerked his head, once, in the direction of the front. Hank walked between them down the corridor and through the metal door. Hall pointed at a messy desk next to a wall of battered green filing cabinets.

"Use my phone," Hall said. "One call. Make it short."

"On a budget?" Hank sat down in Hall's chair.

"Make it short," Hall repeated. He walked away and filled a paper cup at a water dispenser next to the filing cabinets.

Hank glanced at his wrist before remembering yet again that his watch was in an envelope locked away somewhere. A big clock on the wall told him it was twenty minutes before three in the afternoon. He picked up the phone and heard a dial tone.

"Do I have to dial for an outside line?"

"Just dial your number," Hall told him.

Hank dialed. It rang three times and was answered.

"Stainer."

"Pack an overnight bag," Hank said. "I need your help."

7

Karen Stainer sat in the big front window of Mary's Donuts on Bluefield Street and devoured her third blueberry muffin. She pitched into her second super-sized coffee and watched the traffic. It was a pretty town, but Karen was feeling grouchy this morning and wasn't in the mood for pretty.

She'd reached Harmony at just before ten o'clock last night after a five-hour drive. She arrived at the police station to find it closed, the window blinds down and the lights out. Next door was an all-night convenience store. She walked in and rapped her knuckles on the counter to attract the attention of the teenager watching television behind a rack of cigarettes.

"Hey! Clark Kent! Got a sec?"

The kid came over to the counter adjusting his thick black-framed glasses. "Good evening."

"Charmed, I'm sure. Listen, is that the cop shop next door or am I on the wrong planet here?"

The kid looked out the window dubiously. "Yeah it is, but I think they're closed."

"Closed. Christ. What happens if somebody needs a cop in this dump?"

"Uh, they call 911?"

"Okay, so call 911 and tell them an insane bitch is trying to break into their police station."

"Seriously?"

"Yeah, seriously. Tell them I said if there isn't a cop here in five minutes I'm gonna shoot the lock and kick the fuckin' door in. Got it?"

The kid nodded and reached for the telephone. Karen went back outside.

Her husky Texan drawl, which made "here" sound like "hay-yah" and "kick" sound like "kay-yick," would be charming if it weren't coming from a mouth that looked like it might bite a chain in half at any moment. Karen was thirty-seven years old and a sixteen-year veteran of the Glendale Police Department. A Tai-kwon-do black belt with a mean streak, she was five feet, three inches tall, weighed one hundred and five pounds, and had fists like a pair of shoemaker's hammers, small and very hard. Her face was sharp-featured, her blond hair was shoulder-length and wispy, and her eyes, a lovely pale blue shade, tended to fix on people in a laser beam cop's stare.

She wore a navy sport jacket, a pale blue blouse, blue jeans and black cowboy boots. Walking back to the police station, she reached under her jacket and removed the holstered handgun clipped to her belt. She walked over to her red 1979 Pontiac Firebird Esprit, which was parked in one of the empty spaces in front of the police station, and set her gun down carefully on the hood of the car. She leaned against the back fender. Eight minutes later a police cruiser pulled up to the curb and two uniformed officers got out.

The guy getting out of the passenger side spread his legs and put his hands on his hips impressively, but the guy from the driver side swung around the back of the cruiser and quickly took charge.

"You the one asking for police assistance?"

By this time Karen had pushed away from the fender of her car and was holding up the leather wallet containing her badge and identification. "Detective Karen Stainer, Glendale, Maryland Police Department. I'm here to see your prisoner. My firearm's on the hood of my car."

She didn't see any need to mention the Kel-Tec P11 nine millimeter backup that was clipped inside her right cowboy boot.

"Stainer?" The driver, whose name tag said *Orton*, took her identification and examined it with the aid of a small flashlight from his pocket. The passenger, whose name tag said *Collins*, abandoned his authoritative cop stance and hurried past her to grab her gun.

Orton handed back her identification and frowned. "What was that about a prisoner?"

"Y'all got a prisoner, Lieutenant Hank Donaghue. I want to see him. Pronto."

Collins reluctantly returned her weapon as Orton unlocked the front door of the station. He turned on the lights and directed her to sit in one of the visitor's chairs next to a desk while Orton telephoned Deputy Chief Branham.

When Branham arrived he had his own look at Karen's identification and then waved off the two officers, who trooped out the front door to resume their shift. "We gave him his phone call this afternoon. I thought he called his lawyer."

"I'll try not to be too insulted by that," Karen said.

"You work with him, do you?"

"Sure enough."

"Doing what?"

Karen looked disgusted. "Homicide investigation. C'mon, he already told you all that. Don't play fucking games. He's a twenty-year decorated veteran who's a genius on top of it and you're holding him on a case of mistaken identity. You need to release him right now and get your ass after the guy who actually throttled your vic."

Branham spread his hands. "That's Chief Askew's decision, and he can't be reached until tomorrow."

"Can't be reached? What kind of bullshit is that?"

Branham paused for a minute. He ran the tip of his tongue over his bottom lip, looked at his hands, and then smiled faintly. "It's almost ten thirty in the evening and it's definitely a pleasure, Detective Stainer, but you'll have to excuse us if we're a little small-town around here."

"Sure, whatever. Just spring the lieutenant and we'll rock on down the road."

The smile faded a little. "As I said, that's Chief Askew's decision and the earliest he'll consider it is tomorrow morning. His wife was just brutally murdered, Detective. Surely you understand."

"Yeah, I heard, but not by the guy in your cell."

Branham shrugged. "You're probably right. But you know how this works. One step at a time."

"I want to talk to him."

"Five minutes," Branham said. "No touching, no physical contact of any kind, don't try to give him anything."

She had to be content with standing on the other side of the cell door while Branham watched from the end of the corridor. "Christ, Lou, the other guy better look worse than you do."

"Not worse, just uglier," Hank replied. "Thanks for coming."

"No problem. You know how I love to drive."

"Was Sandy okay with it?"

Sandy was John "Sandy" Alexander, Karen's fiancé. He was a special agent in the Glendale field office of the Federal Bureau of Investigation. So far their relationship had lasted almost three years, which was something of a record for Karen, and in May they'd become engaged and moved in together to see how it would go. It was a calculated risk, since they both owned firearms and neither was afraid to pull the trigger, but so far they were still living together and no one had been killed or wounded.

"He's got plenty of stuff to keep himself busy," Karen replied. "I barely see him these days. He's taking a bunch of courses at Quantico."

"Well, I appreciate it." Hank went over the situation in more detail than he'd been able to give her on the telephone. "Eyewitness inside the kitchen at the back of the bar saw a guy who looked like me pass by the window close to the time she was killed," he finished. "He went outside a few minutes later and saw me get in my car and drive away. I haven't seen his statement, that's just putting the pieces together. So there's another guy in the mix who looks like me, because I didn't go around to the back of the place."

"They have any ideas who it might be?"

Hank shrugged. "They're not interested. I look like me, and that's good enough. The fact their witness failed to make a positive ID isn't slowing them down much at this point."

"Christ." Karen shook her head. "So is the kitchen guy a witness or isn't he? He saw you but he didn't see *you*? What is this, amateur hour?"

Branham cleared his throat noisily at the end of the corridor.

"Patience is apparently a virtue," Hank said.

Karen left the station unhappy and drove over to the Harmony Motor Inn, where she checked in and got herself a room. She wandered down to Hank's room but the door was locked and sealed, so she turned in and got some sleep.

Now she was sitting in the big front window of Mary's Donuts on Bluefield Street finishing her second super-sized coffee while watching the morning traffic pass through downtown Harmony, such as it was. As she swigged a mouthful, a big guy with curly hair and a beard walked by on the sidewalk outside. He wore a light-colored dress shirt with no tie and the sleeves turned up on his forearms, black trousers, and black oxford shoes. As she watched, he stepped off the curb and walked around to the driver's side of a dusty white Dodge Ram pickup truck parked in the street just past the entrance of the donut shop. He got into the truck and drove away.

Karen rushed outside but was too late to catch a glimpse of the license plate. She looked around. A young woman and a small girl were approaching her on the sidewalk.

Karen flashed her ID and badge. "Excuse me, did you see the man who just got into that white pickup truck?"

The woman shook her head and hurried past.

"Ma'am?" Karen thought about following her and then changed her mind when she saw a man approaching from the same direction.

"Excuse me, sir, did you see the bearded man who just got into a white pickup truck and drove away?"

"Didn't see nothing."

She went up and down the sidewalk, stopping several other people, but no one had seen anything or would talk to her. She was standing there with her hands on her hips, casting around for another potential witness, when a police cruiser pulled in to the curb, lights flashing. Two cops tumbled out, weapons drawn.

"Police, freeze! Hands where we can see them!"

"Shit on a fuckin' stick." Karen held up the wallet containing her badge and ID.

"Don't you know it's a crime to impersonate a police officer?" demanded the cop whose name tag said *Brooks*. He was about thirty, with short brown hair and thick eyebrows. He snatched the wallet out of her hand while his partner, whose name tag said *Louden*, covered Karen with what she saw was a poorly-kept Beretta 92F. Louden was younger, with a blond brush cut and a trimmed blond mustache.

"Doesn't seem to slow you boys down much."

"Button it, smartass." Brooks took her ID back to the police cruiser and called it in.

A minute later he came back and returned it to her. "Our apologies, Detective Stainer. We weren't informed of your presence in Harmony this morning."

Karen looked at Louden, who was still holding his weapon. "Down, Rover. Play time's over."

Louden glanced at Brooks, who shrugged. He holstered the Beretta.

"Deputy Chief Branham asks if you'd kindly come with us to the station."

"Sounds good," Karen said, turning away, "but I've got my own ride."

Louden followed her across the strip of grass between the sidewalk and the parking lot of the donut shop. When he saw the car she was unlocking, he stopped short.

"That's your car?"

"Yup." Karen opened the door of the Firebird, got in and rolled down the window. Karen's older brother Delbert was an auto mechanic in Houston. He'd bought the car, one of the Redbird editions, ten years ago for three thousand dollars from a regular customer who was short of cash. Delbert put a thousand dollars' worth of work into it and sold it that summer to Karen for four thousand dollars when she was visiting back home. She drove it back from Texas and had driven it every summer since, putting it in storage each winter and switching to a beat-up pickup truck.

"Wow," Louden said, staring at her. "Hot."

Karen looked at him.

"I mean the car. The car. Is hot."

Karen shook her head and gunned the engine into life.

Branham was walking into his office with a cup of coffee in his

27

hand when Karen followed Brooks and Louden into the station.

"Come on in," he gestured to her.

The station was busier this morning than it had been last night. A woman in a lime green dress sat at one of the desks in the central area behind the counter. She stared at a computer monitor, typing industriously. She wore a wireless headset on her right ear. A beefy officer sat at the desk closest to the metal door leading into the back, talking on the phone. His legs were up on the corner of his desk, boots sticking out, and he watched Karen with a bemused smile. To her infinite disgust, he flexed his pectoral muscles beneath his tight uniform shirt and raised his eyebrows.

Karen went in and sat down in the cheap wooden visitor's chair across from Branham's desk. "Didn't we just do this a couple hours ago?"

Branham smiled and held out his cup. "Coffee?"

"No thanks, had some already. I take it you don't have any female police officers in this town."

"No, we don't. Haven't had any applicants, to date."

"Why am I not surprised."

"Although," Branham went on, leaning back and sipping his coffee, "that may change before long. The local college has a pretty good criminal justice program and I've been told the enrollment in the last two years has been forty percent female. Last year was the first year we did a little recruitment thing for the seniors before graduation, and maybe we'll get some interest from female grads if we keep doing it."

"Yeah, well, just make sure you don't send Hulk Hogan out there as part of your recruiting team," she said, hiking her thumb over her shoulder. "No woman in her right mind would want to work with that fucking hippopotamus."

Branham laughed. "Who, Grimes? He's not so bad."

"Says you. You're not female."

"Glad you noticed."

Karen leaned forward and dropped her left palm flat on top of Branham's desk so that her engagement ring made a loud *clack* on the scratched wooden surface.

Branham glanced at her hand and looked up into her eyes.

"Enough fun and games," she said. "Where's this chief of yours who's going to release Lieutenant Donaghue this morning and let us get the hell out of here?"

"He should be in shortly."

Karen leaned back in the chair and looked at him evenly. "I saw a guy this morning you need to bring in. White, tall, maybe six-three, six-four, two thirty, mid-forties, medium length wavy brown hair, beard, yellow shirt, black jeans, black shoes, got into a white Dodge pickup truck parked right near the donut shop and drove west down Bluefield."

"That why you were bothering people on the sidewalk?"

"Know who he is?"

"Know who *who* is?" a voice grated from the doorway.

Branham sat up straighter in his chair. "Chief, this is Homicide Detective Karen Stainer from Maryland. She works with Lieutenant Donaghue in their, uh, Major Crimes division up there. He contacted her with his telephone call."

Askew shifted his weight so that he could look at Karen around the door frame. "Thought he was calling a lawyer."

"Do I look like a lawyer? I understand your case took a major crap when your witness failed to identify the lieutenant. I expect you'll be releasing him in the next five minutes or so."

"Not likely, missy. One witness doesn't make or break a case. Didn't they teach you that wherever the hell it is you come from?"

Karen leaned back and stared at him. "You know," she said slowly, as though speaking to an idiot, "when I was a little girl we moved from Ponder to Fort Worth. We had a little black dog, and one day he got loose from our front yard and ran out into the street. I ran out after it, right into traffic. My daddy pulled me out from in front of a truck just before it knocked me into next week. Turned out it wasn't even our dog. Ours was asleep at the foot of my mother's bed. I learned two things from my daddy that day. One, don't run out into heavy traffic without looking, and two, if it ain't your dog, then Jesus Christ let the damned thing go." She stared at Askew. "You're chasing the wrong dog, pal. Let him go."

Askew shook his head and turned to Branham. "I'll be in my office. If the sheriff's office calls, patch it through to me. I want to talk to them."

"Hang on just a second," Karen said, leaning forward. "We're not done yet. There's a person of interest you need to bring in."

To his credit, Askew didn't move and didn't change his expression. He continued to look at Branham. "Well?"

"Detective Stainer saw someone in town this morning who resembled the physical description given by the eyewitness," Branham explained. "Got into a white pickup truck and drove west on Bluefield."

"Lotta white pickup trucks around here."

"Tall guy with a beard."

"Lotta guys with beards around here. Hillbilly heaven."

"We could check into it."

"Or we could stick with the tall guy with a beard who's sitting on his ass in our cell as we speak," Askew said. "I'll be in my office." He pushed away from the door frame.

"Wait a sec, Chief," Branham said. "I just thought of somebody might fit the description. You know that guy who's in charge of the monastery at Burkes Garden? What's his name again?"

Askew frowned. "The monastery? You mean the guru fellow there?"

"Yeah. What's his name again?"

"Brother something," Askew said.

"Cook?" Branham offered.

"Baker," Askew said. "Brother Baker. Brother Charles Baker."

"That's the guy. Tall, has a beard. Could have been him."

"That could have been who the detective here saw this morning," Askew agreed, "but tell me this: when was the last time you saw a guru monk from a religious monastery hanging around a dump like Gerry's at midnight?"

Branham said nothing.

"And when was the last time that guy in the cell back there was seen hanging around a dump like Gerry's at midnight?"

"Baker could have been the guy Pete saw," Branham said.

"I'll be in my office." This time, Askew left.

"He always this blockheaded?" Karen asked.

"He's a good man and a good cop, and he just lost his wife. Cut him some slack."

"You're right. Sorry." Karen was silent a moment. "The guy should be recused from the case if it's his wife."

Branham stared into his coffee cup and set it aside with distaste. "He and I already had that conversation. It was short and ugly."

"This Baker guy," Karen said, "is worth tracking down."

"I know."

"Didn't I hear you've got a detective around here? Isn't that what he's for? Detecting stuff? Why don't you send him to this garden place to check out the monk?"

Branham shook his head. "I doubt he's available at the moment."

"What the hell does that mean?"

"It means he's not available, Detective," Branham said curtly.

"Then I'll go."

"The hell you will."

"Then you go."

"I've got work to do."

"You've got a killer to catch."

30

Branham sighed. "Yeah, you're right. I'll go. It's worth a look."

"I'll go with you."

"The hell you will."

"We're kinda in a loop here," Karen said.

He shook his head. "What am I thinking? It's a sunny morning in September, Burkes Garden is one of the prettier places around, and a good-looking woman wants to go for a car ride with me. Where's the problem?"

"I'll drive," Karen said, standing up.

"No, you won't. I'll drive."

"This time," Karen conceded, "but you don't know what you're missing."

"I'll bet I do," Branham replied.

8

Branham grabbed the keys to one of the police cruisers, a five-year-old Chevrolet Caprice, and in no time they were heading westbound on Route 460 toward Tazewell. It was a four-lane highway with a flat grass median and wasn't very busy for a Monday morning.

"Burkes Garden isn't very far from here as the crow flies," Branham explained, setting the cruise control at just a hair above the speed limit, "but we have to drive around the mountain to get there, so it takes a bit longer."

"Sure," Karen said, not particularly caring. He was driving, so it was his problem, not hers. She tapped her heel against the black leather shoulder bag on the floor between her feet. She had grabbed it from her car before joining Branham in the cruiser.

"Tell me about the homicide," she said.

"The call came in to 911 at 1:32 a.m. on Sunday from Pete Jablonski, a dishwasher at Gerry's," Branham said. "Responding officers got there about 1:40 a.m. Orton and Collins, whom you've met. Pete said he'd seen a guy walk by the kitchen window earlier, about midnight or so, going around to the back of the place.

"He was rinsing dishes at the time and he says he glanced up at the window every few moments to see if the guy went past the window again, but he didn't. He was curious, so he dried his hands and went out to see if the guy was hanging around back there. He wasn't.

"He went all the way around the building and saw Donaghue get into his car in the parking lot and drive away. He thought at the time it might have been a drug sale or something, because every now and again they had to chase people away from the rear of the bar who went back there to buy and sell weed. He wasn't sure if the guy getting into the car was the same guy he'd seen walk by the window, but he made a mental note of the license plate anyway before going back inside.

"At 1:30 a.m., he said, he took a Coke and a cigarette outside on his break. He looked around to see if he could see anything, litter or something that might explain what the guy was doing back there. He noticed two long, odd-looking scuff marks across a patch of sand on the pavement. He went back inside for a flashlight to take a better look.

The scuff marks angled off in the direction of the ravine. He crossed the paved area in that direction and continued on across the grass toward the ravine."

"Do you know this guy? Is he a credible witness?"

"He's good," Branham said, glancing over at her. "Clean record, originally from Harmony. Spent a few years in Lexington in the horse business, working here and there as a groom, stable hand, whatever, and then came back when his mother got sick. I've known him for a while. He's honest enough. Very serious little guy. No sense of humor whatsoever."

"So he saw these scuff marks and followed them down to the ravine."

Branham nodded. "The ravine runs through town behind the buildings on that side of Bluefield Street. There's an opening in the brush right there and a path leading down into the ravine. Some high grass and weeds on one side had been flattened, so he decided to go down the path a few yards. He found the body on the ground just off the path. He said he didn't touch her, just bent down to try to see her face with the flashlight. When he saw her clothing was in disarray he came right back up and called 911."

"Cause of death?"

"Apparently manual strangulation. We'll know for sure when the autopsy's done. She was strangled behind the bar, dragged for a few yards, then picked up and carried down to the ravine and dumped. Then the guy probably went further on along the ravine, came back up for his car, and drove away."

"What happened to her clothes?"

"Her dress was torn. It was sleeveless, with cloth straps over the shoulders about two inches wide. The straps had decorative buttons on them. The right strap had been torn and the dress was pulled down from the top on the right side, along with the bra, to expose her right breast."

"Rape?"

Branham shook his head. "Doctor said nothing appeared to have happened below her waist. We'll have to wait until the autopsy to be sure. Her shoes were off, and tossed into the grass next to her. Tazewell figures the guy strangled her, started to drag her, and her shoes came off. So he put her down, grabbed the shoes, then picked her up and carried her the rest of the way."

Karen looked at him. "Tazewell figures?"

"We call in the sheriff's office to assist in crime scene processing. They've got a mobile unit for forensic investigation and a couple of detectives who have a lot better training and experience in evidence collection than we do. They did the scene for us Saturday night and also did Donaghue's motel room afterward."

"Then they should have already told you that he had nothing to do with what happened."

Branham shrugged. "We're still waiting for their reports."

"I suppose it's too much to ask that the bar would have video surveillance cameras."

"Not a chance."

After a few minutes of silence they reached the outskirts of Tazewell. He eased onto an off-ramp and took the underpass south onto a two-lane road.

"Just ahead we'll take a left onto Highway 61," Branham explained. "That takes us around the mountain up to Gratton, where we'll turn onto Route 623. That's the only road into Burkes Garden."

Karen grunted. She didn't have a tourist mentality and really didn't give a damn about local points of interest. She had a sense that Branham wanted to play tour guide and she wasn't going to sit there and let him drone on.

"Where are you from, Branham?" she asked. "You're not a local, are you?"

"Louisa, Kentucky," he replied, glancing at her. "Up on the Big Sandy, in Lawrence County. Not all that far from here, really."

"How'd you end up deputy chief of police in Harmony?"

"I started out in the Kentucky State Police. My grandfather lived alone here in Tazewell and when he became sick I got into the Virginia State Police out of Claypool Hill so I could move here and look after him. Then he passed away. I applied for an opening on the town force in Harmony and got in. That was in '01, and I've been here ever since."

Branham stopped at an intersection and put on his left-hand turn signal. "This is the junction of Highway 61. It'll take us to Gratton."

"Pretty small-time around here. You must be bored out of your skull."

"Not really." Smile lines creased the corners of his eyes as he waited for a break in the oncoming traffic. "It's a nice spot. There's not a whole lot of crime to handle, but the people aren't bad. I do most of the administrative stuff for the department, including the budget, shift schedule, that kind of thing. I wanted the experience because it'll help my career if I want to go statie again at a higher level down the road."

"You responsible for training, as well?"

"Yeah."

"Well, your boys need a refresher on firearms care and

maintenance. Louden's carrying a Beretta 92 that needs to be scrapped before he hurts himself with it."

Branham said nothing, concentrating on his driving.

"Where'd you go to college?" Karen asked.

"Eastern Kentucky."

Karen nodded. "EKU is good for police studies, I've heard."

"You heard that, did you? Well, it's true." He glanced at her again. "What about yourself, Detective Stainer? What's your story?"

Karen shrugged. "Not much to tell. Been a cop for sixteen years, the last year in Homicide. Before that there was a long stint in Family-Related Crime, and before that I rode in a patrol car like everybody else for what felt like an eternity."

"Family-Related? That must have been a chore."

"You could say that."

"What's your case load in Homicide like?"

"Heavy. There've been fifty-two homicides in the last six months."

"Wow. I'm surprised you could spare the time to come down here."

"Latest case wrapped up quickly. Suspect got his sorry fucking ass shot."

"Oh?"

She didn't really want to get into it.

The sun was shining brightly through the windshield as they rounded a bend in the highway. Karen grabbed a pair of sunglasses from her bag and put them on. A few minutes later Branham slowed and turned right onto Highway 623. "This takes us up Rich Mountain."

"So who's this guy we're going to see? Brother Charles Baker?"

"He's the head of the Monastery of God in Burkes Garden."

"Great. Religious fanatics. Hopefully they won't start a shootout while we're here."

"Not likely," Branham said. "They're pacifists. Although you look like you're ready to fight the next world war all by yourself."

"No idea what you're talking about."

"Now now," he chided, "full disclosure. Collins mentioned the P-226 you're carrying. You like it, by the way?"

"Love it."

"A friend of mine is a SIG enthusiast and he particularly likes the P-226. Which one is it?"

"The Elite Dark," Karen replied. "I fire the .40 S and W through it."

"With the short reset trigger or whatever they call it?"

"That's right. 'Faster trigger return during high speed shooting,' as the brochure says. I used to carry a Px4 Storm as my off-duty but I doubled up on the 226 instead and I leave the Px4 at home."

"Hmm." Branham glanced in the direction of her feet. "So what do you carry in the shoulder bag?"

"A Kel-Tec P-11. I had it for a while as my oh-shit backup," Karen said, "but I tried a P-32 and it was better, so that's what I'm carrying in my boot." She made a face. "Since I knew you were going to ask."

"You a mouse gun fan or something?"

"Hell, no. If I ever have to fire anything in the line of duty other than this baby on my hip then I'm in deep shit, but I wanted something a little more comfortable in my boot and the P-32 is a quarter inch thinner and half as heavy as the P-11, so I put the P-11 in my shoulder bag when I'm hauling it around and go with the P-32 as my primary backup. I know it's only a .32 compared to the 9 mm P-11, but what can you do?"

"An in-your-ear gun."

Karen laughed. "That's right. Stick it in some guy's ear and it might as well be a cannon."

"So that's it?" Branham asked. "That's everything you have to declare today?"

"You sound like customs." Karen smiled. "Yeah, that's it. I left the rest of the arsenal at home." She shifted in the seat to look at him. "You were telling me about Brother Charles. What's the deal with the garden hideout?"

"Burkes Garden is the name of the place. It's a historical district, the highest mountain valley in the state. Ten miles across. From the air it looks like a moon crater but it has some of the most fertile soil in the area. The Appalachian Trail follows the ridge so they get a lot of hikers and tourists up here. Plus there are some organic farmers with pretty good retail operations, that sort of thing. This brotherhood, the Monastery of God, has a fifty-acre property. They have a small farm operation, a residence and chapel, and they also operate the best free medical clinic in the county."

"Come into town a lot, do they?"

"No, actually, they don't. They usually do business in Tazewell or Bluefield. Occasionally I see a few of them in Harmony and I've talked to Brother Charles once before. I came out here to represent Chief Askew at a charity event and talked to him for maybe five minutes. Other than that . . ."

"So Brother Charles being seen twice in Harmony inside of seventy-two hours is an unusual thing, then."

"A little." Branham paused, choosing his words. "My take on him? Quiet guy, very polite, intellectual. He's the abbot of the monastery, so he doesn't do the manual labor around the place. He's the spiritual leader."

"Gay?"

"If I had to guess I'd say not. They're not celibates, as I understand it, but he didn't come off like somebody with a raging libido, gay or hetero."

"It's the quiet guys you gotta watch," Karen joked.

"I'm just saying I'm not really sold on him as a suspect in a strangulation homicide, that's all."

"So you're just driving all the way out here as a special favor to me."

"I'm driving out here because it's a beautiful day, Burkes Garden is a pretty spot, and a good-looking woman wanted to go sight-seeing."

Karen snorted.

The road wound its way up the mountain, trees lining each side, the sun green and yellow as it filtered through the leaves. Branham slowed at each hairpin turn and accelerated through very short straightaways, slowing again as the road bent once more, right then left, then right. Two lanes only, with a faded solid center line and no shoulders. Karen prayed they wouldn't find themselves behind a slow-moving vehicle or it'd take Branham forever to pass.

Before long they swung south and drove through an opening in the ridge. The road clung to the foot of the mountain slope on the right. On the left through the trees Karen could see a creek and beyond that the slope on the far side.

"This is called The Gap," Branham said. "It takes us into Burkes Garden."

It was pretty scenery, she had to admit.

The Gap began to open up and they reached an intersection where a road on the left crossed a bridge over the creek. "That's Back Road. It loops around the eastern rim of the valley. We'll stay on 623 here because it'll take us directly to the monastery."

After several miles they turned off into a driveway through a large open gate with a sign that said, "Monastery of God: Everyone Welcome." Just inside the gate was a large campus map and another sign that said: "Visitors please report to Reception. Patients may proceed directly to Clinic."

The driveway ran straight for about a hundred feet and then sloped upward. Karen looked at page wire fencing on either side and saw a couple of horses loitering in the field on the left. Ahead there were typical farm buildings: barns, two silos, several sheds, then the driveway branched off to the right. Karen saw a two-story structure with a sign that said *Clinic*, a long, three-story building behind the clinic that was accessed by cement sidewalks, and a typical Virginian farm house on the right with a sign that said *Reception*. Branham eased into an open spot in the visitor's parking lot.

"These people are exemplary citizens as far as we're concerned," Branham said, shutting off the engine. "No records, no reports of anything illegal, no traffic stops, no nothing."

"I get it," Karen said. "Reclusive wackjobs who fly under the radar."

"What I'm getting at—"

"—is that you want me to keep my mouth shut." Karen smiled at him. "Your play, Deputy Chief. I'll be good."

"Thank you."

They got out of the car and Karen followed him through the front door. The exterior might look like a typical farm house, but the interior, Karen saw, had been completely redesigned. They stood in a large reception area that was furnished with armchairs and love seats in an Amish-looking style, coffee tables with magazines, a bookcase filled with books, reading lamps and a side table with a coffee machine, coffee cups, and the fixings. A man wearing a full length white cassock got up from a desk and approached them.

"Deputy Chief Branham, isn't it?" he asked, smiling. "We met last year. Brother Miles."

"Right," Branham said, shaking hands. "This is Detective Karen Stainer. We're here to see Brother Charles Baker."

"Nice to meet you, Detective," Brother Miles said. He waited for Karen to offer to shake hands, and when she didn't, he smiled and nodded before turning back to Branham.

"I'll see if he's available. Is it a personal matter, or business?"

"Police business," Branham said. "A homicide investigation."

"Oh, well, I see. He should be in his office. Follow me."

Brother Miles led them through the reception area to the main staircase. As they went up the stairs to the second floor, Karen stared at the back of the man's head. She'd been put off by the cassock and the oily personality. It was a point in his favor that he'd discarded the receptionist bullshit as soon as Branham told him they weren't there to compare sugar pie recipes, but it didn't do anything to lessen her dislike of the place. Religious fanaticism set her teeth on edge.

On the second floor Brother Miles showed them into a large room furnished with a round wooden meeting table and chairs.

"This is our meeting room," he said. "No phone, no interruptions.

Brother Charles will be with you right away."

Within two minutes they were joined by a tall bearded man who also wore a white cassock. Karen was standing just inside the door and he approached her first.

"I'm Brother Charles Baker," he said, sticking out his hand.

"Detective Stainer," Karen said, hesitating. *What the hell.* She shook his hand. His grip was firm and dry, business-like. He was the man she'd seen this morning outside the donut shop. Up close, he looked nothing like Hank. His face was longer and the skin looked pasty. His nose was hooked like an eagle's beak, where Hank's was straight and normal sized. His brow was higher and his eyes were a watery blue, where Hank's heavy brow gave his brown eyes a brooding look. This guy's reddish-brown hair was short and slightly wavy, where Hank's chestnut brown hair was frizzy, and the monk's beard was quite long, where Hank kept his beard trimmed short. They were about the same height but this guy was about twenty pounds heavier than Hank. Karen could believe that an eyewitness catching a one-second glimpse of this guy through a kitchen window at night might mistake him for Hank from a distance when Hank was getting into his car to leave the bar. Otherwise, though, you'd have to be blind not to see the differences.

"Deputy Chief," Brother Charles said, moving around the table to shake Branham's hand. "Good to see you again. Please, sit down. What can I do for you?"

"Do you drive a white pickup truck, Brother Charles? Dodge Ram?"

"Yes, I do. It's mostly used for farm work, but I borrow it occasionally when the administration car, the Ford Focus, isn't available."

"Were you in Harmony this morning, driving the pickup?" Branham asked.

"Yes, I was."

"What about Saturday night? Were you in Harmony Saturday night?"

"What's this about? Was there a traffic violation or something?" Brother Charles frowned. "I don't remember doing anything wrong."

"Please just answer the question, Brother Charles. Were you in Harmony Saturday night?"

Brother Charles leaned back and sighed. "Yes, I suppose I was."

"About what time?"

"Later in the evening."

"Can you be more specific?"

"Late."

"How late?"

"Close to midnight, I guess."

I guess. Karen eased her chair away from the table a few inches. This guy was definitely going for a ride. She looked at his hands, resting lightly on the table in front of him. They were large hands, with thick fingers. She could imagine them around the neck of some woman, strangling the life out of her.

"Were you at Gerry's Bar about midnight?" Branham asked.

"Yes, I was." Brother Charles spread his hands. "Look, I take it that someone saw me there and reported it to you. I'm guessing this is in connection with the killing of Mrs. Askew. It was in the news. I was there Saturday night, but I didn't see anything that could help you."

"Why were you there?"

"I'd rather not say, if you don't mind. It's confidential."

"We do mind, pal," Karen glared. "This is a homicide investigation." She pointed a finger at him. "The victim was strangled to death right around the time you were there by someone with hands about the size of your hands. Why'd you kill her? Was she going to spill the beans on the affair you two were having, spoil this great setup you guys have got here?"

"No, no," Brother Charles replied, aghast. "Nothing like that at all. Killing is abhorrent. I don't even kill insects if I can avoid it, let alone a human being. I was at that bar, yes, at about the time you mentioned, but there were other men there at the same time. Surely one of them would be the one you're looking for."

"Why were you there?" she snapped.

"To meet someone who needed help."

"Who?" Branham jumped back in. "Who was it you were there to meet?"

"I'm afraid I just can't say."

"Why not?" Branham asked. "Don't you see the position it puts you in? You were at the bar when the victim was murdered, you were seen by an eyewitness walking to the back of the building, where she was killed, and you can't give us a reasonable explanation for your actions. What do you expect us to think? It makes you the most likely person we know of at this point to have killed her. You had means and opportunity, and you seem to be hiding a motive that we'll find out about soon enough."

Brother Charles folded his hands on the table in front of him and stared at them.

"If you tell us who you went there to see," Branham pressed, "they can corroborate your story and clear you. We might be able to keep the specifics confidential. Who was it?"

Brother Charles shook his head. "We help a lot of people at our clinic. Often they ask that we keep their identities confidential, for various reasons. Sometimes," he looked up at Branham before turning to Karen, "they're embarrassed about going to a free clinic instead of being able to afford Medicare. Sometimes, rarely, they have their own Medicare but need to consult someone in greater privacy. Off the grid, so to speak." He turned back to Branham. "We respect and guarantee those requests for confidentiality."

"Are you telling me you went to see someone in Harmony Saturday night who's been getting treatment here at your clinic?"

Brother Charles nodded.

"They were at Gerry's?"

"I was supposed to meet them there, but when I got there I couldn't find them, so I left."

"And you won't tell me the identity of this person to help corroborate your story?"

Brother Charles shook his head. "I'm sorry."

Branham looked at Karen. She hiked an eyebrow. It was obvious enough to her. Branham nodded.

"Brother Charles," he said, getting up, "I'm going to have to ask you to come with me back to Harmony for further questioning."

Brother Charles stood up. "Am I under arrest?"

Karen also got to her feet and moved around the table into a position on the man's left. She knew Branham had a choice and that he would take the high road, but she was going to be ready in case the situation fell apart and she needed to move quickly.

Branham came around the table. "Will you come voluntarily?"

"Yes, of course, although I probably can't tell you any more than I already have. Am I a suspect, then?"

"We'll call you a person of interest at the moment, since you've agreed to come in voluntarily. That way there's no need to arrest you right now and handcuff you and all of that. But I'll tell you up front, if you don't come up with better answers when Chief Askew talks to you, you'll be placed under arrest and charged."

"May I just have a few minutes to arrange things here before we go?"

"Yes, of course. Let's go."

They followed Brother Charles out of the meeting room. He took them down the hall to the desk of a gray-haired woman in a blue dress.

"This is Mrs. Chandler, our volunteer administrator," Brother Charles said. He forced a smile at the woman. "Can you see if Brother David is free?"

"Of course." She picked up the phone and punched a button.

"I'll just make arrangements for Brother David to take over my duties for the next little while," Brother Charles explained to Branham, "just in case. We're in the middle of a budget review and there are a few deadlines coming up that have to be met."

"Budget review?" Karen asked, skeptically.

Brother Charles nodded. "Of course. As abbot I'm responsible for an annual budget of over twelve million dollars."

"Twelve million!"

"Surprised? Most of it is dedicated to the clinic and the farm operation. The profits we realize from the farm are channeled into our charitable works. We're a benevolent order."

"After expenses, no doubt."

"That's correct, but not in a negative sense as you imply. We don't live the high life here. We don't take expensive vacations to St. Lucia or wine and dine every night. We live simple lives, we pay our bills, and everything else goes to our charitable works. When I say we're a benevolent order, I'm not saying we're a bunch of nice guys, I mean it literally. The primary purpose of this order, apart from our own spiritual studies and writings, is to create a vehicle for charitable works to benefit the people of this county who desperately need it. It's the reason we're here."

Karen was about to reply when a short, stocky blond man in another white cassock joined them.

"This is Brother David Wilbur," Brother Charles said. "David, this is Deputy Chief Branham from Harmony and Detective Karen Stainer. They need me to go to Harmony with them. It's about the murder of Marcie Askew."

Karen saw something pass between the two monks, a subtle shift in expression, perhaps, nothing she could put her finger on, but something that made the tiny hairs stand up on the back of her neck. Whatever it was that Brother Charles was not telling them, this Brother David character also knew about it.

"The revised estimates for the clinic expansion need to be signed off by five o'clock," Brother Charles said. "Please act as abbot until further notice. Tomorrow morning, if necessary, chair the committee meeting and get the next steps in the review process approved."

"All right, Charlie. Should I call Garrett?"

Brother Charles hesitated, looking at Branham. "Gordon Garrett's our attorney." He turned back to Brother David. "I'm not under arrest yet, but you might as well let him know what's happening. If I need him, I'll call him." He turned back to Branham. "Fair enough?"

"You've voluntarily agreed to come to Harmony for a formal

interview," Branham said, "so it's your choice whether or not to have your attorney present. Your rights will be respected at all times."

"Then let's go," Brother Charles said.

They stopped at his office on the way, where Brother Charles removed his robe and hung it up in a small closet. "We don't wear these off campus," he explained, "because it puts people off. We want to be able to interact with people without artificial barriers. We wear them here as a symbol of our commitment to the order."

Karen looked around the office. It was unexpectedly small, given that Brother Charles was top dog in an outfit that managed twelve million dollars a year. She looked at a wall filled with books, a simple walnut desk and chair, a small meeting table and chairs on the side, and a leather armchair near the window in the back corner. It looked very much like the office of a professor of religious studies on a medium-sized university campus.

She glanced at the spines of the books on the bookshelf. She wasn't a reader the way Hank was, and she seldom saw a book that she'd actually read, but she was an experienced investigator who knew that the things people kept on their shelves sometimes said important things about them. The books she noticed included *The Pagan Christ* by Tom Harpur, *The Living Goddesses* by Marija Gimbutas, Joseph Campbell's *Transformations of Myth Through Time*, *Liberating the Gospels* by John Shelby Spong and *How Jesus Became Christian* by Barrie Wilson.

"Where's your Stephen King and Dan Brown?" she quipped.

Brother Charles smiled at her faintly. "In my room."

They took him downstairs and Branham guided him into the back seat of the cruiser. No one spoke as they rolled down the driveway and turned onto the highway.

Karen glanced over her shoulder and saw that Brother Charles was looking out the window, his face impassive. She turned back and pursed her lips, rolling it around in her mind. Another guy who happened to be in the wrong place at the wrong time? Or was he a wacko nut job? A sexual predator? A psycho who arranges to meet married women in secret and strangles the life out of them?

Time to find out.

9

Hank was wondering what had happened to lunch when the metal door opened and Officer Grimes came down to his cell.

"Let's go." Grimes unlocked the door and motioned him out.

Hank followed him down the corridor and through the metal door into the office. Karen was sitting in a visitor's chair at Detective Hall's desk while Hall was slumped over another desk in the corner watching a video display and listening to the audio feed through a headset. Branham was in his office, on the telephone. The civilian dispatcher was typing. Officer Grimes dropped into his chair and stared at his computer monitor with undisguised boredom.

Hank walked over to Karen. "What's happening?"

"They're letting you go, Lou. Found a better suspect. Tall guy with a beard. Ring a bell?"

"Christ."

"Guy name of Brother Charles Baker. Runs a monastery outfit not far from here. Their little shrimp eyewitness sat right here in this chair while Askew marched Baker past him into the interview room." She pointed at a closed door on the far wall. "Made a positive ID."

"It's too late for a show-up. Hell, it was too late when he looked at me before. What do they have against lineups around here?"

"Whatever. It got you out of that fucking cell."

The front door opened and two men walked into the station. One was a tall, fortyish man with short, straight white hair and an expensive navy blue suit. His ears were huge and his nose was long and pointed. He carried himself with the unmistakable self-assurance that comes with success in public life. The other man was just as tall but stockier, with trim brown hair and a ruddy complexion. He wore brown trousers and a white long-sleeved shirt and brown tie. The shirt bore large gold and black shoulder patches emblazoned with the words TAZEWELL COUNTY SHERIFF'S OFFICE, a gold badge, and a black name tag that said *Steele* in gold letters. They walked through the cattle door at the end of the counter as though they owned the place and looked into Chief Askew's office.

"Where is he?" the white-haired man in the navy suit asked

Branham, who was walking out of his office.

"Interrogation," Branham replied, offering his hand. "How are you, Mr. Hatfield?" They shook hands and Branham turned to shake hands with the other man. "Sheriff."

"Call him out, will you, Neil?" Hatfield asked. "I understand there's been a development."

"That's right. We've found the individual seen by the witness going behind the bar. The Chief's interrogating him right now."

"Who's this, then?" Hatfield looked at Hank over Branham's shoulder.

"Homicide Lieutenant Hank Donaghue and Detective Karen Stainer, from Glendale, Maryland," Branham said, making the introductions. "This is Assistant Commonwealth's Attorney Donald Hatfield and Tazewell County Sheriff Isham Steele."

"I understand you were also at the scene Saturday night," Steele said aggressively, staring at Hank.

"That's right," Hank stared back, "but I didn't make it to the back of the goddamned building."

"I expect Chief Askew owes you an apology," Hatfield said quickly, glancing at the small bandage on Hank's left cheek and the scabbed nicks on his forehead and lower lip.

"You think?" Hank replied angrily.

"It's a municipal issue. I'll speak to the mayor about it." Hatfield turned to Branham. "Get Billy out here."

Branham knocked on the door of the interview room and let himself in.

Karen looked at Steele. "Did you bring the lieutenant's firearm and personal effects back with you?"

The sheriff ignored her.

The door of the interview room opened and Chief Askew emerged, followed by Branham. Askew was clearly not a happy man. He shook hands with Hatfield and ignored Steele altogether.

"Mr. Hatfield, what can I do for you?"

"You've got another suspect in custody, I understand?"

"Correct. Brother Charles Baker, from the monastery in Burkes Garden."

Hatfield's eyebrows shot up in surprise. "He's the abbot out there, isn't he? Why on earth would you think he's involved?"

"Our eyewitness positively identified him as the man he saw walking past the window," Askew replied defensively, "and the suspect's admitted he was there."

"And this man here," Hatfield nodded at Hank, "that you told me about before, he's not the man seen by the eyewitness after all?"

45

"No."

"I intend to have a word with your mayor about this," Hatfield said, "but if you've got an ounce of common sense you'll personally apologize in writing to Lieutenant Donaghue here and pray he doesn't sue your ass. Has Baker given you anything at all to go on?"

"Like I say," Askew ground out, "he's admitted he was there at the time of the murder, he's admitted he went around to the back of the place, he's admitted he went there to meet with someone but he won't say who it was and he won't say anything other than that."

"Has he been placed under arrest?"

"Not yet."

"Is his attorney here?"

"Not yet. He's been Mirandized and has waived counsel."

Hatfield turned to Steele. "Did your people find any physical evidence at all at the crime scene that might connect Baker to this?"

"No," Steele shook his head gravely.

Askew jumped on it. "How the hell can you answer that question when it's supposed to be my crime scene? When the hell were you planning on letting me know what you may or may not have found?"

"Are you aware of any connection between this guy and your wife?" Hatfield pressed Askew. "Anything that would be a motive for killing her?"

"How the hell would I know?" Askew replied. "He won't give me a straight answer on anything. I sure as hell never heard her mention him before."

"This is the problem, Billy," Steele said, trying to sound sympathetic. "If there was a connection between them it might be real upsetting for you since you were her husband, and you can't be expected to keep a clear head about it."

"That's fucking bullshit and you know it."

"No, it's not bullshit," Hatfield contradicted, "and *you* know it. You know as well as I do it's SOP for a law enforcement officer to withdraw from a case when he has a personal connection." He held up a hand to forestall Askew's protests. "I know, I know. I appreciate your years of experience and professionalism and all that, but I'm having a hard time seeing why this case shouldn't be transferred to the county sheriff's office right this minute."

"It's goddamned politics, that's what it is," Askew growled. "I'm just appointed by the municipality here but you two're elected, you cater to the press and your precious voters, and that means we're not playing on the same field. I'm telling you right now if you start pulling local law enforcement off important cases, every department in this county'll be completely demoralized. You have to give us a fair chance. I can't tell you if there's physical evidence connecting my suspect to the crime scene if this guy sits on it. Plus," he ticked off the point on his index finger, "the autopsy won't be done until tomorrow and it'll take at least a week to process the stuff that was under her fingernails. Plus," he ticked off another point on his middle finger, "nothing physical's been done on Baker yet. I need the crime scene truck to go over to the monastery and turn his room or whatever the fuck he lives in upside down and every scrap of evidence analyzed up the ass. The truck he drove, everything. How the hell can I make any progress when we haven't even worked him yet? You call this fair? You call this professional?"

It was quite a speech. Hatfield shrugged. "I hear you, Billy." He looked at Steele for a moment and turned back to Askew. "You have enough to place him under arrest and keep him in custody?"

"Yes," Askew said.

"Then let's get the warrant to search the residence and vehicle."

"Thank you."

"Don't kid yourself, Billy. This office is hanging by a thread. I want you to tell me right now you'll personally withdraw from any further action directly connected to this case."

"*What*?"

"It's non-negotiable, Billy. If you expect your office to retain control of this case past the next five seconds, you need to say the words. Deputy Chief Branham will have full responsibility for the investigation and you'll stay at arm's length, as you should have right from the get-go. Say the words."

Askew sighed heavily, his shoulders slumping. "All right."

"Say the words."

"All *right*. Branham has the case."

"You'll stay completely out of it."

Askew worked his jaw. "I'll stay out of it."

Hatfield turned to Steele. "Get your team over to the monastery and process everything Branham wants processed as soon as the warrant comes through. And get him reports this afternoon on the findings from Saturday night."

"Yes, sir," Steele said. It was clear he'd hoped for a different outcome.

Hatfield tapped Branham on the chest with a bony finger. "Keep me completely up to date on everything you find."

"Yes sir," Branham nodded.

"Bear in mind you can't keep arresting big guys with beards just because they showed up at some dump on Saturday night. Make this one stick, or it's over. Let's go, Ice."

Askew watched them leave the station, then spun on his heel, strode into his office, and slammed the door.

Karen caught Hank's eye and raised an eyebrow.

Branham stared at the door for a moment and then turned to Hall. "Get the suspect out of there and process the arrest."

He turned to Hank. "If it turns out he did it, we need to make sure we can nail his ass to the wall."

Hank watched Hall get to his feet with an effort and shuffle toward the interview room. He looked back at Karen.

She shook her head microscopically and rolled her eyes.

Not good. Not good at all.

10

They walked across the paved area behind the station to the compound where Hank's Grand Cherokee was locked up. Branham unlocked the padlock, pulled out the chain, and opened the gate. Then he handed the vehicle keys to Hank and cleared his throat.

"Lieutenant, I want to ask you something."

"Sure, why not."

"I understand your feelings about us right now," Branham began, "but I was wondering if you'd consider sticking around for a couple of days until we get something solid on Brother Charles."

"You telling me not to leave town, Deputy Chief?"

Branham winced. "No, not at all. Just the opposite. I was wondering if you'd be willing to offer some assistance. I don't have any budget to pay for consultation services but if you could stay for a couple of days and maybe provide us with some advice and guidance as a gesture of good will, I'd be very appreciative."

"How's your stock of good will these days, Lou?" Karen asked.

"Damned low." Hank stared at the deputy chief. "Do you seriously think I owe you people any favors?"

"No, you don't," Branham agreed, "but I'll be honest with you. I don't think Brother Charles is good for this. He's no more a killer than Barney the purple dinosaur. The real killer's still out there."

"So go catch the guy. What's it to me?"

"Nothing, I understand that," Branham said. "But I basically run this office and I'm not going to be able to spend all my time on this case, and all I've got for a detective is Hall. You've seen Hall."

"I've seen Hall."

"This is what you do for a living," Branham pressed. "Surely to God it bothers you that Marcie Askew's killer's walking around out there thinking he's gotten away with it."

Hank's temper flared. "You've got a lot of goddamned nerve." He turned on his heel and walked away.

Branham looked at Karen. "I didn't handle that well."

"No kidding." She folded her arms across her chest as they watched Hank open the door of the Grand Cherokee and pause, one foot up on the rocker panel. He leaned an elbow on the roof of the vehicle and stared straight ahead.

"When I called Maryland," Branham said, "the sergeant I talked to said Donaghue's the best homicide detective he's seen in twenty years in the job. No offense," he added quickly.

"None taken." Karen shifted her weight. "He's amazing. His IQ would probably scare the shit out of you, but he never lets on. He's a millionaire from a family of big-time power brokers but he never talks about it or makes you feel like he's somehow a cut above. Guy like that, you'd figure he'd be soft in the crunch but he never, ever hesitates to go nose to nose with the worst fuckers you can imagine, and he's the one guy I want covering my six when the bullets start flying."

"I shouldn't have worked the guilt angle. I didn't know what else to do."

"You didn't need to push his buttons," Karen agreed. "He pushes them all by himself without anybody else's help. It's eating him alive that he saw the vic right before she was killed. No cop would like that, but it's bugging him especially bad."

"I didn't mean to piss him off."

"Give him a minute."

They watched Hank drum his fingers on the hood of the Grand Cherokee for several moments. Then he slammed the door and strode back to them.

"What do you think, Detective?" Hank asked Karen, his jaw tight. "A couple of days?"

She shrugged.

Hank looked at Branham.

"A couple of days."

11

The next morning Billy Askew pulled off the highway into a long driveway two miles outside of Bluefield. The driveway was little more than wheel tracks, and Askew's Ford Explorer bounced in the potholes and craters as he worked his way up to the trailer where his sister Pricie lived with her two youngest children and her husband, Jimmy Neal. It was because of Jimmy that Askew was here this morning. He'd decided that he'd seen about as much as he was going to take.

He got out of the Explorer and walked slowly up to the door of the trailer. A car passed on the highway behind him, and he turned to look. It was nothing, just some car that kept on going in the direction of Bluefield. As the sound of the car faded he stood still, listening. A dog barked in the distance and then stopped. Flies buzzed in the early sunlight that lay in strips across the siding that covered the trailer. A blue vinyl tarp thrown over a pile of lumber stirred in the wind. The trailer itself was silent.

He opened the door, which was never locked, and stepped inside. He paused to let his eyes adjust to the gloom. His nostrils expanded at the combination of smells that hung in the air as unpleasant reminders of the poverty in which his sister lived. He picked his way through the stuff on the floor and looked into the kids' bedroom. They were gone. Askew assumed they'd gotten themselves down to the road in time to be picked up by the school bus. They usually did. He walked into his sister's bedroom. The morning sunlight was streaming through the gap between the curtains across her body where she lay turned away from him on the mattress on the floor, covered with a gray blanket. He crouched down and touched her shoulder.

"Pricie."

She moaned but didn't awaken.

"Pricie," he said again, a little louder.

She stirred and turned onto her back. There was an abrasion above her left eyebrow and a black smudge under her left eye. Her shoulder-length brown hair lay flat against her temples and neck. Her eyes fluttered and she looked up at him.

"Billy?"

"Wake up, Pricie."

She closed her eyes and licked her lips, moving her legs beneath the blanket. "What time is it?"

He smelled stale liquor on her breath. "A little after eight."

"In the morning?"

"Get up, Pricie."

"Where's Jimmy?" Her hand moved automatically to the other side of the mattress.

"Sleeping it off," Askew said, "in the jug."

Her eyes opened and she sat up. "Oh God, my head hurts." She rubbed her forehead. "What happened?"

"Bluefield picked him up on a DUI last night. He'll be out this afternoon."

"What day is it?"

"Tuesday." Askew stood up. "Come on, get up. It's time to go."

She stared at him. "Go?"

"I told you the next time he hit you I was taking you out of here. Well, now I'm doing it."

"Oh, Christ, Billy." She drew her legs up under the blanket and reached for a pack of cigarettes on the floor beside the mattress. "You cain't just come in here and expect me to pack up and leave." Her voice was flat, lifeless.

He watched her take a disposable lighter out of the empty half of the cigarette pack and light a cigarette. She put the lighter back into the pack and tossed it aside. Pricie was forty-seven years old, three years younger than Askew. She had seven children. The oldest, Jimmy Ray, was twenty-six years old. He was divorced, had a police record to match his father's, and had disappeared from sight four years ago. The next two, Lorna and Ella, had married and moved out of state, hopefully to somewhere better. Johnny, who was twenty-one, had joined the Army and was currently serving in Afghanistan. Eliza, who was nineteen, had Down's syndrome and was living in a home in Richmond. Perry and Theresa were sixteen and fourteen, respectively, and were still in school, largely due to Pricie's insistence that they complete their high school education before getting the hell out.

"Sure you can leave, it's already done," he told her. "I've rented a place for you in town. It's furnished. All you need's your clothes and the kids' stuff."

She picked up a half-full ashtray and balanced it on her knees. "I cain't."

"Of course you can. Why couldn't you?"

"It's not right."

"We've been through this before, Pricie." He folded his arms across his chest. "The guy's no good. You've stuck with him for how many years now? And look at you. Every time I come around it's the same fucking thing. You've got no money, you're living in a dump, he's never home, you don't eat properly, he's going to seriously hurt you some day, and you've got no Medicare to pay for a doctor. Then what?"

She shook her head slowly, not looking at him, exhaling smoke. "It's not that bad."

"It is and you know it." He shook his head. "Get up and get dressed. Get the kids' stuff and let's get the hell out of here."

"I cain't leave," Pricie said, looking at her cigarette. "Daddy didn't raise no quitters."

Their father had been a man of very high moral standards, true enough. Their mother had died when Billy was eight and Pricie was five, from a stomach infection of some kind. James Askew was an insurance investigator based in the town of Tazewell, responsible for all claims within the county. When his wife died, he decided it was necessary to get off the road and stay at home with his two small children, so he requested a demotion to sales. Within a month one of the salesmen in the company's three-man office in Harmony died from a heart attack and James was offered the position. They left Tazewell and moved into a small rented bungalow on Maple Street in Harmony while James sold insurance policies door to door.

In his previous responsibilities, James had investigated a number of disability claims filed by coal workers living in Harmony and the surrounding area, and had disallowed several. It made him very unpopular in town and the children suffered as a result. Unlike James, who was passive in the face of hostility, Billy learned very quickly how to defend himself with his fists. By the time he reached high school, he was known as a quiet, hardnosed kid who never backed down from a fight and never stopped hitting until the other kid stopped moving or someone pulled him off. He and Pricie had few friends.

Billy was a high school freshman when his father was hit by a car on Bluefield Street driven by a man who had a long-standing grudge against James for disallowing a claim for a back injury that had cost him his job in the mine. The man had contended his injury occurred at work but James proved the man had hurt his back in a bar fight the weekend before. The ruling cost the man a great deal of money and he'd never forgiven James. He'd threatened him several times and finally, drunk at the wheel, was driving through town when he saw James crossing the street ahead of him. He floored the accelerator and ran him down. James died on the way to hospital.

Billy and Pricie left Harmony after the funeral to live with their mother's older sister in Richlands. The woman was very religious and took in the children through a sense of duty to her deceased younger sister, but she was unable to hide her dislike of them. When Billy heard that the man who'd run down his father was acquitted of manslaughter by a jury including people whose claims had been investigated at some point by James Askew, the news drove him deeper into himself. It also strengthened his resolve to fight his way out of any corner in which life cared to pin him. He was damned if people would end up treating him the way they'd treated his father.

Billy finished high school in Richlands, and one day shortly after graduation met an acquaintance of his father's while coming out of the Richlands police station. Billy explained he'd just applied for a job there.

"If you want to be a cop," the man said, "you should apply back in Harmony. They've got an opening right now."

Billy wasn't sure how to respond.

"My cousin's the sergeant there," the man went on, oblivious to Billy's hesitation. "He knew your dad. He'd put in a good word for you."

Something clicked inside his head. He hated Harmony and everything it stood for, but what better way to balance the books than to return as a cop?

"Would you call your cousin?" he asked the man. "Tell him I'll be down in the morning for an interview?"

"Sure enough," the man replied, surprised. "Be glad to."

Billy Askew was hired as a patrol officer a week later. After six years the sergeant retired and Askew was promoted to replace him. He was young, smart, and tough, and he stood out head and shoulders above the other two patrol officers who applied for the position. He remained a sergeant for the next fifteen years until the chief's job opened up. He applied for that job but David Morris, a lieutenant with the Richmond Police Department at the time, was hired instead. That was five years ago.

Morris was a star candidate, a former college quarterback with a graduate degree in criminology, a year with the FBI and seven years with the Richmond PD. He came into town like a celebrity, went to dinner with the mayor at the best restaurant in Bluefield on the West Virginia side, and was offered the job over brandy afterward. Askew never stood a chance.

A year later, Morris resigned in order to run for sheriff in Tazewell. Askew was offered the vacant chief's position on an interim basis. The offer was made outside in the parking lot at five-thirty in the afternoon as Askew stood beside his car, about to go home.

"Interim," Askew repeated.

"Until we can conduct another process," Mayor Blankenship said. "Council would appreciate your help."

"You already conducted a process," Askew replied. "You said I did real fine, only that Morris was a once-in-a-lifetime thing or some such bullshit. You hold another process, I'll do real fine again. Got another Morris up your sleeve? I doubt it. Give me the job straight out or you can shove it up your ass."

He got into his car and drove away.

The next morning a messenger brought a letter of offer to the police station with Askew's name handwritten on the front of the envelope. Askew signed the offer and moved his things into the chief's office. Three months later he laughed out loud when the morning news said that Morris had lost the election for county sheriff.

"I heard about Marcie on the news, Billy," Pricie said, breaking into his thoughts. "I'm real sorry. She was a fine woman."

"Thanks."

"Strangled." Her free hand moved to her own throat.

Askew said nothing.

She drew on her cigarette and slowly blew the smoke into the shaft of sunlight that crossed the room between them. "What'll you do to Jimmy?"

"What?" Askew asked, distracted.

"Are you going to beat up Jimmy again?"

"I'm not going to do nothing to that sonofabitch," Askew said angrily. "I'm getting you the hell out of here, that's what I'm doing. Now come on, let's get moving."

She sighed, shaking her head. "It's not right." She stubbed out the cigarette, put the ashtray and blanket aside and stood up. She was wearing red panties and a stained yellow t-shirt with a Care Bear on it. There were large bruises on the outside of her right thigh and calf where her husband had kicked her after knocking her down.

He turned away. "I'll pick up the kids after school and bring them to the new place. Now get dressed and start packing."

"Just leave Jimmy alone, Billy."

"We'll see about that." Askew turned away.

The way he felt right now, if he saw Jimmy Neal again he'd probably kill him with his bare hands.

12

The office was busy for a Tuesday morning as Hank and Karen pulled up chairs in front of Detective Hall's desk. The civilian dispatcher, whose name was Mollie Roberts, chattered into her headset as she typed on her keyboard. Grimes was reorganizing the office files, carting armloads of file folders back and forth between his desk and the filing cabinets. Branham was on the phone in his office. Askew's door was open but the office was empty.

Hall came out of the washroom next to the interview room and crossed over to his desk.

"I appreciate your helping out," he said, slumping down into his chair.

"You look like something the dog threw up," Karen said.

"Thanks." Hall opened a slim file folder on his desk and glanced at the piece of paper on top. "E-mail to the deputy chief," he said. "Autopsy'll be done today."

"You want to go over my statement?" Hank prompted. "Review the people I saw at the bar Saturday night? Maybe show me some photos? I take it you've identified most of them by now."

Hall said nothing, looking down at the piece of paper.

Hank glanced at Karen. She mimed a drinking motion with her hand and rolled her eyes. Hank nodded. Hall was clearly hung over and struggling to get his body under control. It was a good thing there wasn't much violent crime in the area, if this is what Harmony had to offer in terms of investigation.

Hall looked up. "Billy spoke to Jordan Bickell Saturday night," he said in a low voice. "He was the manager on duty. As soon as Jablonski came inside with his story, Bickell went out with him and took a look, then closed the place down and sent the waitresses home. They close at two, anyways. He told Billy he'd talked to Mullins on the phone, the owner of the place, and Mullins told him not to tell us anything. Billy was about to tear him a new one when he got the word on you and headed right off to the motel."

"So you don't know yet who the waitresses were," Hank said.

"Not yet."

"Nor the customers."

Hall shook his head. "Not for sure."

"Then let's go have a talk to this Mullins," Hank said.

Hall struggled to his feet.

"You okay?" Hank asked.

"I'm fine," he snapped.

Hank led the way toward the little swinging cattle door at the end of the counter. He veered off suddenly and went into Askew's office.

"Hey," Hall protested, following, "what're you doing?"

Hank stopped in front of Askew's desk and looked around. The furnishings themselves were modest enough. Hank looked at a metal desk painted black, large chair upholstered in black vinyl with black plastic arms, two metal visitor's chairs in front of the desk, a four-drawer filing cabinet with a small assortment of photographs on top, and a little table in the corner with a coffee machine, a can of coffee, a jar of whitener, a saucer holding packets of sugar, and a few plastic spoons. A waste paper basket in the corner with nothing in it. Behind the door, a coat rack on which a windbreaker was hanging. The windbreaker had a Harmony Police Department crest on the left breast and CHIEF emblazoned in yellow letters across the back. Askew had a typical power wall going that featured an array of plaques from the Virginia State Police acknowledging this and that, FBI course certificates, years of service awards, and other such tokens of recognition. There was a small window on the opposite wall that looked out into the street.

One of the framed photographs on the filing cabinet caught his eye. It was a picture of the woman he'd seen outside Gerry's Bar on Saturday night. He picked it up. It was a beautiful photograph, taken in a back yard somewhere, under a tree. Marcie Askew smiled at the camera like a sultry angel. Hank felt a tightness in his throat. Swallowing, he turned and showed the photograph to Hall.

"That's her," Hall said. "That's Marcie."

Hank nodded. "She's the one I saw."

"She was a knockout, all right," Karen said, looking at the photograph over Hall's shoulder.

Hank put the photo down. "Let's go."

They went outside and piled into Hank's Grand Cherokee. Karen took the passenger seat up front, and Hall sat in the back on the driver's side. Hank and Karen had already discussed whose car to use for the day and who would do the driving, but she still wasn't happy about it.

They drove to Gerry's. Hank parked in the same spot next to the sidewalk that he'd used on Saturday night. The parking lot was empty except for a black Cadillac Escalade parked near the back. They walked through the parking lot toward it. Hank glanced up at a small window near the rear of the building. It was likely the window through which Pete Jablonski had seen Brother Charles. They rounded the corner and saw that the wooden gate to the garbage corral was open. A short fat man was throwing a bag into the dumpster inside the corral. The crime scene tape had already been removed. There was no sign at all that a murder had occurred here only a few days before.

"Mr. Mullins?" Hall called out. "Can we talk to you for a minute?"

The fat man shut the gate and turned to face them. He was balding and ugly, with a fringe of long gray hair around the back of his egg-shaped head. His nose was large, his eyes were small, and his thick lips twisted unpleasantly.

"Fuck you want, Hall? Cain't you see I'm busy?"

"Very sorry to bother you, Mr. Mullins. We need to ask you a couple things about the murder, if that's okay."

"No, it hain't okay." Mullins was leading them across the pavement from the corral to the back door into the kitchen. He had a business-like waddle that told them he had no time for them and no interest in what they needed to ask.

"Were you here at any time Saturday night?" Hank asked, catching up to Mullins.

"Beat it," Mullins said over his shoulder, reaching for the door knob.

Hank moved quickly and hip-checked Mullins away from the door. He reached out, grabbed the fat man's shirt at the shoulders to keep him from falling and swung him around so that his back bumped against the kitchen door. It wasn't a violent bump, but it wasn't gentle, either. It was firm enough that it focused all of Mullins's attention on Hank for the first time.

Hank smiled down at him. "Sorry, almost knocked you over. Now answer the question. Were you here on Saturday night?"

"If you like being sued, buddy, then just keep doing what you're doing."

"You can file it as soon as we're done talking, but right now you're going to answer the question. Were you here on Saturday night or weren't you?"

"Ansell," Mullins said, looking sideways at Hall, "do you really want this kind of trouble in your life?"

Hank glanced at Hall and was surprised to see emotion flare in the detective's eyes.

"Answer the question, Mr. Mullins. Trouble's a two-way street and you'd sure hate to be on the wrong side of the law. Were you here?"

Mullins pushed at Hank, who didn't move. He glared and shook his head. "You fucking idiots are wasting my time. I wasn't here, that's what I hire people for, to work them kind of fucking hours so I can be at home."

"Your manager, Bickell, was on," Hank said. "Who were the two waitresses?"

"I don't know. I don't have the fucking schedule memorized."

"Well, let's go take a look at it."

"You hain't setting foot in this establishment, mister."

"Let me take a look," Hall said. "It'll just take a minute."

Mullins pushed at Hank again, who took a step back. "Get your fucking ass in here," he said to Hall, "before I change my mind."

He opened the door and Hall walked inside. Karen started in after him but Mullins barred her way.

"Where you think you're going, missy?"

"Where the hell do you think, pal?"

"I don't know you," Mullins said. "You're with him," nodding at Hank, "which means you're staying outside."

He walked inside and slammed the door.

"What the shit." Karen tried the doorknob. "It's locked."

"Never mind." Hank took a few steps around, looking at the pavement. "This was apparently the primary scene."

"Yeah. Someone met her back here, strangled her, started dragging her," she cast her eyes around, "somewhere. I can't see any marks. It's been swept."

Hank nodded. "The whole area back here's been swept. We'll have to rely on the photos."

"Hopefully Hillbilly Central took a few Polaroids before it was too late."

Hank said nothing, walking toward the back. Karen followed. They found the opening in the brush and started down the path.

"There," Karen said, pointing at a spot where the undergrowth had been flattened and trampled.

They looked around but learned nothing new. Hank went further down the path to the bottom of the slope, where he emerged into a rocky crease through which a footpath wound away to the left and right. The ravine was perhaps fifty feet across at the bottom. There was no path leading out of the ravine on the other side. Presumably you'd have to turn either left or right and walk for a distance before finding another path up out of the ravine again on the street side. He turned around and walked back up to where Karen was waiting with

Hall.

"Jablonski was by himself in the back after eight o'clock," Hall told them. "Bickell makes two, and the waitresses were Mary Crutchfield and Debbie Stump."

"Bickell takes his orders from Tub-o-lard," Karen said, "but what about the waitresses? Maybe they're not too scared for their damned lives to talk to us."

Hall shrugged. "I don't know Debbie Stump, but Mary lives a few blocks over. We could go see her."

Mary Crutchfield lived in a rundown bungalow on Spruce Street at the other end of town. A rusted Toyota Corolla sat in the driveway, partially blocking the sidewalk. Hall led the way up the cement walk to the front porch. The screen door was locked. Hall knocked loudly and they waited.

The inside door opened and a teenaged boy looked at them through the screen door.

"Is Mary home, Tommy?"

"She's asleep," the boy said.

"We need to talk to her right now," Karen said impatiently over Hall's shoulder. "We're from the police." *What the hell is it with these fucking people?*

The boy looked at Hall and shut the door again.

They waited.

"Where's the fuckin' SWAT when you need them?" Karen muttered.

Finally the inside door opened again and a middle-aged woman in a housecoat and carpet slippers looked through the screen door at Hall. "What is it, Ansell?"

"We're here to ask you a few questions," Hall said. "About Marcie's murder."

"Some other time," Mary said. "I'm sleeping. I have to work four hours this afternoon at the Kwik Serve and six hours tonight for Mullins. Can't you come back later?"

Karen held up the wallet containing her badge and ID. "My name's Detective Karen Stainer and this here's Lieutenant Hank Donaghue. We're assisting Detective Hall in the investigation of a homicide and your cooperation would be greatly appreciated. Just a few minutes of your time."

Mary sighed. "What do you want to know?"

"Can we come in?" Karen pressed.

Mary hesitated and then unlocked the screen door. Hall opened it and held it for Karen and Hank.

They entered a short hallway. On the left was a half-open door into a bedroom. Hank looked in at an unmade bed. Mary led them through an archway on the right into a small cluttered living room. Hank looked at a television that was tuned to a game show. Watching the television was a man sitting in an armchair. He was in his late forties. He wore jeans, a white sleeveless undershirt, and plaid carpet slippers. He was drinking from a coffee mug with a drawing of a cow on the side. He kept his eyes on the television as they walked into the room. Next to the television was a wooden chair that looked as though it might have been passed down through several generations. It was piled with clothing. Mary moved the clothing and motioned for Karen to sit down. On the other side of the television was a green and yellow sofa. A dinner plate with the remains of an egg sandwich and potato wedges sat on one of the cushions of the sofa. Next to the plate was a gas tank from a motorcycle and an unidentified part that looked like a piston or something. The other cushion was free. Hall sat down there. Hank remained in the doorway while Mary stood uncertainly in the approximate middle of the room.

"This is my husband, Ned," she said.

Everyone looked at Ned. He kept his eyes on the television and said nothing.

"What did you want to know?" Mary asked again, clutching her housecoat a little tighter to her neck.

"We'd like you to tell us who all was there at Gerry's on Saturday night," Hall said over the noise of the television. "Late, when Marcie was . . ."

Mary walked over to Ned's armchair, picked up a remote control and muted the sound on the TV set. Ned looked at her resentfully and then returned his attention to the program, which he could apparently still follow without sound.

"Who was at Gerry's, you said?" Mary slipped the remote into the pocket of her housecoat. "Debbie and me were both on, and Bickell. And Pete. That was all."

"Don't know this Debbie," Hall said. "Where's she live?"

"She's a student at the college. From Kentucky, I think. She lives up above the barber shop near the tracks on Bluefield. I gave her a ride home one night after work."

"Okay, thanks," Hall said. "That's good. Now, at 11:30 p.m. or thereabouts on Saturday night you still had customers, right?"

She nodded.

"Tell me who they were, if you remember."

She thought for a long moment. "A few people, I guess. A couple of guys from town. I'm sorry, I don't remember."

"Regulars?" Karen prompted. "Guys you know from town?"

Mary looked at her. "I really don't pay much attention, I'm sorry. I know it could be important."

"What about him?" Karen lifted her thumb in Hank's direction.

Mary looked from Karen to Hank and back again, confused.

"He was there, right?" Karen prompted.

Mary bit her lip. "He might have been." She looked at Hank. "Were you?"

It was obvious that Mary was so tired, worn out, and run down that she was barely aware of her surroundings at any given moment.

"I was," Hank said, "but that's all right."

"Do you know any of the monks from Burkes Garden?" Karen tried.

Mary shook her head.

"Ever see anyone around Gerry's who looks like the lieutenant, here? Bushy beard, big like him, but from the area?"

She shook her head again.

"Thanks for your time," Hank said. "We're sorry to have bothered you."

Mary returned the remote control to Ned and followed them out into the hallway. As Hall opened the screen door, they heard the sound come back on the television behind them.

Mary stepped out with them onto the front porch. "Sorry about Ned. He's not rude, he's just very depressed these days."

"That's all right, Mary," Hall said. "You don't need to apologize."

"He worked for FabriCorp. He hurt his neck and went on disability, but it just took the life out of him, not being able to work. I worked part time at the flower shop, but after he got hurt it wasn't enough so I got hours at the Kwik Serve and from Mullins to make ends meet. My son left school and he's looking for something. Maybe I can quit Mullins if he can get some hours somewhere."

"Thanks for your time," Hank said again.

Back in the car, Hank looked at Hall. "What's FabriCorp?"

"They're the largest employer in the area. They make mining machinery and equipment. Without them most of the county would be on welfare."

"I thought it was all coal mining around here," Karen said.

"Not any more," Hall said. "Not for a while."

Hank drove back to Bluefield Street. "I turn right to go down to the tracks, correct?"

"Yeah," Hall said.

"What's the college here?" Karen asked, twisting in her seat so she could look back at Hall.

"Lewis Collins College. Liberal arts. I guess they teach the usual stuff."

"Branham said they have a criminal justice program," Karen said. "You guys send somebody over for their recruitment seminars just before graduation."

"Could be," Hall said.

"So this Debbie Stump is a student there," Karen went on, turning to Hank. "Remember seeing her?"

Hank slowed to let a truck creep out into the lane ahead of him from the driveway of a store that sold carpets and flooring. The load in back was covered with a tarpaulin.

"Yeah," Hank said. "Young, cute, flirty. Either a sophomore or a junior, I'd guess."

Karen looked at him. "Flirty, huh? She came on to you?"

"She did not."

"I spoke to Meredith before I left, by the way," Karen said. "Told her you were going to be spending a little more time in Virginia and you'd update her. You better call."

"Tonight," Hank said. Meredith Collier was Hank's friend. He refused to use the word *girlfriend* to describe her, because he felt it was demeaning to a 47-year-old woman. The word *partner* didn't fit because it implied that they lived together, which they did not. *Friend*, however, failed to describe how he felt about her.

They had known each other for four months. Hank had met her while investigating the murder of her only child, Martin Liu. Her husband had died a few years ago and she lived alone. After her son's case was closed, they went out together a few times and became better acquainted. The attraction was clearly mutual, and for the first while they took turns asking the other out, although they refused to call them dates. Middle-aged people didn't date, did they? That was for kids. High school sweeties.

"Hank," Karen said.

"What?" He'd been driving on autopilot, not really focused on where they were going.

"Barber shop," she said, pointing.

"Right, got it." He swung into a parking spot in front of a plumbing and heating storefront two doors down from the barber shop. They got out of the Grand Cherokee. Hank locked it with the remote. He fed a quarter into the parking meter, which bought them fifteen minutes. They walked past a vacant store. The window and door were covered with yellowed newspaper and there was litter and debris accumulated in the recessed doorway suggesting that the front door had not been opened in some time.

Reflected in the window of the barber shop Hank saw a cube van pass in the street behind them, followed by a black pickup truck. Looked like a Dodge Ram. The barber shop was open and Hank could see three chairs, the kind you'd expect to see in any barber shop in America, chrome jobs on swivels with footrest hoops, red upholstery and white linen draped over the back, ready for a customer. But there was no one visible inside. The barber might be sitting in the back, out of sight, reading the paper or listening to the radio to pass the time.

The sign above the door said:

Barber Shop

C. Mastrella

They walked to the next door at the edge of the building. There was a small black tin mail box attached to the wall with the names *Stump* and *Meese* printed with a felt-tip black marker on strips of masking tape. Hall tried the door knob and the door opened. A flight of wooden stairs led up to the second floor of the building. Hall went first. Karen took a step back to allow Hank to go ahead of her. The step took her a foot or two into the driveway.

A tiny horn beeped at her. She stepped forward again just in time to avoid being hit by a red and black smart car that flew out of the driveway and turned left onto the street. The young woman driving the car waved airily as she hummed away.

"Christ," Karen said to Hank, "I almost got run down by Minnie Mouse in a bumper car."

They followed Hall up the stairs.

There was a small landing at the top of the stairs and a single door in front of them. Hall knocked.

"Just a minute!" a female voice called out.

Standing behind Hall, Hank looked at Karen. She raised her eyebrows. He nodded.

The door opened and Debbie Stump stood there looking at them. Her long black hair caught up in pigtails. She wore a black t-shirt with the word *Wumpscut* on it. The t-shirt did not completely cover her stomach, which was a little fleshy. She wore faded jeans low on her hips. Her feet were bare. She was about twenty years old. She smiled at Hall.

"Hi, looking for Rache? You just missed her."

"She just missed me," Karen said.

"Pardon?"

"Are you Debbie Stump?" Hall asked.

"Yep."

"I'm Detective Hall; this is Lieutenant Donaghue and Detective

Stainer. Can we ask you a few questions about Saturday night?"

Hank and Karen held up their identification wallets above Hall's shoulders so that she could see them.

"Okay."

"May we come inside for a moment?"

"Sure." She opened the door all the way. "Yes, of course. Please, come in."

They walked into a small kitchen that was worn out but neat. Hank looked at an old white stove and battered refrigerator, a sink and counter, and a few cupboards with mismatched doors. A space above the cupboards held wine bottles, some empty and some unopened, a glazed ceramic jug, and three small marksmanship trophies. There was a kitchen table and chairs upholstered in cracked yellow vinyl. The floor was covered with ancient linoleum, the walls had been painted many times, and the woodwork was chipped and scarred. It could go either way with students, but these two young women appeared to be conscientious housekeepers who kept the place neat and respectable.

The smell of food cooking on the stove was almost overpowering.

"Is it all right if we talk in here?" Debbie asked. "I'm in the middle of this and I can't leave it right now." She gestured at the counter, which was covered with vegetables, some chopped and some still whole.

"What are you cooking?" Hank approached the big kettle that was bubbling on the stove.

"Nice to see you again," Debbie said. "I didn't know you were a cop. This here's my mawmaw's burgoo. Rache and I are having a few people over tonight and I promised them some genuine Kentucky cuisine."

"Burgoo, huh?" Hank sniffed at the steam rising from the kettle. "You don't have any squirrel in here, do you?"

"Of course not," she laughed. "Mawmaw gets that gamey flavor from mutton, not squirrel. There's veal, pork, and chicken in there, too. I cooked the meats up yesterday and I'm adding the veggies today. It takes about ten hours to make, so I split the cooking into two days."

Hank plucked a wooden spoon from a mason jar filled with utensils. "May I?"

"Help yourself."

He sampled some of the stock. "Oh yeah. That tastes good. You've already added the cayenne."

"Some. The rest goes in as soon as I put the vegetables in. 'Season as you go,' Mawmaw says."

"Amen to that. This is really good. Your grandmother would

be proud."

"Thanks. Wait 'til it's done."

Hall was sitting sideways at her kitchen table with his head in his hand. The smell of food was clearly not as appealing to him as it was to Hank. "We want to ask you a few questions about Saturday night. You were working at the bar when Marcie Askew was murdered, that right?"

Debbie nodded, chopping a carrot.

Karen sat down at the end of the table. "And they sent you home before the responding officers had a chance to talk to you."

"Mr. Bickell said something happened and he was closing up. He told me to go right home, so I did."

"Well, we're going to have that talk now. Can you tell us who was in the place late, say eleven-thirty on?"

"Sure." She hesitated for a moment. "Can I see your identification again?"

Karen opened her mouth to say something sharp when Debbie's tone registered. She fished the leather wallet out of the inside pocket of her jacket, flipped it open, and held it up.

Debbie put down her knife and came around to stand next to Karen, taking the wallet. Karen watched as she pored over the gold badge and identification card inside.

"This is unbelievable," Debbie said. "A real homicide detective. Incredible. Rache would freak." She gave the wallet back to Karen. "She's a criminal justice major and wants to be a cop real bad."

"Well, she drives like one," Karen said. "That's a start."

"I'm a business major," Debbie went on, "but we help each other study for exams so I feel like I know almost as much as she does about abnormal psychology, theories of social deviance, and all that stuff she takes. She'd just die to talk to you, you know, to ask you what it's like to be a woman in law enforcement. To know what she's facing out there."

"Are those her shooting trophies?" Karen asked, looking up at the top of the cupboards.

"They sure are. She's a gun nut and she wins all kinds of competitions."

"Then she'll probably be just fine," Karen said. "Run us through the customers you remember from Saturday night."

"I remember you, right off," Debbie said to Hank. "Mary served you. Did you talk to her yet?"

"Yeah," Karen said, "but she didn't remember him."

Debbie shrugged. "She's middle-aged and married, which is like being dead." She smiled at Hank, looking at his left hand. "You're

66

not married, are you?"

"He's old enough to be your father," Karen said, disgusted. "Who else was there?"

Debbie grinned. "Let's see. Davey was there. Sitting at the bar? A little overweight, never talks? His last name's Toler, I think. He's a regular, almost every night. Mr. Bickell told me his dad's a farmer."

"Eric Toler," Hall said, massaging his eyes.

"Are you okay?" Debbie asked.

"Headache. What time did Toler leave?"

"When Mr. Bickell closed it down, around one forty-five."

"See him go outside at any time and then come back in?" Karen asked.

"No."

"All right. Go on."

"Mr. Fink was there," Debbie said. "He comes in a few nights a week, sits at the same table by himself. I think he's a construction worker or something."

"Henry Fink," Hall said.

"Yes."

"You're from Kentucky?" Hank asked Debbie.

"Me? Yes, from Belfry. That's a tiny little place in Pike County, not so far from here."

"What year are you in?"

"I'm a junior. Oh, I get it. You're wondering how come I know these people. It's something I picked up from one of Rache's courses, actually. Something about how police officers should get to know the people in the area where they work. The regulars on their beat. I thought it sounded like a good principle to follow in business, too, so I've been practicing. I remembered your face, and now I know your name, and the next time we meet I'll be able to say 'hello, Mr. Donaghue.' Sorry, *Lieutenant* Donaghue. Anyway, you know what I mean. It makes an impression on business clients when you remember their names and something about them."

"I'm sure it does," Hank said. "So, Henry Fink." He looked at Hall.

"Forty-six, a carpenter and contractor," Hall recited, "Ace Construction. Has an apartment on Poplar Street. Divorced. I could go on."

"Wow," Debbie said.

Hall grimaced. "What time did Fink leave?"

"When we closed."

"Who else do you remember?" Karen asked.

"Three guys at a table. I see them together a couple nights a

67

week. They take turns paying and use credit cards. Matt Shumate is one, Joseph Wall is another, and, oh damn, I can't remember the third guy's name."

They all looked at Hall.

"Shumate's thirty-seven, lives on Harper Road just outside of town. He's a metal worker at the big plant in Bluefield." Hall sat up a little straighter. "Joe Wall's thirty-eight and a shift foreman at the same plant. The third guy probably also works there."

"Allen," Debbie said.

"First or last name?" Hall asked.

"Last name. I'm sorry; I can't remember his first name."

"That's all right." He realized Hank and Karen were staring at him. "Don't know him."

"What a letdown," Karen said. "When did these guys leave, when Bickell sent everybody home?"

Debbie nodded.

"Anyone else?"

"There were two guys who came in and sat at the bar. One guy had a bushy beard, a ponytail and a lot of tattoos, and the other guy had one of those big long mustaches, a brush cut and the same kind of tattoos."

"The bikers," Hank said.

"Yeah. They left a few minutes after you did."

"Anyone else?"

"No."

"No? You sure?"

She thought for a moment and then her eyes went wide. "Wait, of course. Professor Morris was there. Not very long, but I saw him Saturday night, that's right."

"Professor Morris?"

"Yeah, he's one of Rache's instructors. I think she's a little sweet on him."

"David Morris?"

"Yeah."

Hank looked at Hall, who nodded. It confirmed Hall's previous assumption that the forty-something guy in the black sport jacket and jeans Hank had mentioned had been David Morris, the former chief of police.

"What about a guy with a beard who might have looked like a priest or something?" Karen asked. "Big like him," nodding at Hank, "but a bushier beard, longer face, hooked nose, hair not as curly."

"Not as good looking," Debbie said, smiling. "Yeah, I saw him just for a minute. He stuck his head in the door, looked around and left again. Didn't sit down or anything."

"When was that?"

"I'm not sure. Around midnight?"

"Know the guy?" Karen asked.

Debbie shook her head. "Haven't seen him before."

"But you remember him."

"I'm practicing. When I see a face for the first time I try to commit it to memory right away along with a key word or something to remind me where I saw it first."

"And the key word for this guy?"

She blushed. "Goober."

Karen guffawed. "Goober?"

"G for Gerry's," she explained, "and goober because he looked like one."

"For cryin' out loud," Karen said.

They questioned her for several more minutes without learning anything else of use. Karen gave her a business card and they went back downstairs.

Outside on the sidewalk Hank turned to Hall. "Maybe your uniforms could interview these people, check them out."

Hall nodded.

Karen looked at her watch. "Damned if that didn't smell good in there."

"Lunch," Hank said.

"As long as they don't put squirrels in it," Karen said.

13

Hall didn't feel like eating anything, which surprised no one, so they dropped him off at the station and drove back down Bluefield Street. Hank parked the car at the curb, fed a couple of quarters into the parking meter, and they walked down to a small restaurant called Annie's Diner. It had a dozen wooden tables and chairs, a counter at the back for the cash register and take out, and décor that featured antique tins, crocks, and vintage toys. There was one other customer in the place, a heavy-set guy in a green work shirt and matching trousers who sat along one wall with his back to the room. He was eating a hamburger. The only two other people in the restaurant, from what Hank could see, were a middle-aged brunette who came up to their table and a teenaged girl in the kitchen area.

Hank ordered a club sandwich with extra mayo and a large Coke. Karen ordered a steak sandwich, fries, and coffee.

"I like the bikers," Karen said as they waited for their food. "Have they run the plates yet?"

Hank shook his head. "I don't know."

"People around here are like something out of a cartoon."

"It's a different pace."

"I'd go fucking nuts if I was stuck here," Karen said. "It'd be like having your brain sucked out of your head and put in a jar in a laboratory hidden off in the hills. Then nuclear war strikes, civilization's wiped out, the hillbillies take over, and you sit there, a brain in a jar, waiting for humanity to reinvent the wheel so they can get a fucking move on and rediscover your hidden lab and plant you back into a body so you can do something constructive instead of floating in pickle juice for eternity staring at the wall."

Hank looked at her. "Where the hell did that come from?"

"Well, how would you like to be stuck here doing fuck all while time marches on?"

"I don't know. The peace and quiet might be nice for a change."

"Give me a fucking break. You'd be insane in a week." She stopped talking as their orders arrived. Hank bit into his club sandwich.

It was very good. Some kind of subtle flavor he couldn't quite place.

"Jeez," Karen mumbled through a mouthful of steak sandwich, "this is really good. What is it with this town and food? Anyway, I can see the bikers getting too rough with her and then taking off."

"Hall will check it out," Hank agreed, "but it's a little fuzzy. Granted, they were bikers, but they came off more like businessmen in transit to some kind of convention or something. The stereotype's changing."

Karen snorted and took another bite.

Hank lifted the lid on his club sandwich, took a dab of mayo on his fingertip and tasted it carefully. "Capers," he said. "And sun-dried tomatoes."

"You did what?"

"Puréed into the mayo. It's really good."

"So the bikers are fuzzy, you think. What else have we got at this point? Other than Brother Charles, of course. We have two eyewitnesses placing him at the scene, the guy in the back and little Debbie, and he's admitted to Branham he was there. He just wouldn't say who he was going to meet."

"What's your take on him?" Hank asked.

She shook her head. "I don't know, I really don't. I expected a creepazoid nut case but he seems pretty level-headed. Didn't quote a bunch of scripture, didn't try to convert us, didn't act condescending and know-it-all, like God was his special buddy and we were dog shit on his sandal. Didn't panic at the thought of being arrested but didn't like the idea, either." She shrugged, sandwich poised an inch from her lips. "He doesn't seem to fit for it."

Hank thought for a moment. "We need to work from the victim."

"Minefield," Karen mumbled, chewing.

"Apparently. How far do you think Branham will be willing to go?"

Karen swallowed and took a swig of coffee before answering. "Pretty far, I guess. He wants to be chief, but he's not the kind of guy who'll stab his boss in the back. I'd say he's an honest cop who won't sweep anything under the carpet."

"So he'll support Hall if he works the victimology," Hank said.

"He'd probably have a heart attack if Hall worked anything. Guy must have a liver like a bar sponge."

Hank said nothing, finishing his sandwich.

"We've got almost none of the basics yet," Karen grumbled. "Autopsy's supposed to be today, so hopefully that'll fill in some blanks."

"Maybe Branham would be willing to call and get a verbal from the medical examiner when it's done."

"Worth a try. He needs to get those goddamned reports from the sheriff's office."

"And Hall needs to call the state police and get them to put out a BOLO on the bikers."

They finished their meal and went back to the cash register. It was Hank's turn, so he pulled out his wallet as the middle-aged brunette rang up their bill.

"Are you Annie?" Hank asked, handing her cash.

"In the flesh," she smiled, setting his money on the top of the till and pulling out his change.

"Excellent club sandwich, Annie," he said. "Never tasted mayo done that way."

She gave him his change and looked at him, head tilted to one side. "What do you think was in it?"

"Capers and sun-dried tomatoes," he said.

"Correct!" she grinned. "Congratulations, you've won a free copy of my self-published cook book, *Annie's Best*." She took a spiral-bound book from a pile next to the cash register and handed it to him.

He accepted it, puzzled. "Thanks."

"Gemmie and I have a little contest going," she explained, glancing at the teenager in the kitchen who was wiping her hands on her apron and smiling at Hank. "Anyone who can correctly identify the secret ingredients of the day wins a prize."

Karen looked around Hank's arm at the cook book. "Will it teach him how to boil water? He's dangerous in a kitchen."

"You don't cook?" Annie asked Hank.

"Sorry."

"Yeah, but Merry does," Karen said. "His girlfriend."

"She does?"

"Friend," Hank said. He flipped through the cook book. "She's an outstanding cook. She'll love this. She loves to try new things."

"My website's on the back cover," Annie said. "When she tries a few recipes ask her to send me an e-mail. Or she can tweet me on Twitter. I'd love to get her feedback."

Hank closed the cook book. "Thanks."

Karen laughed when they were out on the sidewalk heading for the Grand Cherokee. "Website! Twitter!"

"She's probably trying to generate reviews," Hank said. "Marketing. Draw people in off the highway."

"Whatever. It's hilarious!"

They drove back to the station and went inside to find Hall

sitting at his desk staring at his computer screen. He looked no better than he had an hour ago.

"Is Branham in?" Karen asked.

Hall nodded.

"Well, look alive, Hoppy. He needs to call about the autopsy and he needs to call the sheriff for the crime scene reports."

Hall sighed, pushed away from his desk, and stood up. He walked across the room and stuck his head into Branham's office, Karen and Hank right behind him.

"Got a minute?"

Branham was typing something on his computer. He waved them in, finished what he was typing, and swung around to face them. "What's happening?"

"Update time," Karen said from the doorway. Hall had taken the only visitor's chair in Branham's office. Hank moved to the far side of the office to lean on the top of a filing cabinet. Karen leaned against the doorframe. "Where's your chief?"

Branham shrugged. "Out."

"Heard from the autopsy yet?"

"It was being conducted this morning."

"Maybe the ME will give you a verbal."

He looked at her for a moment and then nodded. "He might." He picked up the telephone and looked expectantly at Hall, who recited from memory the telephone number of the western district office of the Virginia Department of Health in Roanoke, where the autopsy was being conducted. Branham dialed the number, explained what he wanted, was put on hold, explained again what he wanted, was put on hold again, explained what he wanted a third time, listened, gave his name and telephone number, said thanks, and hung up.

"Dr. Oliver Bailey's the forensic pathologist performing the autopsy," he said. "It's just wrapping up. If I call again in fifteen minutes Bailey will probably be willing to talk to me about it."

"And still no reports from Tazewell about the crime scene?" Karen prompted.

Branham picked up the phone again. This time he punched in the number without consulting Hall.

"Pooch, how's it going?"

Karen looked at Hank and rolled her eyes, mouthing *Pooch?*

"Not bad, not bad," Branham was saying. "Listen, I need you to fax your reports to me now." He listened for a moment. "I thought that's where they'd be, but I need the info ASAP. Could you ask his secretary to fax them?" He closed his eyes and pinched the bridge of his nose as he listened. "Could you at least walk me through the findings?"

"Christ," Hall muttered.

"I appreciate it. Look, I'm going to put you on speaker. I've got Hall with me, and also Detective Stainer and Lieutenant Donaghue. No, he's not. Yes, they've agreed to consult informally with Detective Hall. Yeah, I hear you. Uh huh. All right, you're on."

He punched the speaker button and cradled the headset. "Can you hear me now?"

"I hear you," a gruff voice said. "Afternoon, Hall."

"Detective," Hall replied flatly.

Branham leaned back in his chair. "Detective Stainer, Lieutenant Donaghue, this is Detective Clarence Muncy of the Tazewell County Sheriff's Office. He's been assigned to the Askew case and has agreed to share his findings with us while the paperwork, uh, clears the sheriff's desk."

"Detective Muncy," Hank said, "this is Donaghue. You work with your forensics team, do you?"

"You could say that."

"So you'll make sure my firearm and the rest of my belongings are returned to me today."

"Uh, we'll have to see about that."

"Pooch," Branham said quickly, "the lieutenant was brought in because of mistaken identity and has been cleared. He's agreed to stick around and help out, and we really appreciate it. He and Detective Stainer have a ton of experience in homicide investigation and we'd be nuts not to take advantage of it. I'd consider it a favor if you'd release his things and send them up right away."

"I'm already doing you one favor," Muncy said.

"Then call it two favors."

"Sure," Muncy said. "Whatever you say."

"You were going to give us a verbal walkthrough of the crime scene findings," Hank prompted.

"I've got the reports in front of me now, Neil," Muncy said. "Physical evidence found at the scene included twelve footprints of two different sizes, size eleven men's shoes, brand unknown, size nine men's, brand unknown. You may remember a rainfall moved through the area a couple days ago, so the ground's still a little soft in spots. I'm going down the list from the evidence log. A button, dark green, an inch across, matched the buttons on the shoulder straps of the vic's dress. Three gum wrappers, Trident brand, empty cigarette package, Camel brand, discarded wad of gum, fast food wrapper, Burger King, blah blah, bunch of other stuff."

"The footprints are important," Hall said.

"No shit, Sherlock," Muncy remarked.

74

Hank shifted his weight. "Branham, what size of shoe do Brother Charles and your witness, Jablonski, wear? I'm a thirteen, by the way."

"We'll verify, but Brother Charles is probably larger than an eleven, judging by his physique, and Pete's probably a nine, tops."

"Agreed," Hank said.

"You think one of these sets belong to the killer, Pooch?"

"Could be."

"Tell us about the button," Hank suggested.

"The button, the fast food wrapper, the wad of gum, and the gum wrappers were found at the primary crime scene," Muncy said, "the paved area between the rear of the bar and the pen where Mullins keeps his dumpster. You'll see it on the scene sketch." He was referring to the diagram of the crime scene that death investigators include in their documentation in order to record where evidence is found at the scene in relation to the body, buildings, and other features.

"The button suggests that the vic struggled with the killer right behind the bar," he went on. "Scuff marks were found twenty feet away from the location of the button in the direction of the gap in the brush where the path goes down into the ravine. Trace shreds of leather were found in the scuff marks that match the heels of her shoes, which had corresponding scuff marks, supporting the theory that she'd been dragged from the spot where the button was found through the spot where the scuff marks were found."

"Detective Stainer here," Karen said. "Your assumption is that she was strangled behind the bar and then dragged, dead, rather than dragged and then strangled where she was dumped?"

There was a pause for a moment before Muncy answered. "That's correct, honey. The scuff marks were straight and parallel. If she'd been alive she would have been struggling and kicking and such. I'll bet you're a blond, aintcha?"

"And I'm guessing your pecker's about the size of my little finger, ain't it?"

Hank covered his mouth with his hand.

"Pooch," Branham intervened hastily, "what else is there?"

"I'm trying to do you a favor here," Muncy growled. "Jesus fucking Christ."

"Yeah, I know, and I appreciate it. Take us through the rest of the narrative, can you?"

Muncy paused. "All right," he said finally, "there was grit collected from the lower portion of her dress. Can I say it was on her ass or will it start another fucking ruckus?"

"The grit," Branham prompted.

"The grit matches samples taken from the pavement within three feet of the spot where the scuff marks were found," Muncy said, "supporting the idea that the doer dropped the victim to the ground somewhere just past the scuff marks, likely when her shoes began to come off her feet. No other scuff marks were found past this point, suggesting he picked her up and carried her the rest of the way along with her shoes, which were found with her. The size eleven footprints went in only one direction, down, while the size nines were pointed in both directions. The elevens disappeared into the rocks down there."

"So you figure that the size nines belong to the witness," Hank said, "and the size elevens belong to the killer, and that he didn't come back up after dropping the body."

"Looks like," Muncy said. "He must have walked a ways along the ravine and come back up somewhere else before doubling back to get his car. We couldn't find where, though. Too much rock."

"What did the victim weigh, approximately?" Hank asked.

"About one hundred and thirty," Muncy said.

"So it'd take a physically-fit man to carry her the distance we're talking about," Hank said. "If it's someone with size-eleven shoes, then someone probably not taller than six feet."

"He wasn't sure about carrying her, though," Karen said, "since he started off dragging her."

"Lazy?" Hall offered.

"Could be," Hank said. "In any event, you're not looking at anyone with a back problem or any other physical condition that would prevent him from carrying her."

"What else have you got?" Branham asked.

"Evidence at the secondary location, where the body was found," Muncy said, "suggests that the victim was lowered to the ground and positioned carefully, rather than simply dropped or thrown down by the perpetrator. Her head was lying on the ground between the trunks of two young trees. There was a slender dead branch protruding from the trunk of one of the trees above the body at a height of about three feet. If the perpetrator had tossed the body down, this dead branch would have been broken off. The guy lowered her to the ground under this overhanging branch. We found what looked like a knee print on the ground."

"He carried her down the path until he was out of sight from the parking lot above," Hank said, "found a spot, lowered her down, took a knee because he was still supporting her weight, got her into position, and let her go."

"Sounds right," Branham said. "Anything else, Pooch?"

"That's the highlights. I'll see if I can get the rest out to you this

76

afternoon."

"Brother Charles," Hall said.

"What about Burkes Garden?" Branham asked. "The van got out there, right?"

"We went," Muncy said. "The reports are still being written. We tossed Baker's room and office at the monastery and confiscated the truck. Got dick, I'm telling you right now. The other head guy, what's his name?"

"Brother David Wilbur," Branham supplied.

"That's the guy. Said the truck is used for farm stuff and sometimes by Baker himself. They keep a log for it, which I got a copy of, and he logged it out late Saturday night and brought it back early Sunday morning, two hours later, tops. Thing is, there was a gas receipt for the Getty gas bar on Highway 61 about ten minutes outside of Harmony."

"I see," Branham said.

"He gassed up at 11:49 p.m. We talked to the kid who was on. It was very quiet about then, and he remembered Baker." Muncy paused for a beat. "He couldn't have made it to the bar before midnight."

"I don't get it," Karen said. "How can you be so sure? Couldn't he have been heading back from Harmony after having whacked the vic?"

"The highway's divided, remember?" Branham said, before Muncy could take a shot at her. "The gas bar Detective Muncy's talking about is on the south side, which means Baker was still en route to Harmony."

"The waitress had him there at about midnight," Hall said, "and so did Pete."

"There you go," Muncy said. "Look, we ran the guy through all the systems and got nothing. I'm sure you did the same."

Branham glanced at Hall, who nodded.

"He's clean," Muncy went on, "and there's no physical evidence suggesting he did her. He was there, but then so was your lieutenant and a bunch of other guys. You want to continue holding Baker, that's your call, but in my opinion he's not your guy."

"I hear you," Branham said.

"Just something to think about. I gotta go."

Branham ended the call after getting Muncy to repeat his promises to send the reports up this afternoon, along with Hank's firearm and the stuff from his hotel room.

"We need a TOD," Karen said.

Branham looked at the clock on the wall, punched in the number for the Virginia Department of Health in Roanoke, and navigated his way to Dr. Oliver Bailey's extension.

"Bailey."

"Dr. Bailey," Branham said, "this is Deputy Chief Neil Branham calling from the Harmony Police Department. I've got you on speaker with Detective Ansell Hall and also Lieutenant Hank Donaghue and Detective Karen Stainer, who are assisting us with the Marcie Askew case. We were hoping to get a verbal on your findings."

They exchanged pleasantries and Bailey explained that he had just completed the autopsy. "First time I can recall getting a murder victim from your area."

"We don't have a lot of violent crime here."

"That's a good thing." Bailey shuffled papers and cleared his throat. "The victim measured five foot nine and a quarter inches and weighed one hundred and thirty-four and a half pounds. I'll spare you the metric equivalents. We'll start with cause of death."

There was a pause as he shuffled more papers. "Forgive me, I'm in the middle of preparing my report and my desk is covered with forms and printouts."

"Sorry about this," Branham said.

"Not at all," Bailey responded in a matter-of-fact tone. "Not the first time. All right, cause of death was asphyxia as a result of manual strangulation. There's a pattern of injury that one looks for in these cases, and I'll just take you through the basics. Tissue damage indicates there was considerable force applied to the neck to obstruct the flow of blood in the carotid arteries. The victim would have become unconscious within ten seconds as a result of the loss of blood flow to the brain."

Bailey cleared his throat again, perhaps in unconscious empathy for what had happened to Marcie Askew. "In such a situation, it's possible for a victim to regain consciousness just as quickly if pressure is immediately stopped, but of course that wasn't the case here. The assailant obviously kept on applying pressure after the victim lapsed into unconsciousness, and it was very brutal pressure, indeed. The larynx was crushed and the hyoid bone was fractured, which actually doesn't happen all that often. There was also vertebral damage, there were petechiae found in the conjunctivae—ruptured capillaries under the eyelids—and subconjunctival hemorrhages, or red in the whites of the eyes, suggesting that the victim struggled while she still could. The surface area and the extent of the damage are suggestive of a person with considerable strength and large hands who strangled the victim for upward to sixty seconds."

"I see," Branham said.

"Sixty seconds is a long time in this context," Bailey said, as though Branham had missed his point.

"This is Hank Donaghue, Doctor. May I ask a question?"

"Yes, Mr. Donaghue. No, sorry, that's Lieutenant Donaghue, isn't it? Of course you may ask a question. Ask away."

"Thanks. You're suggesting that since the act of strangulation went on for so long, it was an act of passion? By someone who lost control of themselves?"

"I'd only go as far as to say that the evidence would support such a hypothesis," Bailey said. "Those kinds of conclusion are up to you folks."

"Someone she knew," Karen murmured.

"I couldn't comment on that supposition," Bailey said.

There was silence for a moment before he resumed his dissertation. "As far as other injuries are concerned—related to the cause of death, that is—we collected fibers and tissue from under her fingernails and in two cases from the jagged edges of broken fingernails, confirming a struggle with her assailant. The tissue may belong to her assailant, who may have scratches on his hands or wrists, or it may belong to herself, since her neck and jaw had scratches which would be consistent with her struggling to pry the attacker's hands from around her neck. We've sent everything to the lab for testing."

Hank thought about Askew's hands around his throat while he was lying on the floor of his motel room. Then his mind moved sideways and he remembered the doctor examining his hands and wrists in the cell after being brought to the station. He felt a flash of anger. Dr. Justice had been looking for evidence on Hank's hands to connect him to Marcie's murder, not injuries connected to Askew's beating.

"There was a very slight scratch just above her right breast," Bailey was saying, "that probably occurred when her dress was torn."

"Was there sexual assault?" Branham asked.

"No," Bailey replied. "No indication of recent sexual activity at all."

"What about the time of death?"

"How familiar are you with the techniques used by pathologists, Deputy Chief?"

"Not very," Branham admitted.

"There are six factors we examine when fixing time of death," Bailey lectured. "I'll take you through them now." He shuffled papers.

"First, body temperature, or what's referred to as *algor mortis*. Dr. Justice attended the victim at the scene. He notes that the temperature at the scene was 71 degrees Fahrenheit at 1:40 a.m., so it was a mild night. He further notes that the body was located in a relatively sheltered spot, down the slope of a hill, and that it was still mostly clothed, all of which make the rate of cooling a somewhat more reliable measurement than it might be otherwise.

"He took his first measurement of body temperature at 1:41 a.m. and noted a reading of 95.7 degrees Fahrenheit. He took readings every fifteen minutes and plotted a very precise curve. If we assume a normal body temperature for the victim of 98.6, minimal body cooling in the first hour and a standard drop in temperature of one and a half degrees per hour thereafter, we can estimate that the victim had been dead for approximately two hours, making time of death somewhere around 11:40 p.m."

"How reliable is this estimate, Doctor?" Branham asked.

"Well, it's not as reliable as having her watch broken by the assailant as he murdered her, that's for sure. But conditions were almost optimal, and I think you could work with a window of between 11:15 p.m. and 12:15 a.m., based on body temperature."

"I saw her alive at about 11:20 p.m.," Hank said.

"Did you now?" Bailey coughed and his seat creaked as he shifted his weight. "Very interesting, indeed." He paused for a moment. "There are five other factors, though, as I mentioned."

They heard an odd noise, and then Bailey chuckled. "Sorry, just slurping my tea. Where was I? Um, *rigor mortis*, the stiffening of muscle tissue after death. Interesting process, I must say. Normally there's an interaction of myocin, actin and a substance called ATP within our muscle tissue when we move our bodies, bringing about the contraction and expansion of the muscle tissue. When we move our arm, for example, myocin and actin bind together, causing the muscles to contract and our arm to move. The oxygen we breathe into our system creates the ATP that causes the myocin and actin to disengage, allowing our muscles to expand again. When we die, the supply of oxygen ends, so the production of ATP ends, so the myocin and actin in our muscle tissues remain bound together, so our muscles remain contracted. Hence, rigor. Anyway, you're probably not interested in the biochemistry. Dr. Justice noted very slight rigor in the jaw at the scene, which is where *rigor mortis* normally starts. In the jaw, I mean."

Bailey paused for another slurp. "Excuse me, I like to drink it while it's still hot. Can't stand lukewarm tea. Very slight rigor in the jaw suggests a very recent time of death, less than three hours. It can begin as early as fifteen minutes after death, depending on environmental conditions, but reliably you see very little in the first three hours. It will be accelerated somewhat if the victim struggled vigorously, because this depletes the amount of oxygen available to form ATP immediately before death, and there are indications that this victim did struggle. Anyway, to summarize, rigor is not a terribly accurate measurement for us to predict TOD but we *can* say that in this case it doesn't contradict in any way what was observed with *algor mortis*."

"All right," Branham said, trying not to sound confused.

"Lividity is next on our list," Bailey went on, almost cheerfully. "*Livor mortis*. Rumpole's favorite. Next to blood spatter, of course."

"Pardon me?" Branham said, now completely confused.

"Sorry, don't mind me. Lividity refers to the coloration of the skin after death when hypostasis occurs. In other words, blood circulation stops and the blood settles in the body according to gravity. In this case there's not too much to say, as I believe the body was moved immediately upon death to the location where it was found. In any event, Dr. Justice notes that the victim's skin blanched when he applied pressure to it, confirming a time of death under four hours from that moment. Not precise, again, but not contradicting other findings.

"Putrefaction is the next factor," he continued, "the breakdown of the tissue caused by bacteria and endogenous enzymes."

"Endogenous enzymes?" Karen asked.

Hank saw that she had her notebook out on her lap and was writing in it. He caught her eye and let his jaw drop.

She shrugged. "In case there's an exam at the end."

"Sorry, Detective," Bailey said. "I was referring to enzymes already present within the body. The temperature at the scene was optimal for putrefaction—"

"Dr. Bailey," Branham interrupted, "did you find anything here to change your mind about the time of death?"

Bailey laughed self-consciously. "Well, putrefaction was not terribly advanced, again, given the relatively short time between TOD and discovery. We're going to run a few tests to try to get more accurate data but these will take at least a week to get back."

"Okay," Branham said, "that's all right. Anything else?"

"Well, the last factor to mention is stomach contents, and there was very little to mention. Some fragments of pork and vegetable matter, potatoes and some corn, suggesting that her last meal was consumed about five hours before death and that nothing else was consumed after that. Bottom line? I think you're safe to conduct your investigation on the assumption that TOD was between 11:20, when you say you saw her, Lieutenant, and midnight, which Dr. Justice's work suggests and my findings tend to confirm. If any further evidence comes up to change that, you'll be informed right away."

"We really appreciate this, Dr. Bailey," Branham said.

"Not at all. Beyond time of death, there are other findings that may impact your investigation."

"Oh?"

Bailey shifted in his chair and shuffled more paper. "I've already mentioned the scratches on her neck and chest area. There was a large bruise just above the elbow on her right arm, suggesting she was grabbed firmly by the arm before death. But there were older injuries you may need to know about."

"Oh?" Branham leaned forward.

"I found evidence of a broken wrist, about six months old, and a separated shoulder, about three months old. Also a small hairline crack on the left side of her jaw and two loose teeth on either side of the crack."

"Oh oh," Karen said.

"Yes, Detective?" Bailey prompted.

"I've worked a lot of domestic violence cases in my time," Karen said. "Those are three of the most common injuries."

"Correct," Bailey said. "I've seen a fair share of it in my time, as well, and I agree that your hypothesis is valid."

"Not good," Hall said.

"One more thing, and then I'll let you get back to your investigation," Bailey said.

"Yes?" Branham said.

"The victim was three months pregnant."

Branham hit the mute button on the telephone and looked at Hank. "This is a problem," he said.

"Why is that?"

Branham grimaced. "Billy Askew's sterile."

14

As Branham ended the call with Dr. Bailey they heard noise out in the main office. Heavy footsteps went into the office next to Branham's. The door closed loudly.

"Looks bad," Karen said, glancing at the wall that separated Branham's office from Askew's.

Branham put his foot up on one corner of his desk and stared at the ceiling.

"He was a legitimate suspect right from the start," Karen went on, "but everybody just tiptoed around him because he's chief."

"Bullshit," Hall said.

"It's not bullshit," Karen retorted. "Six out of seven strangulations of women are committed by men, and overwhelmingly husbands are primary suspects in the murder of their wife."

Hall made a face.

"She's right, Hall, isn't she?" Branham asked.

He took a while, mouth working, but finally he threw up his hands. "I'm not an illiterate hillbilly, Stainer. I've read the same studies you have. In cases of spousal homicide, women are more likely to be assaulted or murdered by their husband or boyfriend than by all other attackers combined. Women murdered in pregnancy are killed most often by the biological father of the child, or else by a jealous husband or boyfriend. The murderer has some kind of a temporary psychotic break and kills the one person he claims to love the most."

"It could fit," Karen said. "He suspects she's been messing around and he roughs her up a few times, trying to force the truth out of her. Then when she finally admits she's pregnant, he flips and strangles her."

"I still say it's bullshit. I don't care what the percentages are. I know Billy Askew and he wouldn't do this. He's a good man."

"We're going nowhere," Branham said. "We need to focus."

"You need to look at the victim," Hank told him. "You need to know who she was seeing over the last six months. You need to confirm who it was she was having the affair with, whether anyone can verify that she and Askew were fighting, all of it. Are you certain he was sterile?"

"Yeah, I'm certain. It was the talk of the town for a while. Their little girl had died, they were arguing all the time, blaming each other the way parents often do when they lose their only child. They couldn't have any more kids. Lucy was a difficult pregnancy and Marcie needed some kind of surgery. I don't know any of the particulars, just that Lucy was it for them. If Marcie got pregnant again it might kill her. Then Billy had an affair, they had a fight in public about it, he promised to make it up to her. Had a vasectomy, stopped drinking, stayed away from other women, everything. That was eight years ago. Since then he's been like a servant to her. Her wish was his command. He bought the store for her, set her up in business, paid all her debts, humored her every whim."

"Store?" Hank asked.

"Well, gallery, actually. It was a shoe store that went out of business. Billy bought the building, and she opened an art gallery in it. Bought and sold stuff from local artists."

"Money down the toilet," Hall said. "There isn't much artistic talent around here. He lost a lot of money on it."

"So maybe he resented it," Karen suggested.

"No," Branham said, "just the opposite. He was very proud of her. Every year he held her birthday party in the gallery. Invited the entire town. He paid every one of her bills with a smile on his face."

"Well, I don't know about any of that," Karen said. "I just know that nine times out of ten it's the husband."

"Or boyfriend," Hall said.

Voices were raised outside the office and Mollie Roberts, the dispatcher, edged past Karen in the doorway to look at Branham.

"It's His Worship," she said, her voice heavy with sarcasm. "He's asking for you."

"Oh, God." Branham rubbed his forehead and stood up. "Excuse me for a minute."

Karen put away her notebook. Hank pushed away from the filing cabinet. As he reached the door, Karen glanced up at him.

"This should be interesting."

"What can I do for you, Press?" Branham said. He held out his hand to a short, skinny man who stood in the middle of the office with his hands on his hips, frowning at everyone. He wore a beige windbreaker over a white shirt unbuttoned at the neck, dark brown trousers, and brown suede shoes with thick laces. His head was as smooth as a light bulb except for a fringe of gray that ran around the base of his skull from ear to ear.

Presley Blankenship owned the drug store in Harmony. He had

the fussy caution of a pharmacist who knew his trade backward and front, along with a strong business sense that had translated into the ownership of several valuable properties in town. He'd originally run for mayor to oppose property tax hikes and ended up being re-elected as a result of his opposition to the expansion of town boundaries. He managed the town's bottom line the way he managed his own, carefully and with full attention to detail. He was a good enough public speaker to get by, but had no discernible sense of humor. He had a small circle of friends and made no effort to expand it, but his no-nonsense approach to civic politics drew supporters like flies.

He shook Branham's hand. "I just spoke to Donnie Hatfield. He tells me you're in charge of the investigation of Marcie's murder, that Billy's been recused or whatever it's called."

"He's agreed to withdraw from the case."

"Just as well. I've got a press conference in an hour. Do you know how long it's been since someone was murdered in this municipality? We've got a lot of nervous and upset people on our hands. We need to be able to say the right things to them."

Askew's door opened. Everyone turned to watch him walk across the floor to the mayor.

"Sorry for your loss," Blankenship said, shaking his hand.

"I heard you say something about a news conference."

"In an hour. I want Branham here available to answer questions in case there are any I can't answer myself. Hatfield's going to answer specific questions about the thing, but I want Branham there just in case."

"He don't need to go," Askew said curtly. "I'll be there."

"No," Blankenship replied, "you won't."

"Yes, I will. It's my job." Askew put his hands on his hips.

"Donnie said you've been taken off the case. He's half a mind just to turn it over to the sheriff and be done with it. Don't make this harder than it already is, Billy."

Askew took his hands off his hips and spread his arms wide. "Everybody's just laying down the roadblocks, aren't they? Just hate to see me nail the fucking bastard who did this."

"That's not it at all and you know it. You're too close to this thing. In fact, as of right now you're on administrative leave until it's cleared up. I don't want you to have any burden of responsibility while you're trying to deal with the loss of your wife."

"Administrative leave?" Askew took a step forward. "What the hell you talking about?"

Blankenship refused to give ground. "I'm talking about you going home and letting your man here do this thing for you. Full pay.

Just go home, Billy. Get some space."

"I don't need any fucking space! I need people to support me and watch my back, not cut me off at the fucking knees!"

"Nobody's cutting you off at the knees. Go home, Billy."

Askew went back into his office, slamming the door so hard the clock fell off the wall onto the top of the filing cabinet.

"Like I was saying," Blankenship said to Branham without missing a beat, "we've got the Bluefield *Daily News*, the Roanoke *Times*," ticking them off on his fingers, "the Richlands *Weekly Reporter*, WBBS, and WRPA all sending people. I understand you arrested some out-of-towner right after the murder by mistake and then had to let him go. Hopefully he's long gone by now. We don't need that kind of complication."

"That would be Lieutenant Donaghue here," Branham said, gesturing to Hank. "He and Detective Stainer are experienced homicide investigators from Maryland. They've agreed to assist our investigation."

"Have they, now?" He looked at Hank and mentally shifted gears. "I'm Mayor Presley Blankenship, Lieutenant," he said, shaking Hank's hand. He reached out with both hands to shake Karen's hand. "Detective. Glad to have you on board. 'Assisting the investigation.' Can I say that? Sounds good. We'll skip the mistakenly arrested part. I guess we owe you an apology for that. My office'll have an official letter ready for me to sign real soon, rest assured." He turned back to Branham. "Got any other suspects in mind?"

"We're questioning several people," Branham said carefully, "but at this point it'd be best to say the investigation's proceeding and we're confident it'll be successfully concluded in the near future."

"Sounds all right." Blankenship looked at Hank and Karen. "Glad to meet you, and thanks for the help. Branham, let's go back to my office and sit down with Donnie. We can go over our notes, make sure we're all singing off the same page of the hymn book."

"We need to question Askew right now," Hank told Branham. "We need to get started on the victimology. Is there a problem with that?"

Branham hesitated for a moment. "No," he said finally, "just have Hall with you."

"All right."

When the room cleared Hank explained to Hall what they needed to do. Reluctantly the detective knocked on Askew's door. When there was no answer he cracked it open and stuck his head in.

"Chief, can we talk to you for a minute?"

"Fuck off, Hall."

Hank, standing behind the detective, reached out and pushed the door open. "We need a few answers, Askew. It won't take a lot of your time."

Askew rolled his lower lip under his upper teeth. Hank saw he was going to say *Fuck off, Donaghue*, but thought better of it and swallowed the words. Hank looked at Karen with a warning in his eyes before pushing past Hall into the office. Askew had turned sideways at his desk and was staring out the window as they filed in. Karen dropped into one of the visitor's chairs. Hank went over and leaned against the wall next to the window. Hall stood uncomfortably in the doorway.

"Have you heard from the autopsy?" the chief asked quietly.

Hank understood that although Askew kept his eyes on the window he was talking to Hall, so he waited. When it was obvious that the detective was not going to answer, Hank said "we've heard."

Askew shifted his eyes to Hank. "And?"

"The COD is asphyxiation from manual strangulation. TOD is 11:20 p.m. to midnight."

"And? What else?"

"You need to answer a couple of important questions."

Askew stared at Hank now as though daring him to go ahead and ask them. No doubt he was thinking back to the moment not all that long ago when he'd had Hank in his grasp and had beaten the living tar out of him. Now their roles were about to reverse and Askew didn't like it. He licked his lips and swung his eyes back to the window. "Ask them."

"How would you describe your relationship with your wife?"

Askew let the question hang in the air for a long time. Finally he lifted a shoulder and dropped it again. "Not the best. Been a long time since we were real close."

"Quarrels? Arguments? Fights?"

Askew shook his head. "Not for a long time. Years ago, yeah, we had our brawls like any other couple, but that was a long time ago. I learned it didn't solve a damn thing."

"Ever get physical with her? Hit her?"

"Jesus Christ!" he exploded, half-rising behind his desk. "Is that where you guys are going with this? The husband did it? Fucking son of a bitch!"

"*Sit back down and answer the question!*" Hank shouted, matching Askew's heat. "Did you ever strike or physically injure your wife? Yes or no!"

"No! No! A thousand times, no! Never! That woman was my entire life!"

"And yet you had an affair."

"Yes! Once! Christ, I'm only human! It was a fucking nightmare. Our daughter was dead and we were blaming each other. I needed someone real bad, it lasted a month, couple months. I ended it. That was it. Once. Eight years ago. End of story."

"The autopsy showed a pattern of recent injuries consistent with abuse," Hank said. "Broken wrist, separated shoulder, cracked jaw, loose teeth. Going back three to six months."

Askew leaped out of his chair again and strode around his desk to confront Hall. "What the hell's he talking about, Hall? What's all this fucking bullshit?"

"It's true," Hall whispered. "Somebody was beating her."

Askew raised his fists. "Son of a bitch, I'll . . ." He realized what he was about to say and snapped his mouth shut.

"Do you expect us to believe someone was battering your own wife and you didn't have a clue?" Hank asked, an edge in his voice.

"I," Askew faltered, "she, there was an infected tooth. And she hurt her wrist, I forget how. We haven't seen each other very much lately. She's been avoiding me all the time."

"There's more," Hank said, "so you might as well get a grip and deal with it."

"More? What the hell you talking about?"

"She was three months pregnant."

Askew's eyes grew wide and his mouth opened. He stopped breathing, as though Hank had punched him in the stomach.

"Deal with it," Hank snapped. "You're a cop. Deal with it."

"No."

"You didn't notice she was starting to show?"

"No. No! I haven't seen her much lately. She's never been around the house when I got home, and we haven't been sleeping together for a while. I didn't know! Christ, I didn't know!"

"Did you have your vasectomy reversed?"

"What?" Askew frowned. "No!"

"Were you aware she was having an affair?"

"No!" He looked at Hank. "With who? Who was it?"

"That's the million-dollar question, isn't it, Chief?"

"Whoever it was . . ." Askew whispered, tears forming in his eyes, "he killed my wife."

15

Hank and Karen stood beneath the flagpoles outside the station listening to the flags snap above their heads in the afternoon breeze. There were three flags: the Stars and Stripes; the flag of the Commonwealth of Virginia, featuring the state seal on a blue background; and the flag of the municipality of Harmony, a bright yellow rectangle with the corporate seal of the town in the center. Snap hooks pinged against the flagpoles as the halyards vibrated. Traffic on Bluefield Street rumbled in the background.

"The air smells fresher around here," Karen said.

Askew's Ford Explorer roared around the building from the back parking lot and barreled out onto the street without slowing. He ran the stop sign at the corner and disappeared down the next block.

"He's in an awful damn hurry."

"He's under a lot of pressure," Hank said.

"He's full of shit."

"I'm not so sure."

They had two suspects in front of them. Brother Charles had initially looked solid, given the fact that he'd been there at the time and wouldn't talk about it, but the gas receipt had introduced an element of doubt that could prove fatal to the case against him. Not to mention that they could only guess at a motive. Billy Askew, on the other hand, had motive coming out his ears but no evidence tying him to the scene at the time of the murder.

Hank listened to the flags for a moment and wondered if Karen were right. One of the primary skills a cop develops is the ability to distinguish between honesty and dishonesty. Officers receive extensive training in the detection of verbal and non-verbal indicators of deception. Hank had worked with cops who seemed to possess an uncanny ability to detect deception at a subliminal level, as though they had truth radar built into their brain. When a person said something during an interview, it either *pinged* on the truth radar or it didn't. How the hell did they do it? It was almost supernatural.

Everyone lies. On the other hand, everyone also at some point says something that's true. The art of the investigator is the ability to separate the two and respond accordingly.

One of Hank's favorite detectives, an old-school homicide cop named Cedric Jones, had been particularly good at sensing bullshit, and Hank had studied him closely to try to understand his secret. An important element of Jones's technique was the ability to minimize his own contribution to the noise level around him. When he listened to a suspect he kept quiet and remained as still as possible. No expression on his face, no unnecessary movements. Very still. Very attentive. Asking only short, simple questions with as few words as possible. He created so much free space around them that the suspect inevitably felt compelled to fill it with his own words and body language. The bullshitters usually brought their own rope; Jones merely sat back and gave them the room to hang themselves with it.

Karen used a different technique, preferring to crowd suspects, disrupt their equilibrium, invade their personal space, and suck all the oxygen out of it. Her aggressive, combative approach often caused suspects to respond in kind, and an angry suspect is a careless suspect. Hank had watched her provoke admissions of guilt more than once during the course of a heated exchange.

Different techniques, but backed by the same ability to sense deception and doggedly root it out.

"I don't know, Lou," Karen said. "He's carrying some kind of load."

"Grief."

"Guilt," Karen insisted, "about something."

Hank removed a folded piece of paper from his jacket pocket. It was written authorization, signed by Askew, to provide Detective Hall with complete access to all of Marcie Askew's medical information. Askew had signed it on the understanding that Hall would use it to obtain access to Marcie's medical files kept by Dr. Diane Gervais, her physician in Tazewell, as well as her medical insurance company and any other source that might turn up in the course of their investigation. They also needed to know what Marcie may have told her doctor that she hadn't written down.

Hank handed the authorization to Karen. "Go with Hall to talk to the doctor."

"All right, Lou." She took the paper and folded it in half. "What are you going to do?"

Hank smiled. "I'm going shopping."

16

The house into which Billy Askew had moved Pricie on the outskirts of Bluefield was in fact a duplex, a two-story box originally built a hundred years ago as a rooming house for miners. At some point it had been divided into side-by-side dwellings with two front entrances and short driveways on each side.

After signing the disclosure of information document for Hall, Askew had been fuming at his desk when Pricie called to tell him that Jimmy was there to take her home. One of Jimmy's buddies had apparently seen her and told Jimmy where she was.

"What should I do, Billy?" Pricie asked. "I should go back home where I belong."

"You stay put until I get there," Askew told her.

He parked his Ford Explorer behind the pickup truck in Pricie's driveway and got out. A middle-aged man sat sideways in the open passenger door of the pickup truck, his feet on the ground. He was drinking from a bottle hidden in a paper bag. Askew didn't know him. He stared at Askew and didn't react when Askew pointed at him in warning.

The aluminum screen door opened and another man looked out at Askew as he walked across the lawn to the front porch. Askew didn't know him, either. The screen door closed quickly and opened again as Askew started up the porch stairs. This time it was Jimmy Neal.

"Fuck off, Billy," Jimmy said, glaring at Askew. "You've caused enough trouble for my wife as it is. Now fuck off."

Askew kept moving up onto the porch and with both hands slammed the screen door so that Jimmy's head banged between the metal edge of the door and the door frame like a nut in a nutcracker. Then he jerked the door open as Jimmy went down, braced it open with his hip, and reached down to pull Jimmy out onto the porch.

With both hands he hauled Jimmy down the steps and pitched him onto the lawn, where he stepped into him with a brisk kick in the ribs.

"Hey, fuck, leave him alone, man!" shouted the man behind

him on the porch. "Are you fucking nuts?"

Askew went back up onto the porch, grabbed the guy and threw him bodily off the porch onto the lawn next to Jimmy. He went back down the stairs and kicked the guy in the mouth hard enough to split his lip open.

By this time Jimmy had made it to his knees. Askew grabbed him by the belt and the back of his shirt at the neck and half-carried, half-dragged him across the lawn to the pickup truck. He was vaguely aware that Pricie was on the porch, screaming at him to stop. Jimmy was not a large man, about five-nine and one hundred fifty pounds, and Askew's anger filled his arms and legs with strength, but for the sake of his back he paused, hauled Jimmy upright and draped him over the back of the pickup, then stooped and scooped his legs and swung him over the fender into the box of the truck. Jimmy hit his head against a chain saw. Askew grabbed the chain saw and threw it into the bushes. Then he turned to go back for the other guy.

"Billy, no!" Pricie cried, running across the lawn to get between Askew and the guy, who stood with one hand raised defensively as he spat blood from his mashed lip.

Askew brushed her aside and walked up to the guy, who backed away.

"Whoa, man, easy!"

Askew lunged forward and caught him by the front of the shirt. He pulled him close and stared into his eyes. "Take that piece of shit out of here before it's too late and I finally kill him this time."

"All right, man! You got it!"

Askew pushed him away. The guy's heels caught and he tumbled backwards onto the ground. Askew went back to the truck as Pricie cried. He leaned over the fender of the truck and grabbed Jimmy by the hair, pulling him up so that he could look into his eyes.

"I told you what would happen if you hit her again," Askew said, his voice low and deceptively calm.

Tears began to roll down Jimmy's cheeks. "Christ, Billy, you're crazy. Don't hit me again."

"You fucking bastard," Askew murmured in Jimmy's ear, "I'm going to fucking kill you with my bare hands."

"Just leave me alone."

"How does it feel, asshole? To have somebody hit you and there's nothing you can do about it? How does it fucking feel? Do you like it?"

"Please, just leave me alone."

"Answer me!" Askew shouted suddenly. "How does it *feel*?"

Jimmy cringed, crying.

Askew was aware of a car stopping at the curb behind him. Doors opened and closed. He began to shake Jimmy like a rag doll. "Answer me! How does it feel?"

"Hands in the air!" a voice shouted. "On top of your head! Right now!"

Askew shook Jimmy again and looked over his shoulder. He was surprised to see two Bluefield police officers on the sidewalk, pointing their weapons at him, faces grim. They were men Askew didn't know.

"Right now! Hands on top of your head!"

Askew released Jimmy and took a step away from the truck, raising his hands slowly to the top of his head. He looked at the drunk sitting in the passenger side of the truck. The guy stared back at him over the top of the bag as he took another drink. His eyes were dead, empty.

Askew's anger drained out of his body as though flushed from a toilet.

They cuffed him and frisked him, removed his sidearm from the holster on his hip, recited his rights, and bundled him down to the cruiser. As they opened the back door of the cruiser, Askew saw his own reflection briefly in the car window.

His eyes were as dead as those of the drunk in the truck behind him.

17

Hall seemed to be feeling well enough to drive them to the clinic in Tazewell where Marcie's doctor had her practice, but Karen guessed he was feeling beat up over the results of the autopsy and what they implied about Billy Askew. Hall was obviously loyal to Askew and was having difficulty adjusting his sights from tall suspects with a beard to middle-aged suspects who were married to the victim. He was an odd duck who showed very little that a person would want to like. He came across as an alcoholic loser and unlike Branham, who was open, friendly and receptive to others, Hall was a shields-up, photon-torpedoes-armed-and-ready kind of guy. As they walked up the wide cement walk to the front doors of the clinic, Karen slung her shoulder bag to a more comfortable position and turned to look at him.

"You need this doctor to talk about stuff that's not in the vic's file."

"I know how to do my job."

"I'm just saying. If she needs her ass kicked and you're not up to it, I'll do it for you."

"I don't need you to do anything for me."

They went through a big set of glass doors and found the name of Marcie's physician, Dr. Diane Gervais, on the big board on the wall. There were six floors altogether in the building and Gervais was on the fifth floor. They took the elevator and walked down a carpeted hallway to her office. There were two names on the door, *Dr. D. Gervais* and *Dr. M. Thoney*. They opened the door and walked into a tidy reception area with new modern furnishings, plenty of sitting room, and four people waiting. There was a wall between the reception area and the rest of the suite, with a counter and two windows. They walked up to the window with the nameplate that read *Dr. D. Gervais*. Hall leaned forward to speak to the receptionist through the hole in the glass.

"Detectives Hall and Stainer to see Dr. Gervais." He held up his badge so that it clacked against the glass.

The receptionist looked as though she should have been home baking cookies for her grandchildren. "She's with a patient. Do you have an appointment?"

94

"Yeah." Hall had telephoned before they'd left Harmony. Probably had talked to this same woman, who now was pretending it was all a big surprise.

She looked at her computer. "Oh yes, here you are. It'll be about ten minutes."

"We'll wait." Hall sat down and stared at his hands. Karen sat down two chairs away and watched him. Maybe he could ask the doctor's advice on a good hangover treatment. Or better yet, get a referral to an effective support group.

Karen understood that alcoholism was an occupational hazard in law enforcement. She and Sandy could name at least six people they knew who'd had good careers ruined by booze. One, Sandy's former supervisor, ended up committing suicide after losing both his family and an important promotion to the bottle, a tragic end to a once-promising FBI career. But surely Hall hadn't seen anything out here in hillbilly heaven that compared to what law enforcement officers dealt with on a daily basis in a large city. What was his excuse?

Karen was known for her patience and empathy when dealing with children, a primary asset when she'd worked in Family-Related Crime, but when it came to adult males she had the sensitivity of a chain saw. Her position was simple: be a man and own your shit or get torn to shreds. It was one reason why her relationship with Sandy had lasted longer than twenty-four hours. Sandy was one of the most stable, even-tempered, self-aware men she'd ever met.

The door opened and a woman wearing a lab coat nodded to Hall. "This way, please. The doctor will see you now."

They followed the woman into an unoccupied examination room. Hall sat down in the visitor's chair next to the doctor's desk, and Karen hopped up on the side of the treatment table, the paper crinkling under her butt. "I hope you're not going to take our blood pressure first."

The woman gave her a sour look and closed the door on her way out.

"Just as well," Karen said, looking at Hall.

It took another five minutes for the doctor to make her appearance. She bustled into the room, a short, heavy, middle-aged woman with straight, medium-length black hair shot through with gray. She wore a white lab coat over a navy blouse and skirt combination, black flat-soled shoes, no makeup, and no jewelry. The obligatory stethoscope was draped around her neck.

"Detective Hall," Hall said, holding up his badge, "Harmony Police Department. This is Detective Stainer. Thanks for making time to see us."

95

"It's late in the day," Dr. Gervais said, sitting down at her desk and crossing her legs. "I still have several patients to see." She spoke with a French accent.

"This won't take long." Hall took out the authorization from Askew and handed it to her. "We're investigating the murder of one of your patients, Marcie Askew."

"I saw that in the newspaper," Gervais grimaced as she read Askew's note. "It was a very terrible thing. *Pauvre* Marcie."

"We have to ask you about her recent medical history, Doctor."

"Very well. This appears to be in order." She set the authorization aside.

"When was the last time you saw her?"

Gervais shrugged. "It's been a while." She shifted in her chair and tapped on the computer. In a moment she had opened Marcie Askew's file. "Slightly more than one year ago, it looks."

"We'll need a copy of her file."

Gervais looked at Hall. "A copy?"

Hall nodded. Gervais shrugged and worked the mouse. The printer next to the monitor began to whir. "It'll take several moments."

"That's all right," Karen said, "we don't mind. So how long was Mrs. Askew a patient of yours?"

"Several years. She transferred from a doctor in Bluefield who has retired."

"Been here long?"

Gervais looked at her. "Have *I* been here long?"

Karen smiled, raising her eyebrows.

"It's been more than twenty years that I've lived in Tazewell County. My husband and I came from Montreal originally to Richmond. He was a physician also. We set up a practice there, learned of an opportunity here, and moved. We built this clinic with our business partners seven years ago. My husband passed away two years ago. Now it's just myself and my partners."

"Sorry about your husband," Karen said.

"Brain cancer." She took the printed pages out of the printer and gave them to Hall.

"Thanks," he said, shuffling through the pages.

Karen leaned forward. "Ever see any signs of physical abuse on Mrs. Askew?"

"No! Why are you asking this?"

"She ever discuss her fights with her husband?"

Gervais shook her head.

96

Hall stirred. "Did she talk about other men she might have been involved with?"

"*Mais non*, not at all. Why are you asking me these questions?"

Hall rolled the papers containing Marcie's medical history into a tube and rapped them against the edge of the desk. "Within the last six months she had several injuries that women get when someone's beating on them. Broken wrist, separated shoulder, cracked jaw, loose teeth. You didn't treat her for these injuries and leave them off her record? Or hear about them after the fact?"

"God, no. That's horrible. I don't treat patients off the record, and I didn't hear about this at all." Gervais pressed a hand to her chest defensively. "Was it her husband?"

"That's what we're trying to find out," Karen said. "You have any reason to think it might have been him?"

Gervais shook her head. "Often when a woman is being abused, it is by her husband. But no, I have no particular reason for thinking so in this case."

"She didn't mention anything the last time you saw her?"

Gervais glanced at the screen. "No."

"I take it then," Karen said, "that you also didn't know she was three months pregnant."

"Ah, no. I did not." Gervais sighed. "This would not be good. I remember very well we talked about this subject several times. I thought she understood that unless she made the proper precautions, her life would be at risk."

"Did you know her very well?"

"Not really. She came to me maybe twice a year. I remember she was a very lively person. She would have made an interesting friend, I'm sure, but we never socialized. I only saw her here as her doctor." She stood up. "I'm sorry, there's nothing else I know."

"If you didn't treat her," Karen pressed, "where else would she have gone? To another doctor here?"

"I really don't know."

"Maybe that free clinic the monks run down below here?"

"I have no idea. It's possible, I suppose. I'm sorry, I just can't help you any more than this."

"Thanks anyway," Hall said. He walked past Karen, following Gervais to the door.

Karen rapped him on the arm. "Do you have a card, Hall? In case she thinks of anything else?"

Gervais turned and looked at him.

"Sorry," Hall said, embarrassed, "I don't have business cards with me." He saw a notepad and pen on the desk and grabbed them. "This is my name and number. Call me if you can remember anything else." He tore off the page and handed it to her.

"Thank you." She held out her hand for the pad. "I'll need it for the rest of my prescriptions."

"Oh. Sorry."

Karen rolled her eyes at Hall.

What a knob.

18

Although it was getting close to three o'clock on a Tuesday afternoon, Hank figured there was still plenty of time to stop in a few stores along Bluefield Street before they closed for the day. His wardrobe was still sitting in the evidence locker at the sheriff's office in Tazewell and he needed a change of clothing, in addition to a pair of shoes. He was wearing a pair of ancient Reeboks Branham had borrowed from Grimes, an arrangement that Hank would no longer tolerate. On top of that, he'd spotted a gift shop on Saturday night that might have something Meredith would like. It had been closed then but should be open now.

Hank headed north from the police station, walking past well-kept frame homes with front lawns and modest gardens showing their last bits of color for the season. It was a pleasant afternoon. White cumulus clouds moved briskly through the sky, which was visible intermittently through the trees lining the street. Although the cuts and nicks on his face had healed and he'd discarded the little bandage on his cheek this morning, he still had a few minor aches and pains from the beating that Askew had given him on Saturday night and was glad for an excuse to stretch his muscles and get a little fresh air.

He reached Bluefield Street and headed east toward the center of town. On this block were Blankenship's pharmacy, the post office, and a bank. He went into the bank and used the ATM to withdraw some cash. Then he crossed the intersection and started walking up the next block. He passed a hair salon, a dry cleaning business, an insurance office, and a church on the corner. On the next block he found a clothing store called Mary Ellen's. It appeared to carry only women's wear but he decided it was worth a look.

He walked past racks of summer clothing on sale until he reached the fall and winter wear and still hadn't seen anything for men. He hadn't seen a customer, either. At the back he found a cash register and a woman sitting on a stool behind the counter. She was in her late twenties, with straight black hair pulled back in a pony tail. She wore a brown cowl-neck sweater and jeans. She'd been watching him on a video monitor that showed the entire store from a camera mounted in the ceiling somewhere. She moved lazily on the stool to look at him.

"Help you?"

"Do you have any menswear? Or is it just women's?"

She slid off the stool and came around the counter. "Over here." She led the way to a section at the back on the far wall that had a six-foot rack of shirts on one side and trousers on the other. She pointed to underwear, socks, and pajamas along the wall. "This is it."

"Okay," Hank said.

"Ninety-nine point nine-nine-six percent of our customers are women," she said. "We have a little something for them to buy for their husbands and boyfriends while they're getting their own stuff."

"Guess I'm the point-zero-zero-four that likes to shop for himself," Hank said.

"Yeah." She smiled faintly. "Passing through town?"

"Sort of." He flicked through the rack, surprised to find Joseph Abboud long-sleeved cotton shirts and Lacoste polo shirts.

"You look like a seventeen and a half neck size," she said.

"Correct."

"Sleeve length 34 to 35."

"Correct again."

She shrugged. "It's what I do. It freaks out the ladies, especially since I don't lie and try to sell them something too small just to flatter them. I don't think there's anything here on the rack in your size, since the men around this place tend to be shorter than you are, but there's more stuff in back. What would you like?"

Hank flicked through the rack and stopped at a pale yellow Abboud shirt. "That's nice."

"We've got."

He looked at her. "Other colors?"

"Pale blue and white."

"Okay, one of each. Yellow, blue, and white." He went down the rack. "I wouldn't mind a couple of polo shirts as well. Here's a seventeen and a half. Forest green. Not my favorite color, but I'll take it."

She took it from him and draped it over her forearm. "Lose your luggage?"

"You could say that." Hank went around the rack to look at the trousers. "I'd rather just get a few pairs of jeans, actually."

She leaned back to look at him. "Thirty-six thirty-six."

"Correct."

"Wranglers okay?"

Hank nodded.

"We have." She smiled. "And with jeans, I don't have to ask which side you dress on."

"You don't have to ask that, anyway."

"I could."

"I'll take two pairs."

"Coming right up."

"While you're getting that stuff," Hank said, "I'll look at the socks."

"I can help you with the underwear."

"I can help myself, thanks."

She went back through a doorway behind the counter and came out a few minutes later with his shirts neatly folded on top of the jeans. "Do you want to try these on?"

"No, they'll be fine."

"I like a man who knows his own sizes. It's rare."

He walked over to the counter and put down six pairs of black socks, a plain black leather belt, and three packages of boxers with two in a pack. "I'll take these as well."

He took out his wallet and removed his credit card as she began to ring them up on the cash register. "Seems like a pretty quiet town," he remarked casually.

"Sure is," she said, trying several times to scan the bar code on a package of underwear.

"Did you know the woman who was murdered Saturday night?"

The bar code reader blipped. She set the package of underwear aside and looked at him. "No. Why do you ask?"

Hank showed her his wallet containing his badge and departmental identification.

"Damn!" she said. "No way! No way I had you for a cop. Son of a bitch!"

Hank smiled.

"Let me see it again."

Hank held out the wallet a second time. She took his hand in both her hands and looked at his ID. "Hank Donaghue." She let go of his hand and frowned. "I didn't know her but I knew *of* her, of course. Everybody knew who Mrs. Askew was."

Hank put the wallet away. "Are you Mary Ellen?"

"No," she laughed. "Mary Ellen was my late aunt. My uncle owns this store. Jack Owings. He named the store after her. I'm Sarah Owings." She held out her hand. "Glad to meet you, Hank."

Hank shook her hand.

"Everybody knew Mrs. Askew," Sarah went on, "because she was a real interesting person. And believe me, it's a boring town."

"She had an art gallery, didn't she?"

Sarah nodded, swiping his credit card. "Next block up. Beside Gibson's. It's still vacant."

"She had to let it go, I hear."

"Yeah. No money in art around here. My uncle barely makes enough to pay his bills and pay me on top of it. This isn't exactly Richmond." She gave him back his credit card.

"I noticed. Why was she interesting?"

"Oh, I don't know. She was beautiful and mysterious, the wife of the chief of police. People said they fought like cats and dogs and screwed like minks. Who wouldn't want to be as beautiful as Marcie Askew? She was gorgeous. But she had a tragic life, I guess."

"Well," Hank said.

"Sorry I don't know anything other than town gossip. But you could take me downtown to interrogate me."

"Maybe another time, Sarah."

She bagged the last of his purchases and jotted something on the back of his receipt before stuffing it into the bag. "My cell phone number. In case you think of any other questions."

Two doors down was an army surplus store. He went inside and bought a pair of black oxford lace-up shoes and a black canvas messenger bag. After paying for them he took a moment at the counter to transfer his clothing purchases into the messenger bag and secured the flap. Then he put on his new shoes and stuffed Grimes's decrepit Reeboks into the plastic bag from May Ellen's and asked the man behind the counter to throw it into his waste basket.

"Everybody needs a Jack Sack," said the man, a tall, thin fifty-something with short gray hair and a trimmed white mustache.

"Pardon me?" Hank asked, slinging the bag over his shoulder and shifting it around so that it rested against the small of his back.

"A Jack Sack," the man repeated, nodding at the messenger bag.

"A Jack Sack."

"Yeah, you know. Like Jack Bauer used to carry."

Hank laughed. "Oh yeah, right." He could immediately picture the popular character, a counter-terrorism operative from the former television series *24* who often carried his PDA, gun, explosives, and other tools of the trade in a messenger bag similar to the one Hank had just bought. Welcome to the global village, he thought, where television provides us with universally-understood referents no matter where we are.

Hank wandered down the counter to look at a glass display case containing an assortment of firearms. He was not comfortable without his handgun, which was still sitting in Tazewell despite his best efforts, and he wished he could buy something now to carry until he got it back. He saw a well-worn SIG Sauer P-225 and thought of Karen, who preferred SIGs and favored the 226. He asked to look at it. The man took it out of the case and handed it over. Although it had quite a few miles on it, it appeared to be in good shape. The man handed him an empty magazine. Hank inserted it and dropped it out again. He set the magazine aside on the counter and checked the chamber. He pulled the slide back and locked it in place with the slide stop. He rotated the disassembly lever down, released the slide lock, and removed the slide.

"You know your firearms," the man said, watching him. "You like cop guns?"

"I am a cop," Hank said. "Out of state."

"Oh."

Hank set down the gun and the slide assembly and held out his hand. "Hank Donaghue. From Glendale, Maryland."

The man shook his hand. "Jefferson Milroy Davis."

"Jeff Davis. Like the President of the CSA."

"I'm a descendant," Davis said proudly.

"Is that a fact?"

"Yep." He watched Hank pick up the recoil spring. "It's braided, see?" He pointed at the spring. "Nice piece of engineering. Works well, lasts longer, makes the gun shorter, and it's less expensive to manufacture than a gas system."

Hank nodded. The spring looked fine.

"Don't forget, we've got the instant check system here in Virginia," Davis said. "One call and I can have you approved in the time it'll take you to pick out your ammo."

"I'm not going to buy right now," Hank said, "although it's tempting. What are you asking for this?" He began to reassemble the gun.

"Four-twenty," Davis said. "Because it's you, I'll throw in the extra magazine I've got for it, the SIG carrying case, and a box of ammo." He showed Hank a box of fifty Federal 9 mm jacketed hollow point rounds.

"How long have you had it?"

"I took it in last summer."

"Sell many handguns?"

Davis shrugged. "So-so. I do better with the long guns." He glanced at another display case on the wall toward the back of the store that held an assortment of rifles and shotguns. "I have a few handgun collectors that come in from time to time, but they all pretty much have a SIG in their collection already or else they just aren't interested."

"What about local law enforcement? Any of those guys ever come in to buy from you?"

Davis guffawed. "No, never."

"Oh?"

"They're not exactly a gun-savvy lot. Oh, once or twice one of them'll come in and try to hassle me for selling stolen property or some such shit, but I don't stand for it. I don't sell junk, and I don't buy from just anyone. I'm picky with what I take in. I want to know about the provenance of each piece before I'll buy it. I've told them before; they can run every firearm in the store if they want to. I've got a proving barrel in back. They can test fire rounds from every one of these guns if they want and run them through their system till their fingers bleed before they'll find a problem with any of my stock."

"What about Chief Askew, ever deal with him?"

"No."

"Too bad about his wife."

Davis nodded. "The whole town's talking about it."

"What are they saying?"

"I'm not a gossip."

The hell you aren't, Hank thought.

"All I know is, if I killed Billy Askew's wife I'd be in California by now. I wouldn't stick around waiting for that guy to find me."

Hank raised an eyebrow. "Volatile, is he?"

"Known to be. Never had much dealing with him, myself. Tough guy, though."

Davis put the SIG back into the display case.

"I've heard that Burkes Garden is a nice spot," Hank said.

Davis nodded. "It is. Going to be around next Saturday for the festival? Good music and good food. It's pretty much the only Saturday in the year that I'm closed all day."

"I don't know if I'll be here that long. I understand there's some kind of monastery up there."

"Yeah, bunch of monks have a farm and a free clinic."

"Ever deal with any of them?"

"Oh, yeah. Seem to be a decent bunch, not the sort of wackos you read about in the newspaper. I buy vegetables from them sometimes, so I know a few of them by sight. Now and again they come in here and buy some stuff from me. Pretty much regular guys, other than the super politeness and the clean language."

"What about the abbot there? Know him?"

Davis shook his head. "Never met him."

Hank left the store still thinking about the SIG. Either he got his damned Glock returned to him right away or he was going to go back and buy that SIG.

The next block up he found a small electronics store called Jim's Wireless. According to the signs in their dust-streaked window, they were service providers for satellite dishes and wireless internet connectivity. They also sold electronic devices. Hank went inside and bought himself a prepaid cell phone, since his own cell was currently in Tazewell along with his damned Glock and his clothing, books, bourbon, and everything else he'd had with him when he arrived in Harmony. By sheer chance, another phone just like it had been returned that day because it wasn't working properly. Since the battery in that phone had a full charge, Hank convinced the clerk to swap it into the phone he was buying.

Back on the sidewalk he called Karen and gave her the number.

"How's it going?" he asked her.

"We just talked to her doctor," Karen said. "Got the records and there's nothing for the past year. Zilch. She was taking her injuries somewhere else. Maybe the free clinic, I don't know."

"What's your opinion of the SIG 225?"

"It's good. How much?"

Hank smiled. Karen had an outstanding sense of value when it came to firearms. "Four-twenty with a second magazine, carrying case, and a box of ammo."

"Highway robbery. Is it in decent shape?"

"I wouldn't bother mentioning it if it weren't."

"Right. What ammo's he offering?"

"Federal 9 mm 115-grain JHPs, box of fifty."

"Okay. Want me to take a look at it with you?"

"Maybe tomorrow if I don't get my Glock back."

"No problem, Lou."

He put away the phone and continued down the street. He paused in front of a vacant storefront, which was apparently where Marcie Askew had run her art gallery. It was a single-story brick structure painted red and brown. Newspaper was taped to the inside of the windows. Next door was a two-story brick building painted light brown and dark brown. There was no space between the buildings. There was no space between any of the buildings on this block, as a matter of fact. They were all jammed together like odd-sized cardboard boxes crammed onto a shelf.

The building next door belonged to Betty Gibson, a friend of Marcie Askew. Hank opened the front door and walked inside.

A bell jingled above the door. He closed the door behind him and looked around. It was a gift shop that sold hand-knitted sweaters, leather accessories, and a lot of stuff with feathers and tufts of fur. Hank wasn't an expert in gift shops. He avoided them. They were foreign territory. He looked at a rack of books that were apparently self-published by local authors, but didn't see the cook book from the restaurant. He saw a display of greeting cards in cellophane, hand-painted rocks that resembled turtles, frogs, and other small creatures, stuffed animals from the American Kennel Club that were sold as toys for dogs, and a very attractive display of local jewelry. Hank gravitated toward this last rack, looking for something for Meredith.

Peripherally he was aware of two women sitting on chairs behind the counter along the wall, beyond the jewelry rack. He figured that the rack was located so that they could keep an eye on the merchandise to discourage shoplifters. He looked at brooches and earrings mounted on pieces of cardboard, slowly turning the rack.

It became obvious that neither of the women planned to approach him. He could hear them talking quietly, their voices too low to make out any of the words. He picked out an attractive brooch made of silver with some kind of inlaid material that looked like it might be tortoise shell. He took it down to the cash register at the far end of the counter and looked expectantly at the women.

One of them, sitting in a wooden rocking chair with a thick blue cushion, was quite old, perhaps in her eighties. She wore a green and white plaid shirt with the sleeves turned up, jeans, white socks, and white running shoes. Her long white hair was pulled back tightly and knotted at the back of her head. She stared at him with dark, glittering eyes as she rocked slowly back and forth in the rocking chair.

The other woman stood up and came over to the cash. She was a large woman in her late fifties, tall and heavy, with a dark complexion. She wore an ankle-length black dress with a green and white scarf around her neck. Her long straight black hair was shot through with broad gray streaks. She rang up the brooch and held out her hand for the money. Hank paid in cash. No one spoke.

Hank took his change and the little bag with the brooch and saw that the woman had already dismissed him from her consciousness. He stayed at the counter.

"Are you Betty Gibson?"

The woman turned around. "Who wants to know?"

Hank took out his wallet and opened it up so that she could see his badge and ID. "I'm assisting the local police in the investigation of the murder of Marcie Askew. I understand you were a friend of Mrs. Askew, is that right?"

"Are you with the state police? I don't recognize this ID."

"I'm a homicide detective from Maryland. I happened to be

here when Mrs. Askew was murdered. Deputy Chief Branham has asked me to assist."

There was a hardness in her face that relaxed only microscopically at the mention of Branham's name. "They can use all the help they can get. I don't understand why the state police haven't taken over already."

"The sheriff's office is lending assistance but it's still within the jurisdiction of the municipality. The state police would become involved if asked to by the commonwealth's attorney, but as I understand it he'd rather have the county sheriff provide support. You were a friend of Mrs. Askew?"

"Yes, I was."

"How long had you known her?"

"Seven, eight years." The bell over the door jingled as two people came into the store, a middle-aged woman and a teenager, obviously mother and daughter. "Can we do this another time?"

"I'll wait. It'll only take a few minutes."

Betty Gibson moved around the edge of the counter and made her way to the front of the store. Hank heard her greet the older woman by name. They chatted for a few moments. Betty smiled and nodded at the teenager, leading her over to a display of leather moccasins.

Seeing that Betty planned to remain with them for a while, Hank went down to the other end of the counter, close to the old woman in the rocking chair.

"Nice day today."

The woman stared at him. Her features were distinctly Native American. Her hands were folded in her lap. Hank saw a wedding ring on her left hand and a silver ring with a dark-colored stone setting on her right hand. She wore a copper bracelet on her right wrist, the kind that people wear to ease the symptoms of arthritis.

"I've been shopping," Hank said, pulling his messenger bag around and unfastening the flap. "I'm not much of a shopper, though. I needed some shirts, so I bought this one." He pulled out the pale yellow Joseph Abboud shirt and held it up under his chin. "What do you think?"

"Yellow shirts make you look sick," she said.

Hank put the shirt back. "You may be right. I have a yellow tie that I like to wear sometimes. A guy told me once that it made my teeth look even yellower than they already were. I don't wear that tie around him anymore."

"Yellow ties look nice with blue shirts in summer," she said.

"I couldn't agree more." He pulled out the pale blue shirt and held it up to his chin. "How about this?"

"Much better."

Hank put the shirt back and leaned forward, holding out his hand. "I'm Hank Donaghue."

She took his hand and shook it firmly. "How do, Hank. I'm Louise Coffee."

"Do you live in town here, Mrs. Coffee?"

She shook her head. "Got a farm up on Dial Rock. Drive in pretty much every day when the weather's good."

"You drive yourself?"

"Sure. Didn't you see my truck parked right in front?"

"The red one?" Hank remembered a battered old Nissan pickup truck that was parked in front of the vacant storefront next door.

"Yep. I may be eighty-seven but my eyesight's still sharp and I can drive as good as you."

"I don't doubt it," Hank said. "Are you related to Mrs. Gibson?"

"No. She was my daughter's best friend. When Brenda got real sick with the cancer, Betty stayed right with her. Held her hand, talked to her, read to her. Betty's like another daughter to me. I stop in to visit with her nearly every day."

"Did you know Marcie Askew?"

"Some. She liked to lock up her place next door during lunch and come in to sit with Betty."

"What kind of person was she, Mrs. Coffee?"

"Marcie? Beautiful woman, but troubled."

"Is he bothering you, Louise?" Betty Gibson asked, coming behind the counter with a pair of moccasins in her hand.

Mrs. Coffee closed her mouth tight and looked away, as though feeling guilty for having spoken to Hank.

The mother bought the moccasins for her daughter and when they left the store, Betty went back to her chair next to Mrs. Coffee and sat down.

"I don't think there's anything we can help you with," she said to Hank dismissively.

He didn't move from the corner of the counter. "Maybe not. But you heard about Marcie Askew's murder in the news, I take it."

She nodded.

"You're aware, then, that someone strangled her."

Betty said nothing, looking away.

"She was strangled by someone who used their bare hands to kill her. It's unusual for a woman to be killed that way by a stranger. It's a very personal and unplanned sort of attack, usually happening during an argument or a struggle involving sex. A stranger would tend to use a ligature of some kind, a length of rope or wire. It's impersonal. They plan ahead about gaining control of the victim and they bring the ligature with them, but a man who strangles with his hands most likely knows the victim and believes he already has her under his control. Since Marcie most likely knew her killer, I need to know more about her, including the people she spent time with, so I can narrow this down and find out who did it."

"That's horrible," Mrs. Coffee said.

"He's just trying to upset us." Betty looked at Hank. "I'd rather you just left us alone."

"All right." Hank shrugged, still not moving. "I saw her at the bar, not fifteen minutes before she was killed. She was waiting for someone. Whoever it was, they likely killed her. She stepped out of the shadows in front of the bar to take a look at me, but I wasn't the one she was waiting for. She was definitely upset about something. I didn't know her, walked right past her into the bar." Hank shifted on the corner of the counter, leaning forward to look directly into Betty's eyes. "You don't generally stop and ask a woman what's wrong when you're a strange male in a strange place unless you're looking for trouble. The best policy is to mind your own business and walk right by her, which is what I did. Now I'm in the position of trying to find out the hard way what I might have been able to find out just by stopping and talking to her."

"She would have told you to hit the road," Betty said.

"I know," Hank said. "Things happen the way they're supposed to, ninety-nine percent of the time. I doubt I could have helped her, as you say. I had no idea what was going to happen to her fifteen minutes later, so I made my decision and walked on by. But it's still rationalization. I still feel terrible that I saw her just before someone strangled her to death. Now I have to make up the difference. And I need help from people who knew her."

Betty took a moment to think about it, then sighed. "Ask your questions."

"Tell me about her," Hank suggested. "How you met her, what she was like."

19

At first, Betty began after a long pause, my relationship with Marcie was based on a mistaken impression on my part. I should probably explain what I mean by that before I talk about Marcie herself, because it will help you better appreciate the kind of person she was.

I was born and raised in Williamson, West Virginia, which is about seventy miles from here. Although it's the county seat for Mingo County it's not very large, only three thousand people or so. It sits right on the Tug Fork. Directly across the river is Kentucky. My father, John Roberts, was a handyman and jack of all trades. My mother was a housewife and a quiet drunk. She sat up late at night, smoking and drinking, and slept most of the day. I didn't really know either of them very well. There were eight of us kids, and no one stuck around for very long.

When I was twenty I married Jack Gibson, a man ten years older than myself who sold farm implements for a company headquartered up in Charleston. His territory took him as far south as McDowell County, and occasionally he crossed the state line down into Tazewell County to attend meetings and social events with other people down here who sold for the same company. After ten years of marriage I had two children, a boy of eight and a girl of six that I was pretty much raising on my own. Then Jack announced one day he'd accepted a transfer to Roanoke and we were leaving in two weeks. He'd have responsibility for all of southwest Virginia.

I didn't want to move, but I didn't have much say in the matter. My children were in a school they liked, and I had to manage their disappointment and fears about a new home, new friends, and new teachers all by myself. I had a small circle of friends I depended on to keep me from going insane, and I didn't want to leave them either. Once we got to Roanoke I found I was isolated and alone. I could sense a negative attitude toward us from our neighbors, the store clerks, and the teachers in my children's school, and it didn't take me very long to make a connection in my own mind to our ethnic heritage.

In my spare time after we moved, I'd begun to research my family history. I suppose it was an attempt to maintain contact with the family I'd left behind in Williamson, although if I'm completely honest it was probably more to create a sense of belonging that hadn't previously existed. I'd heard the word Melungeon before while I was growing up, and more in a pejorative sense than anything else. I asked my mother what it meant, since it obviously referred to our family in some way, and I guess I picked the wrong time, an afternoon when she was hung over and very tired, because she got upset about it. I don't remember now exactly what she said, but it was negative enough that I understood not to raise the subject again.

In Roanoke, though, it didn't take very long to find that I was researching Melungeon history at the same time I was researching my own family history. I know that not many people from outside the Appalachian region would understand what I'm talking about. The Melungeons are an ethnic group that appeared in this region in the mid-eighteenth century. We were often referred to as free persons of color or mulattos because it was apparent we were a mixture—a *mélange*, if you know your French—of two, maybe three different races. There's a distinctive physical appearance associated with us: dark complexion, dark hair, eyes that are dark or startlingly green, high cheekbones, distinctly-shaped front teeth, and a bump at the back of our head. Occasionally someone is born with six fingers instead of five. As you can see, I've got the complexion, the dark eyes, the hair, the teeth, and the bump. Only five fingers, though.

Melungeons are not a well-known ethnic group like the Cajuns or Creoles. People sometimes don't even realize they descend from a Melungeon family. I'm a good example. Often when talking about their family, some of the old people who don't know any better will say something ignorant about a "nigger in the woodpile." Or that one of their ancestors must have come over from Spain or Portugal or married an Indian. Cherokee is often a favorite choice. The way it stands right now, in terms of research into Melungeons as an ethnic group, no one really knows for certain our racial origins. Most of the research conducted to date has been done by amateurs, and not very well.

The few anthropologists who've done work on our group will only go so far as to say that the evidence suggests Melungeons originated as a group in central Virginia early in the eighteenth century. And for every amateur who insists that they began as Portuguese settlers or Turkish sailors stranded by Drake, there's another amateur who insists that the "Turk" element actually refers to a Catawba Indian settlement on the border of South Carolina that was known as Turkeytown. Native Americans living in this village were often called Turkey Indians or Turks for short, according to legend. Some who believe the Melungeons have a Native American origin suggest that they had roots among the

Catawbas from this area.

One reason that people tend not to know about Melungeons is that we lack a distinctive cultural identity. We don't have a dialect of our own, separate religious practices, distinctive music or cuisine, habits of dress, or any other cultural element that would make us unique other than our physical appearance. And even in that regard, most families have been assimilated into the melting pot to such an extent that they're considered Caucasians with a dark complexion and nothing else.

My own personal research turned up a story passed down through the generations that claims my great-great grandfather Ike Roberts was the Melungeon son of a woman from the Saponi Indian tribe. It's all anecdotal, with no actual documentary evidence to back it up, but I expect it's the best I'm ever going to do, so I've decided to accept it as my ancestry.

So you can see from my store that I've chosen Native American culture as a core part of my heritage. I promote Native American crafts and small businesses of all kinds. Almost everything in this store has been made by a Native American artisan or artist.

Louise Coffee, here, is a Mingo whose father was one of the mountain people of West Virginia who sold barrel hoops in Pittsburgh back in the old days. An Indian hoopie, she likes to say. When she first said that I was appalled, because I understood hoopie to be a pejorative term, but she laughs when she says it. It's part of who she is. It doesn't hurt that she's one of the biggest suppliers of ginseng in this part of the country. She's worth a lot more than she looks.

She can still speak some of the Mingo language, which has pretty much disappeared today, and she's been teaching me what she knows. I've been writing it down and I plan to publish a book under both our names. It'll go in that rack right there with all the other books published by people in this area.

What does any of this have to do with Marcie Askew? I know I'm being very long-winded in telling my story, but as I said at the outset, my relationship with Marcie began with a mistaken impression on my part. To make a long story short, as I researched my family history and learned more about my Melungeon heritage, I decided it was my ethnic appearance that was causing people in Roanoke to snub me and my kids. By the time my son left home and my daughter followed two years later, I'd had enough of Roanoke and a husband who was never at home. I filed for divorce, packed my belongings, and moved to Tazewell. Later I moved up here to Harmony when I saw an advertisement in the newspaper for a business for sale. I'd gotten a lump sum settlement from my husband, so I used it as a down payment on this store. I've been operating it now for four years.

I first met Marcie at a Harmony Business Association fundraiser the same summer I opened the store. I was very nervous because I didn't know anyone and I had no idea what kind of community Harmony was going to be. They put me at a table with the guy who runs the army surplus store. He's a certified gun nut. All he wanted to do was talk firearms with the other men at the table. The guy sitting next to me owned the tire store down near the college. He didn't introduce himself, and I had no idea who he was until later on. Sitting on the other side of me were Chief Askew and his wife, Marcie. I felt very uncomfortable.

We listened to the mayor's speech, Billy got up to talk about "safe streets, homes and businesses" in Harmony, awards were handed out to various businesses for various things, and then an auction of antiques and sports collectibles began in an adjoining room to supplement the $100-a-plate ticket price. Funds raised were being donated to the local Baptist church that was rebuilding after a serious fire.

When Billy left his seat to deliver his speech, Marcie leaned across and said hello to me. When the auction began and people began to mill about, Billy went off to hang out with people he knew. Marcie slid over and began to talk to me. I can't properly describe the impact she made on me that evening.

It was obvious to me right away that she was a Melungeon. The complexion, the hair, the eyes all gave her away. I asked her what her maiden name was, and when she told me it was Cole I wondered if she might be descended from the Coles of Magoffin County, Kentucky, who were considered a part of the mixed-blood Carmelites of that area, so I asked her. She said she thought her grandfather was from Kentucky somewhere but didn't really know much about it.

You have to understand that at the time I was obsessed with Melungeon genealogy. I asked her a few questions that a person might consider invasive, particularly given that we'd just met and she didn't know me from a hole in the ground, but she was very gracious and patient about it all. That was Marcie, you see. She had a way about her that's hard to explain. She told me her father's name, his birth date, and that he'd been born and raised in Richlands. I filed it all away for later reference. I'm embarrassed to say that I spent quite a few hours researching her family history after that first night. Her father's family was from Hancock County, Tennessee. Sure enough no doubt Melungeons.

I was fascinated by Marcie from the first moment I laid eyes on her. She had a magnetism about her. Underneath her calm, elegant exterior there was a sexuality that was impossible to ignore. I could see she almost overpowered some men just by being in the same room with them.

I hung on her every word that night, and it wasn't long afterwards that she came into my store to ask my advice on the place next door. She wanted to open up a business of some kind and had more or less settled on a tea room. Her husband bought the property and told her she could do whatever she wanted with it. I had my doubts that a tea room would make any money in a little town like Harmony, but I gave her some ideas for marketing and advertising and wrote down the name and number of someone I knew who could help her with interior design.

She opened up the following spring and closed it that December when her sales had dwindled pretty much to zero. By then she was spending more time in here than she was in her own shop. This is a meeting place for a loose-knit group of women from the area, and people like to stop in for a while and talk. In fact, she got the idea to reopen as an art gallery from a couple of my friends who'd stopped in to see if I would carry their paintings. One specialized in flowers, vegetables, that sort of thing, painted right in the garden, and the other did portraits of Native American girls and women. I really liked their work but I didn't think this was the right place for it. It would kind of disappear among all the other stuff I have in here. Marcie came in while we were talking about it. The tea room had been closed for several months, and she was restless to do something else. She took them next door, and they struck a deal right away. Marcie reopened as an art gallery, found several other artists whose work she liked, and went from there.

She carried a lot of native work but took on a number of other artists from the area. She particularly liked young people just starting out, trying to make a name for themselves, and she didn't limit herself just to oil paintings and watercolors. She took in wood and stone carvings, prints, even drawings from a young woman in town who does extraordinary things with colored pencils. It was wonderful for the community. She hosted events and held showings, made connections with some of the staff at the college, and featured the work of their students from time to time. For a year or two, she had something exceptional going. I caught a bit of the spillover, being next door, so I thought it was great, too. But eventually the novelty wore off, and people stopped coming in. This area's not exactly a cultural hotbed.

She and Billy went through a rough patch, and she went for days without opening the store, which didn't help business very much, either. She came in here instead, but even that didn't go too well. She'd sit for a minute and then would head for my washroom in the back room to vomit her guts out. It was obvious she'd been out all night drinking and didn't want to go home to face Billy. I'd make her a cup of

114

tea to settle her stomach and try to get her to eat something, then send her home. It was very sad.

She had several problems that were eating her alive. After I'd been here long enough to become plugged in to the grapevine, I began to hear a lot of negative things being said about her. People made fun of her looks and the sexy way she always dressed, and at first I thought people were ridiculing her ethnic background. That's what I meant about our relationship being based at first on a false assumption on my part. I thought originally that people were discriminating against her because she was so obviously Melungeon. It took me a while to get over my own fixation with ethnicity and to realize that hardly anyone in Harmony gave a second thought to Melungeons, Cherokees, Saponis, or any other such thing. The way they treated Marcie around here didn't have anything to do with her dusky complexion or her family lineage. I'd originally become obsessed with Marcie because I identified with her Melungeon heritage. It took me a while to realize that I was fascinated by her more because she was a tragic figure, a larger-than-life train wreck happening in slow motion right in front of me.

Because she was the wife of the local chief of police she had a certain social standing that many people resented. I often heard people make fun of things she did in the community, charitable events she hosted or participated in with Billy. People would whisper that she was really a piece of hillbilly trash who liked to put on airs and pretend she was something better than she really was. It was very cruel and not at all accurate. For all her beauty, grace, and intelligence she was one of the least egotistical people I've ever met. You could tell that beneath her smooth, elegant surface she had very little self-confidence. She tried hard to please Billy, to be a proper wife of the chief of police. It took everything she had to keep up that façade, more than she had in the end, really.

She wasn't an idiot. She knew what people were saying about her. She kept turning the other cheek, taking everyone's garbage, and trying not to let it show how much it hurt her. Even people she thought were her friends made jokes at her expense that had a certain edge to them which couldn't be covered over.

Her relationship with Billy was her other main source of despair. I guess it pretty much had its roots in the loss of their daughter. I never met Lucy, who passed away eight years ago, but people have told me she was a very sweet child, dark and beautiful like Marcie, very quiet and loving. It was a difficult pregnancy and when Lucy was born, the obstetrician told Marcie she shouldn't have any more children because it would likely kill her. She doted on Lucy, and when they learned that the girl had leukemia they were devastated. She was only twelve years old, a perfect angel, and they couldn't understand why it was happening to them. The poor thing fought for three years before she finally passed away. If it were true that giving birth to another child would have killed Marcie, it was equally as true that losing her only child killed something inside her almost as precious as her own life.

She began drinking heavily and she fought constantly with Billy. It was a mess. Billy had an affair with a woman who was the dispatcher at the station at the time, and everyone knew about it. It lasted about two months until Marcie made a scene and put an end to it. Her neighbor, Mrs. Cully, saw the whole thing. Mrs. Cully was out in her garden after lunch when Marcie came out the front door of the house with a broom in her hand. She began to sweep the front porch. Mrs. Cully called over to her but Marcie didn't seem to hear. Marcie swept the front porch and then swept the cement walk from the porch up to the sidewalk. When she reached the sidewalk, she just swung the broom up over her shoulder and kept walking. They lived about five blocks from the station. Mrs. Cully followed because she was a nosy busybody and she knew something was going to happen. She followed Marcie all the way to the station. Marcie walked into the station, went through the little swinging gate, went right up to the dispatcher, and started flailing at her with the broom. It took a few moments before people realized what was happening, and another few minutes to decide they'd better do something about it. Marcie was very popular among Billy's staff, you see, and the dispatcher wasn't. They let Marcie get a few extra whacks in before they grabbed the broom and got her settled down. Billy came out of his office, and she tried to go after him. He wanted to take her home but he couldn't get near her because all she wanted to do was scratch his eyes out. One of the older officers took her home and sat with her for a couple of hours, just talking her down. Billy wisely got himself a hotel room for a couple of nights, and the dispatcher quit her job and moved out of town.

It took Marcie a while to let Billy come back. I don't like him very much, but I have to give him credit for making a big effort to win her back by becoming a model husband. He started keeping regular hours and always called to let her know where he was. They saw a marriage counselor in Bluefield for a while. He bought her flowers all the time, on the spur of the moment. On the sex front, he walked the straight and narrow; he had a vasectomy so she wouldn't be at risk of getting pregnant again and told her straight out that she was in charge of the bedroom. What she said, went. She told me all about this, you see. I was her confidante for a while, maybe her closest friend. She had so few people to talk to and she needed to explain things to someone, so I was it.

Anyway, he did everything he could to win her back, because the fact of the matter was that he really loved her and couldn't stand the idea of losing her. She told him she was going crazy alone in the house without Lucy to look after, so he bought the building next door when she started talking about opening a business of some kind. He just bought the damned thing, just like that, and told her she could do whatever she wanted with it. So she took a couple of business courses at the college and started off with the tea room.

Having her own business wasn't the solution to her problems, though. It doesn't take a psychiatrist to understand that she felt overwhelming guilt over Lucy's death, as though somehow it had been her fault, and sometimes that's a problem which can't be solved. You can't bring your child back to life, you can't undo what's happened to them, and it's particularly difficult when you didn't do anything wrong in the first place. If you'd actually done something that caused their death, then it would be a matter of atoning for your actions and somehow finding a way to forgive yourself in the long run. But if it wasn't your fault, then there's nothing to make atonement for, but a part of your mind will never accept that. For some reason you never let yourself off the hook.

So you're constantly trying to solve an emotional problem that can't be solved. It nearly drove Marcie insane.

20

"She was so beautiful, so magnetic, and so very unhappy," Betty said, looking at Hank earnestly. "It was very sad to watch her struggle."

"Did she talk to you this past year about being involved with someone?" Hank asked.

"No. She closed the gallery a year and a half ago, and Billy had to sell the property because of the economic downturn. He couldn't afford to keep it, and he really took a bath on it. Press Blankenship bought it, actually, at a fraction of what it cost Billy. Anyway, Marcie hasn't been around very much since the gallery closed. I know she was taking a photography course at the college for a while, and she was considering reopening next door as a photo studio or something before Billy had to sell the place. Other than that, I never heard about her being involved with anyone."

She looked at Louise. "What about you, dear? Did you hear anything?"

Louise pushed out her lower lip and shook her head solemnly.

"Did you know she'd had a few injuries in the past year?" Hank asked.

"Yes," Betty replied. "I know she broke her wrist a few months ago. I saw her when it was still in the cast. She said she fell down the stairs. Had a bit too much to drink."

"She also suffered a cracked jaw in the past year," Hank said, "and about three months ago she had a separated shoulder. Did you know about those injuries?"

"No. I saw her a couple of months ago with a swollen cheek, but that was from an infected tooth. She went to the free clinic to see a call-in dentist there, she said, because her dentist was out of town." Betty's eyes fluttered. "Oh, God. I get it. All those things happening to her. He was beating her, wasn't he?"

"Who was beating her?"

"Billy. Is that what you're saying? Was he beating her?"

"I don't know," Hank said.

"Oh my God, I can't believe I didn't see it, I didn't understand the pattern. Oh my God. Did he kill her? Is that where this is going?"

Hank held up his hand. "No no, not at all, I'm just asking questions. Don't jump to any conclusions. Did you notice her in the company of any other men at any time in the last year?"

"No," Betty said. "She took that photography course, like I said. Maybe she met someone there. She was bar-hopping a lot, though. In Bluefield, other towns, at the Mullins dump. People talked about it. She might have been picking up guys, I don't know. She didn't tell me if she was, because as I said, I didn't really see her very much any more."

Hank stood up. "All right. I appreciate your help." He stopped short. "I wanted to ask you about family. Did she have relatives around here?"

Betty shook her head. "She was born in Bluefield. Her parents are both dead. She had one older brother who died when they were little. No family here at all that I'm aware of. Just Billy."

"All right." Hank moved around the end of the counter. No other customers had come into the store; there was still just the three of them. He debated for a moment whether or not to ask the question he still hadn't asked her.

Sometimes asking a question actually gives away more information than it gets back. Sometimes that's what you want to do, put information into play, have it circulate around simply by asking about it, in order to see where it ends up. This wasn't one of those situations, though. He wanted to ask the question because he wanted to know what Marcie would have done, but he didn't want the entire town talking about the facts of Marcie's case, so he weighed the pros and cons in his mind for a moment before making his decision.

"Did you know Marcie was pregnant?"

Betty was in the process of sitting down in the armchair next to Louise. She froze in place, her bottom four inches from the seat, her eyes locked straight ahead, her mouth slightly open. Then she blinked and sat down.

"Oh, God. No."

"What would she have done about it?"

"My lord. She must have been extremely upset." Betty ran her fingertips under her eyes to wipe away tears that were forming. "What do you mean? I don't understand your question."

"What would she have done about her pregnancy?"

"You mean would she have had an abortion?" Betty leaned back in the armchair and looked away. "Since she wasn't supposed to have any more children, I guess it's a very good question. I really don't know."

"Was she a religious person?"

"Not that I'd say. She and Billy attended Stanley Baptist like a lot of other people around here. After Lucy died they saw the minister a few times for counseling, but Marcie thought he was a dope and didn't bother after that. Would she have had religious objections to abortion, is that what you're asking? Probably not."

"So an abortion would have been an option for her, in her mind."

"Boy, I really don't know." Betty sighed heavily. It rattled in her chest. "She'd have seen it as saving her own life at the expense of her child's life." She took a breath, pinching away the wetness beneath her right eye. "After what she went through with Lucy, I imagine it really shook her up. She probably decided to have the baby and take her chances." Betty shook her head slowly. "That would have been her atonement. It makes a crazy kind of sense."

"This monastery in Burkes Garden," Hank said. "You said she went there for an infected tooth. Likely to have her cracked jaw examined, given the timing. Would she have gone to the free clinic for her pregnancy as well, do you think?"

"She could have. What about her doctor in Tazewell?"

Hank shook his head.

"How far along was she?" Betty asked.

"Three months."

"Oh, no."

Louise Coffee leaned forward and patted Betty's knee. Then she looked at Hank. "People sometimes go to the clinic when something happens they don't want other people to know about. The people there respect your privacy."

"They don't perform abortions, do they?" Hank asked.

Louise shook her head. "Young girls, they sometimes go there if they get in trouble, and the brothers help them through it. Older women, young girls. When the baby is a big problem. They have a psychologist, or a psychiatrist, I don't know which, who comes and listens and helps them understand what they need to do."

Hank frowned. "But they're a Christian brotherhood. Wouldn't they be strictly anti-abortion?"

"What I hear is, if the girl decides she wants an abortion and won't change her mind, they send her to a doctor in Richlands who'll talk to her about it. Then, if it has to happen, it happens with this doctor in Richlands."

"I find it hard to believe that they'd refer women to an abortionist."

Louise shrugged. "It's what I heard."

"Who's this psychiatrist or whatever, Mrs. Coffee? What's his name?"

"I don't know, I just heard about her. It's a her, not a him."

"What about Brother Charles Baker, the abbot there? Do you know him?"

Louise smiled. "Sure, I know him. He's a very nice man."

"Louise, you're such a darling," Betty said through her tears. "You have at least a hundred clients, and I swear you have something nice to say about each one of them."

Louise chuckled. "Maybe not all of them."

"What about Brother Charles?" Hank prompted. "Do you deal with him a lot?"

"Sure," Louise replied. "I'm one of the vendors at the fall festival in Burkes Garden every year. Are you coming? It's next Saturday."

"I might, if I'm still here. What kind of person is he?"

"Shy. Quiet. Very polite. Smart, too. Two years ago he sat with me for an hour at my booth at their festival, and I taught him to say some things in Seneca. I talk Seneca better than Mingo, even though I'm Mingo. Nobody talks in Mingo anymore." Louise waved her hand. "Anyway, I was saying I taught him some Indian talk. The next time I saw him, he talked to me back in Seneca and used words I hadn't taught him. I couldn't understand how he could do that until he told me he'd sent away for books and was teaching himself more Seneca."

Hank raised his eyebrows. "Interesting."

"Couldn't talk it worth a damn, though," Louise grinned. "I could hardly tell what he was saying, he had the words all wrong. So I taught him better pronunciation. Now I can understand him."

"They're celibates out there, aren't they? Like Catholic priests?"

"I don't think so," Betty said. "I'm pretty sure there are two or three married couples. I think it's a matter of personal choice."

"Is this Brother Charles a cult leader type of guy? Does he tell them all what to do?"

"I can maybe answer that question better than you," Louise said, looking at Betty. "They have like a council that does all their business. The council votes on everything. I know because I have a little partnership with them for a couple of my products. I had to talk to their council about it and wait until they voted. Brother Charles signed the papers with me, but it was the council that made up their minds on doing the business. I don't know about religious stuff, I go to a different church than them."

"What about Marcie? Did she know Brother Charles?"

Betty looked at Louise and shrugged. "Hard to say. She might have."

"I didn't know Mrs. Askew much," Louise said. "Not good enough to know the answer to that kind of question."

"I appreciate the help you've given me, Mrs. Coffee," Hank said. "You have a good day, now."

"Maybe I'll see you on the weekend."

"Maybe you will."

Betty walked with him to the front door. "I'm sorry if I was a little hostile at first."

"That's all right. I understand."

She looked at him. "You might, at that. You sure you're a cop?"

"Very sure." Hank paused with his hand on the door. There was no one visible outside on the sidewalk, and Louise was rocking in her rocking chair, looking up at the ceiling pensively. "You asked me earlier if Billy had been responsible for Marcie's injuries. Do you think he'd be capable of that kind of violence with her?"

She grimaced. "I'm not sure. I was upset, I guess. He's a hotheaded guy sometimes, and I know he's hit a few people, you know, criminals or whatever. But now that I've calmed down, I'd have to say that I doubt it. I really believe he loved her."

"Could he have lost his temper about the pregnancy? Hit her despite himself?"

"Or strangled her?" Betty looked at him. "Is that what you're asking?"

Hank stared back.

"No. Maybe. I don't know."

"What about Brother Charles? He strike you as the kind of guy who'd get sexually involved with a married woman and knock her around and maybe panic and kill her when he found out she was pregnant with his child?"

Betty stared at him. "Him? I doubt it."

"No?"

"I doubt it."

"But maybe Billy."

"I don't know." She hesitated. "Maybe he did, after all."

21

Because Hall was driving, and because he was driving like someone's grandmother all the way back from Tazewell to Harmony, staying in the right-hand lane and keeping the speedometer needle dead on the speed limit, Karen had plenty of time to stare out the window and think about things.

Karen was not a person who indulged in introspection or self-analysis. There were a lot of things she put out of her mind and kept out of her mind. She saw herself as a law enforcement professional first and foremost, and she worked hard to keep her attention between the lines and on the playing field. Her personal relationships, whether with family, friends, or lovers, came second to her responsibilities as a police officer. That's who she was, and Sandy wouldn't have it any other way. As an FBI field agent who was being talked about as the next Special Agent in Charge of the Glendale office, Sandy was also a full-focus professional who kept things in perspective and gave the job whatever it asked of him.

How would they make out as a married couple? Karen found herself asking that question on a regular basis, and it bothered her. She wasn't the kind of person to second-guess herself. She'd decided to marry Sandy, she'd gotten over that hump, and it was now a done thing. She'd admitted she loved the little bastard, she knew without a shadow of a doubt that he was crazy about her, and the situation didn't need any more analysis than that. They got along well together, they were a fit, and their personalities were different enough that they complemented each other nicely, end of story. The sex was great and she knew that he would remain faithful to her for the duration. He was that kind of guy. For her part, while passion was something she liked to throw herself into whenever she was with him, and while she doubted the sexual attraction would ever diminish, sex didn't rule her life and wouldn't interfere with their relationship no matter what.

Having a kid, though, was something she wasn't ready to think about. It was too far down the road and too frightening a topic to lose time on when there were more pressing matters demanding her attention. That's what she told herself, but thoughts of children inevitably led her to thoughts about her mother. Should she have children knowing the kind of person her mother was and knowing the potential that she herself could become the same kind of person? And knowing she could pass it on to her own children?

Her mother lived in a mental institution in Dallas. Karen had to confront the subject at some point. In particular, she had to discuss it with Sandy before they tied the knot. Make sure he was okay with the scenario.

My mother has what the doctors call disorganized schizophrenia, dear. She can't live outside an institution and there's a possibility I could still go off the rails myself. The doctors said it generally shows up in women between the ages of 25 and 35. Since I'm 37 I made it past that one but there's another window between 40 and 45, just before menopause, so there's a chance I may flip out on you three years from now. You okay with that? And oh yeah, it apparently can be passed on to our kids, if we have any. You okay with that, too?

Christ. She bit her lip hard, staring out the window. Focus. Hank. Good friend. Talk to him about it. He'll understand. He understands you better than anyone else, maybe even better than Sandy. Why? Why does he understand you so well? What makes him so special that he can see through you like that? And why does he give a shit?

They reached the off ramp to Harmony. Hall slowed the car to a crawl.

"Jesus, Hall, you drive like my gramma on tranks."

The blanket of silence covered them again until they walked into the station. Hall went over to Grimes.

"Bring Baker out and put him in the interrogation room."

"Is there a point to this?" Karen asked, sitting down in his visitor's chair. "Your beloved chief's starting to look real good for it."

Hall fussed with the computer so that the live feed from the interrogation room was visible on the monitor. "Baker was there. He won't explain why. He won't explain who he was going to meet. I think it was Marcie. I think he killed her."

At that point a door opened and a short bald man in a brown plaid suit emerged from the little washroom next to the interrogation room. He spotted Hall and made a beeline for him.

The detective wilted.

The metal door to the cells opened. Brother Charles emerged, followed by Grimes. The abbot's hands were cuffed in front of him and he looked as though he'd missed a lot of sleep. The man in the brown plaid suit changed course in mid-stride and hurried over to the abbot.

Hall looked at Grimes. "Why didn't you tell me Garrett was

here?"

Grimes gave him a malicious grin. "Oops."

Karen saw Mollie Roberts shake her head in disgust, her eyes focused on her computer screen. "What's going on?" Karen asked. "Who's Garrett?"

"Detective Hall," the man snapped, "is it your intention to question my client right now?"

"That's right, Mr. Garrett," Hall replied wearily. "Can we just go into the room and do it? I have a few questions I need answered."

"I've been trying to get in touch with the chief and the deputy chief," Garrett went on. "I can't reach anyone. It makes absolutely no sense to hold my client without a scrap of evidence. I demand you release him immediately."

"I'm not going to do that, Mr. Garrett." Hall gestured toward the interview room. "If you don't mind?"

"Not without some sort of explanation from Chief Askew. Where is he? I want to speak to him first."

"Chief Askew's been recused from the case by the assistant commonwealth's attorney," Hall said reluctantly.

"Deputy Chief Branham, then."

"He's with the mayor and the ACA right now. There's a press conference going on."

"Right now?"

Hall glanced at the clock, which someone had returned to its place on the wall after Askew had knocked it down when he slammed his office door. "I don't know. It started at three." He took Brother Charles by the arm and led him to the interview room.

As the door closed, Grimes dropped into Hall's chair, put his feet up on the corner of his desk, and picked up the headset. Karen got up and moved around so that she could see the monitor.

The door from the employees' area at the back of the station opened. Branham walked in, followed by Assistant Commonwealth's Attorney Hatfield.

"Looks who's back," Karen said.

"What's going on?" Branham asked, walking over.

"Hall's trying to interrogate the abbot," Karen said. "Lawyer's with him. Might be interesting to hear if ol' sack-o-shit wasn't hogging the audio."

Branham slapped Grimes hard on the leg to knock his feet off Hall's desk. Grimes removed the headset, startled.

"Put it on the speakers and go lock the front door," Branham snapped.

Mollie Roberts followed Grimes with her eyes, her mouth set, as he shuffled over to the door and locked it.

As the audio came on, Hatfield sat on the corner of the desk. "I deeply regret," he said to no one in particular, "that I quit smoking three months, six days, and ten hours ago. I could really use a cigarette right now."

"Look, I appreciate that," Hall was saying to Garrett, his voice sounding thin through the speakers on each side of the monitor, "but it's only a few questions. We want to know why he drove into Harmony on Saturday night. We want to know who he went there to see."

"I don't see how it's in my client's interest to answer anything," Garrett replied.

Hatfield's cell phone purred. He took it out, glanced at the call display, and thumbed a button. "Hatfield."

He listened for several long moments and closed his eyes. Then he opened them again. "I assume it was on the Virginia side."

He listened again and nodded.

"I appreciate the heads up. Yep. Thanks." He ended the call and looked at Branham. "Your chief's been arrested in Bluefield. He's refusing to talk, refusing to call a lawyer, being a general pain in the fucking ass. That was Johnson." Laura Johnson was the assistant commonwealth's attorney in Bluefield. "He's been booked on two charges of assault. They're holding him."

Branham closed his eyes and pinched the bridge of his nose.

"So what about it, Baker?" Hall asked in the interview room. "Who'd you go see on Saturday night?"

"Marcie Askew," Brother Charles replied uncomfortably.

Branham's eyes snapped back open and focused on the computer monitor.

"Why on earth would you be meeting with a married woman at a bar on Saturday night? You like the bar scene, do you? Like to mix with married women?"

"Of course not. She called me and asked me to meet her there."

"Why would she do that?"

"She was meeting someone there and . . . was a little nervous about it. She wanted me to be there with her, for moral support, I guess."

"Who was she meeting?"

"I don't know."

"You don't know?" Hall repeated, incredulous.

"No, I'm sorry, she didn't say."

"Okay, why was she meeting this person? She tell you that much, or were you going into the entire thing blind?"

126

"No, I knew more or less what was going on. She . . . uh, was pregnant."

"And?"

"You don't seem surprised by that."

Hall snorted. "Never mind me, Baker. I'm not the one suspected of murder. Spell it out for me. She was going to Gerry's to talk to someone about the fact that she was pregnant, is that what you're telling me?"

"Yes."

"And who would that have been, the father of the baby?"

"I don't know."

"Okay, explain why she called you. Why'd she call you, Baker, of all the people she could call?"

"She was a patient at our clinic. I shouldn't say anything else because of privacy of information concerns."

Hall patted his jacket and reached inside to pull out a folded piece of paper.

"Funny you should mention that," Hall said, handing the paper to Gordon Garrett. "Her husband gave us permission to get whatever medical information we need for our investigation."

Everyone sat still for a moment as Garrett scanned the document.

"Tell him whatever he needs to know," Garrett said to Brother Charles.

"I wasn't involved in her case at first," Brother Charles said. "Originally it was Dr. Long."

"Who's he?"

"Brother Benjamin. Dr. Ben Long. He's our chief administrator at the clinic, and he also takes a regular turn with walk-in patients. About six months ago she came to us with a broken wrist. Dr. Long treated her. She told him she'd fallen down a flight of stairs, put her hand out to break her fall, and snapped her wrist. He noticed the absence of bruising on the heel of the hand which normally accompanies that kind of fall. Then about three months ago she came back with a dislocated shoulder. Again, it happened to be Dr. Long who treated her. She told him she was walking a friend's dog, a Saint Bernard that wasn't very well trained."

"I'll want copies of your records on this," Hall said.

Brother Charles looked at Garrett, who nodded.

"Then what?" Hall prompted.

"Then two months ago she came in looking beaten up," Brother Charles went on. "Her face was swollen on one side. She had a black eye, and the x-rays showed a cracked jaw. This time it was another doctor, Dr. Orlov, who was on duty. After looking through her file, he told her it would take a while to process the x-rays and called Dr. Long and myself. We discussed it, and called Dr. Margaret Huntley, a psychologist in Bluefield who does volunteer work for us on an ad hoc basis. Dr. Huntley wasn't able to come down but gave us a couple of timeslots for the following week when she'd make herself available. Then we sat down with Mrs. Askew and got her to pick one of the times for an appointment with Dr. Huntley."

Karen looked up as someone tried to open the front door of the station. Hatfield frowned in irritation. Grimes stirred, but Branham shook his head.

"Did she show up at the appointment?" Hall asked.

Brother Charles nodded. "She saw Dr. Huntley twice at our clinic."

"Were you involved with these meetings?"

"You mean, did I sit in? No, of course not."

"But by this time you'd become friends with Mrs. Askew, is that it?"

"No. We knew each other. We'd spoken several times."

Karen's cell phone purred. She took it out and looked at the call display. "Stainer."

She listened for a moment and then laughed. "Yeah, we're here. Invitation only." She listened again, still grinning. "Okay, if you insist." She ended the call and looked at Branham.

"It's Lieutenant Donaghue at the front door. He wants to know if he can come in."

Branham sighed and gestured to Grimes, who got up with a big show of annoyance to unlock the door for Hank. As he headed back, Grimes noticed Mollie Roberts staring at him and scowled. She showed him her teeth in a sardonic grin.

"Howdy," Karen said to Hank. "Come join the party."

"What's going on?"

Karen brought him up to speed as Hall continued to question Brother Charles about how well he'd known Marcie Askew. Hatfield grew irritated and shushed her.

"So what you're telling me," Hall was saying, "is that you knew about Mrs. Askew's case, you knew she was pregnant and was being abused, but you don't know who was hitting her and you don't know who the father of the child was. Have I got that right?"

"I'm sorry," Brother Charles replied, "I know how frustrating it must be, but that's the truth. I have no idea if she told Dr. Huntley who it was, you'd have to ask her, but Mrs. Askew didn't tell me, and according to Dr. Long and Dr. Orlov she didn't tell them, either. I have no reason to doubt their word. I just don't know who it was."

128

"Sounds like you're assuming the person beating her and the person who fathered the child were the same guy."

Brother Charles spread his hands helplessly. "I just don't know. I'm sorry."

"Okay," Hall said. "Back to Saturday night. When did you arrange to meet her at Gerry's?"

"She called me about seven o'clock. She said she was going to be meeting someone at eleven-thirty and wanted me to be there."

"As a witness? Because she was scared of the guy?"

"I guess so."

"So you said you'd be there."

"Yes."

"So walk me through the evening."

"After her call I had a meeting to chair. We've been doing a budget review, and Brother David and I had a number of details to iron out."

"A meeting? On a Saturday night?"

"It's what we do, Detective Hall. We don't punch a time clock and put in for overtime. Our work is our lives."

"Okay, all right. So you had this meeting. What time did it end?"

"It went late. Brother David and I disagree on a few things, and we debated it back and forth for quite a while. When I looked at my watch, it was already past eleven o'clock, which was when I said I'd meet her. She was supposed to meet this person there at eleven-thirty or something and wanted me there. She wanted to explain to me first what was going on."

"So you're saying she wanted you there when she met the guy because she was afraid of him?"

"I suppose so."

"Looks like she had good reason to be, doesn't it? So okay, you left your meeting at eleven. Then what?"

"I got in the truck and drove to town."

"Did you go straight to Gerry's or did you go somewhere else?"

"I went straight there. I was already late." Brother Charles frowned at Hall. "No, wait. I had to stop for gas along the way. The last person to use the truck is supposed to gas up, but they didn't. I was running on empty. I stopped at the all-night Getty along the highway."

"What time was that?"

"I don't know. I was late, that's all I remember."

"Okay. Go on."

"I drove to Gerry's and parked in the front lot. She said she'd be out front, but she wasn't there."

"What'd you do?"

"I looked inside, just opened the door and looked around, but she wasn't there."

"She could have been in the washroom."

"I suppose, but it didn't occur to me at the time. I went around the back to see if she was there, but she wasn't. So I gave up and left. I didn't feel very comfortable and wanted to get out of there. I thought she'd probably changed her mind and left, or she'd had her conversation with the man and they'd left together. Either way, there was nothing for me to do, so I left."

"Go back for a second. Tell me in detail about going back to the back of the bar."

"In detail?"

"Walk me through it."

"Uh, I came outside again, she still wasn't out front, so I thought I'd better look around, so I walked along the side of the building. There's a pen for garbage back there, a security light up on a pole, it's all paved. I got to the corner of the building and looked around the corner and saw no one there. So I came back up and got in my truck and drove away."

"Did you go all the way back behind the bar?"

"No, I just kind of peeked around the corner and left again. I felt extremely uncomfortable being there. I just wanted to get out of there and go home."

Hatfield turned to Branham. "This guy didn't do it."

"I don't know," Branham said.

"He wouldn't hurt a goddamned flea, Neil. Look at him."

"His feet are too big," Hank said.

Hatfield frowned. "What?"

"His feet are too big. The prints at the crime scene that the sheriff's criminalists have connected to the killer are from a size eleven shoe. Mine are thirteen, and I'd say that his are probably the same. He didn't drag Marcie Askew across the parking lot and carry her down the path into the ravine. The footprints don't match. He's not your guy."

Hatfield looked at Branham.

"Go ask him to show you his shoe," Hank said to Branham.

Branham looked at Hatfield.

"Do it," Hatfield said.

Branham went into the interview room. Everyone leaned closer to the monitor to watch.

"Gordon," Branham said, "what size shoe does your client wear?"

"What? Shoe?"

"Thirteen," Brother Charles said.

Branham held out a hand. "Can I see?"

Brother Charles looked at Garrett, who shrugged. "Give him one of your shoes."

Brother Charles bent down, removed his right shoe, and handed it to Branham, who looked it over. Hall squirmed in his chair on the other side of the table.

"I'll be right back," Branham said. He walked out of the interview room with the shoe in his hand.

"Grimes," he said, coming toward them, "where's a measuring tape? Have you got a tape?"

Grimes went to his desk, pawed through a drawer, and produced a small measuring tape. Branham held up the shoe. It was a well-worn, slightly warped black oxford wingtip shoe with a smooth thin sole.

"There's a bunch of stuff that was stamped inside but it's worn off," Branham said. He turned the shoe over and Grimes measured the sole. "Thirteen and a quarter inches."

"Cut him loose," Hatfield said. "Give him back his goddamned shoe and get him the hell out of here."

Hank and Karen drifted back to the far corner of the office to watch as Brother Charles was brought out of the interview room and seated at Hall's desk. Grimes processed the paperwork and gave Brother Charles the envelope containing his personal effects.

Karen glanced at the messenger bag on Hank's hip. "Shopping went well, I see."

Hank nodded. "Got some clothes." He glanced at his watch. "Maybe tomorrow we'll go take a look at that SIG."

"My pleasure."

"Talked to Betty Gibson, a friend of Mrs. Askew. No luck on who Marcie was having the fling with, but there seems to be a sense that Askew could be violent if provoked enough."

Karen snorted. "News bulletin, Lou. He's sitting in jail in Bluefield as we speak for beating on somebody's ass up there."

Hank looked at her. "Are you serious?"

"Completely. Hatfield just got the call not ten minutes ago. I think he's starting to like Billy Askew for this."

They watched Brother Charles and Gordon Garrett leave the station. Then Hatfield turned to Branham.

"Do you know where Chief Askew was on Saturday night before the call came in?"

Branham looked uncomfortable. "His cell phone was turned off. We had problems getting hold of him."

"So we don't know yet if he has an alibi." Hatfield bit his lip. "Alibi or not, I don't like the looks of it. This arrest for assault is just the frosting on the cake." He put his hands in his pocket. "I'm not going to put you in the position of investigating your own chief. As of right now, this investigation is transferred to County. Have all your case material transferred to Tazewell first thing in the morning and make arrangements for you and Hall to brief Sheriff Steele and his investigators on everything you've covered to date."

"Now wait a minute, Mr. Hatfield," Branham started.

"No." Hatfield held up his hand like a traffic cop. "That's it. You're done. You've got a promising future, Neil. Step back and let Steele take it from here. That way nothing'll get splashed on you." He looked over at Hank. "You folks are free to leave. Thanks very much on behalf of Tazewell County for your cooperation."

"But they've been providing invaluable help," Branham said.

"I'm sure they have." Hatfield walked over to Hank and put out his hand. "Thanks again."

Hank shook his hand. "You're welcome."

"Please accept my verbal apology for your treatment on Saturday night. Under the circumstances, as we now understand them, Chief Askew had no right to handle you the way he did." Hatfield patted Hank's elbow. "We have your address on file and will be sending a written apology to you right away, and I understand the town will be doing the same. I hope that'll be sufficient."

"To avoid a lawsuit?" Hank asked.

"To avoid any further trouble," Hatfield said. "If we can do anything else to set things right, just let me know."

"You could start by having Steele courier my stuff back to me immediately. Including my firearm."

"Everything will be delivered to this office by mid-morning tomorrow. Will that be soon enough, or will you be leaving now?"

Hank shrugged. "I thought I'd stay on through the weekend. I'd like to go to the fall festival on Saturday at Burkes Garden." He looked at Karen. "What do you think? Sound like fun?"

"A fall festival with a buncha monks?" Karen rolled her eyes. "Can't wait."

"I see. Well." Hatfield shrugged and stuck out his hand to Karen. "I appreciate your assistance, Detective. Lieutenant. But please remember, this case now belongs to Sheriff Steele, and he has all the expertise he needs. Just stay out of his way and let him do his job. All right?"

Hank smiled. "No problem," he said.

22

Where Tuesday had been a busy day, Wednesday by contrast was dead. When Hank called Karen just after 9:00 a.m. to see if she'd had breakfast, he discovered she was already on the road.

"Nothing happening, so I thought I'd take a little solo time, Lou. Go for a drive, look around."

"All right," Hank replied. "I'll call you if anything comes up." He heard her grunt and mutter. "You okay?"

"Fucking grannies around here. Four lane divided highway and they still drive below the speed limit in the left lane. How the hell are normal people supposed to pass?"

Hank thought about it for a moment and decided not to comment. "Will you be back later in the day?"

"Not sure," she said. "I'll call you, all right?"

"All right."

"Stay outta trouble, Lou."

When he arrived at the police station, Branham was out. Louden was working the desk, and Grimes was off. The dispatcher, Mollie Roberts, looked up as he leaned on the counter.

"It's deader than a doodle bug around here," she said. "Courier brought your stuff."

"Great."

"Come on back. I put it on the table in the interview room so you can make sure everything's there."

"Thanks."

The first thing he went for was his firearm. After giving it a close inspection, he clipped the holster onto his belt and felt better. He then went through the rest, which was packed in three large cardboard boxes. He checked off each item on the list, signed the form, and handed it to Mollie, who kept a copy for herself.

"Like bourbon, do you?"

"They're for my mother."

"Just don't let Hall see them or they'll disappear on you."

"I'll keep that in mind."

"You do that."

Hank looked at her closely. Her shoulder-length dark brown hair was wavy and twisted in a style that looked careless, but probably had been done in a salon. Her bright tangerine dress hugged her plump form in the wrong places. She wore a necklace of glass and wooden beads, three bracelets on her left wrist made of woven hemp, and several large rings. Her dark-brown eyes stared back at him with a directness that made it obvious she had something she wanted to say. He raised his eyebrows.

"This is what you do, right? Investigate murders?"

He nodded.

"You've done it for a long time?"

"For a while, now."

"You think Billy did it? Killed Marcie?"

"I don't know," he said. "I really don't."

"He's got a mean streak. You found that out the hard way."

"True enough."

"You're sure the religious guy didn't do it?"

"He didn't do it. How long have you worked here, Mollie?"

"Almost a year. Neil was the one hired me." She paused. "He's nice. Some of these guys I could punch in the mouth, but Neil treats me like a human being instead of a . . ."

"Dyke?"

"Hunh." She tilted her head. "Figured that out, did you?"

He smiled faintly. "I'm a cop, Mollie."

"Yeah, but you're okay." She looked away. "My partner's a dentist in Richlands. We live just outside Wittens Mills. I'd rather get something down there and commute with her, but there's not a lot around these days." She looked at him again. "Do you think it's dangerous for me here? I mean, whoever did this, would he do it again to somebody else?"

"We're not really sure right now," he replied carefully, "but Marcie's murder looks more like an act of passion, something strictly between Marcie and her killer, than something done by someone stalking women."

"An isolated incident," she said.

"That's how it looks. But it wouldn't hurt to be careful, just the same. Stay safe, be aware of your surroundings, and don't take any unnecessary risks until this is resolved. We'll find out who did it and put them away."

"All right," she said, clearly not feeling any better. "If you say so."

23

As Karen pulled into the visitors' parking lot outside the reception building of the Monastery of God, she felt a brief twinge of doubt. Maybe this wasn't such a good idea after all. She shut off the engine of her Firebird and looked at the car in the parking space next to hers. It was a two-year-old black Mercury Grand Marquis that she'd seen yesterday parked in front of the Harmony police station. It belonged to Gordon Garrett, who was no doubt here to follow up on yesterday's events with Brother Charles. They'd be making copies of Marcie Askew's medical records and debating the merits of a lawsuit for wrongful arrest. She'd be an unwelcome visitor, showing up at an awkward time.

She got out of the car and went inside. There was a different guy in a white robe at the reception desk than on Monday. This one called upstairs and told her that Brother Charles was in a meeting. It would take about ten minutes for him to come downstairs. She was welcome to wait in the comfortable seating area on the right. Would she like a cup of coffee or tea?

She felt like asking for a beer but settled for a cup of Earl Grey tea, black, one sugar.

As she sipped the tea, served in a bone china cup with matching saucer, she watched the hustle and bustle around her. This time as she'd driven into the valley she'd taken more notice of the signage and what not for the fall festival coming up on Saturday. Preparations were obviously well underway. A few monks in white robes were evident on the monastery grounds, but mostly she saw regular people in street clothes carrying boxes and files and plastic sacks, yakking nonstop about this and that. Volunteers, probably. Many of them were young, likely students from the college. While she sat there, she counted three separate courier deliveries, one of which was also a pickup. It was noisy and busy. She liked it. The tea was hot and damned good. Her stress level went down a notch. Maybe it was a sign.

Brother Charles came down the stairs and threaded his way through the bodies toward her with a guarded expression on his face.

"Y'all are going full bore around here," she said, grinning up at him. "On account of the festival?"

"That's right, Detective Stainer. There's so much to do, and so little time to get it done. Thank goodness for volunteers. The festival committee has given us most of the responsibility for organizing things this year and we're swamped. What can I do for you?"

"Just a few minutes of your time," she said, ignoring his tone. She set aside her tea cup and stood up.

"We sent our copies of the medical records to the sheriff's office. They were just picked up by the courier. Was there something else?"

"I'd like to ask a couple more questions. Maybe talk to Dr. Long, if he's around."

"I understood that the investigation has passed to the sheriff and that you folks are no longer involved."

She shrugged. "This is what I do. Can we go scare up Dr. Long?"

"Actually," Brother Charles said, fingering his beard uncomfortably, "Ben's in Rome right now attending a conference."

"Rome, as in Italy? Are you guys Catholics?"

His eyes widened. "God, no. What made you think that?"

"Rome?"

He blinked for a moment, then abruptly laughed. "Oh, Rome as in the Vatican. Hell, no. He's speaking at an EU conference on public health. Free clinics are a hot topic in Europe these days."

"You swore."

"Pardon me?"

"You swore," Karen repeated. "You said 'hell.'"

"I did?" He made a face. "Sorry, I hope I didn't offend you."

She snorted. "No. So if I swore, it wouldn't offend you?"

"Not especially."

Thank fucking Christ, she thought. The effort to keep her language clean had been half-killing her. "Okay," she said, "what about the other guy who saw Marcie, this Dr. Orlov. He around?"

"He is. I'm sure he'd spare a few minutes for you. Come on, we'll go over to the clinic and see."

They left the reception building and set off along a cement sidewalk that wound across the campus toward the clinic. Karen noticed that as the mid-morning sun fell across his face Brother Charles brightened perceptibly. His shoulders dropped, his fists opened, and his facial muscles relaxed.

"Nice day," she said.

"It is." He glanced at her. "When I came out this morning to say my prayers, I counted six different kinds of birdsong. We have a little pavilion behind the residence. That's where I like to go when the weather's nice. I haven't heard many birds the last couple of days."

It was a swipe at those responsible for tossing him in jail, but she didn't bite. "So if you guys aren't Catholics, what are you?"

"Odd ducks."

"My fiancé is with the FBI," she told him. "He took a course on cults last year. I read through the handouts they gave him. Stack this high." She held her hands about a foot apart. "I don't remember you guys being mentioned there."

He looked sideways at her, tilting his head. "The FBI."

"Uh huh."

He was obviously trying to decide whether or not she was yanking his chain, so she held up her left hand to show him the ring.

"Congratulations," he said.

"He's a cute little sonofabitch."

"Glad to hear it." He clasped his hands behind his back. "Actually, the FBI categorizes us as an NRM, a new religious movement. Ironically, it's our Christian cousins who refer to us on a regular basis as a cult. A 'dangerous, heretical cult,' to be precise."

"You sound like you've had contact with the FBI before."

"I've met several times with Special Agent Lucas Peppers. He's an instructor at Quantico. He was doing research on NRMs and came down to see us a couple of times, maybe two years ago. We still exchange e-mails on a regular basis."

"Don't know him," Karen said. "Sandy probably does. Anyway, you didn't really answer my question about what you guys are, besides odd ducks."

Brother Charles preceded her up the front steps of the clinic and through the automatic sliding glass doors. "It would take quite a few minutes to explain, and you're probably not interested."

He walked up to the reception desk and asked them to page Dr. Orlov. Orlov telephoned the receptionist back within thirty seconds to say that he was in his office on the third floor. Brother Charles led the way down the corridor to an elevator.

"In addition to the walk-in clinic," he explained, "we also schedule appointments with patients. Dr. Orlov's likely between consultations; otherwise it would have taken him a little longer to answer the page."

They left the elevator and passed a lone receptionist on their way down the corridor to Dr. Orlov's office. The door was open. Brother Charles peeked inside.

"Are we disturbing you?"

"No, not at all, come on in."

Brother Charles led the way into a smallish office that contained a desk, two visitor's chairs, a filing cabinet, and a small bookshelf that held a collection of medical and pharmaceutical reference manuals. The man sitting at the desk was about forty. He was stocky with wavy black hair, a trimmed black beard, thick black eyebrows, and surprisingly pale blue eyes. On second glance, Karen realized that he was sitting in a wheelchair.

"Dennis," Brother Charles said, "this is Detective Karen Stainer, from out of town. She's been assisting the Harmony police in the investigation of Mrs. Askew's murder. Detective, this is Dr. Dennis Orlov."

Karen shook hands with him and sat down. "Appreciate the time," she said. "This won't take long."

"Not a problem." Orlov folded his hands across his stomach and smiled at her. "From out of town?"

"Out of state, actually. Maryland."

"That's hardly a Maryland accent."

"No sir, it's not. I'm Texas born and bred."

"Thought so." Orlov glanced at Brother Charles. "Was there anyone waiting out in the reception area?"

Brother Charles shook his head. "No one but the receptionist. I don't think I've met her yet. I didn't recognize her."

"It's her second week. Was she eating anything?"

"No." Brother Charles looked puzzled.

"Volunteers," Orlov said to Karen. "Some are more professional than others. Cynthia has a bad habit of eating junk food when it gets quiet. There were all these grease stains on the forms she was typing for me. I had to say something." He glanced from Karen to Brother Charles. "I *hate* saying anything to volunteers, since they're good enough to donate their time and skills in the first place, but forms tend to get rejected if they're smeared and hard to read."

"I could have a word with David," Brother Charles offered. "He's our volunteers coordinator," he explained to Karen.

"No, don't bother. It's been okay so far this week."

"So are you another monk?" Karen asked.

Orlov shook his head. "No, actually I'm a volunteer as well. My story's boring, though. I won't waste your time."

"Dennis is one of the best diagnosticians in Virginia," Brother Charles said. "He made a pile of money at the top hospital in Richmond, published a ton of papers, one book . . .?"

Orlov winced. "Two. Sorry."

"Two books, I stand corrected, then was sideswiped by a speeding police car while driving home from work one night. Suffered an irreversible spinal injury."

"Oh oh," Karen said.

"It was very late," Orlov said. "The officers were chasing a hit and run suspect. The guy passed me at over a hundred miles an hour and the police car followed, but they hit a very large puddle of water in their lane just as they were about to pull away from me. Touched my front fender just enough to send me into a spin. I went into the ditch and rolled so many times that my car looked like it had been shredded by the time it stopped. I was wearing my seat belt but got hurt anyway. It was unavoidable."

"I'm sorry to hear that."

"Don't worry, I'm not a cop hater. An elderly woman died at the scene of the hit and run. Never had a chance. The guy was stinking drunk and didn't even know that the cruiser was already behind him when he ran the red light and hit the poor dear. I was very angry at the time, of course. No one wants to end up like this. But I didn't let it make me bitter. And the police department bent over backwards. My lawyer was very surprised. So when everyone had settled on the right numbers, I was able to retire and do whatever I wanted with the rest of my life. I'd already met Ben and knew about the work he was doing here. Suffice it to say that he talked me into giving it a try. So I volunteer about thirty hours a week and spend the rest of my time working on my next book."

"How's it coming, by the way?" Brother Charles asked.

"Not bad, thanks for asking." Orlov looked at Karen. "I'm writing a book on the psychology of bird watching. Charlie here was my immediate inspiration, although I must admit I've gone off in a different direction now." He looked at Brother Charles again. "I think you'll still find it very interesting."

"You got bored by the spiritual insight."

"Let's just say I got fatally distracted by the physics of birdsong."

"This is over my head, fellas," Karen said. "Let me just ask my questions, and I'll get the hell out of your hair."

Orlov chuckled. "Feel free."

"You treated Marcie Askew on a couple of occasions, as I understand it."

"That's right," Orlov nodded. "I read through her file again this morning, since we were making a copy for the sheriff. I thought the investigation was in their hands now."

"Yeah, but I've been consulting on it and just need to tie up a loose end." Karen leaned back and stared at him. "Did she tell you who it was that was beating on her?"

"No," Orlov said gravely. "Understand, Detective. The first time it was a broken wrist, and her story was thin but plausible."

"She fell down the stairs and put her hand out to stop herself."

"Correct. The second time, with the separated shoulder, the story was less believable."

"Right. She dislocated it while walking somebody's dog."

"Yes. A shaggy dog story. She went on and on about this dog, trying to make a joke of it. Again it was Dr. Long, but this time he was becoming concerned."

"Made him suspicious?"

"Yes. He questioned her closely, but she stuck to the dog story."

"That was three months ago."

"Correct. Then a month later she was back with a cracked jaw, loose teeth, and a black eye. Before seeing her, I read through Dr. Long's notations in the file, and as soon as I saw her I knew we had a problem."

"You called in Brother Charles."

"That's correct. And Dr. Long. While the x-rays were being processed, we discussed it and decided to call Dr. Huntley."

"The psychologist in Bluefield."

"Yes. As I understand it, she met with Mrs. Askew once or twice after that. I think Mrs. Askew talked to you about it, didn't she, Charlie?"

Brother Charles nodded. "Yes, she did." He looked at Karen. "We asked her to make a full disclosure of the abuse, to go to the police and file a report, but she refused."

"Did you ask her if it was her husband?"

"I did," Dr. Orlov said. "I asked her if that was why she didn't want to go to the police. She denied that it was him."

"She did."

"Yes. She said he'd never laid a finger on her in his life. She was pretty emphatic about it."

"Well who in the flaming bejesus was hitting her if it wasn't him?"

"We wanted to know just as badly as you do," Brother Charles said, "particularly when she told me the last time we spoke that she was pregnant. I asked her how her husband felt about it. She admitted that she hadn't told him, and that he wasn't the father."

"She told *you* that?"

Brother Charles shifted uncomfortably. "It's the robe. It makes people think we're priests. They want to confess, get absolution, move on. You'd be surprised what people have told me, right out of the blue. We don't do confessions, though. We leave that to the Catholics."

"So she didn't tell either of you who the father was?"

Both men shook their head.

"Or who was abusing her?"

They shook their head again.

Dr. Orlov's phone buzzed. "Excuse me," he said, and picked it up. "Yes?"

He listened, hung up, and looked at Karen. "It's my next appointment."

She stood up. "That's all right, I'm done." She gave him a card. "Call my cell number if you think of anything else."

Outside, Karen shoved her hands into her pockets as she and Brother Charles walked back across the campus. "I worked several years in family-related crime," she said. "As far as I'm concerned, abusing women and children is the lowest, filthiest, and most despicable crime there is. Worse than murder. At least when you kill someone, that's it, it's done, lights out, game over. But when you abuse someone, they suffer from the after-effects for the rest of their lives. An entire life, when it's kids. A never-ending torture that warps their minds. Eventually I had to get out. I was getting too intense." She made a face. "Actually, they threw me out."

"I'm sorry to hear that."

"Not that I want to confess my failures or anything, Padre."

He chuckled.

After a moment's silence, Karen cleared her throat. "Can I ask you something?"

"Of course."

"I mean, not related to the Askew case. Something else."

"Sure."

"You believe in life after death, right? Being a Christian monk, and all?"

"Actually we're not Christian. But yes, I believe in an afterlife."

"Oh. I thought you were Christian. Monastery of God, and all."

"We believe that Jesus probably actually lived, and probably was an important prophet in his time. After that it gets pretty complicated."

"Oh. Okay." Karen chewed her lip. "Do you believe in reincarnation?"

"You mean as in the Hindu belief that the soul repeatedly dies and is reborn into another body?"

"Yeah. Do you believe in that?"

"No."

141

"Oh. Too bad."

"Why?"

She gave him a look. "It's complicated."

They walked for a while in silence. Brother Charles turned to her. "Did you want to talk about something?"

"I don't want to take up any more of your time."

Brother Charles took out his PDA and worked it with his thumbs. "My scheduler's synchronized with the monastery network," he explained. "Apparently I'm free for the next hour. We can talk, if you like."

"You guys are networked?"

"For crying out loud, Detective, we're not Luddites. We use the best tools we can get our hands on to manage our time, since our time is one of the most important commodities we give to other people. That's not egotism or excessive pride, just unadorned fact."

"Okay, okay. Sorry I asked."

"Come this way." Brother Charles led her down an adjoining sidewalk that took them around a large, square brick building. "This is our residence." They walked around the back of the building into a garden, the centerpiece of which was a large gazebo. The gazebo contained enough patio furniture to seat eight people comfortably. He led her up the stairs and through the screen door.

A brass plaque above the door told her she was entering the Abbot Ahrenson Pavilion. She dropped into a very comfortable patio chair. He settled down across from her.

"Who's Abbot Ahrenson?"

"He was our original abbot." Brother Charles folded his hands together. "He passed away quite a few years ago."

"And you replaced him?"

He nodded. "I was appointed."

"How long has this place been here?"

"The monastery? Since 1972."

"So it was like a hippie commune, was it?"

He smiled. "Something like that. No drugs or promiscuity, but lots of music, so I understand."

"When did you come here?"

He thought for a moment. "Sixteen years ago, I guess. Time flies."

"You said you were elected."

"That's right. You were talking earlier about cults. One of the supposed characteristics of a cult is that it has a single, charismatic leader to whom the group is completely loyal. Fanatically loyal, I guess. Well, the abbot is our leader. When the monastery was first founded there was no actual leader. Everyone had a vote, and majority ruled. Once it became clear, though, how they wanted to operate the commune, that they were going to have small farming enterprises to pay for expenses, they created a council to help keep things organized, with a chair person. It took almost ten years for the religious side of the commune to solidify, after which the chair person became an abbot. It's an administrative position, but the abbot is also the spokesperson for the monastery on matters of philosophy. Just the same, decisions remained collective, including decisions about belief. The founding members wrote up a set of guiding principles, a code of conduct, policies on how the monastery would be run, and a set of basic religious tenets on which their beliefs are based."

"That was before your time?"

He cocked his head sideways. "Yes, this was all done by the original founders. I was six years old when they came here, Detective. I was in Grade One at Millhurst Elementary School in Sebring, Ohio and didn't have a clue. They really were hippies. It was kind of cool, actually. It was the sweetest sort of idealism that came out of that era, a back-to-the-land movement coupled with a surprisingly pure spiritualism. One of the originals was a Zen Buddhist, and the others were Christians whose beliefs were heavily cut with Taoism, various flavors of Zen, and a whole lot of other stuff. If they had a cult leader back then, I suppose you could say it was Alan Watts."

She looked blankly at him.

"The writer and philosopher? Alan Watts? He wrote a number of books? *The Watercourse Way, This Is It, The Way of Zen, The Wisdom of Insecurity*? No?"

Karen shook her head.

"That's all right, it's not important. Apparently he spoke here once. It was a very big thing at the time." He smiled. "This is longwinded, I know, but I *am* trying to answer your question. You see, when I came here I was part of the second wave, people who'd heard about the monastery or met some of the originals, sort of like the Next Generation. David and I came here together. We were close friends, roommates at college, devout Christians at the time but not satisfied with the Church. We were both training to become Anglican priests; it was a shared decision to walk out and look for something better. David was friends with someone who'd come here so we drove down for a visit. We spent a week and asked to join. The rest is history. But I have strong administrative skills, you see, that eventually led me to this position. The council needed to replace the late Abbot Ahrenson, and I was the best choice."

"You said you guys are not Christian. So what are you?"

He chuckled. "Ah, the human urge to categorize. We're all taxonomists at the end of the day. We have to fit everything into its appropriate box in order to understand it."

Karen gave him one of her unamused cop looks.

"Sorry. I wasn't making fun of you. We normally just tell people we're a non-denominational benevolent religious order and they let it go at that." He folded his hands together. "We're not atheists, for starters. Or humanists. We don't believe, as Feuerbach did, that humanity's love was misdirected to God and should rightly be directed to humanity itself. We don't believe that the human species, through science and technology, can continually improve itself to the point that it might actually achieve divine status itself.

"We believe in God. A single, omnipotent, omniscient creator. We believe that science is our way of understanding the tools and materials God used to create existence and that mathematics is our attempt to construct a language that might describe this creation in terms that are understandable to us. Jesus, Mohammed, the Buddha, Isaiah, Abraham, all these people made very important efforts to steer us in the right direction as a species. What they taught has value that we need to appreciate and apply in our own lives, but we're so far away from them now in terms of time and culture and technology, and there have been so many layers of interpretation, extrapolation, and sheer fabrication laid on top of their efforts that it's a lifetime commitment to excavate the truth out from under all the bullshit.

"However, there's a definite movement in this direction, Karen. More and more scholars are examining holy scriptures in the context of figurative and allegorical teachings, rather than literal descriptions of historical events, and understanding how these prophets have contributed to a universal set of religious beliefs that probably extend all the way back to our beginnings as a species."

"So you haven't taken Jesus into your heart, son, as your personal savior?" Karen asked in her best Texan twang.

Brother Charles smiled. "Well, actually I did as a young man and I have to say truthfully he's still there. I suppose I could say I've come to terms with the improbability of what I was taught about Jesus and have kept him in my heart as a personal symbol instead of a *deus ex machina* who'll bail me out of this mortality thing at the last second." He let the smile fade. "But you're asking me about my beliefs primarily because you're trying to decide whether I have the answers you're looking for, aren't you?"

Karen shrugged. "I suppose."

"So what about yourself? Did you have a proper Christian upbringing?"

She shook her head. "No. Daddy wasn't a churchgoer. We weren't that kind of family."

Brother Charles said nothing.

"Not that we were atheists, either," she went on after a while. "Daddy taught us to believe in God and Jesus and the Ten Commandments and all that stuff. He made sure I had a proper upbringing, and he'd whup my ass if I did anything wrong. He was a cop. A Texas state trooper. He believed in the law and in right and wrong, and he made sure I was the same. I became a cop because of him and so did Darryl, my oldest brother."

"What about your mother?"

Karen took a while before answering. "She's spent most of her life in a mental institution. I haven't a clue if they've got church there or not. Wouldn't matter worth a damn, anyway."

"I'm sorry."

"Don't be. It's not that big a deal to me. She's been there since I was what, ten years old? Daddy paid a cousin of his, Auntie Myrtle, to come over three times a week to do housework and all that female stuff, because I sure was no good at any of it. But to make a long story short, no, I didn't have what you'd call a Christian upbringing but that don't mean I'm not God-fearing in my own way."

Brother Charles crossed his legs and folded his hands on his knee. "Sounds like a difficult childhood."

Karen glanced at him sideways. "I wouldn't say that. Daddy was a real good father to us. I was the only girl, the middle child, with two older brothers and two younger brothers, but Daddy didn't treat me any different. I had to do chores just like them, I got my ass whipped when I broke the rules just like them, I played sports at school just like them, and I got decent grades or else explained why just like them. He taught me to shoot when I was big enough to handle a gun just like them, only I turned out to be a helluva lot better shot. Darryl can drive a car better than any of us, Delbert can fix cars better than any of us, Bradley can build a house better than any of us, and I can shoot better than any of them."

"What about your fourth brother?"

"He can break the law better than any of us. Let's just leave it at that." Karen's youngest brother, Jimmy Bob, was currently serving time for armed robbery.

"Okay."

"You're sure you guys don't believe in reincarnation?"

He smiled at her patiently. "I'm sure."

Karen told him the story of Taylor Chan, the three-and-a-half year old boy in Glendale who suddenly began to talk about his past life

145

as Martin Liu, his mother's cousin. Martin had been murdered four years earlier. Precocious to begin with, little Taylor soon began talking about his "before mother," Meredith, who had blond hair and was not Chinese like the rest of them. Meredith Collier was Martin's mother, but Taylor had never met her. As well, he somehow he knew that Martin's eyes had been green. He talked about time he spent as Martin with Peter Mah, Martin's cousin, things they'd done together, places they'd gone such as a traditional Chinese theater and a member's-only club in a basement underneath a hairdresser's salon. He could describe the Triad tattoos Peter wore on his chest, tattoos his parents never talked about. He also described his death in chilling detail, including the first names of two of the men involved in his murder.

Karen told him about talking to the boy at his daycare, how he described the murder to her, and she tried to explain how badly it had shaken her. A murder victim's voice seeming to come out of the body of a three-and-a-half year old boy. She admitted that the boy had birthmarks which corresponded to the gunshot wounds on Martin Liu's body, a birthmark on the front of his leg that matched the entry wound and another birthmark on the back of his leg that matched the exit wound.

She talked about how she still didn't sleep very well at night. She had a lot of dreams about children asking her for help. She told him she was going to get married, that Sandy was level-headed and easy-going and didn't really have strong religious beliefs, but was firmly grounded in modern rationality and didn't have much interest in metaphysical issues such as life after death or reincarnation.

"Have you talked to him about the case involving the little boy?" Brother Charles asked.

"Yeah," Karen said. "A bit."

"Did you talk about how you felt about it? That you were trying to decide whether it was actually true that the boy's spirit was the reincarnated soul of the murder victim?"

"Not really. I mean, he knew I was upset about it at the time." Karen shrugged. "He asked, but I didn't really want to talk about it. You know. We're going to be married, and he doesn't want a flake for a wife. And if we have a kid, he sure as hell doesn't want a flake for his kid's mother."

"Have you talked to him about your mother?"

Karen frowned. "What do you mean?"

"About her condition, the fact that she's in an institution, and how you feel about all that?"

"No. But look." She moved forward in the chair, getting ready to stand up. "I'm not the kind of woman to talk about feelings. I don't do that thing, the Weepy Wendy crap. And he doesn't want to hear about it. He wants me to be a stand-up person, reliable, dependable. That's who I am."

"I don't know him, of course," Brother Charles replied, "but I know it helps to talk to the people we love about the things that bother us. If they truly love us, they won't be judgmental about what we tell them. They'll actually feel good that we care enough about them to trust them with our inner feelings."

"You could be right," Karen said.

"If not your fiancé, then maybe a close friend."

She thought again about Hank. "Maybe." She stood up. "Anyway, thanks for listening. I didn't mean to take up your time."

Brother Charles stood up with her and led the way out of the gazebo. "No trouble at all." Back on the sidewalk, he put out a hand to stop her. "By the way, just so you're clear about something."

Karen looked at him with calm blue eyes, her expression neutral.

"The way we just talked? That's the kind of conversation I had with Marcie Askew. No more and no less."

Karen stared at him for a moment, then nodded. "I get the message, Padre."

24

The next morning, Thursday, Karen picked up Hank outside his motel room and drove across town to Mary's Donuts for breakfast. They sat at the same window seat in which Karen had been sitting on Monday morning when she'd seen Brother Charles for the first time. She described to Hank her conversation with the abbot and Dr. Orlov.

"So she didn't tell them who it was," Hank said.

Karen shook her head, draining her coffee cup.

"You believe them? Are they telling the truth?"

"Yeah, I'm pretty sure." Karen picked at her muffin. "Orlov's not one of the brothers or monks or whatever. He's just a rich doctor in a wheelchair who donates most of his time. Pretty straightforward guy. No bullshit." She downed what was left of the muffin and crushed her napkin in her fist.

"What's your take on Brother Charles?"

She dropped the napkin into her empty coffee cup. "Same thing. Straightforward. Truthful. He went there because she asked him to, he didn't see her because she was already lying dead in the ravine, he didn't know who was beating her or who fathered the child. It's believable. He didn't kill her and doesn't know who did."

"All right," Hank said. "So we've pretty much come to the conclusion that the eyewitness who saw the big bearded guy has ended up pointing everybody in the wrong direction."

Karen nodded, amused.

"That leaves us with Askew." Hank ran a hand through his frizzy hair. "His whereabouts at the time of the murder are currently unknown, he had all kinds of motive, he's a violent guy who uses his hands, he's strong enough to have carried her back to the ravine, and remorseful enough to have eased her down under the tree branch."

"All we need is a single scrap of evidence placing him at the scene and putting his hands around her neck," Karen remarked, staring out the window.

Hank said nothing.

"So do you want to go look at that SIG?"

"I don't think I need to," Hank said, touching the holster on his hip beneath his jacket.

"We could look anyway. It'd be an improvement on that Gleeyuck you carry around now."

"We'll see." Hank drank the last of his coffee and went over with her once more his interview with Betty Gibson. "She was back and forth on whether he was capable of beating Marcie," he finished. "On the one hand he became a model husband and on the other he has a bad temper and might have been capable of losing control. But we don't know enough yet. There's someone else still out there."

She slid out of the booth. "Lover boy."

He nodded, getting up. "Physical evidence either turns up or it doesn't. But until we know who the other guy is, we don't know enough."

She pushed the door open and held it for him. "What do you want to do?"

"Go to the college. See if she met with someone there."

"When she was taking that course."

"Right."

They got into the Firebird. Karen flew out of the parking lot and into the street as though propelled from a giant catapult.

The college campus was fairly large for the size of the community it served. Karen stopped at the booth just inside the main entrance and asked the uniformed security guard where they'd find the registrar's office. He directed them to Lancaster Hall, which turned out to be a Greek-style building with a large cement staircase, columns with scrolls on the top, and two cement lions sitting on blocks on each side of the front doors. They went inside and followed the signs to the registrar's office where a young man with a cheerful smile and bright eyes nodded at the badges they held up and brought out a course calendar from the spring term.

"This is the only photography course we offered that term," he explained, folding the calendar at the appropriate page and pointing to the listing.

"No prerequisites," Hank said.

"That's right," the young man said. "It's a general elective that pretty much anyone can take. Graphic design students need the credit for their program and so do most students taking other Media Studies programs, but a lot of people take it just for interest."

"Bird course," Karen said.

He looked at her, smile steady.

"We need a list of students who took it this spring," she said.

The smile didn't falter. "I don't think I could do that, sorry. We don't normally release that sort of information. Privacy

149

considerations."

"It doesn't list the instructor," Hank said, tapping his finger on the course calendar. "Can you tell us who taught it?"

"Sure, I guess. Professor Brogan is our photography instructor."

"Where's his office?"

"*Her* office is . . ." he flipped open a binder and turned a few plasticized pages, "H building, second floor, room 216."

Out in the corridor, Karen gritted her teeth. "Do you have to have some kind of surgery to keep a smile on your face that long? Christ, it was like talking to the fucking Joker."

"He was just trying to be polite," Hank said.

"Yeah, well he acts like he's psychotic."

"You're way too hard on people."

They walked out the rear entrance of Lancaster Hall and followed the signs across the concourse to H building. It was a long, square, four-story building made of bricks and glass. They tramped up the staircase to the second floor and found room 216. It was empty. They backtracked to the main office of Media Studies and got the attention of the woman behind the front counter.

"Professor Brogan?" Karen asked. "She wasn't in her office. Is she in class?"

The woman shook her head and pointed to a doorway down at the far end of the office. "Faculty lounge."

It was a typical lounge with comfortable furniture, a glass case displaying faculty publications, a single window with heavy dark drapes, a coffee machine, a Coke machine, and a little kitchenette with a microwave oven, kettle, and mini fridge. Two women sat in armchairs on either side of a round pine coffee table. One was small and athletic, in her mid-thirties, her straight red hair pulled back in a severe ponytail, her face plain and her eyes bright and penetrating. She wore black slacks and a black long-sleeved t-shirt. A black jacket was lightly folded on the table in front of her.

The other woman, in her late thirties, had a medium build. Her straight chestnut brown hair fell across her shoulders and her brown eyes were soft, with crow's feet showing at the corners. She wore a coffee-colored suit and white blouse. The skirt came just below her knees. Her dark brown shoes were flat-soled and sensible.

Hank looked at Karen. She looked back at him without expression. He nodded.

"We're looking for Professor Brogan," Karen said, holding up her ID and badge.

"I'm Erica Brogan," the redhead said.

"Detective Karen Stainer. This is Lieutenant Hank Donaghue. We need to ask you a few questions about Marcie Askew."

Brogan frowned. "Of course. I heard about what happened to her. What a terrible thing."

"We understand you taught a photography course this spring that she took. Is that correct?"

"That's right."

"What can you tell us about her?"

"I don't know," Brogan shrugged. "She was a nice person. She seemed to enjoy the course. She attended every class, participated in the field trips, got along very well with everyone else."

"Was her class work any good?"

"She finished with an A, which is not all that hard to do, really. Attend the classes, take notes, get all your assignments in on time, and show that you're learning the basics and you'll probably get an A. We're not exactly looking for the next Annie Leibovitz here."

"Anyone in particular she seemed close to?" Karen asked. "In the class?"

Brogan thought for a moment. "I don't think so."

"She come across like the big fish in a small pond? Being the wife of the chief of police and all?"

"No, nothing like that. She had a good sense of humor, liked to laugh, asked questions, took notes. She was completely normal."

Karen looked at the other woman. "And you are?"

"Dr. Jane Morley."

"What do you do around here?"

"I'm the director of our criminal justice program." She tapped her forehead with a long, slender finger. "I'm taking mental notes right now."

"Good for you." Karen turned back to Brogan. "Was she the same way from beginning to end in the class? Easy going?"

"Well, no, actually," Brogan replied, pursing her lips. "After a while she seemed to withdraw into herself a little bit. Got a little more quiet. I thought maybe she was worried about her grade but she said no, nothing like that. She said she'd planned on opening a photography business in a little store her husband owned, but he sold it and she wasn't sure what she was going to do. Her motivation for the course might have dipped after that."

"She give any indication she was having marital problems?"

"No. We weren't friends; it was strictly professional. She was a student. We didn't talk about personal things at all."

"Can you give us a list of the other students taking the course? We'd like to talk to them as well."

"Ask the registrar's office. They have it there."

"They balked," Karen replied. "Privacy concerns."

"Well, I'll give you a copy from my files. I'll get it for you in my office before you leave."

Karen looked at Jane Morley, whose expression remained neutral and mildly interested. "What about you? Did you know Marcie Askew?"

"Only by sight," Morley replied. "I never spoke to her."

"Ever deal with her husband?" Hank asked.

Morley shrugged. "Once or twice. I spoke to him briefly at a job fair we held last year. They had a booth. Maybe once or twice after that. Two-minute conversations. Nothing memorable."

"This is a small community," Hank said. "Neither of you heard talk of Marcie having problems with her husband?"

A frown flitted briefly across Morley's face. "No. Sorry."

"You're more likely to hear gossip about people here on campus than people from town," Brogan said. "A college in a little place like this is kind of like its own little universe. Closed in and shuttered. They could set a bomb off downtown, and you'd probably hear about where the Dean spent last weekend before anybody'd get around to mentioning an explosion. It's that kind of place."

"So just to make sure we're asking all the right questions, then," Hank said, "did either of you hear anything connecting Marcie Askew with anyone on campus?"

"No," Brogan said.

"Sorry," Morley said.

"All right, well, thanks," Karen said. She looked at Brogan. "Maybe we can get that list now."

"Of course," she said, standing up.

Karen gave Morley her card. "If you do hear anything, call."

"I'll be glad to, Detective," Morley said, looking at the card.

"Oh, by the way," Karen said, turning back. "I understand you have a student by the name of Rachel Meese. That right?"

"Rachel? Yes."

"We were talking to her roommate, Debbie Stump. I understand Rachel's an excellent shot."

"Yes," Morley replied. "The best in class, by far."

"How are her grades?"

"Top three," Morley said. "She's an excellent student. She should make a very good police officer."

"Glad to hear it," Karen said.

25

Hank leaned against Hall's car in the employee parking lot behind the Harmony police station, talking through the window to the detective, who was about to go home. Karen was inside, giving Branham a summary of their conversation with Erica Brogan. Hank asked Hall if he'd had a chance to interview the other customers who had been in Gerry's on Saturday night when Marcie was murdered.

"Not my problem anymore," Hall said. "All the files were sent to County. Done deal."

"I get that, Hall," Hank said. "I'm just asking if you or your uniforms talked to them all."

"I talked to all the locals," Hall replied.

"They have anything useful to say?"

"No."

Hank waited.

"Henry Fink spent a lot of time describing you," Hall finally said. "He thought you probably did it."

"That's the best you could do?"

"I'm off the case, Lieutenant. And I'm tired. I'm going home to get some sleep."

Hank could no longer ignore the strong odor of alcohol coming from the open car window. "It's two in the afternoon, Hall. You really need to pull it together."

"Thanks for the advice."

Hank was thinking about Gerald Mayburn, a former partner of his when he was still the Golden Boy of the department. Hank was twenty-eight years old at the time, and as part of his development he'd taken courses from the famous Behavioral Science Unit of the FBI at Quantico. He'd impressed his instructors as serious minded and highly motivated. One day after a class on the management of death investigations, he went for a drink with one of the instructors, Ed Griffin. They talked about the toll the job can take on even the toughest, thick-skinned individuals.

"It can eat away at you," Griffin said, leaning back on his bar stool to poke himself in the stomach. "From the inside out. Ulcers, heartburn, high cholesterol, hemorrhoids, you name it. You bottle up the stress inside your body and it keeps trying to get out. And up here, too." He moved his finger up to his temple. "You end up spending all your waking hours either thinking about what you've seen or trying your damnedest *not* to think about what you've seen. You can't sleep at night because when you do fall asleep, you dream about what you've seen when you're awake. Then you turn to this." He lifted his beer glass off the bar and set it down again. "You think that maybe a drink now and then will tone it down some, take the edge off, give you a little peace between the crime scenes and autopsies and interrogations and court appearances. Then it's a quart every night. Then a mickey during the day to get you to the quart at night. Then you're gone."

"My partner's like that," Hank said.

"I'm sorry to hear it."

Hank found himself telling Griffin about a recent case and how he'd blown up at Mayburn in the Homicide bullpen, making a fool of himself in the process. Mayburn was a twenty-seven-year veteran who'd worked in Homicide so long no one really remembered where else he'd been before that. They closed a few cases together, and quite a few others remained open. His relationship with Mayburn was almost non-existent. The veteran was solitary and unfriendly, and refused to call Hank by his name, referring to him only as "Golden Boy." Realizing how it was going to be, Hank kept their interactions to a minimum. Then the homicide of Solomon Black fell into their laps.

Solly Black owned a chain of liquor stores and was known as a rough and aggressive competitor who wasn't afraid to do business on both sides of the law. He was inspecting one of his stores in upper Midtown early one evening when a man entered, pulled out a gun, and told the female clerk behind the counter to hand over the cash in the register. In the back room, Solly saw what was happening on the video surveillance monitor and marched up to the front as the clerk was explaining that the seventy-five dollars she'd handed over was the most they were allowed to keep in the till at one time. When the robber threw the cash back down on the counter and demanded to be taken to the safe, Solly came up to him, pushed him hard on the arm, and told him to get the hell out of his store.

At that point the robber could have done any number of things. He could have been surprised at Solly's aggressiveness and backed off, even run away. He could have stood his ground and forced Solly to take him to the safe. What he decided to do, though, was grab Solly, wrestle him into a headlock, drag him outside of the store, force him down onto his knees on the sidewalk, and shoot him through the right ear. Then he calmly walked to a car parked at the curb a few yards away, got into the back seat, and was driven away.

Hank lived fairly close to the scene and was the first to arrive. He took charge and spoke to the responding officers about what they'd found and what they'd done to secure the scene. He spoke to the medical examiner, did a walk-through with crime scene technicians, and began talking to witnesses before Mayburn showed up. His partner prowled around the scene for several minutes, listened to Hank question the clerk, and then made his pronouncement.

"Some out-of-work loser hoping to score enough to pay off his bookie. Did we get him on the video?"

Hank shook his head. "Looks like he knew where the camera was and kept his face averted."

"Well, maybe the bullet will tell us something. They find it yet?"

"No, they're still looking."

Mayburn spread his hands. "I don't know what to tell you. These things happen all the time. Guys hold up liquor stores and never get caught. We're wasting our time here."

Hank wasn't so sure. He interviewed a witness from across the street, a woman who was closing up a delicatessen directly across from the liquor store. She'd gone out to bring in her sandwich sign from the sidewalk and had seen the whole thing. She described how the assailant dragged Solly outside in a headlock, how he forced him to his knees, how he put the gun to Solly's ear and fired the shot, and how he got into the back seat of a car at the curb and was driven away.

"He got into the car and drove away," Hank repeated.

"He got into the *back seat* of the car. There was someone already behind the wheel, waiting for him. This other man drove the car away."

"The car was directly in front of the store?"

"No, it was two doors up."

"He got into the back seat? Not the front passenger seat?"

"Something wrong with your hearing? I told you, he calmly walked away from Mr. Black and got into the back seat of the car, behind the driver, on the driver's side. When the car pulled away from the curb I saw the two of them, one in the front driving and the other in the back seat behind him."

The street was one way, running east to west. Left to right, from the woman's perspective. The car would have pulled up to the curb on the driver's side, closest to the store but two doors up so that the liquor store could be approached without giving warning to anyone inside. It was not unusual for armed robberies to be carried out by a pair, one going into the store and the other driving the getaway car, but when the hold-up guy came out he usually ran like hell around the car and threw himself into the front passenger seat next to his partner. Hank couldn't recall a case where an ordinary stick-up punk calmly walked to the car and got into the back seat after leaving the money behind on the counter where he'd thrown it. It suggested that what had happened was not a robbery at all but an assassination. A hit.

Hank stayed with it for two weeks. The bullet was found but told them nothing. The video surveillance tape from the store confirmed that the shooter appeared to be a man in his early forties, medium height, a bit stocky, white, unhurried, calm. Hank watched the tape over and over again and decided early on that the anger with which he'd thrown the cash back down on the counter had been contrived, that the demand to see the safe had been an excuse to get to Solly, who'd made it easy by coming up from the back room on his own. In addition, the gunman had dragged Solly outside onto the sidewalk, rather than shoot him inside the store, in order to make a public statement.

Fuck with us and this will happen to you, too.

So who were they, and how had Solly fucked with them?

Mayburn resisted this line of inquiry with the stubbornness of a mule, first with inaction and uncooperativeness and then by openly ridiculing Hank in the bullpen whenever he had an audience. Hank took it for a while, then finally lost his temper one afternoon. He'd pretty much wrapped up the case on his own, without his partner's help, and was trying to fill Mayburn in on the details. He'd tracked down the driver, who turned out to be a Russian with known connections to organized crime elements in the city. He'd been picked up during a raid on a club by the Anti-Gang Unit and had suddenly decided to get a few things off his chest. It seemed he had relatives in America and wanted to stay. When he mentioned Solomon Black during the course of his debriefing, they called Hank to sit in. The driver talked about a hit man he'd picked up at the airport, driven downtown to the liquor store, and then had driven back to the airport immediately afterwards. He didn't know the hit man's name. He didn't know which city he'd come from or which city he'd departed to, didn't have a flight number or even an airline. It didn't work that way. But he assured them that his own gang leader, a man named Urilov, had ordered the hit. Solly had apparently offended Urilov in some way.

"Golden Boy's invented a pretty story to explain why he wants to dump it," Mayburn said, playing to the bullpen audience.

Hank said a few things about the alcoholic fog in which Mayburn himself had lost most of their cases, Mayburn tried to take a swing at him, they got pulled apart, and the captain gave Hank a not-so-polite lecture about respect for fellow officers and working cooperatively with others.

Telling this story to Griffin, Hank felt embarrassed. He fell silent, studying the ring of foam at the top of his glass of beer.

The Quantico instructor shrugged. "You could have handled it better. The thing about drunks you have to understand is that they live in a world of their own, a world with big thick walls around it. Nobody else is allowed in. They do whatever they have to do to protect themselves and their little world."

"I don't know how to deal with him," Hank said. "Have you ever worked with a partner like that?"

"No," Griffin said. "However, I've seen a lot of cops go down that road. *I* went down that road a ways myself, a few years ago. That's why this is non-alcoholic beer, my friend." He sipped from his glass. "How to deal with guys like him? Some people try to help them, but that almost never works and eventually everybody just ends up leaving them the hell alone. Only your partner can help himself, and believe me, guys like him are already in the process of destroying themselves, help or no help. Be there if he needs you, like a good partner. Otherwise, leave him the hell alone."

Mayburn ended up taking his own life about a year later. It wasn't until Hank shook Mayburn's ex-wife's hand in the parking lot of the church after the funeral, and looked into the faces of his two teenaged daughters, that his former partner's story finally came into focus. The survivors were three vulnerable people who'd fled long ago to save their own lives after finally accepting the fact that they couldn't save Mayburn's. His ex-wife looked older than her years and beaten down by life, even though she'd been divorced from Mayburn for nearly a decade. She'd continued to buy his groceries for him, clean his apartment, and do his laundry despite having left him. Mayburn had only been fifty-seven years old when he'd died. He'd looked a hell of a lot older. He'd been a complete wreck. His wife had gotten the two girls out while they were still young enough, had built a new life for them that excluded their father, but had come back to do what she could to keep him alive. She kept trying to help him, but nothing worked. The pressures Mayburn felt finally pulled him under for good.

To this day, Hank still believed there was something he didn't do that he should have done. Perhaps Griffin's advice had been focused on how Hank could help himself rather than help Mayburn, to keep him clear of the whirlpool that Mayburn was creating around himself. If Hank had waded in, would he have made a difference? Could he have pulled Mayburn out of his downward spiral? One half of his brain told him that it might have turned out that way, if only he'd forced the issue. The other half of his brain told him that Mayburn didn't respect him, and without that respect would never have listened to anything he'd said. Griffin unfortunately was right. Only Mayburn could have saved Mayburn.

Now, leaning against the car, Hank watched Hall break eye contact and turn away, moving his hand to the gear shift. Hank walked around the car and got in on the passenger side.

"What the hell are you doing?" Hall demanded, his hand still on the gear shift.

"Humor me. Tell me about the witness interviews."

Hall sat for a moment. "I don't see the point. I'm tired, Lieutenant."

"Tell me about the interviews, Hall. Tell me what they said."

Hall thought about it, then sighed, shifted, and backed out of the parking space.

As they drove through the parking lot and out onto the street, Hank rolled down the window to let a bit of fresh air into the interior of the car. Hall drove up to Bluefield Street and turned left. He went three blocks down Bluefield and turned right onto Chestnut Street. They were in a residential section that looked like any other town in America, lined with brick bungalows and two-story frame homes. Hall slowed and turned left onto Booker Street. At the corner was a white frame church. Hall drove down a long slope and turned left onto Magnolia Street. On the left was the wide expanse of lawn behind the church and on the right was a weed-covered empty lot. Hall drove slowly up the slope, passing small houses on either side. He turned into a driveway on the right side and shut off the engine.

The house was a two-story Colonial-style structure with an enclosed front porch and a tiny lawn in front. The gray exterior looked like asbestos siding. The lot on which it sat was small, maybe forty feet by one hundred. Hank looked out the windshield at a small white garage. It was so small that Hank doubted it would be possible to open the car doors inside the garage after you drove in.

"This where you live?" Hank asked.

"I spoke to Dave Toler first. He was at the bar from approximately 9:20 p.m. until it closed and Bickell threw everybody out. He told me about a conversation he had with Debbie Stump. He remembered that Henry Fink was there, talked to Joseph Wall briefly in the washroom, and noticed you, although he couldn't describe you very well and didn't know when you arrived or when you left. He couldn't place anyone else there. He said he concentrates on his drinking and minds his own business. Sounds about right, since he had no recollection of the two bikers who sat at the bar just down from him."

"Okay," Hank said.

"Henry Fink arrived at the bar at about 9:10 p.m. He saw Dave Toler arrive, and the others, including you. He gave me a very good description of you, as I mentioned before. He thought you looked very suspicious. His theory was that you were an ex-con who was passing through, looking for women to prey on. A serial killer type."

Hank smiled.

"Dave Morris confirmed that he arrived around 11:25 p.m., as you said. He had one beer and left. He said he'd been out of town for the day, shopping in Bristol, and got home late. Stopped in for a beer because he didn't want to go home right away. He lives alone. Said he wanted a little company and was hoping to see someone he knew. He didn't know any of them, so he finished his beer and went home."

"Okay."

"Do you want me to keep going? None of them had anything useful to say. No one mentioned anyone who hasn't already been accounted for. There were no glaring contradictions, nothing worth spending any more time on."

"Is this where you live?"

"Yes, it's where I live."

"Relax, Hall."

"I am relaxed. In fact, as soon as you get out of my car I'm going to go inside and relax some more."

"My car's back at the station," Hank said.

"It's not too far to walk."

"That's not very hospitable."

"Hospitable's my middle name," Hall said. "Just not today."

"Live alone, do you?"

"I'm not going to do this, Donaghue." Hall took the keys out of the ignition and unbuckled his seat belt.

Hank looked through the windshield at the enclosed front porch of Hall's house. "Looks like you've got a couple of chairs there. How about inviting me in. We can talk."

"Maybe another time."

"Tell you what," Hank said. "You're thirsty. I get it. I wouldn't mind a beer myself. Get me a beer, we'll sit on the porch, we'll talk, and then I'll walk back to the station. Won't take long."

"For godsakes," Hall said, getting out of the car.

Hank followed him across the lawn and waited at the bottom of the stairs while Hall unlocked the metal screen door of the enclosed verandah. Hall let himself inside the house as Hank sat down in one of the big rocking chairs, looking out onto the street. It was a pleasant street, quiet and tree-sheltered. Hank felt that it would look better with sidewalks, but he understood that a town could afford only so much.

After a while Hall came back out onto the verandah carrying a serving tray. On the serving tray were two bottles of beer, a quart of corn whiskey, and two tumblers. He set the tray down on a table between the two rocking chairs and handed Hank one of the bottles of beer. He removed the top from the quart of whiskey, poured himself a generous drink, and tipped the bottle toward Hank.

"Just a little," Hank said.

Hall poured more than just a little into the other tumbler and set it close to Hank's hand, then sat down in the other rocking chair.

They watched a car drive past the house. It slowed and turned into a driveway three houses up, across the road.

Hank watched an elderly man get out of the car with a plastic shopping bag in his hand. The man walked up to the front door of the house and let himself in.

"Do you really have a photographic memory? Or is it just bullshit to impress the girls?"

Hall snorted.

Hank watched an elderly woman get out of the passenger side of the car. She slowly walked up to the front door of the house and let herself in. Hank wondered why the hell the old man hadn't had the courtesy to wait for her so that they could walk into their home together.

"Actually, what I have is hyperthymestic syndrome." Hall took a large gulp of whiskey and coughed. "Enhanced autobiographical memory. People like me remember everything that ever happened to them." He chased the whiskey with beer. "Every fucking minute of every fucking day."

Hank sipped the corn whiskey. It tasted harsh against the back of his throat.

"Photographic memory," Hall went on, "a.k.a. eidetic memory, is supposed to be total recall of visual images recorded in the brain. Some people believe that eidetic memory's a myth, that people who claim to have it simply have a very good memory and that's all. I don't know about that, I'm not an expert. I do know about hyperthymesia, though. It's too goddamned real."

Hank chased the whiskey with beer, looking out at the street. A bird flew across the yard from left to right.

"It means I can remember everything that's ever happened to me, right back as far as I can remember. I can recall complete conversations, which is why I can tell you everything a subject said to me in an interview. I could recite it verbatim, but that's too weird. I only do that when I've had too much, just to get under people's skin."

"You remember things clearly from your past?"

"I remember every day of my past. In detail. Name a date and I can tell you what the weather was like, what clothes I wore, what I ate, who I saw, what we talked about. When I was eight. Or eighteen. Doesn't matter. Memory is highly associative, too, so I'm constantly getting flashbacks to previous experiences. Which is to say it's not just passive, sitting there waiting to be recalled, but active, pushing into my brain constantly even though I don't want it. But don't ask me questions to test me, just take my word for it. I'm not a goddamned trained dog."

"I won't ask," Hank said.

They drank in silence, watching the street.

"My dad taught high school physics here in Harmony. He had an exceptional memory as well, although I don't think it was this kind. He was just like a computer for facts, names, dates, instrument readings, measurements, any kind of numbers."

Hall poured himself more corn whiskey and waved the bottle at Hank, who shook his head.

"He built this house," Hall went on, putting the bottle down on the table a little too hard. "I grew up here."

"It's a nice street."

"Yeah, but it's worth shit. Two years ago I decided to put it up for sale. I was going to get the hell out of here. The real estate agent said it would list for forty-five grand, and I'd probably have to settle for forty, tops. It wasn't worth it."

"That's too bad."

"Asbestos siding." Hall waved a hand at the house behind him. "That's a killer, right there. And the rooms are all small. Basement's unfinished. Steam radiators, and I need a new water heater. The roof leaks. It's a dump."

"Sorry to hear that."

"Yeah, well, it's not your problem." Hall pulled at his drink as though it were serious business that could not be put off any longer.

"Don't you think you should go a little easy on that stuff?" Hank asked.

Hall shook his head and refilled his glass. "You wanted to hear about it, didn't you? So shut up and listen."

26

I probably inherited my memory from my father. My mother was just an ordinary person with an ordinary mind. Housewife. Worked part time in the drug store to help my father make ends meet. She was nice. They were both nice. I had a decent childhood. They were pretty good. No booze. No abuse.

I was an only child in a quiet house, so I grew up with an introverted personality. I didn't make friends easily, and today I can say in all honesty I don't have a single friend in the world. That's not something that bothers me at all; it's just the way my life is.

My father, when it came down to it, was my best friend. I miss him to this day because he helped me as much as he could with my problems. You see, Fate couldn't leave me alone with just the hyperthymesia, it also had to deal me another joker from the bottom of the deck by the time I was twenty: chronic depression. Back then, the medication available to treat depression was worse than the condition itself. My father kept me off of it and spent a lot of time with me instead. I would tell him whenever I was crashing, we'd talk, and he'd hold my hand until the worst of it had passed.

Naturally my perfect memory became the perfect weapon I could use against myself when the depression became bad. I would dredge up every small, negative thing that ever happened to me. Things I'd done wrong that had made me look stupid or feel guilty, things people had said that were nasty, all the negative stuff. I turned it all against myself and made the whole thing worse. It was a nightmare. My father was a saint. He spent long hours trying to talk me through it. I can't imagine how difficult it must have been for him, looking back on it now.

My grades in high school were outstanding, given my perfect memory, and I was offered several academic scholarships. I chose law enforcement. We all have different reasons for wanting to become police officers. Mine, I'm embarrassed to say, is because my favorite television program at the time was *Hill Street Blues*, and I wanted to be Officer Andrew Renko, the character played by Charles Haid. He was so different than I was, so full of energy; I just thought he was cool and

I wanted to become a cop like him.

I managed to get through college, earn my degree, and come back home in one piece. It took a while, but I finally got hired by Harmony PD as an officer.

Six months later my father was on his hands and knees in the lab at school, trying to reach a steel ball bearing that had rolled under a table, when the janitor came in with some equipment on a lift jack. He didn't see my father until the last minute, swerved, and banged into the table. A motor that was sitting right on the edge of the table fell over and hit my dad on the back of the head, knocking him out. Three weeks later a blood clot in his brain caused a massive stroke and just like that, he was dead.

For the next ten years it was just my mother and I. I put off going back to the doctor to have the depression treated, and my mother tried her best to replace my father as my sole support mechanism but she didn't really understand what I was going through. She knew I had a very good memory and she knew I often got upset about things, but she didn't have my father's depth of understanding and couldn't reach me when things were at their worst.

Then I began to notice little changes in her. Fits of temper. Forgetfulness. A lack of focus. She became paranoid and insisted that people were playing mind games with her and doing things behind her back. They forced her to quit her job at the drug store because she kept having lapses and it was causing problems with customers.

Finally, I came home late one afternoon and found her crawling around in the back yard on her hands and knees. She said she was looking for the key to the garage, that she wanted to put something in the garage but had somehow lost the key in the grass. I got her back in the house and saw that she'd left her breakfast half eaten on the kitchen table. She'd been out there all day, crawling around on her hands and knees, missed lunch, didn't take her midday medication, looking for a key that was hanging on the hook inside the back door where it always was.

"Did you put it there?" she yelled at me. "Why didn't you tell me you found it this morning?"

I finally took her to the doctor, and she was diagnosed with Alzheimer's disease. It took her seven years to die from it.

I thought it was cruel to have complete personal memory recall. Imagine how shocked I was to learn that the opposite is just as horrible. I watched as everything she knew slipped away. It was a nightmare. She kept denying there was anything wrong with her. She'd have a lapse and be all upset and I'd tell her it was because of the Alzheimer's and she'd scream at me, "I don't have Alzheimer's!"

One afternoon we were out here taking the air. She was sitting in that rocking chair you're sitting in now. She looked at me and said, "I suppose some day I won't know who you are anymore."

It was the closest she ever came to admitting she understood what was happening to her. We sat there, not saying anything else for quite a while. Eventually she started talking about something else, and I got the sense that she'd already forgotten that she'd been upset. It was like a bubble of lucidity that had floated through her consciousness, popped, and disappeared.

I learned the hard way to depersonalize it. A mind afflicted with Alzheimer's disease compensates for memory loss by constructing plausible stories to fill in the gaps. She'd look at a knick knack on the buffet, couldn't remember where it came from, and concoct an elaborate tale about finding it in a second-hand store in Roanoke when in fact I'd given it to her for Christmas when I was in high school. At first I corrected her mistakes, but it made her angry so I stopped and let her mind do whatever it needed to do to try to stay above water. But that meant I had to abandon our real relationship, a normal, caring relationship between a parent and child, and accept a different relationship based on agreeing with whatever version of reality she needed to live with that particular day. When I walked in the door after work, I had to leave my real self out in the car and become this untruthful, agreeable guy who didn't react to her highs or lows but just let pretty much everything go in one ear and out the other. I had to force myself to stop getting upset, stop getting depressed, and stop hoping that her brief periods of lucidity meant she was fighting it off and might actually be plateauing for a while. By the time I was able to do all that, I was a completely different person to her. I was shallow, superficial, and phony with her. It was like she wasn't my mother anymore but some stranger to whom I was painfully polite. I hated it.

I kept her at home and looked after her as long as I could, but eventually it got too much for me. I'd made detective by then and although there's not a lot of heavy duty crime around here, they kept me busy. Plus I had started drinking fairly heavily and had had a few episodes myself. It finally became too much and she had to go into the hospital in Richlands. I couldn't afford to put her in a nursing home. My dad was under-insured when he died, and after the funeral expenses there wasn't much left. I just couldn't do everything for her anymore. There's not only the memory loss but also a loss of cognitive skills. She forgot how to operate simple things like the washing machine, microwave, even how to dial a telephone number. She couldn't prepare a meal anymore. On top of that, there's a physical component. She lost the ability to wash herself, feed herself, dress herself, go to the bathroom herself. She couldn't walk without help, couldn't keep her hands from shaking. I couldn't stay on top of it, so I had to put her in Richlands where she'd get constant care.

I drove down there every day to see her. One evening I could tell she didn't know who I was. She was very polite and we had a nice visit, but I could tell she wasn't connecting the dots. The next day she asked me what my name was and said we'd never been introduced but she was pleased to meet me.

That night I got stopped by a statie for driving under the influence. I showed him my ID and he let me off, but I got stopped twice more in a month and finally Billy brought me into his office and read me the riot act. The division commander in Wytheville had called Billy as a courtesy to explain that they couldn't keep letting me go and that either it stopped or they'd start charging me and it would end up costing me my job.

Billy could have fired me but he didn't. He stuck by me. Started riding shotgun on my ass, checking on me. He arranged for counseling sessions and got me into AA. None of it worked, but he kept trying. I appreciated it. I really did. But I was too far gone. I couldn't handle it any more.

Not long after my mother died, I went for a little vacation. I was gone for ten days. Here's the funny part: I don't remember all of it.

I drove to Cincinnati. I remember being there a few days. I decided to drive to Cleveland. The first night on the road after Cincinnati, I stayed in Columbus. Then I woke up one morning in a motel in Zanesville, and it was four days later. Somehow I'd lost four days out of my life. I couldn't believe it. That had never happened to me before. It shocked me sober and scared the hell out of me.

What had happened during that time? What did I do? Something bad, something I'd regret? I turned around and came right back home.

I went easy on the booze for a while after that, because I was scared. But at the same time it was fascinating. Like a cavity in a back tooth you keep sticking the tip of your tongue into. You just can't leave it alone, you have to keep feeling it. Still there. Yeah, still there. I kept going back to that hole in my memory. I'd discovered it was possible *not* to remember every goddamned thing.

So was that a good thing or a bad thing? I didn't know; it just confused me. I couldn't make up my mind. I kept going back to it, trying to make up my mind if having gaps like that, the way normal people sometimes do, would be good or bad.

On the one hand, I'd always hated having perfect recall of every goddamned moment of my life. I'd wished every day for a break from it. But on the other hand, I'd seen what gradual, brutal, inexorable memory loss had done to my mother, and I was scared to death at the thought of ending up like that. With hyperthymesia I have a painfully clear understanding of exactly who I am based on the sum total of all my experiences, thoughts, and perceptions, available in real time at any given moment, but with Alzheimer's disease I would be left with absolutely no awareness of who I'd been and what I'd done, good, bad, or indifferent. I would be no one. Nothing. A worm in a bag of water.

I just can't decide what I want. Some of that gap eventually came back, a little fuzzy around the edges, but there's still a hole of about two days that are apparently gone for good.

So now I drink, I guess I'd have to say honestly, because I don't know what to do. Alcohol takes the edge off. It inhibits the instant recall just enough that consciousness is tolerable. I can still remember whatever I need to remember just by reaching for it and pulling it out, but once I've had enough to drink the involuntary memory tones down just enough that I can get through the day.

At the same time if I drink too much, I know I can destroy something of myself in there, so I drink right up to the edge, I flirt with it, then I get scared because I'm not quite ready to commit suicide just yet. There's still a primitive survival mechanism that keeps me from going all the way. Usually I think of my father and how disappointed he'd be. Then I have one more drink because I know he'd be damned disappointed in me anyway, and I leave it at that.

The result of which is what you see in front of you now, a shit cop with a bad reputation who's a joke all over the district.

27

Hank walked up to Bluefield Street and leaned against a telephone pole on the corner. He took out his cell phone and called Karen to come pick him up. While he was waiting, he watched the traffic pass and memorized license plates for practice. When Karen skidded to a stop in front of him, he slid into the passenger seat of the Firebird and barely had time to close the door before she rocketed away from the gravel shoulder back into traffic.

"Dark blue Malibu, probably '06, West Virginia license number 657Y45," he said, buckling up.

"What's that?" Karen frowned, stomping on the brakes and pulling a hasty U-turn in front of a tractor trailer.

It was the license number of the first vehicle he'd seen after calling Karen. "Nothing," he said. "Question for you: would you rather remember absolutely everything that ever happened to you every minute of your life whether you wanted to or not, or forget everything five minutes afterwards and never be able to remember it again no matter how much you wanted to?"

"Huh? I don't know. What the hell kind of question is that?"

"Never mind." He watched a pedestrian hurry across the street as they shot through the intersection of Bluefield and Chestnut. "Who's first on the list?"

"Some guy named Peter Allen." She fished a piece of paper out of her jacket pocket and handed it to him. It was the list of students who'd taken the photography course with Marcie Askew. "First guy on the list, first guy I got a hold of on the phone. He's a nurse at the hospital. Said he'd meet us outside the Emergency entrance for a smoke."

There were twelve students on the list, including Marcie. "How many did you talk to?"

"Four. Allen, the woman Dillon, the man McCarty and the woman Smith."

Peter Allen turned out to be a thirty-year-old father of three girls who remembered nothing at all about Marcie Askew that was useful to them. He was obviously more interested in what they might be able to tell him about the investigation than in what he might be able to tell them.

Selena Dillon was a waitress working at Mary's Donuts who recognized Karen and was delighted to learn that she was a detective from out of state, but had nothing more useful to tell them about Marcie Askew's interactions at the college than Allen had been able to supply. They sat in Karen's usual booth at the front, looking out onto Bluefield Street, drinking coffee for which Hank had paid.

"She was a beautiful woman," Selena remarked in a light Appalachian accent, "and it was a darned shame, her getting killed like that. Everybody in class liked her."

"Any of the men in the class seem to like her more than normal?" Karen sipped her coffee casually, eyes moving from the street to Selena's face as though by accident.

"No, not really." Selena said. "It was kind of a disappointing bunch, if you know what I mean. Not a real good looker there at all."

"At least you learned a whole bunch about photography."

"Sure, I guess. Leastwise I took better pictures of my kids last Christmas than the year before."

Jim McCarty sold cars at the General Motors dealership on the highway just outside of town. He was a thirty-something who'd been given the responsibility of setting up a website for the dealership and had convinced the owner he needed the photography course in order to take attractive photos of the cars they would be listing online. He remembered Marcie Askew as having been beautiful, sexy, vivacious, and completely disinterested in his advances.

"Kind of a stuck-up bitch that way." He leaned against the fender of a four-year-old lease-return, low-mileage Impala that was loaded with options. "Beautiful but haughty."

"Haughty." Karen tried to force her face into a neutral expression and failed.

"Did she show interest in any other males in the class?" Hank asked.

McCarty shook his head. "I thought at first maybe she'd be looking for a little fun, but that wasn't the case. She pretty much ignored every one of us guys."

"What about other men on campus?"

"I only saw her during our classes. Once she blew me off, I dropped it. When a woman says no, I move on. No sense beating a dead horse. No pun intended."

Hank noticed Karen's right hand moving involuntarily toward her hip. He thanked McCarty for his help before Karen could draw her firearm and shoot him. They drove back into town to look up Jean Smith, a real estate agent with the Colonial Real Estate Company on

Spring Street, right next door to the Dairy Queen.

"If this one's dry," Karen said to him, slamming the door and walking around the front of the Firebird to join him on the sidewalk, "you're buying me a banana split. *Comprende?*"

"I'll buy us both one," Hank promised.

Jean Smith was a square-faced woman in her late forties who examined their credentials with a severe expression before allowing them to sit down in her tiny office. "You don't have any jurisdiction that I can see," she pronounced. "I don't know why I should answer any of your questions at all."

"We've been asked by the Harmony Police Department to assist in their investigation," Hank replied, not untruthfully.

"Not by Chief Askew, I hope," Smith retorted, "since I heard on the news this morning he was arrested in Bluefield and transported to Tazewell yesterday. They say he may be charged with his wife's murder."

"We've been working directly with Deputy Chief Branham and Detective Hall," Hank said. "If you'd feel more comfortable calling them before you talk to us, we'll wait."

She glared at him, chewing on her lower lip. Hank thought she'd probably make a better prison matron than a real estate agent, but there were several award plaques on her wall that suggested otherwise. She probably threatened prospective clients with a severe pounding unless they bought one of her listings.

"I suppose it won't do any harm," she said finally. "Mrs. Askew was the center of attention, needless to say. A beautiful woman like her can't help but attract notice, and she certainly didn't do anything to discourage it." Smith stopped herself and held up a hand. "Don't misunderstand. I'm not saying her behavior was ever inappropriate. She was quite aware of her local status and did nothing improper. All I'm saying is that the men's eyes never strayed very far from her, and she remained the focus of their attention throughout."

"Well, okay," Hank said. "Did she seem particularly interested in any of them? Did she spend time talking to any one of them more than the others?"

"I understand where you're going," Smith replied coyly, "and I don't think you'll have much luck there. The men in the class—there were five of them, altogether—were a collection of pitiful losers who couldn't hope to buy her a cup of coffee, let alone get into her panties. If she had a relationship with any of them, I think I'd fall over dead from a heart attack."

"All right." Hank didn't dare look at Karen, even peripherally. "What about anyone else on campus? Do you know if she had any friends that she might have spent time with on campus, male or female?"

Smith leaned back in her chair and eyed him speculatively. "Mmm. Interestingly put. Was she bi?"

"Excuse me?" Karen popped, shifting her weight suddenly.

"Well, the way he asked it, the inference was that she had a lover who might have been female. Is that what you're saying?"

Hank took a deep breath. "No, I'm just asking questions, Ms. Smith. If you can't answer them, that's quite all right."

"*Miss* Smith. I'm not ashamed of my singularity. And to answer your question, yes, I saw her on several occasions lingering after class with men. But never women. If you're suggesting she was bi, I'm afraid I can't help you there. We women seemed to be pretty much beneath her notice altogether."

"Which men in particular?"

Smith pursed her lips. "There was Sam Hanshaw, director of the college's finance department or something. He's also on the town council and a friend of the Askews. She'd sometimes meet him in the cafeteria after class for coffee. I know him well because I sold him the house he's in right now, a beautiful four-bedroom up on Ridge Road. Then there was that other fellow, the former chief, David Morris. I saw her leaving with him a few times. Getting a ride home, no doubt." She rolled her eyes. "And as well I saw her a few times with George Rudy, who's head of the college's fine arts department." She shrugged. "That's pretty much it, I suppose."

Back in the Firebird, Hank and Karen discussed strategy. Jean Smith was correct; Askew had been transported from Bluefield to Tazewell in the custody of the sheriff. Branham had told Karen he would be charged with his wife's murder within a day.

Meanwhile, Richmond police had found the two bikers and questioned them, but Branham wasn't very enthusiastic about the outcome. Sheriff Steele had sent one of his deputies to Richmond to interrogate them again, but no one felt very strongly about where it might go. Everyone had high hopes that the test results on the tissue recovered from beneath Marcie's fingernails would point directly to the killer, and neither biker had as much as a shaving cut on him. Still, DNA samples had been collected, and the bikers would be kept as long as possible. Originally the lab tests on the tissue had been scheduled to be completed next Monday, but Steele was making a lot of noise to have them bumped up in the queue, given the nature of the crime.

They didn't know at this point if Billy Askew had scratches on him that could reasonably be dated to last Saturday night.

"Steele's probably gonna hold on to him as long as he can, anyway," Karen said, "since he's already got the assault charges pending. It's a toss-up if a judge will grant bail right now with the murder investigation ongoing like this, and Askew looking real good for it. Hatfield should be able to convince a judge to keep him indoors for a while."

"Meanwhile," Hank said, "I don't think the sheriff's bothering to find out who's responsible for Marcie's pregnancy."

"Yeah, he really has a hate on for Askew. He's probably trying to whup a confession out of him even as we speak." They were parked at the curb outside the real estate office just above the railroad tracks on Bluefield. "We've got three names. We should check these guys out; see if one of them likes to use his hands as much as Billy Askew does."

"The sheriff should be doing it," Hank complained.

"Sure enough. You just call him right up and tell him. I'm sure he'll appreciate the input."

Hank looked at her in mock amusement.

"Three guys, Lou. One of them is probably gonna ring the bell. We're talking about hanging around this one-hole outhouse until the weekend anyway. I say we look them up and see if they'll trade possum soup recipes or something. Come on, it'll be fun."

He shook his head. "Let's talk to Branham and run it by him. He can call your new friend Detective Muncy and pass along the names, get a sense of their level of interest in that angle."

"Deputy Dawg. I'm sure he'll bark real loud when Branham tosses him that biscuit."

"You're probably right; he probably won't give a damn. We can play it by ear, but we've got to make sure we don't step on toes here. It's the Golden Rule, right? Don't screw with another cop's investigation if you wouldn't want them to screw with yours."

"Yeah, yeah. All right." Karen threw the Firebird into gear and twisted around to watch for a break in traffic. "Here's the thing, though. To get to the station we have to drive by that army surplus store. I'm not going by there again without looking at that SIG you were talking about. If you don't buy it, I might."

28

Neil Branham looked at his watch. It was 4:27 p.m. He'd just hung up the phone after talking to Detective Muncy in Tazewell, who had shown tepid interest in the three potential boyfriends of Marcie Askew that Hank and Karen had turned up. When Branham offered to interview them as a favor, Muncy made the expected noises about jurisdiction and reasonable grounds before relenting.

"I appreciate the help," he grumbled.

Branham pulled the phone book out of the bottom drawer of his desk, looked up a number, and dialed it. When the main switchboard at Lewis Collins College answered, he asked for the extension of Sam Hanshaw. He was put through and spoke briefly with Hanshaw, who was still at his desk. He'd be there for another hour. Branham explained that he was with Hank and Karen, and they'd stop by before he left. Then he got Hanshaw to pass him back to the switchboard and asked for David Morris. Morris's line went to voice mail. Branham hung up. After dialing Morris's home phone number with the same result, he redialed the college and asked for George Rudy. Rudy's phone also rang and went to voice mail, but Rudy's message included a cell phone number, so Branham hung up and called the cell phone number. Rudy answered immediately and told Branham he was coaching the volleyball team and would be in the gymnasium until six o'clock.

Branham hung up and grabbed his uniform jacket off the back of his chair. "Let's go," he said, nodding at Hank.

"I'll drive," Karen said.

Branham shook his head. "We'll take the chief's Explorer. Looks more official that way."

Sam Hanshaw was a thin, cadaverous sixty-year-old who was just locking his office door as they walked up.

Branham badged him, introduced Karen and Hank, and folded his arms across his chest. "I thought you were going to be here until five o'clock."

Hanshaw jingled his keys. "I finished up early. My wife and I are going out tonight and I don't want to keep her waiting."

"This won't take long," Karen said, her tone casual. "Witnesses tell us you were pretty chummy with Marcie Askew before she was strangled. Care to explain that?"

Hanshaw blinked at her. "We were friends."

"Pretty good friends, were ya? Sack buddies and all?"

Hanshaw looked at Branham. "What on earth is she talking about?"

"Tell us about the nature of your relationship with Mrs. Askew," Branham suggested.

"We were friends, as I said." Hanshaw shifted his black leather briefcase from one hand to the other. "Actually, she was closer to my wife than to me. We socialized occasionally with them. I dealt with Billy from time to time on committee work, you know, for the town council, and we spent Sunday afternoons together whenever Billy's work permitted. The girls played backgammon, and Billy and I watched football. That's pretty much it."

"You knew she was taking a photography course out here a while ago?" Karen asked.

Hanshaw nodded.

"Ever see her while she was on campus?"

"Yes. Sometimes she'd stop by my office after class. We'd have a cup of coffee in the cafeteria before she went home."

"She was closer to your wife than to you, but she'd go out of her way to look you up for a cup of coffee." Karen's tone made it clear that she didn't believe a word he was saying.

"Yes, well, it was only a few times. Once, she wanted to know what to buy Marjorie—that's my wife—for her birthday. Another time I left a message with her instructor, Professor Brogan, to have her stop by my office after class because I had some documents for Billy and it seemed the most convenient way to get them to him. Things like that. Nothing at all inappropriate, as you seem to be implying."

They worked him for a while longer and then let him go. As they walked across the grounds toward the gymnasium, Karen looked at Hank.

"That guy's got about as much sex appeal as an old tube of toothpaste. No way she was romping in the sack with *that*."

Hank nodded. "Probably not physically fit enough to have carried her down the ravine."

"No scratches that I could see from struggling with her," Branham added.

They found George Rudy sitting in the bleachers as two teams of female players battled on the volleyball court in front of him. He was a chubby, balding, middle-aged man with a whistle around his neck and a perpetual grin on his face. He wore a gray Lewis Collins

College sweater, red track pants with white stripes down the legs, and white Nike sneakers. He shook everyone's hand without getting up and motioned them to sit down as a violent spike on the court scored a point for the team on the right-hand side of the net.

Rudy stood up abruptly and blew his whistle, nearly deafening Karen, who was still standing next to him.

"Mandy! You were out of position for the block! Remember, keep your feet moving at all times and be ball aware! Ball aware!"

"I'll bet you're a ball aware guy, aren't you?" Karen asked him, rubbing her ear.

"They need repetition to remember the basics," Rudy smiled, sitting down again.

"Sorry, I couldn't hear what you said on account of you deafening me," Karen said, "but reading your lips I thought you said you were real close friends with Marcie Askew. I get that right?"

"Huh? Marcie?" He looked from Karen to Branham. "This is about her murder, isn't it? You wanted to ask me some questions about her?"

"How well did you know her?" Branham asked.

Rudy shrugged apologetically. "Not nearly as well as I wanted to, that's for sure."

"You ever meet with her around here?" Karen asked.

"Yeah," Rudy's eyebrows went up enthusiastically, "a couple of times. I'm director of fine arts, so I step in for the first few minutes of the first class for our courses, make a little speech about Lewis Collins being a great place for liberal arts and creativity and imagination and all that. Give the instructor a bit of a boost. I noticed Marcie right off in Brogan's class that day. I recognized her, knew who she was, and asked around a bit. Someone thought she was separated from her husband or something, so I accidentally on purpose bumped into her after one of her classes and bought her a coffee. Excuse me."

He leaped to his feet, blew the whistle and pointed. "Again! Run that set again. Pam, you and Ann need to get your timing together. Try it again!"

He sat down and grinned. "Sorry. Where was I?"

"You were coming on to the wife of the chief of police," Karen reminded him.

"Oh. Yeah. Right. I'm divorced, and I thought she was available, but she set me straight right away. She was real nice about it, let me recover gracefully, and we had a nice chat. I bought her coffee one more time after that, just to make sure I'd understood her correctly, if you know what I mean, and I *had* understood correctly, so it was just a nice chat and have a good evening, see you later. Only I didn't.

174

Unfortunately."

"You ever see her socially away from campus?" Karen asked. "In town? At bars or somewhere like that?"

"Good heavens, no!" Rudy laughed. "I prayed, but no such miracle ever happened. Look, I know I'm no Lothario. They don't sigh and melt when they see me coming. So when a woman says she's not interested, I move along without an argument. And you'll notice, Detective Stain, I said woman and not girl." He pointed at the volleyball court. "They're girls. Kids." He tipped his hand back and forth. "More or less. Not yet women, really, because they're not in complete control of their own lives yet. Not interesting to me, in case you were wondering. There's nobody female around here who's willing to coach volleyball, and I happen to love the sport. I'm forty-three years old. Anyone under thirty is way too flighty for me. Does that answer your question?"

"It answered about six of them," Karen said. "And the name's Stainer, not Stain. You always talk this much?"

He grinned back at her. "Know any mature single women who are good listeners?"

Walking back across the parking lot, following Rudy's directions to the building where David Morris's office was located, Hank looked at Branham, who shook his head.

"I don't think so. He didn't come across as someone prone to violence."

"More like the Pillsbury Dough Boy," Karen said.

"Didn't notice any scratches from a struggle," Hank said.

Karen shrugged. "Wouldn't hurt to do a background on him, I guess."

"That would be Muncy's call," Branham said.

David Morris's office was locked. They asked around and were told that he had already left for the day.

"Hall already interviewed him," Branham said. "Didn't come up with anything out of the ordinary."

"Hall's lucky to be able to find his ass with both hands," Karen said.

On the way to the stairwell she heard someone call her name. It was Dr. Jane Morley, director of the criminal justice program. Morris's boss.

"I found your business card. You remember, you gave it to me earlier in the week when you were interviewing Erica. It gave me a great idea. I'm teaching a third-year Criminal Investigation course, and our class tomorrow is on interrogation. We try to bring in guest speakers whenever we can on Fridays, and I was wondering if you might be willing to make a short presentation, maybe ten minutes or so, on your experiences with effective interrogation techniques? Then take a few questions from the students?"

"Whoa," Karen said, "I'm no teacher. You'd probably do a lot better with someone else."

"With all due respect, Detective, I have to disagree. You're an experienced detective from a large city force, and no doubt you've interrogated quite a few subjects in your time. Plus, you're a woman, and I've got a lot of female students in my class who'd benefit from listening to a successful female police officer. It's a rare opportunity for them and I'd really appreciate it."

"I don't know." Karen looked at Hank.

"Do it," Hank said.

Karen frowned. "Will Morris be around?"

"David?" Morley nodded. "Yes, of course. There are only two of us on faculty for Criminal Justice, David and myself, and we both attend the Friday presentations. Why?"

"Just wanted to make sure he wouldn't have a problem with me presenting a female point of view," Karen lied.

"Of course not. In any event, I'm the director and I think it's a wonderful idea."

Karen accepted Morley's invitation and agreed to be there at 11:00 a.m. tomorrow.

Out in the parking lot she pointed a finger at Hank.

"You have to tell me what to say. I don't know what the hell to say to a bunch of kids."

"About interrogation?" Hank pretended to be astonished. "After all the war stories I've heard you tell?"

"I don't tell war stories. I just kick asses."

"You'll be fine," he said. "Besides, I have an idea. Maybe the same one you have. If Morris is going to be there, we might have an opportunity to press him."

Branham raised an eyebrow. "Let me call Muncy." He took out his cell phone and thumbed the number. He explained to Muncy Hank's idea to apply pressure to Morris during tomorrow's class at the college.

"I don't know," Muncy groused. "Sounds pretty dubious to me."

"Drive up tomorrow morning anyway," Branham said. "Breakfast's on me. We can talk about it some more."

He put away the phone. "He'll be here."

"We need more info on Morris," Karen said. "If we can't talk to him, we should talk to some people who know him."

"How about his former boss?" Hank suggested. "The mayor?

He seemed to have a pretty high opinion of Morris when he hired him as chief of police. Be interesting to see if he still feels that way about him."

Branham looked at his watch again. It was nearly 5:30 p.m. "He might still be at the drug store."

"Let's find out," Karen said.

Press Blankenship was still working behind the counter at the back of his pharmacy, filling prescriptions.

"Press," Branham said, leaning his hip against the counter, "got a minute?"

Blankenship nodded and finished what he was doing, then gestured toward a waiting area off to the side where there were several hard plastic chairs, all currently unoccupied. "What can I do for you?"

"We'd like to ask you a few questions about David Morris," Hank said.

Blankenship looked at Branham. "I understood that with the case moved to the sheriff's office and Billy in jail down there, we don't have a role anymore. Are these two helping Sheriff Steele now?"

"Detective Muncy asked us to conduct a couple of interviews to assist," Branham said. "We want to talk to David Morris, but we can't get in touch with him right now so we thought we'd have a word with you."

"About David? I don't understand."

"We'd like a little background," Hank said. "He was there at the bar the night Mrs. Askew was murdered, and as a potential witness he needs to give a statement to us. I'd like a little better understanding of him first."

Blankenship studied him. "You obviously know that David and Billy didn't see eye to eye whatsoever. You figuring that David might color his testimony to prejudice the case against Billy?"

Hank shrugged noncommittally.

"Can't see it," Blankenship said flatly. "Nothing to gain by doing so. Billy's pretty much put the noose around his own neck without help from anyone else."

"You think pretty highly of this Morris guy." Karen put her hands on her hips and cocked her head at him curiously.

"Yes, m'am, I guess I do. Wouldn't have hired him as chief of police otherwise."

"It must have pissed you off when he quit to run for sheriff."

"I wouldn't quite put it that way. More disappointed, I'd say. David was a star candidate, the kind of man you don't see very often around here."

"What was his background?" Hank was familiar with the high

points but wanted to hear it from Blankenship.

"He's from Charlottesville." Blankenship sat down in one of the plastic chairs and motioned them to do the same. "Did a degree in criminology at the University of Virginia, my alma mater."

Hank sat down next to him and casually crossed his legs. "He was an athlete, wasn't he?"

"That's right. Football. Quarterback, as a matter of fact. Second string, but he started three games his senior year when the starter got hurt. He wasn't drafted after he graduated, but the Bears signed him to their practice squad for a year. When they released him he went back to U. Va. to do a graduate degree, then joined the Charlottesville police. After three years he applied to the FBI and got in. Spent two years with them and moved to the Richmond police. He was promoted a couple times, I believe to the same rank you have, Lieutenant. Then he saw our notice for chief of police and applied down here. Five minutes into the interview I knew we had our man."

"This is a lot smaller community than Charlottesville or Richmond," Hank said. "How'd he fit in around here?"

"Oh, I don't know." Blankenship shrugged. "He had a big-city swagger to him, all right, which ruffled some feathers here and there, but I figured it was all good, you know? Having a lot of self-confidence in a job like that, running the law in a community where there ain't a lot of jobs and money to go around and people might be thinking about stepping over the line a little to make ends meet, is a good thing because it makes the law high profile and in everybody's mind all the time. They all knew who he was and what he was here for, and as far as I'm concerned he didn't need to fit in and be everybody's pal, he needed to represent law and order. That's what I hired him for."

"Did he like the rough stuff?" Karen asked.

"What do you mean?"

"Come on, you know what I mean. Ever have any problems with him getting too physical with people, knocking them around a little, that sort of thing?"

Blankenship glanced at Hank. "It tends to go with the territory in a small place like this, as you learned, Lieutenant. Sometimes it can't be helped. Billy has a hair-trigger temper, that's for sure."

"We're talking about David Morris right now."

"Sure, I suppose. There were a couple of incidents, guess you could say. They got smoothed over, and everybody went home happy."

"Any of those incidents involve women?" Karen asked.

Blankenship looked up at her.

Karen stared back. "You make it sound like it was just hillbilly

DUIs or kids trying to jimmy parking meters," Karen said impatiently. "What about women? He have any problems roughing up women that had to be smoothed over?"

"Of course not. David's single, and the girls think he's good-looking, I guess, but I don't know of anything along the lines you're talking about."

"Sure about that?"

"Sure, I'm sure about that." Blankenship stood up. "If there's nothing else, I have to get back to work."

Hank stood up and offered his hand. "We appreciate your help."

They walked single file through the pharmacy toward the front door, Karen leading, Branham in the middle, and Hank bringing up the rear. They passed rows of cold remedies and pain relievers on the right, and toothpaste, toothbrushes, and mouthwash on the left. At the front of the store, a woman came around from behind the cash register as Karen headed for the door. She was about sixty, tall and bulky, wearing a flowered dress, flat-soled shoes, an elegant-looking wrist watch, and a small pendant on a thin gold chain around her neck. Her hair was medium length, nicely styled, and colored to a shade somewhere between coffee and caramel.

"Just a moment," she said to Karen, holding out her hand. "Can we talk for a minute?"

Karen stopped on a dime. "Talk? Sure."

Branham nearly ran into her from behind.

"Just outside, please." The woman led the way through the front door out onto the sidewalk, then moved several paces down until she was beyond the plate glass front window of the pharmacy.

"I'm Desiree Blankenship," the woman told Karen, folding her arms protectively in front of her. "Folks call me Des."

"What did you want to talk about, Mrs. Blankenship?"

"Just Des, please." She worked her jaw for a moment before plunging ahead. "I heard you asking Press questions about David Morris. He bought a bill of goods from that man and that's all there is to it."

"You've got a different opinion of him, do you?"

Des Blankenship was several inches taller than Karen, and so she stooped a little as she moved forward, lowering her voice. "He don't know the half of it. That man was horrible, just horrible. I was hoping against hope he'd just get on back to Richmond after he lost the election, but instead he got that job at the college. The men all think he's just wonderful, one of these macho police types, former football star, all that." She glanced meaningfully at Branham. "But women know better.

179

Least, they eventually do."

"What are you saying, Mrs. Blankenship?" Hank asked, straining to hear her soft voice. "Were there problems between Morris and some of the women in the community?"

"You could say that." She looked defiantly at Branham. "I'm sure you wouldn't agree, would you, Deputy Branham?"

"M'am, I never heard anything official about Chief Morris along those lines."

"Oh, that's right pretty." Des Blankenship put a hand on her hip. "Just what does that mean, exactly?"

"Yeah," Karen agreed, glaring at Branham, "what the hell *does* that mean?"

"Just that I was never aware of any complaints against Chief Morris filed by women," Branham said defensively. "There was a lot of talk about him being a lady's man, but I don't pay a lot of attention to gossip."

"I thought that was a policeman's job," Des retorted. "To pay a lot of attention to what's going on around him."

"All right," Karen said, "you've made your point. Have you got something to tell us that we need to know?"

Des continued to glare at Branham. "You went and arrested your own chief for killing his wife when he never done a single thing to that poor woman except try his best to make it right for her." She shifted her gaze to Karen. "You got to understand, Press and I spend a lot of time at social functions and gatherings and the like with all the various people in this town. Town councilors and their wives, the town manager and his wife, Chamber of Commerce, folks at the college, on and on. It's a whole lot of work and a lot of time, and us wives don't have much say in it. So I've been around Mr. Morris quite a bit since he come down here, and Billy and Marcie too. I seen stuff Press never did, and I heard stuff Press never heard. David Morris is an oily, two-faced rodent who can't keep his hands to himself. Women either love that or they hate it. Hell, he even pretended to flirt with me, and look at this." She passed her hands up and down her body. "Then I let on how much it made me want to puke and he got the idea. Just ignored me completely after that, which I was glad of. But it's the man's nature, don't you see? There ain't a female alive he don't think he can charm right into the sheets."

"An oily rodent," Karen mused. "You see any indication he was bothering Mrs. Askew that way?"

Des looked away for a moment. "I'm afraid so. That poor woman wasn't too good at hiding what she was thinking. I could read her like a book when she was around that man, and it wasn't a book I liked to read very much. Not that any of the men had a clue, mind you." Another disgusted look at Branham. "They're just plain thick, even when it's their own spouse he's hitting on."

"They were having an affair?" Branham asked.

"Hain't I just said so?"

"Was he rough with her?" Karen asked. "Did you see any signs he was hitting her?"

"Oh, my." Des looked away again, worrying her lower lip between her teeth. "Another man's wife, and he treated her worse than you would a dumb animal. She kept always making excuses for her swollen face and broken wrist and the like, and Billy seemed to believe her stories but I sure didn't. I knew better just by watching her and Morris when they were in the same place at the same time. He just plain owned her. Could do whatever he wanted with her, and likely did. I just couldn't understand how some women seemed to need that. It sure turns me off."

"I hear ya," Karen said. "Big time."

29

There were eight cells in the wing of the county jail in which Billy Askew was incarcerated, but only one other was currently occupied. A man in his sixties had been brought in on a DUI and had passed out on the cot. They were letting him sleep it off. A young guy in his twenties, wearing a stained wife-beater and jeans, had made a brief appearance but they'd moved him out again a while ago. Askew had recognized the kid as a drug dealer with a record for possession with intent to traffic, possession of stolen property, and assault. Not that he gave a shit. He'd stopped paying much attention to his surroundings.

He sat on the edge of his cot and stared at his hands, which were clasped between his knees. The time passed as it always does, regardless of what we do or fail to do, and Askew let it pass without protest. His mind wandered. He knew he was in a blue funk. A corner of his mind chewed away at him to snap out of it and do something, solve the problem, kick somebody's ass, and get the hell out of there, but the blue funk enveloped his brain and kept him where he was, motionless, almost weightless, like a Styrofoam cup snagged in a half-submerged tree limb in a stream.

There was a dim light in the corridor from a lamp over the door at the far end. Other lights came on, but Askew didn't give a shit. On a certain level he knew it was late, but he hadn't been able to sleep so he just continued to sit there and didn't stir when he heard the door open. Footsteps stopped outside his cell. Someone banged a folding metal chair on the floor and sat down in it.

"Evening, Billy."

The dickhead, Muncy. Askew clasped his hands a little more tightly between his knees.

"I realize it's late, Billy, but I was here doing paperwork and thought I'd have a little talk with you before I went home."

Good for you, dickhead.

"You should've at least talked to your attorney, Billy. You're in a real bad spot. You should take help when it's offered."

Askew stopped listening after the word "attorney." He'd kept his mouth shut ever since being transported from Bluefield down here to Tazewell. Ice Steele had pounded away at him for a good hour, but Askew had just blocked him out and eventually Ice had given up and gone away. Then Judd Witten, Askew's lawyer, showed up. He'd heard about Askew's arrest and subsequent transfer on the radio news and came down as soon as he could get free. Askew wouldn't talk to him. Wouldn't even acknowledge his presence. Witten had gone away, saying he was going to arrange for Askew's release on bail, but hadn't come back. Not that Askew gave a shit. The blue funk was like a drug. He surrendered himself to it and stayed motionless as time flowed on around him.

"–during the autopsy," dickhead Muncy was saying. "When the lab tests come back we're gonna know whose tissue it was under her fingernails from the DNA, right, Billy? If it's yours, you're screwed, right? You know that, don't you?"

Askew said nothing, but unfortunately he was now paying attention.

"If it's somebody else's then we're wasting time trying to grill your ass while the real killer's getting away with it. It'd be a big help if you'd just explain where you were on Saturday night so we can separate the wheat from the chaff and find out who killed your wife."

Askew couldn't help himself. "You see me missing any tissue, dickhead?"

"No, sir," Muncy promptly replied, "and that's the real truth. The doctor who looked you over confirmed you got no marks anywhere except the fresh-skinned knuckle and torn fingernail from your little dust-up in Bluefield. The only thing is, the lab may find that the tissue was only Marcie's, since she scratched her own neck trying to pry the guy's hands off of her. Sorry, Billy. I know that's graphic."

Askew said nothing.

"Best case," Muncy went on, "we find both her DNA and the killer's DNA in the samples. Worst case it's only hers and we got to have something else, like a confession or a witness or something."

Askew said nothing.

"If you could tell us where you were Saturday night, and we could confirm it in some way, it'd go a long way toward getting you out of here. Ice don't feel real good holding a fellow law enforcement commander here in jail with the drunks and druggies."

Askew unclasped his hands and flattened them on his knees. "Ice is laughing his fucking head off."

"No, he's not, Billy."

"He ain't had this much fun in a long time."

"No, that hain't true, Billy. We're all real upset about this. You

183

gotta help us out. Tell us where you were on Saturday night."

Askew stood up and walked over to the bars to look out at Muncy. "That's personal, and I'm not about to tell a dickhead like you."

"Would you tell Ice? I could ask Ice to come back down. He'd talk to you right now, if you like."

Askew pursed his lips. Something in him shifted a little. It was as though the current had flipped over a bit and the Styrofoam cup had become unwedged. "What time is it?"

Muncy looked at his watch. "Almost midnight. Eleven-fifty."

It was late. Steele was probably already in bed. Next to his wife. Snuggled up comfortable. Maybe already asleep.

"Get him down here before I change my mind," Askew said.

It took forty minutes for Ice Steele to show up. He wore jeans, scuffed deck shoes, and a faded gray Carolina Panthers sweatshirt. His brown hair was tousled, and the bags under his eyes looked as though they were stuffed with cotton. Askew was sitting cross-legged on the cot with his back against the wall. Muncy shifted the metal chair in front of Askew's cell door. Steele sat down on it while Muncy moved a few steps away with his arms folded across his chest and a serious look on his face, as though he'd just orchestrated a high-level diplomatic intervention between warring countries.

"Muncy tells me you got something to say," Steele growled. "So say it."

"Nice of you to come down, Ice. Hope I didn't disturb your beauty rest."

"You did. So cut the crap."

"I was at my sister's on Saturday night. The trailer where she was living with her piece-a-shit husband on 102 just outside of Bluefield. Got there maybe nine-thirty and stayed until about one-forty, when I got the call from Dispatch."

"The way I understand it," Steele said slowly, "your people were trying to get a hold of you when they first got the call but they couldn't reach you. Your cell phone was out of service or some damned thing."

"I had it turned off."

"That something you do on a regular basis?"

Askew shook his head. "I was knee-deep in shit and had to deal with it."

"What kind of shit we talking about?"

Askew said nothing for several moments. This was the crux of his reluctance to say something in his own defense. He was a man of enormous pride, and it cut him deeply that his sister had sunk to the level of trailer trash, victimized by her worthless, drunken husband.

184

He'd always kept Pricie carefully compartmentalized from the rest of his life. He was ashamed of her; at the same time he was ashamed that he was ashamed of her. Now the entire thing had become a trap that was costing him his reputation and his liberty.

Complicating the situation, to the point of paralyzing him, was the fact that someone, some other man, had been abusing Marcie for the last year and he'd completely missed it. He'd had no idea she'd been stepping out on him, and worse, he'd completely missed the signs of abuse he had no trouble recognizing in his own sister. They'd seen so little of each other in the last while that Marcie had almost become a stranger to him. When she said she fell down the stairs and broke her wrist, he'd believed her. When she said she'd hurt her shoulder walking someone's dog, he'd believed her, absent-mindedly wondering if she were becoming accident prone. When she said she had an infected wisdom tooth and the dentist was rough pulling it out, he'd believed her, thinking he should go have a word with the damned clumsy dentist. What a fucking idiot he'd been.

Sitting here alone, punishing himself for his stupidity and his failure to protect both his sister and his wife, he'd become numb. He'd stopped thinking. But now he knew he had to do it. He had to let go of Pricie, stop trying to correct her failings for her, stop trying to push her life into a shape that matched the picture in his head of how his sister's life should be. He had to let her go and free himself at the same time.

He needed to let go of Marcie, too. She'd been gone longer than he'd known, and it was rough to find that out the hard way. Now he needed to save himself. There was nothing else left to do.

"My sister's a victim of domestic abuse," he said. "Long-term. Bluefield's been out there often, I've been out there too, but you know how it works. There's not a lot you can do when the woman keeps smoothing it over." He paused, aware of the irony in his statement when applied to his own wife. "Last Saturday he'd beat her again and I went out there looking for him. Lucky for him, the sonofabitch had taken off. I stayed with Pricie as long as I could. Tried to talk her into leaving. Eventually she just fell asleep, so I sat with her for a while. Then I went out to the kitchen to fix myself a drink, turned on my cell, and it rang right away. Like to scare the fuck right out of me." He paused. "Marcie was gone. So I got the hell out of there."

It was like trying to fix up something on one side, and while your back was turned something infinitely more precious got destroyed on the other side. You couldn't win. You just couldn't win.

"I suppose this sister of yours'll corroborate everything you're saying."

"I don't want her bothered." Askew pushed away from the wall and stood up. "You understand me, Steele? I don't want her name in the papers, reporters knocking on her door, bothering her kids, talking to that fucking Neal. I want her left out of it." He grabbed the bars and shook them. "Leave her the fuck alone!"

Steele crossed his legs calmly and folded his arms across his chest, craving a cigarette. It was his jail and he could break the rules and smoke if he wanted to, but unlike the man in front of him he was stronger than his cravings, stronger, smarter, more ambitious, more successful, with a higher ceiling. A better man.

"If she's your alibi and she don't come forward," Steele pointed out, "you could be screwed. Hatfield can make a case against you tomorrow that's good enough to get you the death penalty even without DNA evidence."

Steele's last words hit hard, reminding him that Marcie had been pregnant when she'd been killed. Murdering a pregnant woman was a capital offense in Virginia.

"Leave Pricie alone," he repeated.

Steele considered the possibilities for a moment. "Muncy could drive up there, have a quiet word with her. Corroborate your story. If it's true and the investigation leads somewhere else, she's not a factor and she stays out of it. We just tell the press something vague and non-specific."

What he left unsaid was that if Askew were charged and the case went to trial, she'd be dragged into it regardless by Askew's own lawyer as a witness for the defense, and she'd not only become a focus of attention for the media but fair game for Hatfield to destroy as he saw fit. Steele knew what was on Askew's mind. He just didn't give much of a shit, one way or the other.

"I don't like it at all," Askew said.

Steele shrugged. In ten seconds he was going to stand up and go back home to bed.

"I could check on her," Muncy offered. "See if she's okay. Have a word with her husband; let him know somebody's still watching him. Ask her about Saturday night while I'm there."

Askew opened his mouth to tell Muncy to butt the fuck out of it, then closed it again. "Mmm."

I *can* be discreet, Billy. Believe it or not.

Askew stared hard at him, then nodded. "Okay."

Muncy nodded back. "Okay."

Steele stood up and walked out without another word.

30

It was getting late, but Hank was restless and couldn't sleep. He lay in bed staring up into the darkness, watching headlights crawl across the ceiling as cars drove by on the highway. He hoped it wouldn't be all that long before he was able to fall asleep in a motel room again without half-expecting the door to be kicked in at any moment. It was no consolation that the primary door-kicker around here, Billy Askew, was safely behind bars. Any door could be kicked open at any time by anybody, when you really thought about it.

Hank mulled over Billy Askew as a suspect and didn't really like the way it fit together. Unless he could satisfactorily explain his whereabouts on Saturday night when his wife was killed, Askew would be Donnie Hatfield's best bet for a conviction at this point, depending of course on what kind of physical evidence came out of the lab tests ordered by the medical examiner, but Hank felt uneasy. The compass in his head was slowly swinging toward David Morris. There was reason to believe that Morris was the other man in Marcie's sex life and that he was the father of her child. There was talk about him being physically abusive of women. He was at Gerry's on Saturday night around the time that Marcie was murdered.

It bothered Hank that they hadn't been able to find him. Hall said he'd already interviewed Morris and that the former chief of police had had nothing useful to contribute to the investigation. Branham, when asked today about his relationship with Morris and his assessment of Morris's potential as a suspect, had been vague and uncomfortable. He'd only known Morris for a year while the man served as their "star" chief. He hadn't liked him all that well, hadn't socialized with him off-duty, hadn't really gotten to know him before he'd resigned to run for sheriff. They hadn't really spoken since then.

Hank threw himself out of bed and went into the washroom. When he came back out he sat on the side of the bed and deliberated. What about Hall? Hank realized he had no idea what Hall's attitude toward Morris might be. His loyalty to Billy Askew was clearly evident, but it occurred to Hank that Hall had never expressed an actual opinion of Morris. Perhaps Hall knew more than he was letting on.

Making up his mind, he got dressed and drove over to Hall's house. The lights were all out. Hall was likely in bed, since it was now past midnight. Hank pulled into the driveway and pounded on the locked metal screen door of the enclosed porch.

A dog in someone's back yard began to bark, causing another dog farther away to begin barking as well. Hank pounded again.

"Hall! It's Donaghue! Open up!"

The closest dog began to yodel an octave higher than before, excited by the sound of Hank's voice in the otherwise quiet neighborhood. The light came on in the enclosed porch. The inside door opened.

"What the hell are you doing? It's late at night. I'm trying to sleep."

"Open up, Hall," Hank said. "We need to talk."

"Are you psychotic? It's after midnight. Get lost."

"Let me in, Hall. I want to talk to you about David Morris."

Grumbling and grousing, Hall came out and unlocked the screen door. Hank followed him inside into the kitchen, where Hall gestured to a round wooden table with four woven place mats and matching napkins in wooden rings set neatly in front of four oak press-back chairs.

"Sit down, Lieutenant. Want some coffee? I'm going to have some."

Hank noticed a subtle difference in Hall's demeanor. "With a whiskey chaser?"

Hall poured water into a coffee machine and shook his head. "Not tonight. Tomorrow night, but not tonight. You said you want to talk about Morris. What about him? I told you already he didn't have anything useful to say about Saturday night."

"Branham, Karen, and I conducted a few more interviews this afternoon. We asked them who Marcie Askew might have been messing with. Morris's name came up. It's possible he was the father of her unborn child."

"It's actually a double homicide, isn't it, Lieutenant?" Hall said, scooping coffee into the basket and shoving it into the machine. "Nobody's mentioned that small detail yet. The Virginia Criminal Code has a section covering fetal homicide, although at only three months the fetus probably wouldn't be legally accepted as a separate victim. Just the same, morally, the killer's responsible for two deaths, not just one, and it's a capital offense on top of that."

"I see what you mean." Hank turned one of the chairs sideways and sat down, resting his elbow on the table. "You worked for David Morris for a year. Is he that kind of guy? Someone who'd have an affair with another man's wife, physically abuse her, lose his temper, and strangle her to death?"

"I don't know." Hall switched on the coffee machine and leaned against the counter. "I just got to sleep when you started pounding. I feel like dog shit. After you left, I put the booze away and ate some supper. I had a little nap, watched some TV, didn't have anything else to drink, went outside and stood in the backyard for a while, remembered the names of all the constellations my dad had taught me when I was a kid, wondered what the names of the other ones were that he didn't tell me about, came in, went to bed, stared at the insides of my eyelids for a while, fell asleep, then woke up when all hell started to bust loose. I was dreaming I was dating some woman. The woman had a dog, and the dog didn't like me. It kept barking at me. Turned out it was only you and the dog down the street."

"What did you think of Morris, Hall? How did you get along with him?"

Hall rubbed his forehead and nodded. "I agree, Lieutenant. Let's not dwell on personal stuff we can't change overnight. I'll have a drink tomorrow, just not right now. I didn't like Morris one bit. He was a stuck-up, self-righteous, greasy little fucker that no one liked, least of all me. He treated me with complete contempt. I'd been a detective for a few years by the time he came along, but I'd started drinking by then and it was showing. He had this sneery, superior attitude I couldn't stand. The way Grimes and some of the other uniforms treat me? They picked it up from Morris, the prick."

"Were there ever any conduct complaints against Morris filed by women?"

Hall shook his head. "No. But some of the guys, like Grimes, Collins, and Brooks, liked to talk about his 'way with women.' That's how they like to put it. He had a 'way with women.' I may be a bachelor who wouldn't know one end of a woman from the other, Lieutenant, but I'd never treat a woman the way Morris treated them."

"Rough? Control freak? Dominating?"

Hall took two coffee mugs down from a counter. "You could say that. How do you take your coffee?"

"One sugar. Cream if you have it. Did you hear of any connection between him and Marcie Askew?"

Hall took a carton of coffee cream out of the refrigerator and put it on the table in front of Hank, followed by a sugar bowl and a spoon. "No. Nothing. But they wouldn't say anything about Marcie even if they knew. Too scared that Billy would hear them."

"Think he's been involved with women at the college?"

"Is the sky blue?" Hall took the carafe out of the coffee machine and filled Hank's mug. "It's like a joke to men around here. College women are supposed to be like these horny minks running around throwing themselves at every man they see." Hall snorted. "In their dreams." He poured his own coffee, then sat down across from Hank. "Morris didn't like women, that much was obvious."

Hank fixed his coffee and moved the carton of cream closer to Hall. "What makes you say that?"

Hall shook his head. "I take it black. Real black." He sipped and winced as it burned his lips. "He liked to screw them, sure enough, but he had no use for them otherwise. Neil wanted to start recruiting women into the job back then, just as one example, but Morris told him flat out to forget it. Had no use for the idea at all. Typical, too, that he'd promote a guy like Neil and then never listen to any of his ideas."

"Branham was promoted to deputy chief under Morris?"

Hall nodded, looking into his coffee mug. Then he met Hank's stare and shook his head. "No, don't get the wrong idea. Neil was by far the best candidate for the job. Even the mayor liked him. Neil didn't have any more use for Morris than I did, but Neil's very astute politically and knows how to keep his mouth shut. I don't know what he's told you about Morris, but there's no misplaced loyalty there. He was just as relieved as I was when the guy resigned and Billy took over."

"Branham was already deputy chief when Askew was promoted over his head?"

"People around here treat me like I'm invisible, Lieutenant. Like I don't exist. So I hear stuff I'm not always supposed to hear. When Morris quit, Blankenship came in to talk to Neil about taking over. Neil turned him down flat and said they'd be nuts to pass over Billy a second time. The mayor didn't like it, but Neil said he wanted to stay as deputy chief for a few years to learn the administrative side of the job first. Blankenship agreed and gave the job to Billy. There was no intrigue there. It happened the way it should have."

"Okay," Hank said. "Back to Morris. Is that it? Is that the only reason you say that Morris didn't like women, that he vetoed Branham's idea to recruit them to the force?"

Hall grimaced, gulping at his coffee with something just this side of desperation. "There was other stuff."

"Such as?"

"I don't know, stuff. We had a drug bust one time over on College Street. I got a call from a guy I knew with the state police saying a car load of dope was coming into town from Roanoke, their cruiser had been involved in an accident and could we make the bust for them? An informant told them it was going to be delivered to this house being rented by a couple of college kids, two young guys." Hall took another swig of coffee and closed his eyes. "I hung up the phone and told Morris.

He got this look on his face, like a predator, and I had to run after him to keep from being left behind. He didn't tell any of the officers, so there was no backup. On the way, though, he called a newspaper reporter friend of his and told him where it was happening. When we got there, we were early. His reporter friend showed up, and Morris told him where to wait so he'd get the best angles for his pictures. Then the car gets there and it's three kids. Two males and a female driving. The two males get out, go to the door of the house, and come back to the car with the two guys from the house. They open the trunk of the car, start taking bags out, and Morris springs into action."

Hall drained his coffee mug and poured himself another cup from the carafe that had been sitting close to his elbow. "Sorry if I sound a little sarcastic. I followed Morris across the street. He had his gun out and was yelling at the boys to get down on their knees with their hands on top of their heads. All this time his reporter friend was taking pictures. I took out my gun to cover them just as the girl got out of the car and started running across the lawn. Morris lit out after her and tackled her. He rolled her over and punched her four or five times. It was totally uncalled-for." Hall stared at Hank. "She was just a kid, Donaghue. Nineteen, maybe twenty. Somebody's daughter. None of them had a record, they were just kids moving weed. See, he wasn't rough with the boys. He joked around with them, made fun of them, that sort of thing, but with the girl it was nasty. Vicious. Like it was personal for some reason. At the time I wondered why he was being that way, but I didn't dare ask. I was skating on thin ice already with my own problems as it was."

"Didn't the girl file a complaint?"

Hall shook his head. "Turns out she was the daughter of a Methodist minister in Roanoke. They were so shocked they kept it as quiet as they could. Afterwards I heard they left the state altogether. Moved to California."

"Was he ever married?"

"Divorced while he was in Richmond. Married for three years. No kids, thank God."

"Anything else, Hall?"

Hall put down his coffee cup and rubbed his eyes with the heels of his hands. "Tomorrow I'll go back to drinking, Lieutenant. I heard the point you were making this afternoon loud and clear, believe me. I figured I'd stop drinking tonight just to prove to myself that I could, so that's what I'm doing right now. But don't ask me any more questions, okay? You're trying to fit Morris to your profile of Marcie's killer, and I have to admit that although at first it never occurred to me, once I think about it, it might be plausible. You might be on to something, weird as it seems. But don't ask me any more questions about what I remember about him, okay? For godsakes. Right now my brain is like a hurricane of memories. I remember every moment I spent with the guy. All these associations to things. I can't even talk about them right now. They're coming so fast I can't process them all properly. I feel dizzy. I'm gonna throw up."

He paused, hands pressed to his eyes, and sobbed. "Stop. Stop. I need a drink. Just stop."

"Isn't there medication you can take for it, Hall?"

"Yeah." Hall put his head down on the table. "In the cupboard at the end. A fresh bottle of Wild Turkey. Don't bother, though, I'll get it myself later."

Hank sat there for a long while, saying nothing, then quietly got up and let himself out.

31

Karen had never been much of a student. As a Criminal Justice major she'd struggled through the math and statistics prerequisites, obtaining the required C only through a great deal of last-minute cramming, and she hadn't done much better in the psychology and sociology courses. She'd flourished in the criminology-specific courses, however, and had graduated with an overall B average. When she entered the academy she was in her element, as though the extraneous frills had been pared away, leaving only what she considered the important stuff. She'd graduated with the second-highest grade average in her class and received her badge with a sense of pride and accomplishment. She lacked the patience for calculus or Jung's theory of archetypes, but had all the time in the world for ballistics and criminal profiling. She wasn't a brainiac like Hank, wasn't very well-read and didn't give a damn about it, but she was a smart, experienced law enforcement officer and she knew it.

Before the class, Dr. Jane Morley introduced them to the others who'd be sitting in. Cynthia Witherspoon was the vice-president of Academic Affairs. She was about fifty, short and thin, with neat, wavy copper-colored hair and gold wire frame glasses. She was all business and shook Karen's hand without offering a smile, but Karen saw that her hazel eyes were alert and appraising. Dr. Colleen Richardson was a young, doughy-looking blond from Pennsylvania who was the director of the Sociology department and attended all presentations given by the Criminal Justice Friday guest speakers. Professor Brogan, Marcie's photography instructor, was also there.

"Because she won't take no for an answer," Morley joked.

Brogan shrugged, a little embarrassed. "Wouldn't miss it."

"I'll try not to be boring," Karen said.

"And this is David Morris," Morley said, "the other member of our Criminal Justice faculty."

Karen saw that he was exactly as previously described, a forty-year-old former athlete with short black hair, a thin face, and pale blue eyes that looked at her with frank interest. When he shook her hand, he squeezed it twice, as though to make sure she understood how friendly he was.

"Cut yourself shaving?" Karen asked, looking at a scratch on his left cheekbone that was several days old.

His smile didn't dim as he touched it with his finger. "Must have, I guess. I don't remember."

As the sleeve of his jacket pulled down and his shirt cuff dropped, Karen saw similar marks on his wrist and the back of his hand.

Hank tapped her on the elbow. "Just got a call from Branham," he said quietly into her ear. "He wants a few minutes with us downstairs."

"We'll be right back," Karen told Morley, starting for the door.

"We're about to begin," Morley said.

"Won't be long."

They rode the elevator down to the main floor, where Branham and Detective Muncy were waiting for them. Karen found it interesting that Clarence Muncy accurately fit her mental image of him based only on the telephone conference call from Tuesday. He was about thirty, stood six feet tall, and was shaped like an eggplant. His head was shaved, and his scruffy goatee failed to hide a double chin. He wore a cheap green suit, his lace-ups were brown, and his tie was pale blue with yellow flowers on it.

"Pooch drove up to Bluefield this morning," Branham said, after the introductions were made. "Billy's sister has alibied him. Billy was up at her place on Saturday night when Marcie was killed."

"She's not gonna be the strongest witness in the world," Muncy said. "A good lawyer'd pick her apart like last Thanksgiving's turkey leftovers, but it feels right to me. I think she's telling the truth. He wasn't in Harmony when his wife was strangled."

"I gave Pooch the rundown on our interviews late yesterday," Branham said.

"You folks talked to this Hanshaw and Rudy," Muncy said, looking at Karen.

"That's right," she bristled. "You guys need to pull your head out of your ass and start looking at who got her pregnant, because that's who killed her."

"Back off, Tex," Muncy said, raising a palm, "I hear you. Neil tells me that according to the mayor's wife, David Morris sounds like a possibility."

"He is," Hank said. "We'd like to put him on the spot this morning. Apply some pressure and see what happens."

"Neil told me." Muncy frowned, shaking his head. "You really think this is a bright idea? Questioning a suspect in front of a class of

194

students?"

"Why not?" Karen replied airily. "Should be good for a laugh."

"I don't think so." Muncy stared at her. "I don't like it."

"Morris is an experienced law enforcement officer," Hank said. "If you put him into a room and try to sweat him he'll ride it out. He'll pull a shell around himself and look for mistakes in everything you do. This way we might catch him off-guard. He'll be in his hail-fellow-well-met university instructor persona, not his tough-guy cop persona. Maybe we can exploit that."

"Or we can wait for the lab to finish processing all the evidence we gathered and see if his DNA matches. Helluva lot simpler."

"What if you come up empty?" Hank looked at him. "What if the tissue under her fingernails was her own, and you don't have any conclusive physical evidence?"

Karen was about to mention the scratches she'd just seen on Morris's face and wrist, then kept her mouth shut. She *wanted* this chance to put the screws to the sonofabitch in front of an audience. Muncy hadn't seen Morris and wouldn't know that it was probable the bastard had donated his DNA to the investigation. She balled up her fists and clenched her teeth.

"I still don't like it," Muncy complained. "It could be a serious violation of his rights."

"We'll manage it," Hank said.

Muncy looked at the ceiling.

"Give it a chance, Pooch," Branham said. "Pull the plug if you don't like where it's going."

Muncy reached out and punched the elevator button. "Let's get on with it."

Morley's third-year Criminal Investigation class consisted of sixteen students, ten male and six female. It wasn't a very big room, maybe twenty-five by twenty-five feet, with a whiteboard and projection screen on the wall and the instructor's lectern at the front. Each row consisted of two student tables seating two students each. There were five rows altogether. Male students sat with male students, and female with female. Morley began the class by introducing the guests, who'd lined up along the back wall. Then she introduced Karen.

As the class clapped, Karen walked up to the lectern and leaned on it with a casual hand.

"Thanks. Glad to be here. Y'all are in third year, so by now you've probably studied all that stuff about communication, verbal and non-verbal behavior, body language, listening skills, the difference between open questions and closed questions, blah blah blah, drone drone drone."

She stared at them as they got the titters out of their system. "It's all good stuff. All very important. Your professor here, Dr. Morley, said you've been reviewing the difference between an interview and an interrogation, and she wanted me to talk about interrogation techniques, so that's what I'm here for.

"She would've made it clear to you already if you're just interviewing some guy, if you're just asking him some questions to see if he knows something important, then you'll use a bit of technique on him to make him comfortable enough to talk. Make a little small talk, check him out, ask good questions, remember his answers. If you're like my lieutenant back there, you'll be sure to take notes while you're at it."

She waited for the ripple of laughter to pass. "But if you're interrogating somebody, you've only got one thing on your mind. You think he did it, or else he knows who did it, and he's gonna tell you what he knows or there's gonna be hell to pay."

She saw a look of concern jump across the face of Colleen Richardson and gave her an aw-shucks, down-home Texas shit-eatin' grin. "Don't get me wrong. I know everybody's got their constitutional rights and all that stuff, and I know a confession has to be admissible in court or else it's no good. I get that, and so does every other experienced law enforcement officer out there. I'm just trying to make it clear that an interrogation isn't some polite conversation over tea and biscuits. You're trying to break somebody's will. You're trying to outsmart him, out-think him, and out-tough him. It's you against him. You're the good guy and he's the scumbag. Show one sign of weakness and he's gonna eat your damned lunch."

Karen let go of the lectern and walked around it. "I guess a lot of people don't like the word 'interrogation.' I can see your Sociology professor is one of them, just from the look on her face."

Several students turned around to glance at Colleen Richardson at the back of the room.

"Frankly, Detective," Richardson said, frowning, "you're right. I don't like the word. If it were me, we'd be discussing interviews and advanced interviews. I'll even bet that the rooms in which you question people back in Maryland are called interview rooms. Isn't that right?"

Karen nodded. "That's exactly what they're called, and we do a lot of interviews in them, too. Only now and again, we get some bastard we just *know* was there with the guy who shot the eighty-year-old woman in her studio apartment and stole all the money she'd hid in her underwear drawer, and we need to get a little firm with him. Just a little firm. Make it clear that we've got his sorry ass right where we want it, and he needs to cough up his accomplice or it won't go well for him.

So we interrogate him. Firm-like."

She sat down on the corner of the nearest table. The two students sitting at that table were female, one a redhead and the other, sitting closest, had long, glossy brown hair pulled back into a ponytail. Karen looked for a moment at the one with the ponytail.

"Being good at interrogation is a skill," she went on, turning back to the class. "It takes practice. You need experience with all that stuff I mentioned at first, reading body language, noticing what their eyes are doing when they talk, listening to the words they use to tell their lies, and there aren't a lot of people who are really good at it right out of the box. It'll take some time for you to develop your own style with it, so stay patient. One thing I've found is that it goes real well if you work with a good partner."

She pointed at Hank. "Take the lieutenant. No offense to anybody else in the room, but you'll never find a sharper, smarter cop than him. I've been real lucky to be able to work with him, and we've grilled a few suspects in our time. It's probably not hard to guess that our approaches are completely different. He takes notes, he likes to sit in the weeds, be analytical, surprise them with an angle they don't expect. I'm more up front and in their faces. Not good-cop bad-cop because everybody's seen that on TV a hundred times and it gets tired real fast. But it's a question of rhythm. Right, Lou?"

"That's right," Hank said. "It's important to reach a point with a suspect where he's going to be willing to tell you what really happened. Sometimes he'll feel more comfortable with only one other person in the room, he'll even be willing to establish what he thinks of as a relationship of trust with you, and that's often easier to do if there's only one officer asking the questions. But what Detective Stainer is describing in a two-officer scenario is entirely true, and as she says, it works best if you avoid the good-cop bad-cop thing altogether and use something called the expressive-cop silent-cop cycle. That's where one officer establishes a relationship with the suspect and holds his attention at all times while the other officer just listens and takes notes. Then at an appropriate moment, the two officers trade roles. The second officer then uses a different technique or introduces a completely new set of questions."

"You get a sense of when it's time to slap hands and jump in," Karen said. "Maybe he's sticking to his story and needs shaking up. Maybe you want to catch him off guard and get him to answer something he thinks is harmless but is going to take him somewhere he's not gonna like."

"Isn't a two-officer interview just an expression of police paranoia?" asked the redhead. "A mistaken belief that everything you do has to be corroborated by another officer or it won't be found to be credible in court? Isn't a partner really just a crutch that limits a police officer's initiative and self-confidence?"

Karen twisted around to look at her. "I'll bet you don't believe in having a study buddy, either." She looked at the brunette with the ponytail. "Are you her study buddy?"

The brunette shook her head.

"Thought not." Karen kept her eyes on the brunette, letting her feel a little of the heavy weight of an experienced law enforcement officer's stare. "You're Rachel Meese, aren't you?"

The brunette nodded.

"Thought I recognized you. You almost ran me down the other day."

Rachel blushed furiously. "Sorry about that."

"No problem." Karen moved her gaze back to the redhead. "No, to answer your question, a two-officer interview, or interrogation, is not an expression of police paranoia; it's just teamwork, pure and simple. Nothing says you can't question a suspect all by your bitty self, particularly since most interrogations are recorded nowadays anyway. Sometimes your partner's busy in the other room talking to your suspect's buddy. But if you've got the opportunity to work a suspect with a good partner, you'd be nuts to pass it up. That's all I'm saying. A good partner is almost as important as a reliable firearm." She winked at Hank. "Almost."

She casually stood up and moved back to the lectern. "Let me give you an example. The lieutenant and I were recently assisting Deputy Chief Branham in the investigation of a murder here in Harmony. At that time we had occasion to interview, and I do mean interview in this case, Professor Brogan, who's with us this morning. Right, Professor?"

At the back of the room, Brogan looked mortified. "Uh, um, yes it is."

"Right. Now, we don't need to get into too many specifics because the case has been transferred to Detective Muncy, who's standing right there, and it's up to him now what should or shouldn't be said about it. But we've got a good opportunity here to get some feedback from a real, live interviewee." Karen gestured at Brogan. "So why don't you tell the class what you thought of our interviewing technique, Professor Brogan. Did you find it effective?"

"Um, yes, I suppose so."

"The victim, Marcie Askew, happened to have been in one of the professor's photography classes a while ago," Karen told the class. She looked at Muncy. "I suppose it's all right to tell them that, isn't it, Detective?"

Muncy shrugged grumpily.

"How did you feel," Karen asked, turning her gaze back to Brogan, "when we were asking you all those questions? Stressed? Pressured?"

Brogan looked surprised. "No. Not at all."

"You felt comfortable telling us what you knew about Marcie Askew?"

"Yes, of course."

"So apparently it was an appropriate tone for an interview," Karen said, her eyes flicking briefly at Colleen Richardson before returning to Brogan. "Who asked the questions, do you remember? Did I, or did Lieutenant Donaghue?"

"Um, uh, I think you did."

"So I was the expressive cop and the lieutenant was the silent cop, that right?"

"Yes, actually, I think that's right. I see what you mean."

Karen nodded, then shifted her posture to look at the class. "Let's try something interesting now, just for fun. A little case study to demonstrate good interrogation techniques. Let's say the lieutenant and I wanted to question two people as part of a case we're working on. Say they were brought in together but we need to question them separately."

She turned around and looked at Morley, who was sitting on a chair against the wall below the projection screen. Amused by the puzzled look on Morley's face, Karen pointed. "Let's say we're gonna start with you, Professor Morley. How about that?"

"Uh," Morley frowned.

The class clapped their encouragement, as Karen knew they would. There wasn't a student in the world that didn't enjoy seeing their teachers put on the spot now and then.

"So we're gonna start by separating them." Karen turned back to the class. "How about it, Professor Morris? Would you mind playing along with us for the fun of it? Maybe you could step out of the room for a few minutes."

Morris chuckled. "Sure. Why not?" He walked toward the door at the front of the classroom.

"Hold on a sec." Karen snapped her fingers at one of the male students in the back row, a tall, muscular-looking kid with short blond hair and red cheeks. "You, there. What's your name?"

"Adamson," the kid replied.

"All right, Adamson. How about you play the role of a uniformed police officer for us? Your job is to stay with this here person of interest." She waved airily at Morris. "Keep him on site until we call for you to bring him into the interrogation room. Sorry, interview room. Meaning in here. Okay?"

"Sure." Adamson stood up and shuffled over to Morris. He was at least four inches taller than his teacher. "Should I handcuff him?"

"Maybe later," Karen said over the laughter of the class.

When Morris and Adamson closed the door behind them, Karen beckoned to Morley. "C'mon over here, Doc. We'll do this right." She looked at Rachel Meese and the redhead next to her. "Think you two could give us your table for a few minutes?"

"All right," said Rachel, closing her notebook and standing up.

Karen looked at the redhead. "What's your name, darlin'?"

"Brenda McCoy."

"Brenda, do you mind if you and Rachel just stand there against the wall while we do this?"

"Not at all."

Karen gave the two students a moment to gather up their things and move over to the wall, then she dragged one of the chairs around to the front of the table and gestured to Morley. "Have a seat, Doc."

"Lawyer up!" one of the male students chirped from the back.

Morley smiled bravely as the class laughed. She sat down in the seat facing the class as Karen sat down across from her.

"Anybody who wants to move closer," Karen said over her shoulder, "feel free. Since this is a practical demonstration, you'll want to make sure you can see and hear."

She waited a few moments as movement started behind her. In her peripheral vision as she kept her eyes on Morley's face, she saw Hank drape his haunch over the corner of the table next to her. Branham and Muncy slid up the wall to stand next to Rachel and Brenda. A few other students also moved closer.

"Now, Doc," Karen began, "we had a brief interview a couple days ago, that right?"

"Yes." Morley frowned. "I'm not sure I'm comfortable with—"

"Relax, it's just a demo. Get into the role, have some fun with it. If I'm not mistaken, you have law enforcement experience, isn't that so?"

Morley hesitated. "Yes, that's correct."

"What kind of experience was that?"

"I was with the Arlington PD. I made sergeant there."

"What made you leave the job and get into the academic world? Too much stress?"

"No! I love teaching. It was a golden opportunity, the pay was double what I was making, and are you actually taking notes of what I'm saying?"

Hank looked up, feigning surprise. "Of course I am." He wagged his pen in the air. "Isn't it supposed to be a practical demonstration, Dr. Morley?"

"Oh, for crying out loud."

"Doc, try to stay on point," Karen snapped. "Did you know Marcie Askew?"

"No. Yes. I knew her by sight, of course. But we weren't friends or anything."

"Ever socialize with her? Have a drink with her in town or anything like that?"

"No, of course not."

"Were you aware of any relationships she might have had with anyone here on campus?"

"Relationships?" Morley folded her arms across her chest. "What do you mean?"

"C'mon, Doc," Karen scoffed, "you know what a relationship is. You've probably had a few, yourself. Did Marcie Askew have a relationship with anyone here on campus?"

"Not that I know of. I didn't know her well. I told you that already."

"So you're saying you don't know anyone here who was having a sexual relationship with the victim?"

Morley stared at her. The classroom was silent. "No."

"Were you aware," Hank interjected, "that she was having an affair with your colleague, David Morris?"

Several students gasped. One of the male students laughed. Morley glared up at Hank. "What kind of a question is that?"

"Answer it," Hank said. "Did you know that Marcie Askew and David Morris were having an affair?"

"I don't find this at all appropriate."

"What would you say," Karen said, "if I told you we have eyewitnesses who swear they saw Morris and the deceased meeting up in bars late at night going as far back as last March, sucking beer in the corner and gnawing on each other's tongue?"

"Oh really," Cynthia Witherspoon protested, speaking up for the first time. "I'm all for case studies but I think you're carrying this too far. I agree with Dr. Morley. This is not at all appropriate. Please move to a hypothetical case study and leave faculty out of it."

Detective Muncy cleared his throat. "I'd like to hear her answer the question."

"Go ahead," Karen prompted Morley, "answer the question. Did you know Dave Morris was banging the wife of the chief of police?"

Morley opened her mouth, closed it again, and looked at

Witherspoon.

"This is hardly necessary or appropriate, Detective," Witherspoon said to Muncy. "As vice-president of Academic Affairs, I think I should call the sheriff and voice my concern."

"Call the sheriff if you want," Muncy said uncomfortably, "but I need to hear Professor Morley answer the question."

"It's absurd," Morley said. "The idea that David was involved with Marcie Askew."

"And yet we've got witnesses," Karen said blandly, leaning back in her chair.

"They're deluded, or lying."

"What about someone else on campus?" Hank pressed, leaning forward. "Has Dave Morris been having an affair with anyone else here? We heard there was someone on staff he was involved with."

In the silence that followed, Erica Brogan's sharp intake of breath from the back of the classroom was heard by everyone.

Karen glanced over her shoulder. "Sounds like a yes from your friend back there, Doc. How about it? Were you and Morris getting it on?"

"I don't have to answer that question, or any other question, so I'm not saying anything else," Morley said, standing up. "There's nothing more to talk about, and this class *is* over."

"Should we treat you as a suspect, Dr. Morley?" Hank asked.

"No! This is ridiculous."

"Did you find out that Morris was screwing Marcie Askew?" Karen pressed. "Did you get jealous and arrange to meet her at Gerry's Bar to tell her to stay away from your man? Did things get out of hand? Did you kill her without meaning to?"

"No, no, NO!" Morley was shouting.

Karen waited a beat. "Were you and Morris involved?"

"Yes!" Morley screamed, losing her cool. "All right! Fine! Yes! But I didn't know he was having an affair with her, too! Although it figures, given his overblown ego. He thinks he has a divine right to screw everything in a skirt. Son of a *bitch*!"

"There, that wasn't so hard, was it?" Karen soothed.

"Jane?" Witherspoon stepped forward. "I think this should end right now."

Hank stood up and touched her lightly on the elbow. "Please take a seat, Mrs. Witherspoon."

Karen jumped to her feet and clapped her hands together. "Great! Okay, now it's time to bring in the other person of interest, don't you think?"

"Sure," Hank said.

Branham walked past Brenda and Rachel. He opened the classroom door. He beckoned and Morris walked in, Adamson right behind him. Morris looked around, a little puzzled by the supercharged silence in the classroom.

Karen stepped forward. "How'd it go, Officer Adamson? He give you any trouble?"

"Nope." Adamson pushed out his lower lip.

"Did he say anything while y'all were waiting?"

"Yep. We talked about an assignment that's due in his class next week. I asked him a few questions about it."

There were a few nervous titters.

"Anything about today's class?" Karen asked. "The presentation or the case study we're running right now?"

"Nope."

"Go sit up there," Karen said to Morley, pointing at the chair at the front of the classroom. "Morris, come and sit down here. Hurry up, let's not drag our ass, huh?"

Karen shooed Morley away and got Morris seated. She stayed beside him, on his side of the table, staring down at him.

"So, Dave, we've been asking your co-worker there, Jane Morley, a few questions about the recent murder of Marcie Askew. Now it's your turn. Did you know Marcie Askew?"

"Don't say anything!" Rachel Meese suddenly shouted. "They know about you and her!"

"Ah, Christ," Karen muttered.

"Be quiet right now," Detective Muncy ordered, stepping in front of Rachel and leveling a finger at her, "or I'll have you charged with obstruction of justice." He turned back to the class. "That goes for the rest of you, as well."

"What is this?" Morris asked mildly. "Seems kind of odd for a case study."

Karen looked at Muncy. "You want to do this?"

"Yes." Muncy sat down across the table from Morris as Karen walked over to stand next to Rachel Meese.

"Professor Morris," Muncy began, "I need you to understand that we're done with the case study thing. I'm going to ask you real questions about the homicide of Marcie Askew. Are you willing to answer those questions now of your own free will?"

"This is definitely irregular. What's your name again?"

"Detective Clarence Muncy from the Tazewell County Sheriff's Office." Muncy tapped the badge pinned to the wallet draped over the breast pocket of his jacket. "Detective Stainer and Lieutenant Donaghue have been assisting in the investigation of the homicide of

Marcie Askew, but right now I'm going to be asking the questions. You can answer them here or we can go to Tazewell and you can answer them there in private. Your choice."

"I've got nothing to hide," Morris said.

"Since you're teaching criminology," Muncy went on, "you should be aware of your Miranda rights, but how about if I remind you of them now?"

Morris laughed.

Muncy recited Morris's rights. "Now, am I to understand you're waiving these rights and will answer questions here and now, or shall I place you under arrest and transport you to Tazewell where you'll answer them there?"

"This is bizarre." He looked around the class. "I hope you're all taking notes. There's an important dividing line between custodial and non-custodial questioning, and it'll be on the final exam. Pay close attention."

"I think this should be done in Tazewell," Muncy said, standing up.

"You might be right," Hank said, sliding off the table and putting his notebook away, ready to assist.

"Don't be stupid," Morris said, waving at them with a superior expression on his face. "I'll answer your questions. I knew Marcie. That's about it. We may have spoken once or twice in the halls." He looked at Rachel Meese, standing against the wall next to Karen. "I'm not sure what Rachel thinks she knows, but she's obviously confused about things." He rubbed the side of his nose and yawned.

"Did you ever meet with Mrs. Askew late at night in a public place?" Muncy asked.

"No, of course not."

"We have eyewitnesses who tell us different."

"They're mistaken." He looked again in the direction of Rachel Meese.

"About recognizing a former chief of police in a community this small?" Hank scoffed. "Not a chance. And no, Miss Meese is not the eyewitness."

Karen stirred. "Did Dr. Morley, your other squeeze, find out you were bonking Mrs. Askew? Did she go ballistic on you? Threaten to reduce the competition?"

"Good lord," Morris said, looking around until he found Cynthia Witherspoon. "Don't you think this has gone too far?"

Witherspoon chewed her lower lip. "I don't know what to think right now, David."

"Answer Detective Stainer's question, Professor Morris,"

Muncy said, sitting down again. "Did Dr. Morley find out you were having an affair with Mrs. Askew?"

"Who says I was having an affair with Mrs. Askew?"

"Were you?"

"It's completely ridiculous."

"Are you having an affair with Dr. Morley?"

"That's personal and private and none of anyone's business."

"I'll take that as a yes," Muncy said. "Were you at Gerry's Bar on the night of Saturday, September 17, between eleven and midnight?"

"I might have been."

"You were," Hank said. "I saw you there. You arrived at 11:25 p.m., drank a beer, and stepped outside for a smoke at 11:35 p.m. You were taking out your pack of cigarettes as you walked to the door."

"If you say so," Morris said dismissively.

"I say so." Hank shoved his hands in his pockets. "You stepped outside for a cigarette and didn't come back in. Why'd you leave?"

"To go home. I went to bed. I was tired."

"What size shoes do you wear?"

Morris rolled his eyes. "Eleven. Why?"

Muncy cleared his throat. "We found size eleven shoe prints leading from the spot where Mrs. Askew was murdered down to the spot in the ravine where her body was dumped. Care to comment on that?"

"No. Do you have any idea how many people wear size eleven shoes?"

"Would you be willing to provide us with the shoes you wore Saturday night to Gerry's?"

"Not without a warrant, I wouldn't."

"Dr. Morley," Karen said suddenly, stepping toward the front of the classroom where Jane Morley sat with her hand in front of her mouth, "the victim, Marcie Askew, was manually strangled. That's a very violent, brutal act. The killer had both hands around her throat and he squeezed hard enough to crush her larynx. There was enough light back there for him to watch her die. To see the life empty out of her eyes. The autopsy also showed that Mrs. Askew had a series of injuries dating back more than six months that correspond to a pattern of physical abuse. A broken wrist, a separated shoulder, a cracked jaw, loose teeth. Did David Morris ever hit you? Has he been physically abusive during your affair?"

Morley stared at Morris, tears rolling down her cheeks.

"Oh Jane," Brogan said from the back of the room. "Oh, no."

Rachel Meese began to sob.

"Did you break Mrs. Askew's wrist, Morris?" Muncy demanded.

"Did you ask her husband that question?" Morris retorted. "Everyone knows what kind of temper he's got."

"He denies it," Muncy said, "and the funny thing is, I believe him."

"You shouldn't,' Morris scoffed. "You've got him in custody already. You're wasting your time talking to me; you should be practicing your interrogation skills on him. God knows they need improvement."

"Did you know Marcie was pregnant?" Karen interjected. "And that she wanted to have the baby even though it was a huge risk to her life? Did you know that her husband was sterile, and it'd be obvious someone else was the father? Did you go to the bar Saturday night because she wanted to talk to you about it? Did you figure out she was going to refuse to abort it? Did you find her at the back of the bar? Did you argue with her, lose your temper, shut her up with your hands around her throat, then just keep on going because it felt so good? Is that how you got those scratches? From her trying to pry your hands away from her neck? Are we gonna find your DNA under her fingernails?"

"You bastard!" Morley shouted, launching herself at Morris.

Hank intercepted her and pushed her back against the projection screen. Cynthia Witherspoon and Colleen Richardson materialized beside him, trying to calm her down. Behind him, everyone seemed to be on their feet and talking at once. Hank turned around to see what was happening.

"Leave him alone!" Rachel shouted at Karen. "Stop trying to trap him!"

Adamson shouldered his way up to Muncy. "Back off Professor Morris right now! Just back off and leave him alone!"

"Stand aside, kid," Muncy warned.

Adamson put his hands out, as though to shove Muncy aside.

"Don't do it," Muncy growled, putting his hand on the butt of his gun.

Branham stepped forward to block another male student from joining Adamson.

"You're just being mean and vindictive!" Rachel protested. "David's wonderful. He loves me and we're going away together after I graduate to start a new life away from this hole!"

"Rachel," Karen said, putting a hand on her arm, "calm down."

"Don't tell me to calm down! He loves me and I won't put up with you slandering him like this!"

"Oh, shut up, you stupid child!" Morley shouted across the

206

room.

"Quiet," Hank growled at her.

"Leave him alone!" Adamson ordered Muncy.

"Lou!" Karen shouted. "Do you have a twenty on Morris?"

Hank swung around. Morris was no longer in sight. Hank spent a few precious seconds hunting for him among the milling bodies in the classroom before spotting the open classroom door. He caught Karen's eye and pointed with his chin.

She nodded and turned away from Rachel.

"Muncy! Your suspect's in the wind!"

32

They wasted time looking for Morris on campus, rushing to his office, which was unoccupied, searching classrooms, lounges, the food court, and gymnasium. Officers Brooks and Louden, accompanied by Ansell Hall, arrived and joined in the search, followed about fifteen minutes later by two Tazewell deputies. Karen doubled back to the classroom to ask Rachel where Morris might have gone and found that she, too, had vanished. Students loitered in the hallway, chattering among themselves and texting the juicy news to friends. Adamson made a brief attempt to interfere with Karen's forward progress, thumping the butt of his palm into her shoulder, but a brief martial arts thumb-bending thing convinced him that Karen's mood would only get worse if he persisted in being stupid.

No one seemed to know where Rachel had gone. For the most part, they probably wouldn't tell her even if they knew. It reminded her once more of the significant gap between students taking law enforcement courses and police officers enforcing the law. These kids clearly had a lot of ground to cover before making it to the other side.

She headed for the parking lot behind the building and found Hank circling around from the north side, having had the same idea. Rachel's smart car was nowhere to be seen. Instead, they discovered Jane Morley hurrying across the lot toward her own vehicle. They caught her just as she unlocked the door and threw her purse onto the passenger seat. Karen tugged her back while Hank closed the door with his hip.

"Where is he?" Karen held the sleeve of Morley's jacket with terrier-like tenacity as Morley tried to pull away. "You called him, didn't you?"

"Let me go! Let me go or I'll sue you!"

Karen laughed. "You'll what?"

The posse approached, threading their way through the parked cars. "Dr. Morley!" Muncy called out, "stay where you are! Stainer, don't let her go!"

For a beefy guy, Muncy had good wind. When he reached them, his breathing was more or less normal. He narrowed his eyes and put his hands on his hips. "Where is he, Dr. Morley? Where'd he go?"

Muncy's deputies bracketed her meaningfully as Karen let go and moved to one side.

"You talked to him, didn't you?" Muncy prompted. "Where is he? What'd he say?"

Morley looked around at the circle of faces and sagged. "He went home. He's getting a few things and he's going to go away for a while."

"Where?" Muncy demanded. "Where's he going?"

"I don't know." Morley chewed on her bottom lip. "Meese showed up before he could tell me. He had to end the call to get rid of her."

"Meese?" Karen repeated. "Rachel Meese is there? At Morris's house?"

"Where does he live?" Hank asked.

"Route 784," Hall piped up. "Civic number 16232. It's a dead end road at the foot of the mountain."

"What the hell are we waiting for?" Karen asked.

The deputies bundled Morley into the back of their cruiser and everyone piled into their vehicles, Hall squeezing reluctantly into the back of the Firebird. As Karen burned rubber leaving the parking lot, she directed Hall to reach down behind Hank's seat for the dual strobe light. He handed it to Hank, who clipped it onto his sun visor and plugged it into the cigarette lighter. Strobes flashing, they hurried down several blocks to the ramp onto Highway 460. Karen floored it as they kept pace with Muncy's unmarked gray Impala along the highway. Eventually they reached the off-ramp leading to Route 784.

A few minutes later they found themselves at Morris's property. The road ended in a loop that allowed vehicles to escape the dead end. Morris's house sat at two o'clock on the loop, a nice two-story frame structure with a short driveway leading up to the garage. It was the only house at this end of the road.

A black Lexus sat in the driveway closest to the garage. The driver's side door of the Lexus was open. Behind the Lexus was Rachel Meese's smart car, unoccupied. In the loop, blocking the driveway behind the smart car, was the Harmony PD cruiser that Officer Brooks had driven, and behind the cruiser was Muncy's Impala. Karen pulled over onto the shoulder of the loop close to the Impala. She and Hank piled out, leaving Hall to fend for himself in the back seat.

Officer Louden stood next to the open door of the Lexus with his sidearm drawn. A chime was sounding inside the car. "It's out of gas," he said to Karen. "Key's in the ignition, that's why you hear it dinging, but it died in Park."

"Some fugitive," Karen said. "Runs out of gas in his own driveway."

"Guess he didn't check the gauge until it was too late," Hank said.

"Or was too scared to stop between the college and here in case we caught him right away." Louden pointed at the house with his weapon. "The others are inside."

"Do me a favor," Karen asked him.

"Sure."

She gestured at his Beretta. "Holster that thing before you hurt someone with it. Either take better care of it or get a new one."

Louden looked crestfallen. It was obvious he had a crush on her and was devastated by her criticism, but she was having none of it. "Take a course or something, for chrissakes. It's disgraceful."

"Yes, m'am."

Karen and Hank went up the three steps onto the small porch and through the open front door of Morris's house. In the hallway Officer Brooks turned at the sound of their footsteps. "Looks like he's gone."

Karen's eyes shot to the staircase on the left leading to the second floor, where they could hear the room-to-room search in progress.

A sheriff's deputy appeared in the doorway on the right that led into the living room. His name tag said *Charleton*. "Nobody on the main floor."

They could hear sirens approaching in the distance.

"What about the basement?" Hank asked.

Charleton shook his head. "Haven't gotten there yet. My partner's checking the garage. I just finished the kitchen."

Hank nodded at Karen. "Let's go." He squeezed between Brooks and Charleton. There was a door just before the entrance to the kitchen. He drew his gun and glanced over his shoulder. Karen was there, her SIG held at high ready. She gave him a look, wanting to precede him, but he shook his head and opened the door. The stairs leading down were dark. There was a switch on the right. He flicked the lights on.

"Police!" He called out. "Show yourself at the bottom of the stairs with your hands on top of your head! Now!"

He waited a beat; heard nothing.

"Police, Morris!" he called out again. "We're coming down! Place your hands on top of your head and keep them there!"

He went down the stairs cautiously, and as soon as possible he squatted and peeked. No one. He went down two more steps and squatted again. Nothing. He could hear the sirens outside grow loud and then stop. He went to the bottom and surveyed the basement, his gun following his eyes. Karen came down behind him and moved across the floor on his right.

The basement was small and unfinished. They saw a water heater, a stack of plastic storage tubs, cardboard boxes, a rocking chair with a broken arm, a washer and dryer, but nothing to hide behind and no one in sight. They headed back upstairs.

"Basement's clear," Hank called out as he approached the top of the stairs. "We're coming up."

Charleton eyed them as they emerged into the hallway. "Not in the garage. My partner's outside briefing the staties. It's getting crowded out there."

"Let's go see," Hank suggested, holstering his gun.

Muncy thundered down the stairs. "We're setting up a command post outside." He gestured at Karen. "Branham's upstairs; there's something he wants you to look at."

"Sure." She holstered her weapon and went upstairs as Hank followed Muncy outside.

"Stainer?" Branham called out. "That you?"

"Where are you?"

"In here."

She followed his voice into a room at the end of the hall that faced out on the front of the house. It was fixed up as a study with a glass-and-aluminum desk holding a computer and printer, a bookshelf holding catalogs and text books, a green filing cabinet, and a metal gun cabinet, the door of which stood open. Branham stood in front of the gun cabinet with his arms folded. He turned around and raised an eyebrow.

"Take a look."

"It's empty," Karen said.

"It is. Also expensive. A Browning gun safe; costs more than a grand. Combination lock, optional dehumidifier, optional pistol rack. My brother-in-law bought one like this to reward himself for making it to forty in one piece."

Karen stepped up next to him for a closer look. There were wire fixtures on the inside of the safe door intended to hold long guns. They were empty. The interior of the safe was divided into slots on the right to store two more long guns—empty—and shallow shelves on the left to store ammunition, binoculars, or other such items—also empty. At the top was a shelf that held the optional pistol rack. Empty. "So what do you figure was in here?"

"Hard to say for sure but maybe you can tell," Branham replied, pointing behind the desk. "Look."

Karen crouched down to look at several rifle rounds on the floor. Morris had evidently dropped the box, spilling the rounds on the floor, grabbed most of them, and left the rest. She pointed at one of the cartridges. "Three-seventy-five Remington Ultra Mag. Nasty."

They heard several more vehicles arrive outside. Branham folded his arms across his chest. "For big game, right?"

Karen looked at him. "You could stop an elephant with one, if you were brainless enough to want to do that kind of shit."

"All right. You're the expert. What kind of rifle does he have?"

"I don't know, but there aren't a lot of possibilities. Remington or Savage, basically. The Remington 700 XCR. That's a center fire bolt action extreme condition rifle. Helluva recoil."

"I don't know much about long guns," Branham said, "but I figured you would."

"I'm into handguns," Karen said, "but my brother Delbert's a hunting nut and the XCR's on his Christmas list."

"What kind of range are we talking about?"

Karen stood up. "Everything else here looks high end, so he's probably got a high-end scope, too. Range? At two hundred yards the .375's like you just fired it. At three hundred yards, with a real good shooter, still no problem for accuracy or punching power. A great shooter? Farther."

Branham grimaced. "Let's go downstairs. We need to know where he's gone."

"Maybe the cavalry's already got it figured out for us."

Outside they found the loop crammed with vehicles. A folding table had been set up on Morris's front lawn. A crowd stood around it as someone unrolled full-sized topographical maps.

Karen found Hank and rapped his elbow. "When did the circus hit town?"

"Sheriff Steele's been working the phones." Hank glanced at Branham. "Called everybody except the Navy." He gestured at a van and trailer nearest to them on the loop. "State police tactical operations team."

They watched an all-terrain vehicle back out of the trailer. "They brought a canine unit with them, too. They're behind the house checking the shed. The other van and trailer are from the Forest Service. That's the woman with the maps. Her partner's bringing out their ATV."

"They figure he went up the ridge," Branham said.

Hank nodded. "Shed doors were found open with fresh tire tracks leading out and up that way." He pointed south toward the ridge. "Muncy's theory is he was blocked by Rachel, ran out of gas in the car while they argued, knew he couldn't escape pursuit on the highway in that little thing of hers, and decided to get to higher ground."

Branham took a few steps across the lawn, shielding his eyes with his hand as he stared at the ridge behind them. "If he went all the way to the top, he could conceivably follow the trails right over the other side to Route 61. Maybe he's thinking he could flag down a car over there."

"Is that possible?" Hank asked.

Branham turned to look at him. "Depends on whether he's decided to run or turn and fight."

"He might have quite an arsenal with him," Karen told Hank. "Definitely a long-range hunting rifle with big game rounds. Maybe other long guns as well, and handguns. He's packing."

"Sounds like he might hole up and try to fight it out, at least short term." Hank put his hands in his pockets. "The state police have a Cessna flying up from Abington that's going to do a recon, and they also have a helicopter that'll get here in a couple of hours. No expense spared on this one."

They watched the Forest Service ATV back out of the trailer.

"They're fixing to go up there after him," Karen observed.

Muncy rounded the house with the dog handler and dog and a state police detective. While the others headed toward the command post, Muncy veered over to Branham.

"We were concentrating on Rachel Meese," he said, hands on his hips. "The dog showed some interest up to the shed behind the house, then nothing else. It's a poured cement floor, several years old, no signs of having been disturbed. We went all over the back around there and no sign of her, no signs of digging, nothing. We figure she's still alive and with him."

"Voluntarily?" Branham asked.

"That's the five-dollar question." Muncy folded his arms. "We have to treat it as a potential hostage situation unless something tells us otherwise."

"Sounds like the best way to play it," Hank said.

"Two empty gas cans in the shed," Muncy said.

"You'd figure he'd have put it into the car," Hank said.

"I checked and both cans are dry," Muncy said. "It probably would have been a good idea to keep a supply on hand, you know, for emergencies."

Karen shook her head. "What a tool."

Muncy introduced them to the crowd around the table, which included Forest Service officers Ann Taylor and Jim Billings, Team Leader Kevin Stanley of the state police tactical operations team, state

Tactical Officer Bill White, a counter-sniper, and state police Detective Justin Savage.

"We're going to recon up the slope a bit," Stanley said. He thumped his finger on the topographical map spread out on the table and weighted down at opposite corners with fluorescent yellow portable radios. "There's a trail running up this gully that we think he may have used. We're going to take one of the ATVs and see if we can find his tracks. Then we can spot the aviation unit for their fly-over."

"I'll drive," Jim Billings said. "I can take one of your guys with me."

"That's okay," Stanley replied. "If he sets an illegal fire we'll let you know. Otherwise it's a police matter and we'll handle it."

Billings looked at him. "What the hell kind of an attitude is that?"

"Tell Jackson to bring the ATV over," Stanley said to Bill White, ignoring Billings.

Muncy held up his hand. "Wait a minute. It wouldn't hurt to have Billings make the first run up there, since he knows the trails and can help figure out where Morris is going."

"I'm going to have Jackson and White do the recon," Stanley said calmly, "because that's what they're trained to do."

Muncy rolled his eyes. "We've already had this conversation. Your captain agreed that the sheriff's office had jurisdiction, and Sheriff Steele has placed me in operational command. Once we've got him located, I agree that your team will take point, but right now I don't see the problem with the Forest Service guy driving a goddamned fucking ATV up to the foot of that gully for a look around. Which one of your men will ride with him?"

Stanley turned away. "Jackson!"

One of the uniformed men standing around a state police SUV trotted across the lawn. He had a Colt M4 rifle slung over his shoulder. He was a tall, slender African-American in his mid-twenties with a trimmed mustache and an expectant expression.

"Ride with Billings, here," Stanley ordered, "and do a recon up toward that gully. We want to pick up his trail and figure out where he's headed. We'll have a fly-over shortly and then we'll have a better idea if he's holed up or what the fuck. If you see him, do *not* engage. Understood? Just report in and we'll take it from there."

Jackson nodded.

Billings picked up one of the fluorescent yellow portable radios and handed it to Jackson. "Use this. More reliable than yours." He looked meaningfully at the portable radio that Jackson wore on his left hip.

Jackson looked at Stanley.

"Take the fucking radio and get moving," Stanley snapped.

Hank caught Karen's eye and nodded in the direction of the driveway. Detective Hall was sitting sideways in the front seat of the Harmony police cruiser, his feet outside and his elbow resting on the steering wheel. He was chatting through the cage with Jane Morley, who was still confined in the back seat.

Karen rolled her eyes.

They left the mob gathered around the table and strolled across the lawn. Hall looked up without expression as they stopped in front of him.

"What's her take on it?" Hank asked.

Hall slid out of the driver's seat and quietly closed the door. "She says there's a cabin or shack up there that he uses occasionally during hunting season. Been there a long time, apparently abandoned. Morris fixed it up for his own use. It's sitting on the edge of a clearing looking down into the gully. He took her up there once. He keeps supplies and stuff in a footlocker inside the cabin."

"Does she think he might try to cross the ridge and hit the highway on the other side?"

"She doesn't know. She says he isn't the kind of guy you feel comfortable asking a lot of questions. He was quick with his hand if she said something he didn't like."

They looked up at the sound of a light aircraft passing over the house in the direction of the ridge.

"Cessna 182," Hall said, shielding his eyes to follow it into the distance. "The state aviation unit has four of them, last I heard. Four-seater, maximum speed of 150 knots, a ceiling of about 18,000 feet, and a range of over a thousand miles."

"It's like hanging out with Mr. Spock," Karen said.

"He told her about it," Hall said casually, his eyes slowly meeting hers.

She stared at him. "You mean Morris? He confessed to her? When?"

"When she called him."

They waited, but Hall continued to look at Karen without expression.

"Come on, Hall," Hank urged.

"You think I'm such a screw-up," Hall said to Karen. "I couldn't possibly detect like a big-city pro like you."

Karen snorted. "What the fuck?"

"Hall," Hank said, stepping between them, "she's an equal-opportunity misanthrope. Don't take it personally. What'd he tell her?"

Hall shrugged. "He went there Saturday night after Marcie called and wanted to meet him. He had a beer, like you said, expecting her to show up inside. When she didn't, he went out and found her around the back. I assume she'd gone back there to avoid being seen by anyone else after deciding Brother Charles was going to be a no-show."

"And?"

"She told him she'd decided to have the baby."

"So he already knew she was pregnant," Karen said.

"Yeah. He insisted she have an abortion, she refused, they argued. She started to get loud and, according to Dr. Morley, Morris just wanted to keep her quiet. Then she hit him, and he lost his temper."

"Some temper," Hank said.

"Yeah, consistent with his pattern of abuse." Hall leaned back against the cruiser. "He claimed to Morley it was accidental, that she scratched and fought him, and he was just trying to subdue her."

"Bullshit," Karen said.

"Yeah. I agree."

They wandered back across the lawn toward Muncy, who took a portable radio from Stanley. He raised it to his ear as he stared at the Cessna, which was inching across the horizon above the ridge.

"Tell him to look for a cabin or shack," Hank said.

Muncy frowned at him. "What?"

"Hall was talking to Morley," Hank explained. "She told him there's a cabin or something up there that Morris is known to use." He turned to Hall. "About how far up do you think it is?"

Hall shrugged. "Hard to say. She said it took about twenty minutes to get there on the ATV. Climbing up like that you wouldn't be going very fast. It's just hard to say for sure."

Muncy turned away and relayed the information to the Cessna. He received a reply and stepped over to the table. "Taylor, you know of anything up there that would fit the bill?"

"Where are we talking?" Taylor asked. "It's a big mountain."

Hall shook his head. "She couldn't give me specifics. About twenty minutes from here on the ATV, that's the best she could do. The edge of a clearing looking down into the gully."

"Not much help. That could be anywhere." She started to pore over the map, Stanley on one side and a state police detective on the other.

The radio crackled. "Command, this is AU-3. Got a visual on a structure, turning now to approach."

"AU-3, copy that," Muncy said. "Approach with caution.

Suspect is armed and dangerous."

"Roger that."

They waited for several long moments until the radio crackled again. "Command, this is AU-3. Got a visual on what looks like a red all-terrain vehicle parked outside the cabin. Someone just stepped outside. Stand by and we'll make another pass."

"Copy," Muncy said. "Proceed with caution."

"Will he fire at the plane?" Taylor asked.

"How would I know?" Muncy growled.

"I've got a visual on two individuals," the spotter in the Cessna radioed back after a few moments. "They're moving to the edge of the clearing where it looks down into the gully."

Muncy asked for the coordinates and Taylor quickly found the spot on the map. "Right here. Elevation at that spot is about 4,000 feet, roughly 240 feet from the top." She slid her finger down the map. "We're at 3,120 feet here."

"Bit of a climb," Hank said.

They all jumped as the fluorescent yellow radio sitting on the corner of the map sputtered to life.

"We're taking fire! Ann, are you there? Come in!"

Taylor snatched up the radio. "Billings, what's happening?"

"We're taking fire, we're taking fire! The state trooper's been hit, we need backup!"

"Jesus Christ!" Stanley exploded. He spun around and slapped White on the arm. "Bring the ATV over here. You and I are going up there."

"Jim!" Taylor yelled, "What's happening?"

"The trooper's okay," Billings replied, more calmly now. "The shot barely grazed him on the right arm just above the elbow. I dressed it and I think the bleeding's almost stopped. He's okay. We've taken shelter behind the ATV. Send backup to get us out of here!"

"Are they still shooting at you?"

"No, it's stopped. There were a couple of other shots but they missed. Since then we haven't moved–"

The rest was lost in the growling of the state ATV as White drove up to the table to pick up Stanley. Taylor frowned and waved him off, turning away. "Repeat, Jim! Repeat last!"

Stanley yelled at White to kill the motor on the ATV.

"–said we haven't moved since the last shot was fired a couple of minutes ago and there's been nothing since. The trooper's conscious and talking. He's okay. It was almost a complete miss."

"Suppressing fire," Karen said.

"What?" Stanley looked at her.

"Suppressing fire. He's just pinning them down. Not trying for the kill."

"He shot my man! How the hell do you figure that to be suppressing fire?"

"He's dealing with a helluva recoil," Karen shrugged. "Could be he was trying to disable the vehicle with his first shot and missed. The other shots are just to keep them from moving up any farther."

"Command, this is AU-3," Muncy's radio came to life again as the Cessna checked in. "We're taking fire and are withdrawing at this time to a safer distance."

"AU-3, copy that," Muncy replied. "Were you hit?"

"Ah, roger, Command, we heard a little thunk somewhere aft. No problems presently but I had a visual on a suspect at the edge of the clearing and he was pointing a rifle at us."

"Copy, AU-3. Get to safety and stand by."

Stanley looked around. "Williams!"

The dog handler hurried over.

"White and I are going up the mountain. I need you to handle comm and liaison. Get EMS out here right away for Jackson. He's coming back down with a gunshot wound."

"Hang on," Muncy said. "Just what do you plan on doing up there?"

"Look," Stanley growled, "we're too far away here to be effective." He stabbed a finger at the map. "We're here. We need to be up here." He poked again. "We move the command post, extract my wounded officer, and bring him back down here to the highway for transport, then effect our hostage rescue. You and the Forest Service stay down here and meet EMS when they arrive, contain the media if they show, all that."

Muncy shook his head. "Not me. I'm going up there."

"I'll stay here," Branham told Muncy. "Your deputies can stay with me for crowd control."

"I like it," state police Detective Savage said. He turned to Taylor. "How do we get up there? Drive?"

"I wouldn't take the SUVs off-road here," Taylor replied. "If we're moving forward we'll have to use the ATVs."

"We've got two," Stanley said. "We'll have to shuttle it. When we get there we'll send Billings back on his. That'll give us three."

"Lou," Karen said, tapping Hank lightly on the arm.

Hank followed her away from the discussion around the table. A car was approaching at high speed on the highway. "Media?"

Karen shook her head. "Betcha five bucks it's not."

They strolled down to the end of the driveway, watching the

car approach.

"Poor judgment," Hank said quietly.

"What's that?"

"Poor judgment on my part." Hank ran a knuckle across his mustache, eyes on the car. "I should have let Muncy take him to Tazewell. He should have been questioned in a controlled environment. Now lives are at risk unnecessarily."

Karen made a noise. "Disagree, Lou. You told Muncy if he put him in a little room with no windows he'd just tough it out and give them nothing, and you were right. If they come up empty on the physical evidence, they've got zip. This way, he's made his move and it's out in the open. Anyway, it's pointless to second guess."

A battered gray Toyota Camry pulled over onto the shoulder and parked behind Karen's Firebird. Debbie Stump got out and hurried over to them.

"Where is she? I talked to her. She said the police were after Professor Morris and she wasn't going to let them get him."

"Hold on now, hold on." Karen held up her hands to stop her. "What's all this about you talking to Rachel? When was this?"

"About ten minutes ago," Debbie said.

Hank frowned. "Ten minutes ago? How'd you get here so fast?"

"I was already on my way. Everybody's texting everybody about what happened."

"Slow down," Karen urged her, "just slow down a sec. Did you call her or did she call you?"

"I texted her," Debbie said. "I've *been* texting her since it went viral. She finally answered ten minutes ago."

"You've got cell coverage out here?" Hank asked, incredulous.

"Actually, yeah. There's a tower right close by, near Wittens Mills. The dead zone is about five miles from here and it zig-zags along the top of the mountain, but where we are right now, there's coverage."

"Amazing." Hank turned to watch a state trooper jump into his cruiser. He drove it about fifty yards back up the road from the loop and parked it cross-ways to block the road. He lit up his roof rack and got out to watch as Brooks drove the Harmony PD cruiser up to join him, making a two-vehicle barricade. Debbie's car would be the last that would be allowed to get through to the loop.

"How did she sound?" Hank asked. "Was Morris holding her against her will?"

"No, she's helping him."

"Helping? How?"

"I don't know. She just texted that she was going to hold them off so he could get away."

"Omigod," Karen said. "She's the shooter."

"All those trophies," Hank remembered.

"White, Lou." Karen looked at him. "He's their counter-sniper. They'll take her out."

"They may," Hank agreed.

"She's just a kid." Karen started toward the command table. "I gotta get up there."

Over the next half hour Karen begged, pleaded, and bullied, all to no avail. Neither Muncy nor Stanley would give her the time of day, even after she explained to them that it was Rachel who was laying down the suppressing fire, according to Debbie Stump. They remained focused on moving the command post and setting up their operation.

It took several trips on the ATVs to convey everyone who was moving forward up to the new command post, which was established inside the gully about 800 feet away from the spot they figured was Rachel's sniper position. Stanley and White made the first run, and Billings returned with Jackson sitting behind him, looking pale, upset, and blood-spattered but otherwise all right. Given the rounds that Rachel was firing, he was lucky to be alive. Williams took him inside the house and got him to lie down while they waited for EMS to arrive. A Richlands radio crew got there first, however, followed closely by a reporter from the *Clinch Valley News* and a crew from the television station in Bluefield on the West Virginia side. Branham strolled up to make sure they respected the barrier.

The Cessna continued to circle around the spot from a safe distance, reporting that one of the suspects could be seen moving back and forth between the cabin and the ATV.

Billings had just returned from his latest shuttle run on the ATV when his borrowed state police radio received a transmission from the helicopter, announcing that it was five minutes out. Billings got off the ATV and helped guide the helicopter to a landing in the field east of Morris's house. It was a Bell 407 helicopter bearing the markings of the Virginia state police, with a crew of two and seating for up to five passengers. Only one passenger climbed out of the cabin, however: Tazewell County Sheriff Isham Steele.

Billings trotted forward to meet him. Steele walked briskly up to the command table, now virtually abandoned except for Hank, Karen, Hall, and Debbie Stump. The Forest Service maps remained on the table, as Taylor had taken another set forward with her.

Steele approached the table with the air of a field general about to take command of a battlefield. Billings showed him on the map where the cabin was located, where Rachel was thought to be pinning down the team, and where the new command post had been established. He paused as they all turned to watch the arrival of another television crew down at the barricade.

"Tactically," Billings finished, trying to impress Steele with his knowledge of law enforcement terminology, "what your people first thought was a hostage scenario is now a straight fugitive apprehension scenario with two suspects, both armed and dangerous."

Debbie Stump stepped forward. "Rachel is *not* a suspect. You can't hunt her down like a criminal, you just can't."

Steele looked at her for the first time. "You a friend of hers? That why you're here?"

"Yes, I'm her friend."

"You help her do this?" Steele moved toward her and looked at Hank. "Has she been questioned? Why hasn't she been placed under arrest?"

"She's not involved," Karen said. "She got here just a minute ago. She's worried about her friend. Plus, she's reached the girl on her cell. She's your comm link to the shooter."

Steele stared at Karen for a moment, then turned to Billings. "I want to talk to Detective Muncy."

Billings called Stanley on the state police radio. On the other end, Stanley gave his radio to Muncy as Billings handed his to Steele.

"Detective Muncy."

"Here, Sheriff."

"Muncy, were you aware that this girl down here has been in touch with the female suspect?"

"Yeah, Sheriff. So I heard."

"Why haven't you made contact, then? To talk her down?"

"Uh, Detective Savage advised that the tactical team should get into position first before we established contact."

Steele opened his mouth to say something when he saw over Karen's shoulder that Deputy Charleton was trotting down the road toward them. "Stand by," he said into the radio.

They crossed the lawn in a group to meet Charleton at the edge of the loop.

"Crowd's getting a little unruly, Sheriff," the deputy said, a little out of breath. "We've stopped a couple of them from trying to get around us on foot, but they won't take no for an answer much longer."

"Call for backup," Steele ordered.

"I did. They're en route. Maybe if you talked to them, made some kind of a statement that would hold them for a while longer?"

Steele was an elected official and it didn't take him very long to make up his mind. He turned to Hank and pointed at Debbie. "Get her up to Muncy and establish communication with the suspects on the double."

Hank watched Steele walk up the road toward the barricade. His eyes slid to Billings. "Never mind your ATV. We'll take her up in that." He pointed at the helicopter.

At that moment they heard over the radio that the Cessna was pulling out and that the helicopter would assume aerial coverage of the scene.

"We'd better hustle," Hank said, "or we'll miss our ride."

"Goddammit," Karen complained, staring at the helicopter. "I hate those things."

33

They ascended the ridge and touched down in a patch of bare ground about a hundred yards short of the command post. The pilot turned and motioned them out the cabin door. "Best I can do!"

Karen found the ATV tracks that marked the path into the trees above them and led the way, cursing at the slope, the fact that it was now mid-afternoon and she hadn't eaten since breakfast this morning, idiot ex-cops who thought they could escape accountability, her shoes, damned helicopters, and everything else she could think of. Debbie Stump followed, glancing over her shoulder occasionally at Hank, who brought up the rear.

Hank smiled his patient smile at her.

After a long walk they reached the new command post, which had been established at the edge of another small clearing with an unimpeded view of the top of the gully where the cabin was supposed to be located. They couldn't see the cabin, nor could they see Rachel Meese, but Muncy assured them that both were definitely up there.

Hank leaned against a tree to catch his breath. He heard the helicopter report that the ATV had left the cabin and was climbing to the top of the mountain. Stanley checked with his team and was informed that they still hadn't reached their flanking positions.

Muncy cursed. Morris was trying to escape along the top of the mountain. "We've got to get up there and head him off!"

"Helicopter," Hank said.

"Good idea." Muncy pointed at Stanley. "Call him back. He can take me up and drop me off. There's a road or something up there, right?"

"He can't land here and pick you up," Stanley said. "It's not like calling a taxi, for chrissakes."

"Back where he let us off," Hank said. He pushed away from the tree. "I'll go with you."

"Let's go," Muncy said.

"What about the girl?" Detective Savage interjected. "Is she still in position or did she pull out with him?"

"How the hell would I know?" Muncy complained, anxious to

get into the air.

"Text her," Karen said to Debbie.

Debbie took out her cell and began to compose a message.

"We can't wait," Muncy said. "Call the bird, tell him we'll be down at the clearing."

"You'll need tactical support up there," Stanley said.

"Never mind, I'll go with them," Savage said. "Stay here, find out if the girl's still covering his escape, and deal with her if she's still in position."

Hank took a deep breath and led them back down the trail toward the clearing where they would meet the helicopter.

Debbie sat down with her back against a tree trunk and worked the keyboard of her cell phone. Karen crouched beside her, watching.

r u s t?

Karen frowned. "What does that mean?"

y.

"I said, 'are you still there?'" Debbie explained without looking up from the phone, and she answered 'yes.'"

poms.

ihu.

ruok?

Udh82bme clm.

"Translate, translate," Karen said. "What's she saying?"

"I told her you were watching over my shoulder, she said 'I hear you,' then I asked her if she was okay."

Karen stared at the last entry, biting her lip. "'You'd hate to be me,'" she guessed. "And the rest?"

"'Career-limiting move.'"

"Call her. I want to talk to her."

"I don't think she'll talk to you."

"Ask her. Tell her I want to help her."

Debbie hesitated, head tilted sideways as she stared at the screen.

cm, she typed. Call me.

They waited in vain for a response. Stanley walked over and stared down at them. "What's the word? She still there?"

"Just about to find out," Karen replied calmly.

"I've got White getting into position. Either she gives herself up right now, or he's going to take the shot as soon as he's got it."

"Whoa, hold on now, partner," Karen said, standing up, "easy does it. Give us a chance to establish communication and talk to her, all right? She may be too scared to know what to do. Give me a chance to talk her down."

Debbie's cell phone began to play music, the unexpected sound punching at their taut nerves.

"Rache!" Debbie cried into the phone. "What are you doing? Are you insane? These people are going to kill you!"

"Hold on, sweetheart," Karen said, crouching down again and holding out her hand. "Let me talk to her."

"The woman cop wants to talk to you," Debbie said, wiping at tears with her free hand. "Yeah, I think so." She looked at Karen. "Stainer?"

Karen nodded.

"Yeah. Maybe you should talk to her, Rache. She's trying to help you."

Karen waited out several minutes of crying, coaxing, and pleading, during which she turned to Stanley. "Give me one of your radios."

Stanley reluctantly handed one over. She clipped it to her belt at the small of her back, under her jacket. "How about some cuffs?" Stanley hesitated, then passed her his handcuffs, which she slipped into her jacket pocket. When she turned around, Debbie was holding the phone out to her. Nodding, she took it and lifted it to her ear.

"Rachel, this is Detective Stainer. Are you still in the same position up there at the top of the gully?"

"Why should I tell you that?" Rachel replied, her voice taut with stress. "You've probably got snipers ready to shoot me in the head."

"Honey, I won't lie to you, there's a tactical team from the state police here and they're in position to respond, but don't you give them any reason to, all right? Just put that rifle down and show yourself with your hands on top of your head. You won't get hurt if you do what I say. All right?"

"They'll shoot me. I shot that cop. Is he dead?"

Karen began to walk forward to the edge of the clearing. "No darlin,' you barely nicked his arm. He's fine. The bleeding had already stopped by the time he got back to the house. EMS looked him over and he's fine." She chuckled. "What was up with that shot, anyway? I thought you were an expert marksman."

Rachel cried for a moment into the phone. "I was . . . afraid I'd . . . killed him."

Karen passed between two trees and slowly moved out into the clearing. "Naw, he won't even get any time off work. You should have shot him in the foot, made it worth his while."

Rachel laughed through her tears. "I didn't mean to hit him. I was shooting at the tire."

"You missed, honey."

"Yeah." It took a moment for her to regain her composure. Finally she said, "I'm really sorry about all this."

Karen kept moving slowly uphill through the clearing. "I know you are, darlin.' We all make mistakes in judgment, especially when it comes to men."

"Wait! Stop! I can see you!"

Karen stopped dead. She slowly raised both hands over her head, showing Rachel the cell phone and an empty left hand, then lowered them again. "It's just little ol' me. My sidearm's holstered and it'll stay that way as long as we can do this easy, okay?"

"Take your gun out of your holster right now and put it on the ground," Rachel ordered.

"Can't do that, sweetheart," Karen said calmly. "Sorry. You can't ask an experienced cop like me to separate herself from her best friend in the world now, can you? Besides, it'll get dirty lying on the ground, know what I mean? What's your favorite? What do you like to fire best of all?"

"What?"

"I saw your trophies back at the apartment, so I know you're a real good shooter. What's your favorite?"

"My favorite?"

"Yeah. The one that feels better in your hand than any of the others. The one you'd want to have with you when you walk down a dark alley at three o'clock in the morning."

"I have an S and W M66."

"You gotta be kidding me," Karen exclaimed. "You fire the .357 or the .38 special?"

"Both, but I like the .357 better."

"Well, I'll be damned. That's my barbecue gun, girl."

"It is?"

"Hell, yeah. Ivory grips, just a real beauty." Karen took a few experimental steps forward. She could see where the ATV trail swung off to the right into the trees up toward the cabin. "Tell me something, what's that rifle you got with you up there?"

"It's a Remington."

"The model 700 XCR, right?"

"Yes, that's right," Rachel said. "How'd you know?"

"Saw some rounds on the floor back at the house and figured it out. Fired it before?"

"Actually, no."

"Helluva recoil, huh?"

Rachel laughed with embarrassment. "Yeah, that's why I missed the first shot. Please, Detective Stainer, don't come any closer."

"Call me Karen."

Static burred across the line for a moment, then cleared. "Don't come any closer, Karen," Rachel was saying. "I don't want to have to shoot you. This is horrible enough already."

"Morris has already high-tailed it over the ridge, darlin.' He's gone. Your delaying tactic worked. He got away. There's no more need for you to stay there, holding us off. It's over."

"No, I've got to make sure he gets away."

"I understand, sweetheart, but I'm telling you he's gone already, and you need to give yourself up right now."

"If I show myself they'll shoot me."

"Hang on a sec. I'm gonna take out a radio and talk to the tactical boys. All right? Just hang on a sec. I'll let you listen in." Karen lowered the phone and turned around, slowly removing the radio, knowing that Rachel was watching her through the scope. It gave her a crawly feeling that she forcibly suppressed. She saw Stanley standing between the two trees at the edge of the clearing, watching her.

"Team Leader Stanley," she said into the radio, holding it at an angle with the cell phone close to her mouth, "copy?"

"Copy," Stanley replied.

"Lovely. This is a 10-62," Karen said, using the police 10 code that referred to an unauthorized listener, "but I want her to hear this conversation. Copy?"

"Copy, Detective."

"All right. If the girl shows herself in order to give herself up, does she have your word that your marksmen won't shoot her?"

"Does she intend to surrender?"

"Well, what the hell do you think I'm talking about? I'm asking her to show herself, leave her weapon on the ground, and walk out to me with her hands on her head. If she does that, will you guarantee her safety?"

"If she does all that, nice and clean, we'll hold our fire," Stanley said, "but she has to keep her hands in plain sight on top of her head at all times."

"Did you get that, Rachel?" Karen asked, raising the phone to her ear again, thumb back on the transmit button of the radio so that Stanley could listen in.

"Yes," Rachel replied.

"So, how about it?"

A sigh was all that Karen heard over the phone for several long moments. Static flared and subsided.

"What should I do?" Rachel finally asked in a small voice.

"Here's the best way," Karen said. "Let me come up to you. I'll come all the way up to your crow's nest, you put your rifle on the ground and any other hardware you're packing, put your hands on top of your head and walk into view, and then I'll bring you the hell out of there myself. They won't shoot if I have you under control. You know the drill."

They had to wait a moment for the crying to subside before Karen got her answer. "Okay."

"Okey doke, let's do it. Team Leader, are we copasetic?"

"You're on, Detective. But stay frosty."

"Always." Karen took her thumb off the transmit button of the radio and clipped it to her belt, then began to walk briskly toward the spot where the trail re-entered the trees. "Let's stay on the phone while I'm coming up, okay?"

"All right," Rachel said.

Karen made it into the trees and began to climb the slope. "Damn, you couldn't have picked flat ground to do this on, could you? This climbing shit is for the birds."

"Sorry," Rachel said, half-laughing and half-crying.

"S'okay, I need the exercise."

"Karen?"

"Yes, darlin'?"

"My career is seriously fucked, isn't it?"

"You might say."

"I don't want to go to prison. I can't stand the thought of having to be in prison, in a tiny cell, showering with other women, eating garbage food with them. Oh, God!"

"Now hold on a sec," Karen said, increasing her pace, "don't think about all that stuff right now, okay? Just think about doing the right thing, and then you'll have the whole rest of your life to make up the difference and do good."

"My life is *over*."

"No, it ain't, honey. You got your whole life ahead. You're just a kid, for cryin' out loud, you'll come back from this. You'll see. Where the hell are you? I'm at a big-assed boulder and the trail goes right and a footpath or something goes left. Where do I go?"

No answer.

"Rachel!"

Silence, then, "Left."

"I go left? That what you're saying?"

"Mmmm."

"You all right, Rachel? You staying with me, now?"

"I'm all right. I'm sorry."

Karen took the footpath to the left and hurried through the trees, aware after a minute or so that she could see the gully below her through gaps in the brush on the left.

"Wait!" Rachel said.

Karen heard her over the phone and through the air at the same time. "I'm putting the phone in my pocket now, honey, then I'll show you my hands," she said. She put the phone in her pocket, raised her hands to shoulder level and continued along the footpath to a clearing. In front of her was an outcropping of rock that looked down into the gully. Rachel knelt behind the outcropping, pointing the rifle at her.

"There you are," Karen said. "Man, I'm glad to see you. Now put the rifle down and we'll get out of here."

"I won't go to prison," Rachel said.

"Rachel, you're a hell of a lot tougher than you think. The alternatives all involve getting shot, and believe me, you don't want that. You can get through this fine."

"No, I can't."

"Yes, you can. You're tough and you're smart and I'll help you."

"You won't help me."

"I just said I would, didn't I? I'm gonna give you my cell phone number and I expect you to call me anytime, day or night, from this minute on. Understand what I'm saying? When you don't call me I'm gonna call you or come see you. Until you're through this and out and starting your life over again. Then when you choose what you want to do with your life, I'll be there if you want advice, a helping hand, whatever. Got it?"

"You won't do all that."

Karen bared her teeth. "Jesus Christ, girl, didn't I just say I would?"

Rachel cried. "I'm sorry, really. I just really, really, need help right now."

"You got it. Now put the rifle down like I told you."

Rachel gently set the rifle down on the ground.

"Hands on top of your head, sweetie."

Rachel put her hands on her head and stood up.

"Easy, easy."

"Okay," Rachel said, upright.

"Walk slowly toward me," Karen ordered, "and keep your hands on your head."

Rachel walked out from behind the outcropping of rock toward her. Karen knew that White now had the girl in his scope and was waiting for the word from Stanley.

"I'm gonna pat you down, girl. You got anything else on you?"

Rachel nodded miserably.

"Fuck. All right, here we go." Karen moved forward. "Where

is it?"

"In my waistband behind my back. I'm sorry."

"It's okay." Karen reached her, plucked a Beretta M92 from behind Rachel's back, dropped out the magazine, cleared the chamber, and slipped the gun and magazine into her jacket pocket.

"I'm gonna pat you down now. Just hold still with your hands on top of your head like you are. Am I going to find anything else?"

"No."

Karen patted her down and found her cell phone but nothing else. "Now I'm gonna cuff you, Rachel. So they know you're completely in my control and you don't pose any further danger. Okay?"

Sobbing, Rachel nodded.

"I'm just taking out the cuffs." Karen removed them from her jacket pocket, plucked one hand off the girl's head and applied the cuff, then grabbed the other hand, pulled her arms behind her back, and completed the job. She gripped her by the elbow and took out the radio.

"Suspect secured. We're coming down."

"Good job, Detective," Stanley replied.

Karen guided Rachel back down the path. When they were into the trees, she said, "repeat after me, darlin,' four-ten."

"What?"

"Just say it. Four-ten."

Rachel repeated it.

"Eight-six-seven."

Rachel repeated it.

"Twenty-six seventy. That's my cell number. Now say it again. Four-ten."

Karen made Rachel repeat it over and over as they walked down the trail to the clearing where Stanley waited to take her into custody, hoping it would distract her from the horror that was about to swallow her whole.

35

The passenger portion of the helicopter cabin seated five passengers. There were two seats facing the rear, immediately behind the pilot and co-pilot, and a bench seat facing forward that could accommodate three people. Hank climbed into the cabin first and slid along the bench seat all the way to the far side, so that he was sitting behind the pilot, facing forward. Savage got in next, took one look at Hank's knees pressing against the seat in front of him, and chose the seat immediately behind the co-pilot, facing back. Muncy sat down facing Savage. The seats were not especially luxurious, being covered in cheap cloth upholstery, and their view of the ground below was limited to what they could see through the windows on each side of them.

Hank stared at a poster on the pillar next to Savage entitled "Bell 407 Safety" that explained how not to be decapitated when you entered and exited the helicopter. They lifted off and swung around slowly to approach the summit of the mountain from the southwest. Hank could see the cabin below them in a small clearing about 200 feet from the top. A strip of trail wound through the trees from the cabin to the summit. The top of the mountain was shorn of all its trees, like a tonsured monk, to accommodate power lines that ran all the way along the mountain to the West Virginia border. Running parallel to the power lines was a dirt road, and as they skimmed over the point where the trail leading up from the cabin met the dirt road at the top, the co-pilot leaned forward and pointed.

"There he is."

Hank adjusted his headset and moved the mike closer to his lips. "Where?"

Muncy pointed. "There. Moving northeast on the road."

Hank saw Morris bouncing along the dirt road on his ATV. He threw a look over his shoulder, then hunched down.

"He can't see us," said the co-pilot, whose name was Phillips. "We're coming at him right out of the sun."

"But he can sure as hell hear us," Savage said.

"Ain't that a fact."

They passed over Morris and kept on going along the mountain, following the road until it suddenly forked. The branch on the left angled off toward a cluster of buildings farther down along the summit. Hank leaned over and saw that the one on the right headed toward the power lines and a hydro tower in a small clearing. He reached over and tapped Muncy on the arm, then pointed at the buildings on the left. "What's that?"

"Damned if I know." Muncy leaned forward, frowning. "Phillips, what are those buildings and shit over there?"

The co-pilot shrugged. "Weather station or something."

"It's a test facility," answered the pilot, whose name was Davis. "They're talking about putting windmills up here but there's a lot of controversy. The power company owns most of the mountain that isn't part of the national forest, bought it up a while ago, and they built that test facility to measure the weather, see if there was enough wind to make it viable."

"Are there people working up here? Right now?"

"I don't know. I suppose. Scientists, I guess."

"Meteorologists," Savage said.

"Maybe he'll go the other way at the fork," Hank said.

"We'll swing around and see." Davis banked slowly, and they retraced their flight path back to the fork. Morris was still racing along the road, a few hundred feet from the fork. This time he could see the helicopter coming straight at him.

"Don't forget he's armed," Hank warned.

"He's firing at us," Phillips said calmly from his co-pilot's seat. "A handgun."

"We're all right." Davis put a little more air beneath them as they passed over Morris. "Never fear." He swung them around in a lazy arc and came back to the road in time to see Morris choose the branch to the left.

Muncy got busy on the radio with Stanley down on the ground, coordinating the movement of backup units from the state police and the sheriff's office to block any escape routes at the other end of the dirt road. From what Hank could gather, there were several points at which Morris could descend and make his way toward Bluefield, where he could steal a car and cross the state border. They needed to seal off each of these escape routes while Stanley and his team raced around to intercept him.

"By the way," Muncy said, turning to Hank, "Stanley says your detective brought the girl down for us. She walked right up there and talked the kid into giving herself up. Put her ass on the line for Stanley and his team."

"That sounds about right," Hank said.

"They were all set to put a round right through the kid's head," Muncy said. "Stainer saved her life."

"Stanley's en route, is he?" Savage asked.

"Yeah," Muncy replied, "but I doubt he's going to get up here in time."

Savage reluctantly agreed.

"We have to take him ourselves," Hank said.

"I think so," Muncy said.

"Not from this helicopter," Savage disagreed.

"We need to set down ahead of him," Muncy said, "disable the ATV when he reaches us and take him down."

"Where?" Savage frowned at him. "Where do we do that?"

They'd over-flown Morris again. Davis swung around over the test facility.

"How about here?" Hank pointed at a tower beneath them that was festooned with microwave dishes and other assorted ornaments. The tower was the first thing Morris would pass as he entered the station compound. "We could wait for him right there."

"Sounds good." Muncy relayed their plan to Stanley, who had his own ideas. As they debated it back and forth, the helicopter passed over Morris again and swung around to approach him once more from the rear.

As they came up behind him, Phillips suddenly leaned forward. "He's stopped."

"Uh oh, he's got a rifle," Davis said. "Climbing."

Before they could ascend out of range, however, one of Morris's rounds punched through the floor, passed between the co-pilot's legs on an angle, traveled over his shoulder, and clipped the left side of Savage's headset in the back seat before passing through the roof above Muncy's head. Savage grabbed at his left ear as his headset was blown sideways, half-across his face. Hank and Muncy ducked as shards of plastic flew everywhere.

Davis looked over at Phillips and did a double-take. "Pete!"

"I'm all right! It missed me! Let's get the hell outta here!"

"Christ," Savage said, scrabbling at the headset and looking at blood on his hand. "What the hell happened?"

"We've been hit," Hank said, freeing his right ear from the headset. "Everyone all right in front?"

"Jesus, my ear hurts," Savage said. "I can't hear anything!"

"He nearly killed me!" Phillips yelled.

Muncy removed his headset, unbuckled, and moved forward to examine the left side of Savage's head. "Your ear's cut. Maybe from a piece of plastic." He took out a handkerchief, wadded it up, and gave

234

it to Savage.

"Look." Hank pointed at a hole that had been punched above Muncy's head. "That's where the round went."

"Jesus fucking Christ!" Savage exploded, "the bastard nearly killed me!"

"You're okay," Muncy soothed. "It was close."

"Too fucking close! Jesus Christ!"

Muncy frowned out the window. "Hey, we passed the station. Pilot, where are you going?"

Davis didn't reply as the helicopter altered course and began to leave the ridge on a northwest heading.

Hank put his headset back on. "Davis, where are you going? We need you to set us down back there at that station."

"Fuck this," Davis said. "We're outta here."

"Get us back there right now!" Hank shouted.

Davis said nothing, staring straight ahead.

"Savage," Hank said, "put your headset on and order him to turn around! Now, before we lose Morris!"

Muncy handed Savage his headset before putting on his own. Gritting his teeth, Savage held the right earphone to his ear. "Davis, turn around and put us down where we told you. That's an order."

"Negative. Too dangerous."

"Look, set us down and then you can get the hell out of here!"

They went back and forth for another angry minute before the pilot reluctantly banked around and returned to the top of the mountain. He refused to bring them right to the main compound of the test facility, dropping them off instead at an outlying building about 150 yards from the spot they'd chosen as their ambush site. They scrabbled out from under the rotor wash and watched the chopper lift back into the air.

"We're too far away," Muncy complained as they reached the shelter of the building.

"He may have already reached the compound," Hank agreed, drawing his gun. "Let's go." He led them around the building and down the driveway to the dirt road.

They paused, looked both ways, saw nothing and turned left, trotting up the road toward the next building, an open shed containing a pickup truck, a backhoe, and a panel truck. Seeing no one in the shed, they trotted on.

"Truck tires," Muncy said, pointing at fresh tracks in the dirt, "but no ATV."

Savage nodded. "Right. He hasn't gotten this far yet."

Hank looked at him. "You all right?"

Savage felt his ear gingerly, then looked at his hand. The blood had already stopped flowing. "Yeah. But I'm definitely going to beat that bastard to an inch of his fucking life."

They slowed as they entered the compound. On the left were two portable buildings that likely contained offices and workstations used by the staff. There were several privately-owned vehicles parked in front of them. On the right, at the edge of the road, was another portable building surrounded by small sheds. Hank could see an assortment of meteorological measuring devices, suggesting the sheds were specialized weather stations. The door of the portable building opened as they came up.

A man wearing a white hard hat frowned at them. "Who the hell are you? What's going on with that damned helicopter?"

Savage held up his badge. "State police. Go back inside and lock the door. Anybody else up here right now?"

"Yeah, of course, everybody's here today."

"Get them the hell inside and lock all your doors. Call all your people right now and tell them."

"Why? What the hell are you doing up here?"

"Tazewell County Sheriff's Office," Muncy said, holding up his badge. "There's a fugitive loose on this ridge. Now shut the fuck up and get back inside."

"Make them calls!" Savage repeated.

The man went back inside and slammed the door.

"Look," Hank said, pointing down to the big tower that had been their destination. "There's the ATV."

The four-wheeler was sitting in the compound just past the tower. There was no one in sight.

"Shit." Muncy began to move forward.

Hank grabbed his arm. "Wait. Look."

Behind the tower was a Quonset hut. A man in a yellow hard hat emerged through the front door of the hut. Right behind him was David Morris, restraining him in a choke hold, a gun pressed against his right temple.

"Easy does it!" Morris shouted.

Savage suddenly broke right, heading for a waste barrel sitting at the side of the road. He was six feet away from it when Morris reached around his hostage and calmly shot Savage in the left leg. The detective went down heavily, weapon flying. He rolled behind the barrel and lay still.

"All right, all right! Muncy shouted. "Hold your fire, Morris! Let's talk this thing through!"

"There's nothing to talk about. Throw down your weapons and

236

walk slowly toward me, both of you, hands on your head. A little further apart. Now!"

Hank obeyed, dropping his Glock, and began to walk slowly across the compound. Muncy was on his left. Hank took a step to his right for every two steps forward, approaching Morris on an arc that soon put the sun directly behind him.

Muncy got the idea. "We've got the girl in custody," he called out, to draw Morris's attention. "You're by yourself now, no more backup. Let's just do this easy. Let the guy go."

"Not a chance, buddy. Hey!" He swung around and pointed his gun at Hank. "Stop the horseshit and walk straight toward me."

He was squinting, so Hank knew he'd succeeded in positioning himself so that the sun was in Morris's eyes when he looked at him. He half-expected to be told to move back to his left, but instead Morris swung the gun over to Muncy again, who was now about fifty feet away from him. "Far enough. Stop there. I want your backup guns out, right now. Index finger and thumb only. You first, Muncy. Draw it and toss it over here to me."

Muncy slowly lifted his right trouser leg, removed his backup weapon, and threw it toward Morris. It landed about halfway between them.

"Show me the other leg."

Muncy slowly lifted his left trouser leg to show Morris there was no weapon strapped there.

"Last chance, asshole," Morris said. "If I search you and find something else, I'm gonna put a round through your fucking knee, understand?"

"There's nothing else," Muncy said in a bored monotone.

"Now you, Maryland."

Hank reached down and pulled up his right pant leg. "No backup here. I don't like them."

"Bullshit. All cops carry a backup. Show me the other leg."

Hank showed him the other leg, which was also bare. "Nothing here, Morris. I don't like guns."

"Your funeral. Now down on your knees, hands on your head. Both of you!"

Hank knelt on the ground, his hands lightly touching the crown of his head. He saw that Morris's gun was large, a revolver of some kind. He couldn't tell for certain what it was from this distance. Morris also had a knapsack on his back and a rifle of some kind slung over his left shoulder. It was probable that there was ammunition in the knapsack, perhaps another handgun. Morris might also have another gun in his pocket or tucked into the waistband of his jeans. The odds were pretty good, even without factoring in the hostage, that Morris could outgun them in a short-term stand-off.

The hostage wore a plaid shirt, jeans, and scuffed work boots. He had a tool belt buckled around his waist that contained several electronic devices as well as a hammer and other tools. His hands gripped Morris's choking forearm. As Hank watched, Morris used the barrel of the revolver to knock the man's hard hat off his head onto the ground. He pressed the muzzle against the man's temple.

"Let go."

The man immediately lowered his arms.

"That's better." Morris looked at Muncy, then Hank. "Either of you give me any trouble, I'll shoot you like a dog. Got it?"

"Sure," Muncy said.

Morris peered into his hostage's face. "What are you, some kind of worker?"

"I'm a lineman. I came up to do some work on the tower."

"Well, this is your lucky day, isn't it?" Morris moved him around, trying to see what was in his tool belt. "You got something I can tie these fuckheads up with?"

"I don't know. There's spools of wire back in the hut."

"Yeah, well that's back there, not out here where I need it. Down on your knees, asshole. Make any moves I don't like and I'll blow your head right off your neck."

"Okay." The man knelt down on the ground as Morris eased his chokehold.

"Put your hands on top of your head. Now, let's take a look."

With his gun stuck in the middle of the man's back, Morris made a quick search of the tool belt. "Hey, look here!" He removed a bundle of plastic locking straps that were held together by an elastic band. "Long ones! Just what the doctor ordered."

He removed one of the locking straps with his teeth and dropped the bundle behind the lineman onto the ground. "Okay, bring both hands slowly down and behind your back. Too fast and I'll shoot you dead."

"Yes, sir."

"You two fuckheads don't move a muscle or he dies, got it?"

"Sure," Muncy said again.

He knelt behind the lineman and used his free hand to cross the man's wrists, then took the locking strap out of his mouth and bent it around the underside of the lineman's wrists. "Good. Long enough." With a warning look at Muncy and Hank, he used his gun hand to cup the strap underneath the wrists while he looped the end through the cap with his free hand and jerked it tight.

The lineman winced.

"Hurt?" Morris grinned. "Good." He retrieved the bundle of locking straps, stood up, gun out, and looked at Hank. "If you move, I'll kill you."

"Okay," Hank said.

Morris waved the gun at him a couple of times, as though firing, then turned and began to walk toward Muncy.

Hank dropped his right hand down from the top of his head, reached behind and under his jacket, removed from the holster at the small of his back the SIG Sauer P-225 he'd bought this morning from Jeff Davis's army surplus store, and shot David Morris in the ribs.

Morris's revolver went flying as he jerked sideways and fell, striking his head on the ground. Hank scrambled to his feet and raced across the intervening fifty feet. He stomped on Morris's right wrist as Muncy tugged the rifle from Morris's left shoulder and threw it aside. Muncy did a hasty pat-down, found a small pistol in his left jacket pocket and threw that aside as well.

Morris opened his eyes and drew in a ragged breath. The wound was bleeding copiously. Hank looked at Muncy, who shook his head.

"Why'd you do it, Morris?" Muncy asked, crouching low so that he could look him in the eyes. "Why'd you kill her?"

"Didn't mean to."

"You choked her to death, you bastard."

"She," he coughed and swallowed, "beautiful. Ever saw."

"You strangled her, Morris. Watched her die."

"Didn't. Mean to."

"Was it because she was pregnant? It was your kid, and she wouldn't have an abortion? Was that it?"

Morris grunted, blood flowing out of his mouth.

"She was a beautiful woman and you killed her, Morris," Muncy growled. "You goddamned son of a bitch."

"Muncy," Hank said.

"All she wanted to do was live her life and you killed her. I should let her husband come up here with a hunting knife and skin you alive, you bastard."

"Muncy," Hank repeated.

"What? What the hell?"

"He's gone. Let it rest."

36

Saturday was a beautiful day that featured a deep blue sky, scattered white cumulus clouds, and pleasant temperatures. After checking out of his hotel room, Hank followed Karen into Tazewell and turned in the Grand Cherokee, loaded his stuff into the trunk of her Firebird, and strapped himself into the passenger seat.

It was a little after nine o'clock in the morning. Karen turned onto Highway 61, and they settled down for the drive to Burkes Garden. Traffic was much heavier than the previous two times she'd been here because it was the day of the fall festival. By the time she reached Gratton and turned onto Highway 613, she'd resigned herself to a slow, winding drive in the middle of a stack of traffic with no opportunity to pass.

"It's nice along here." Hank uncurled his fists and rubbed his sweating palms on his thighs. "Good day for a pleasant, slow drive."

"Yeah," Karen groused, "we could walk there faster than this."

Hank watched her worrying her lip, wanting to talk about something. He watched the scenery and waited, but it didn't happen so he let it ride.

The festival was in full swing when they reached the elementary school and adjacent community center. Deputy Charleton was directing traffic in and out of the parking lot. When Karen reached him she stuck her elbow out the window and grinned at his fluorescent vest.

"You look like you're having fun."

"You folks stopping in here or going on to Sunset Farms?"

"Dunno," Karen said. "What're they doing in here, running a day care?"

Charleton shrugged. "There's stuff for the kids, but this is where the crafters and quilters set up shop."

"Quilters?"

Charleton stared at her. "Traffic's waiting."

"Can we look?" Karen asked Hank.

"Sure."

"Lemme through, Deputy Dawg," she said.

Charleton stopped oncoming traffic to allow her to turn into the school parking lot. They browsed among the vendors outside and then went into the gymnasium where the majority of the quilters had set up their booths. Karen bought two quilts, a large one for herself and a smaller one that she said was for her mother. She talked Hank into buying a beautiful specimen featuring a pattern that Karen said was called the North Star.

"Slaves used something called quilt codes," she told him as he paid the woman and bundled the quilt under his arm. "They'd make quilts with patterns that were actually coded messages, then hang them outside as though they were airing them. Escaping slaves following the Underground Railroad could read the quilt and know what was waiting up ahead of them."

Hank was familiar with the subject but didn't let on. "So what did the North Star say?"

She raised an eyebrow at him. "North Star, Lou. You know. Head north? Duh."

"I didn't know you were interested in quilts."

"Too girlish?"

"No, not at all," Hank replied carefully.

"I'm such a cop lifer I can't have any side interests like a normal human being?"

Hank looked at her. "Is there anything I can say right now that won't get me a kick in the ass?"

"Not really."

They walked next door to the community center, where they met Neil Branham. He looked very casual in jeans, an untucked white shirt, and a pearl-colored linen jacket. His belt buckle was a large pewter oval with turquoise inlay in a catchy western pattern. He was smoking a skinny black cigar and holding the hand of a petite blond woman whom he introduced as Janice Riley. Riley rolled her eyes and released his hand.

"I'll wait for you in the car."

Branham shrugged as they watched her weave through the crowd toward the parking lot. "It's just the third time we've been out together. She's not sure she likes being around law enforcement people."

"She's a loser," Karen said flatly. "Dump her."

Branham gave it a moment, then stuck his hands in his jeans pockets, the movement brushing aside the edges of the linen jacket to reveal the off-duty weapon holstered on his belt. "The sheriff's office transferred Billy Askew back to Bluefield. He still has to face the assault charges up there, but he's been released on bail."

"I feel bad for him," Hank said.

"That's very generous of you, given the beating he laid on you that first night."

"Surely to God he's not coming back to work," Karen said.

Branham shook his head. "He's been relieved of his duties."

"Fired. Sounds right. So where's that leave you?"

"Town council voted to remove the interim tag and appoint me chief of police," Branham said. "I decided to accept."

"Well, congratulations," Karen grinned, shaking his hand. "That's great."

"Ditto," Hank said. "I've got a question for you, though."

"Ask away."

"What do you plan to do with Hall?"

Branham thought about it for a moment. "Not sure, as a matter of fact. I know Billy tried to help him before and didn't get anywhere."

"He might be ready now, if you decide to try again."

"I'll keep it in mind," Branham said. "By the way, Muncy told me the lab report came back positive for Morris's DNA under Marcie's fingernails."

Hank said nothing, uncomfortably aware that if they'd waited for the results Morris would still be alive. He knew from Branham's tone, though, that the new chief was simply pleased to have received solid physical evidence that wrapped up the case.

"So what's going on in here?" Karen asked, pointing at the community center. "Anything worth looking at?"

"Mostly promotional kiosks for local businesses. Okay if you like collecting keychain giveaways and four-color brochures. The real fun is at Sunset Farms. That's where the best food is and the best music."

"Sounds good," Hank said. "What are we waiting for?"

"Hot air balloon rides, too," Branham added.

"There you go, Karen," Hank said. "Just what you wanted."

"Not a chance. Forget it."

"You're not afraid to fly, are you?" Branham couldn't believe it. "You flew in the helicopter."

"I'm not real crazy about it. Four wheels on pavement, that's me."

"Let's go check out the music, anyway," Hank said.

Branham's personal vehicle was a silver 2009 BMW 335. They followed him several miles down the road, creeping along in the heavy traffic until they reached the entrance to Sunset Farms. Another sheriff's deputy was directing traffic, and Karen drummed impatiently on the steering wheel as Branham shot the breeze with the deputy for half an eternity before finally turning into the driveway. Karen swung in behind him. They crept up to the field where volunteers were pointing out empty parking spots. She parked next to Branham and when they piled out he wasted no time grabbing Karen's elbow and steering her toward the next field where a large blue and red hot air balloon sat tethered, waiting for its next load of passengers.

"No way," Karen protested, "not a chance. Don't make me hurt you."

"Bullshit," Branham scoffed, "you'll love it. You can see the whole mountain from up there, it's unbelievable." He looked over his shoulder. "Are you coming, Janice?"

Riley shook her head. "You two have your fun. I'm going to find the beer tent."

"Suit yourself. Lieutenant?"

"Maybe later."

As they watched Branham and Karen disappear among the parked cars, Riley turned to Hank. "Your girlfriend sure likes Neil a lot."

"She's not my girlfriend," Hank said, looking at the hot air balloon. "She's a colleague. Engaged to an FBI special agent."

When he turned back, the woman had already walked away.

Hank slung his messenger bag over his shoulder and wandered toward the sound of live music. A bandstand had been set up in a field behind the barns. A group of four musicians were playing a blend of bluegrass and country. Hank joined a small but appreciative crowd. A young woman with long, straight brown hair gathered into a bun at the back of her head sang lead vocals and played the guitar. A heavy-set young man with a ponytail and beard played banjo, an older woman with short black hair played fiddle, and a gray-haired man played an acoustic bass fiddle. Hank stood through several songs before catching the eye of the woman next to him.

"Who are they?"

"They're called The Hillside Revival Band," she said, "from Tennessee."

"They're good."

She beamed at him. "You think so? The guy on the string bass is my husband, Terry James." She held out her hand. "I'm Mary Ellen James."

"Hank Donaghue," he replied, shaking her hand. "Have they recorded anything?"

The woman reached into the big handbag looped over her left forearm and produced a compact disk. "Just the one, so far. It's twenty dollars, if you're interested."

Hank gave her a twenty and slipped the CD into his messenger

243

bag. The set finished, and Mary Ellen hurried off toward the stage.

Hank's nostrils twitched. The odor of barbecue smoke was coming from somewhere on the other side of the bandstand. He decided it was time to find the food concessions. He followed the milling crowd to the edge of the bandstand and found himself next to the woman who had been singing on stage. She was unstrapping her guitar, her guitar case open on the ground in front of her. Hank admired the guitar and found himself making eye contact with her.

"That's a Wayne Henderson," he said, nodding at the guitar. "It's beautiful." The guitar was made of Brazilian rosewood and spruce. Its shaded top was golden and ruddy brown, tones that complemented the tortoiseshell pick guard, bright chrome tuning pegs, and the Henderson logo inlaid in the headstock.

She looked at him, mildly surprised. "Yes, it is. Do you know him?"

"No, not at all. I've never actually seen one of his guitars before, and definitely never heard one live before. It has a beautiful sound."

"It sure does. I won it in a statewide songwriting contest when I was in high school. I could never have afforded to buy it on my own."

"You play it very well," Hank said. "You do it justice."

"Why, thank you. And what's your name, again?"

"Hank Donaghue."

She stuck out her hand. "Martha Dexter, Mr. Donaghue. Visiting the area, are you?"

"From Maryland. On vacation."

"What do you do for a living?"

"I'm a cop."

"No you're not."

He pulled the CD out of his messenger bag. "Would you mind autographing it for me?"

She smiled. "Sure. Why not?"

Hank found his pen, peeled the cellophane from the CD, slipped the front booklet from the jewel case and handed it and the pen to her. She signed the booklet and gave it back to him. He put the booklet back in the jewel case and returned it to his messenger bag. Then he took out his wallet and gave her one of his business cards. "If you ever pass through my neck of the woods and need anything, give me a call."

She took the card and looked it over. "Goodgodalmighty, you are a cop. Lieutenant Hank Donaghue." She slipped the card into the back pocket of her jeans.

"Thanks for the autograph." Hank nodded and walked away.

The crowd led him to an area where local farmers were selling fruit and vegetables. He spotted a large kiosk with a sign on it that said *Dial Rock Ginseng* and sure enough, Louise Coffee was sitting in a rocking chair behind the kiosk while a girl in her late teens served customers.

Pleased to see him, she stood up and came around to the front of the kiosk. "Heard you took care of that bad business with Morris."

"Yes," Hank said.

She put her hands on her hips. "Had it coming to him. Good thing there are men like you who know what to do when the time comes to do it."

Hank changed the subject. "These are the products you sell through your business, are they?"

She grinned and took hold of his forearm. "I'm sure you'll find something you'll like." She pulled him over to the girl. "This is my granddaughter, Tammy Hartnell. Tammy, this is Lieutenant Donaghue, a real important police official who's visiting from Maryland. Why don't you show him what we're selling today?"

Tammy looped her hair behind her ear and picked up a jar. "This is our one-hundred per cent pure ginseng berry juice, from ginseng berries. Of course it's from berries, if it's berry juice, right? Sorry. Anyway, it's really good for reducing blood sugar." She set the jar down and picked up a white plastic bottle. "These are powdered ginseng capsules. They're very high in ginsenoside, that's the active ingredient in ginseng that gives you an energy rush. Well, not a rush, exactly, but more energy."

Louise patted his forearm. "A fellow your age needs to think about a little help that way, now and again."

Hank bought a bar of ginseng berry soap and a jar of the juice. He put them in his messenger bag and gave Louise a business card before saying goodbye. He strolled past other kiosks, nostrils flaring at the smell of grilling meat somewhere nearby. Karen and Branham materialized next to him.

"Back already?"

"It was a blast, Lou, an absolute blast. You have to go up. It was like being able to fly." Her face was flushed with excitement. She looked like an eight-year-old girl with a new pony.

"I thought you hated flying."

"Nah, I hate airports and I hate airplanes, not fussy about helicopters either, but that was great. I just held on real tight."

"Where's Janice?" Branham asked.

"I'm not sure," Hank said. "She said she was going to look for the beer tent."

"There isn't one," Branham replied. "It's a dry event. Anyway, it's lunch time and I'm starved. Let's get something to eat. Maybe she's having a cup of tea over there."

"Lead the way, Chief," Hank said.

"I like the sound of that." Branham led them through the crowd to the area where the food vendors had set up shop. Everywhere Hank looked, it seemed, middle-aged men in white aprons were grilling meat on everything from charcoal-fired barbecues to monstrous propane outfits to home-made barrel barbecues fashioned from 55-gallon drums. It was as though he'd died and gone to barbecue heaven.

"Heart attack central," he grinned at Branham. "Where the hell do I start?"

"Anybody here know how to grill real Texas-style brisket?" Karen asked.

"I doubt it, but you can probably get a very good hamburger," Branham said.

"Step aside." She set off in search of the largest burger she could find.

"Excuse me," Branham said to Hank, "I think I see Janice over there. I'd better go. If I don't see you again before you leave, thanks again for all your help."

Hank shook his hand. "No problem. Think about what I said about Hall."

"I will," Branham promised, then turned away to look for his errant girlfriend.

Alone again, and as happy as he'd felt since he'd strolled out of the Emporium tobacco shop on Bluefield Street a week ago with a big cigar in his mouth and nothing but time on his hands, Hank wandered among the stalls until he found himself watching a middle-aged woman serving very large burgers sided with seasoned potato wedges.

"Smells good," Hank told her.

"They're rosemary lamb burgers," she said. "Care to try one?"

"Lamb?" Hank was dubious.

"You'll be surprised at the taste, sir. There's a secret about good lamb that I don't mind letting you in on."

Hank laughed. "All right. I'm game."

"Very funny." She removed a burger from the grill and slipped it onto the heel of a large bun. "Normally I'd ask how you want it dressed, but I think maybe I'll do it for you just this once." With brisk, practiced movements she built the burger in front of him. "There's rosemary, oregano, and lemon zest right in the burger already, so I'm just going to top it with this here chutney made with black and green olives, roasted red peppers, and sun-dried tomatoes, then top it off with some of this crumbled feta cheese and we'll call it done. Side helping of rosemary potato wedges, and there you go. Take a big bite of that burger and tell me what you think."

Hank accepted the paper plate from her and took a bite. It was delicious, without the gamey lamb flavor he'd expected.

The woman handed him a napkin. "You got some bits in your beard, right there. Good, isn't it?"

Hank nodded, chewing.

"Now I'll let you in on that secret. Lamb doesn't need to be so strong-tasting as people think. We raise our own lambs right here on Sunset Farms, and they're every one of them grass-fed each day of their lives. Most growers finish them off with grain to fatten them up, but sheep are ruminants, know what I mean? They naturally eat grass, not grain, and it makes a big difference in the taste. Plus, our sheep are bred for burgers and not for wool, which also makes a huge difference."

"It does?" Hank managed between swallowing and biting.

"Sure enough. Sheep bred for wool have a lot of lanolin, that waxy, oily substance? That's what gives the meat such a strong smell and taste. Sheep bred for eating are low in lanolin, and if they're sheared and slaughtered properly you keep the lanolin away from the meat altogether and there you are. A delicious burger or chop or what have you. Plus, they're antibiotic free and pasture-raised. They don't live in little cages. You can see the pasture yourself on the other side of the barns, if you're interested." She grinned at him. "Good, huh?"

Hank nodded. "Got a Coke?"

"Coming right up."

A few kiosks over, Karen was sitting with Brother Charles Baker at a picnic table, munching on a regular beef burger and sipping from a can of Mountain Dew.

"You'll be driving back to Maryland soon," Brother Charles said, leaning his elbows on the table.

"As soon as Hank's done looking around." Karen swallowed. "He really digs this stuff."

The crowd thinned for a moment. Across the way they could see Hank standing by himself with a paper plate and can of Coke in one hand, half-eaten burger in the other hand, looking back in the direction of the bandstand where the next performers were tuning their instruments in preparation for their turn on stage. Karen's mouth quirked fondly. He looked like someone's uncle, big and frizzy-haired, his worries momentarily forgotten.

"I never did have a chance to talk to him," Brother Charles said. "He seems like a good man. He carries a lot of tension, though."

"He's upset about the woman. He saw her only ten or fifteen minutes before she was strangled, and it's eating away at him."

"How could he know what would happen?"

"Exactly. He thinks he should be telepathic or something. Plus, he had to shoot the guy who killed her, and he hates that. He sees it as a failure. But he's a helluva cop, he does what he can, and that's the best any of us can do." She drained her Mountain Dew and set the can down on the picnic table with a clack. "He's tough enough, just the same. Not as tough as me, but tough enough. He took a round in his shoulder only a couple months ago, and he doesn't show it. He hates to make a fuss about himself." She nodded in Hank's direction. "That's how he does it. How he stays sane. He just forgets who he is for a few minutes and has a good time."

"Do you think you'll talk to him, Karen? About your mother, the things you mentioned to me before?"

Karen ate the last bite of her burger. She stood up from the picnic table, put the empty can on her paper plate, carried them over to a nearby trash receptacle, and dropped them in. "I guess I'd better."

"You're not Superwoman, just as he's not Superman," Brother Charles said. "You're just two people trying to do what's right."

"I guess." She allowed him to embrace her and kiss her on the cheek.

"Stay in touch," he said. "Send me an e-mail. And drive carefully."

"Well, that last one won't happen, but we'll see about the e-mail."

He disappeared into the crowd.

She made her way over to Hank. He was dumping his garbage into the trash bin and looked as though he wanted to head back to the bandstand, so she rapped him sharply on the forearm.

"Come on, Lou, we gotta hit the road. Time's a'wastin.'"

It took a moment for his eyes to focus on her, but after two heartbeats he was back within himself, the familiar weight of self-awareness once again settled across his shoulders. "You're right. Let's go."

She led the way back down to the field where they'd parked. They got in, she started the engine, she put her hand on the gear shift, and turned to look at him.

"Something I wanna talk to you about, Lou."

"Okay. Right now?"

"No, not right now. Right now I just wanna get out of this fucking place and hit the interstate."

Hank slouched down and closed his eyes. "Wake me up then, whenever."

As they bounced out of the field onto the driveway and she edged slowly down to the road behind a passenger van loaded with kids, she glanced over at him.

I will, she promised herself.

I will.

Acknowledgements

As always, I'm very happy to be able to thank my team of manuscript readers, who provide me with a wide range of very valuable feedback during the preparation of this novel. Thanks go out to Gwenda Lemoine, Margaret Leroux, Danielle Rapone, and Larry Sudds.

I owe an enormous debt to my wife, Lynn Clark. A former professional editor, Lynn donated hours of her life that she can't get back to critiquing, copy-editing, and proofreading this novel. In addition, as my business partner in The Plaid Raccoon Press, she has been very supportive of the incredible amount of time I've spent marketing *Blood Passage*, the first in the Donaghue and Stainer Crime Novel series.

Oh, oh. Here we go again!

About the Author

Michael J. McCann lives and writes in Oxford Station, Ontario, Canada on seven acres in the Limerick Forest south of Ottawa. A graduate of Trent University in Peterborough, ON and Queen's University in Kingston, ON, he worked as an editor for several years with Carswell Legal Publications before spending fifteen years with Canada Customs (CBSA), where he was a training specialist, project officer, and program manager at national headquarters in Ottawa. He is married and has one son.

Mike is the author of *Blood Passage*, the first Donaghue and Stainer Crime Novel, and *The Ghost Man*, a supernatural thriller.

THE DONAGHUE AND STAINER CRIME NOVEL SERIES

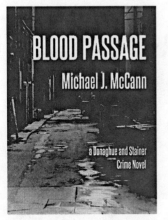

Blood Passage
by **Michael J. McCann**

ISBN: 978-0-9877087-0-0
      (paperback)
      978-0-9877087-1-7
      (e-book)

Would you believe a little boy who claims to remember the men who killed him in a previous life?

Praise for *Blood Passage*

"Got an hour? Because that's how long it'll take to describe all the great things about this book. . . . This book's got everything: a great main plot, interesting and not overwhelming subplots, believable characters, true-to-life dialogue, and a satisfying ending that leaves you with just enough unanswered questions (it is a crime novel, after all)."   — *Mark Lee, The Masquerade Crew*

"*Blood Passage* is an exciting murder mystery that will keep you turning the pages. . . . I especially loved the character of Karen Stainer, a no-nonsense tough woman who is not afraid to get nose to nose with the criminal element, but does have a soft side to her. . . . A very tense edge-of-your-seat type of page turner that will keep you guessing to the very end." — *Kathleen Kelly, CelticLady's Reviews*

"Action filled and worthy of its own television show. . . . I thoroughly enjoyed this book." — *Melanie Carrico, Have You Heard Book Reviews*

AVAILABLE FALL 2012

A DONAGHUE AND STAINER CRIME NOVEL

THE
FREGOLI DELUSION

MICHAEL J. McCANN

CPSIA information can be obtained at www.ICGtesting.com
Printed in the USA
LVOW060702301012

305014LV00001B/13/P